8/15

P9-DOE-936

CROOKED

ALSO BY AUSTIN GROSSMAN

Soon I Will Be Invincible

You

CROOKED

AUSTIN GROSSMAN

MULHOLLAND BOOKS

Little, Brown and Company

New York Boston London

Copyright © 2015 by Austin Grossman

Mulholland Books/Little, Brown and Company
Hachette Book Group
1290 Avenue of the Americas
New York, NY 10104
mulhollandbooks.com

First Edition: July 2015

Mulholland Books is an imprint of Little, Brown and Company, a division of Hachette Book Group, Inc. The Mulholland Books name and logo are trademarks of Hachette Book Group, Inc.

The publisher is not responsible for websites (or their content) that are not owned by the publisher.

The Hachette Speakers Bureau provides a wide range of authors for speaking events. To find out more, go to hachettespeakersbureau.com or call (866) 376-6591.

ISBN 978-0-316-19851-6
Library of Congress Control Number 2014956721

10 9 8 7 6 5 4 3 2 1

RRD-C

Printed in the United States of America

Despite all the official probes, the trials of the miscreants involved, and the massive efforts of scholars and reporters, no one has ever convincingly established the motive for the Watergate break-ins.

—Anthony Summers, *The Arrogance of Power: The Secret World of Richard Nixon*

PART ONE

CHAPTER ONE

JUNE 1972

THE OVAL OFFICE always smelled of cigarette smoke, of medical disinfectant and a faint undercurrent of sage. I just hope no one ever puts the great seal under a black light. Near the end, we had to steam-clean it after each new moon. The walls were a pale yellow, and on summer evenings like this the flags hung limp like so much damp laundry. There was nothing to do but wait, all night if I had to, looking out at the black Washington, DC, sky and my own reflection in the window, an old man's reflection now. I couldn't help sweating in the June heat, my shirt and wool jacket sticking to my back. It was always remarked that I never took it off publicly. I don't like to come across as too informal. That, and there was some custom tailoring in there that it wouldn't do for people to see. A hidden pocket that held a small-caliber revolver with a speed-loader. Regular bullets, no silver-plated nonsense. My insurance policy, along with a vellum scroll held to my thin, pale, old man's calf with a rubber band.

A knock at the office door.

"Do you need anything else tonight, Mr. President?" It was one of the interns.

"No. Go to sleep, son."

"Yes, sir."

I locked the door behind him.

The clock on the wide wooden mantelpiece read 12:07 a.m. The first minutes of June 18, 1972. A mile to the west, on the sixth floor of the Watergate Hotel, Team A was finished with its work. Team B would be waiting in the hotel suite two floors below, checking their watches, smoking, bullshitting for eight more minutes.

I had been there three hours ago for the briefing. In person, over Henry's strenuous objections, I was snuck in at the last minute in a waiter's uniform, head bowed to hide my face. The face that, absurdly, had become one of the most recognizable in the world.

I arrived to join fourteen other men crowded into one hotel room. I leaned against the wall and the others sat on chairs, perched on the bed, watched from the bathroom doorway. Henry stood as always in a patch of quiet; no one ever liked to be within two feet of him. Liddy, quietly in command but glancing over at me every few minutes for encouragement, and Barker, who'd come through the Bay of Pigs fiasco with most of his body scarred. Gonzales, a locksmith. McCord, requisite FBI, glancing around as if he'd walked into the wrong room. Martinez, with quick eyes, and Sturgis, who listened without comment.

An eclectic array of equipment lay spread out on the bed—cameras, lock picks, tear gas, listening devices, duct tape, surgical gloves, thermite. Silver medallions, a small bag of salt, a Bible. Bundles of dollar bills, two hundred dollars each for everyone there. It all felt amateurish and haphazard, more like a strangely outfitted sleepover party than a clandestine operation.

Agent Hunt broke it down for them: "We recovered a few pages from a DNC research project," he told them. "We knew they were polling behind, and it seems like they're a little more desperate than we thought. They've started drawing from a different playbook."

He held up a Xeroxed page of densely written Cyrillic, the word *Gregor* circled in two places.

"Maybe some of you recognize that name. If you do, you know it's not politics as usual anymore. Nobody likes going outside the law, but I assure you, the president is fully behind us on this one. We clean the place out. This time tomorrow you'll be on your way and no one will ever hear about what happened." He glanced at me. There were people in the room who already knew this was not true.

The first team went out, Henry and the rest of them, and the second team, the ones whose names you will know from the newspapers, were left. After a while McCord went upstairs to tape the locks on the fire doors, and I came back here to wait.

It had been my office for four years. I cleared everything out when I arrived because of Kennedy. Kennedy's desk was nice but I wanted a broader writing surface, and I like a darker wood, and I don't like to sit where he sat. God knows what went on here.

The new desk was supposed to have been Woodrow Wilson's, a man I admire. The twenty-eighth president was a sorcerer of no small ability within his limits, better than Eisenhower, if you ask me, until in 1918 he went too far, made a pact that brought the Great Plague. His dyslexia held him back, not to mention his education—there are some things they don't teach you at Princeton.

The Wilson desk was a PR coup until—and it took fucking Safire to point it out—we found out it wasn't Woodrow Wilson's at all, it was *Henry* Wilson's, a vice president who served under the Great Butcher, who, incidentally, had the least human blood of anyone to serve in the office.

The desk, I found, had several secret compartments. One contained papers handwritten in an unknown alphabet and bearing the signature of James Madison; another held a bronze dagger inscribed with the opening words of the Declaration of Independence. A third one was empty, and objects placed inside it for longer than eight hours would reliably vanish, I never found out to where. Nothing is ever the way you think it's going to be, not even the job of your dreams.

I lit a cigarette.

Pat would be asleep by now. No one awake but me and the security guards.

Franklin D. Roosevelt built the modern version of the Oval Office in the thirties. He had some strange help, and it still has some strange properties. At this hour it can feel like a time machine going back, back to the barren swampland that once was here, the square miles of muck and still, black water. In November 1620, five hundred miles to the north, a hundred and two British settlers arrived and started dying. Half of them went almost immediately, from diseases caught during the journey coupled with no food and a killing winter. Only four adult women survived that first year. Fugitive Protestant mystics, Tilleys and Martins and Chiltons, they huddled together in half-built log halls, reading by firelight on the edge of a frozen continent next to a dark forest that stretched westward all the way to the Mississippi. They couldn't even bury their dead. Outside, the snow had fallen six feet deep, and there were moving shapes in the night. They were fifty-three people without a country watching one another die until one of them, we will never know who, walked out into the darkness to do what none of the others would. The colony at Roanoke had died. Plymouth would live.

I stubbed out the cigarette and took off my jacket. The

phone rang, once. It meant that Henry's shadow team was climbing the hotel stairway to the eighth floor. As I later heard it, the Egyptian went first, clearing the hallway and sniffing out anything dead in the adjacent rooms. Henry followed, shambling. He always looked vaguely apologetic in his eternally rumpled suit, but if there's anything on this side of the Atlantic that can destroy him, I'd like to know about it. Nothing was going to be the same after what happened at the hotel. I was used to calculating through events but I wasn't used to anything on this scale. There were deep scratches on my forearms. I was shaking a little. Presidents didn't do this kind of thing. Not by a strict constructionist view of things, at least.

It was time for me to do my part. I closed the blinds, knelt down, and rolled back the carpeting to reveal the greater seal of the office, set just beneath the public one. I rolled up my left sleeve and cut twice with the dagger as prescribed, to release the blood of the Democratically Elected, the Duly Sworn and Consecrated. I began to chant in stilted, precise seventeenth-century English prose from the Twelfth and Thirteenth Secret Articles of the United States Constitution. These were not the duties of the U.S. presidency as I had once conceived of them, nor as most of the citizens of this country still do. But really. Ask yourself if everything in your life is the way they told you it would be.

My family started a lemon farm in Southern California after they moved there in 1910. I wasn't born yet, of course. Just my father and mother and my brother Harold. They thought the land was empty, and who wouldn't have? Southern California was clean and dry, the sun shining every day on grassy hills, so hot and bright it seemed all the poisons of history must have been bleached out of it long since.

The land had just been sold to the Janss Investment Company, and the executives named it Yorba Linda. The year I was born the company dug a reservoir four miles from our house. There's photographs of workers lining it with concrete, letting the river drain in, four and a half million gallons of water for farms like the one my parents started. You can see the mayor standing there, waving at the camera.

People were building all over the place. They were throwing up houses everywhere, staking claims, digging basements like they were the Earth's first inhabitants. My parents just wanted to grow lemons.

Maybe it was the reservoir driving out something that had slept undisturbed for long millennia. Maybe the diggers touched something under layers of parched earth. Maybe my family brought it with them from Ohio.

I hear they've drained the reservoir. They turned it into a park, and they didn't find a damn thing. The whole place is housing developments now. Whatever's there has dug itself deeper, waiting for someone digging a well or subbasement to stumble on it, or just waiting for the right words to come, to tell it to come out. Some nights I think it followed me all the way back across the country. Most of the lemons never grew, and the ones that did, we had to burn. Jesus, but that land was rotten.

I speak the words, light the incense, and try to clear my mind, but it isn't easy. The first time I was here was with Eisenhower in 1953. He was a different kind of man than you find now, the last president born in the nineteenth century. He smelled different. Up close you could see the seams where he had been sewn back together, a clumsy job by some Kansas doctor. He and I used to sit up nights in here listening to the crickets on the lawn. Just talking, drinking, and waiting for whatever call was coming. Like when the *Trieste* hit bottom in the Mariana Trench in 1960, and we waited for the news. The black phone rang, and he brought it to his ear; I could hear the midshipman's voice squeak, and Eisenhower shivered in the heat. He knew things almost nobody knows now. He remembered waking up at dawn to pray to ancient gods of small-town Texas. He told me a lot about the war, things that no one will ever know. He said he wasn't afraid of the future, just the past.

I put my jacket back on, thinking ahead to what would be in that room on the eighth floor of the Watergate Hotel. Chairs pushed to the walls. A dead man in a wool suit seated in the lotus position in the exact center of the room, eyes closed. It was freezing inside, outside the heat of a June night in Washington. Packing crates marked in Cyrillic. Black feathers.

Afterward the Cubans would do their part, the cleanup and set-dressing, before we staged the next act. They'd be found and the police summoned, and the team would be revealed as amateurish hired hands caught in the wrong place. Liddy would do his comic turn as the loose cannon. History would take its turn, and my public life would begin to unravel.

But I survived. I outlived the hippies; I outlived Elvis and Marlene Dietrich and the Soviet Union itself. It's been twenty years since I was forced to stage my own death. The tiny silicon disk on the moon that bears my name is slowly gathering dust. I lived to see myself become a laughingstock, a cartoon villain, the place in the august roll call of presidents where history pauses and snickers.

This is the story of the great con game that was the late twentieth century, of American history's worst presidency, of how I learned to lie. It is not history as you know it. Suffice it to say that there are at least three sides to this story, and I'm telling both of mine. I promise you I will show the same contempt for the historical record that it has shown for me.

My name is Richard Milhous Nixon. I swore an oath to preserve, protect, and defend the Constitution. I was educated at Whittier College in Whittier, California, and I have seen the devil walk.

CHAPTER TWO

NOVEMBER 1946

THIS IS THE true story of the Watergate break-in. It's the story of the original crime, of course, and the hapless cover-up that followed, but there were other things we covered up, worse things, and other crimes. This is the version that will be redacted and concealed for the next thousand years or hundred thousand if the limestone vaults beneath the Nixon Library survive that long and remain undiscovered. But to understand it all you have to begin much earlier, as long ago as 1946, in the dawn of the American era and my final few days as an honorable man.

The Nixon of 1946 was clear-eyed and righteous and hungry for whatever the world had to offer. At thirty-three years old, I lived just fifteen miles from my birthplace. I had a law degree from Duke University and the remnants of a law practice I'd begun before the war. I wanted nothing more than to leave, but after the adventure of the war, I had nowhere else to go.

My parents built the house we lived in on a bare patch of dirt scorched clear by the unrelenting Southern California sun. When my father planted a tree, he'd dig down through three or four feet of red clay and crumbling sandstone before the first hint of damp. October to March it was a little cooler, and every few weeks there were torrential rains that ran and pooled on the clay soil. Red rains, sometimes, and black rains, even a

11

yellow rain one year. Growing up, I thought we were the first people ever to live there since the world began.

An Orange County childhood was nothing like the ones in the children's books in the library. My family was Frank and Hannah, my older brother, Harold, and three younger ones, Arthur, Donald, and Edward. Electricity came in the year I was born, the first paved road when I turned four. There was a small school. Two kids who apparently lived in the woods. A family of eight who spoke a language no one ever identified; the youngest daughter translated when she had to, until the morning their house was found standing empty and they were never seen again.

There were no white Christmases or meadows or scented pine woods, no bears or foxes. There were rattlesnakes and black widow spiders we boldly stomped on when we found their messy little webs. It was the west, but it wasn't wild at all, or romantic. It was dusty and lonely and weird and I dreamed obsessively of getting away, even before the worst of it began.

Even for that world the Nixons were a strange race, quiet and inward. My father and mother read too much; my father taught Sunday school, and I was singled out for it. There was a silence around our house; other children did not come over to play.

The faint smell of rotting lemons seemed to cling to everything we owned, our clothes, our hair. There are still moments when I will smell it, out of nowhere, and feel the fatal dust of Orange County between my fingers and remember that bleak, sunny place. No one was surprised when we began to fall ill.

It was as if something were stalking us. Arthur died first, when I was twelve. No one ever determined what the cause was. Tuberculosis or meningitis, one of those unanswerables. They held prayer meetings for him. Arthur had never been strong, and it was 1925. Kids died.

But then there was Harold. Four years older than I, Harold wasn't shy like me; he liked to be with people, and he could talk to girls. He'd stay out late in the warm nights in Yorba Linda's meager social world. Harold flew airplanes. After Harold had one especially late night, Dad sent him to boarding school in Massachusetts, unimaginably far off. I never found out exactly what he'd done. I was fourteen and maybe they didn't think I should be told.

When they sent Harold back six months later, he wasn't well. He'd lost weight, he coughed, he couldn't stay warm. I was, I guess, too young to understand what was happening. Arthur's death might have made sense but Harold getting sick was like something had gone wrong with the sun. They called it tuberculosis, and maybe it was. We moved him to a sanitarium nearby and then to another in Arizona. He died when I was twenty.

Later my mother would say that losing Arthur and Harold was the source of my precocious seriousness, that I was trying to make up for the loss and do the work of two brothers. She said it because that's the kind of thing you say to the press, but I don't think my mother could have been confused about this: I worked to stay out of that Yorba Linda dirt. I worked to get out.

The only good thing Orange County ever gave me was Pat, and if anyone in the Nixon White House was less well understood than me, it was her, a woman who passed through history leaving behind only a ghostly parody of herself. A reporter once wrote, "She chatters, answers questions, smiles and smiles, all with a doll's terrifying poise . . . Like a doll, she would be smiling when the world broke." No one in Washington ever saw Pat for what she was except, perhaps, Dwight D. Eisenhower, and he never told.

I met Pat when I was twenty-five, when both of us were cast in a community theater production of *The Dark Tower,* a justly forgotten stage play. According to the script, Pat was supposed to be a "dark, sullen beauty of twenty, wearing a dress of great chic and an air of permanent resentment." I was a "faintly collegiate, eager, blushing youth of twenty-four." Neither casting was a stretch. In the play we supposedly had a great rivalry—I was naive, she was charismatic and manipulative, we had made-up fights and said absurd things to each other, and that was our introduction.

When biographers tell the story of our courtship, the emphasis is on my prolonged, almost pathologically dogged pursuit—everyone dwells on the fact that I would chauffeur her anywhere she liked, even on dates with other men. History has managed to make even the great romance of my life a snide humiliation.

Not that I knew what I was doing. I was in my middle twenties but this was the beginning of my romantic life and I had only very vague ideas about what I was looking for. I was absurdly passionate about her but I had no insight whatsoever as to why.

I'd like to say that love made me a better man but it didn't, and I don't actually see how love could ever make anybody better.

All I learned at the time was that when I wanted something I behaved with all the dignity of a rookie soldier panicking in a foxhole. I courted her with exactly the same no-brakes determination with which I later ran for public office.

Like an eons-buried elder god or a vast extradimensional intelligence, the heart lives by unreadable codes and incomprehensible motives, knows nothing of dignity or humanity, and more often than not brings only destruction and madness on those who are exposed to its baleful cravings. You could say we recognized each other. She sensed that I was as desperate as she was, as angry as she was, and that I was struggling to go places and would maybe do something stupid and interesting.

It took me years to learn that Pat's life made no more sense than mine did. Pat's father started as a miner, failed at that, and then became a failed farmer. He and her mother both died before she was sixteen. She'd dug in the dirt on her parents' farm and worked at department stores and cleaned at a bank and driven an elderly couple across the country for money; she'd cared for tuberculosis patients and been an extra in films and taught bookkeeping at Whittier Union. She was enormously intelligent and uncomfortably aware that it didn't matter, that she was going to be poor her whole life, and on some level she was on the verge of going insane.

We didn't know how to be in love, or live together, or any of it, so we made it up. We were grown-ups, yes, but young ones. Still with a great deal to find out about ourselves and each other, secrets that would take years and decades to come out. Still with ample room to make a lifetime's worth of stupid decisions as our partner looked on. We moved in together, we set up house and tried to make a home that looked roughly like our parents' homes, partly as a kind of private joke, mostly because it was time to act like grown-ups and we didn't know how else to do it.

We'd been married only a few months before I left for the war. We'd write to each other while I was in the Pacific. I wrote her long, intense, almost hallucinatory letters about my ambitions, about what we'd do, about who I thought I was and what my purpose was. What I thought we were. Hers were more polite, remote. She was keeping house, working in the war administration.

When I saw her next we were like college friends meeting up again, a couple of years later, to see who we'd grown into. To see if we were still friends. To see what we had to contend with, now that we were suddenly in the same house together again, husband and wife. Or were we even friends?

This is a tale of espionage and betrayal and the dark secrets of a decades-long cold war. It is a story of otherworldly horror, of strange nameless forces that lie beneath the reality we know. In other words, it is the story of a marriage.

At thirty-three I had come back to Whittier. My family expected I would settle myself but I couldn't shake the idea that my life hadn't really begun yet, not the real one. It seemed as if this were my last great chance: I would reinvent myself or else close myself off forever.

I read Tolstoy and Joseph Conrad and Somerset Maugham, anything at all for a glimpse of a faraway place. I went to the public library and found a directory of law firms in New York and wrote them long, courteous letters while picturing myself in a glamorous snow-covered city with sophisticated men and women. I mailed in an application for work at the FBI. None of them wrote back.

But one day a letter arrived from the Republican National Committee inviting me to come in for an interview. They were looking for someone to run for Congress against the Democrat Jerry Voorhis. It didn't take much in those days; I was a lawyer and a former lieutenant colonel in the U.S. Navy; no criminal record.

The first thing I did was bring the idea to Pat.

"You mean Congress as in government?" she said. "You're going to be in an election? Oh, honey, no. You can't."

"Of course I can. I was class president, wasn't I?" I told her.

"But you're . . . I love you, Dick, but you're not . . ."

"Not what?" I asked.

"I mean, you're not exactly a statesman, are you? You're, well, you have to know things for that, don't you? About oil prices and unwed mothers and foreign-exchange rates. And people have to vote for you."

I knew what she meant, however she meant it. I was grimly competent at making small talk because I'd learned it by rote and strenuous self-coaching. At larger functions I strained heroically for the effect of joviality and bulled through any surface awkwardness by force of will.

"It's just an interview. Is it all right if I go in for that?" I asked.

"Go on, go ahead. My blessing."

I did go, along with the other would-be Nixons, local businessmen, eminent lawyers, a minor-league baseball player, a crowd of hopefuls in the waiting room of history. I was chosen to run.

It turned out I had natural advantages that applied to politics and no other situation whatsoever. I had a slyly acute sense that we were moving into an interesting historical moment. The war had concluded triumphantly. Peace would reign; the great rebuilding would commence. Europe was exhausted and devastated but Roosevelt, Churchill, and Stalin would set up the international chessboard again with the rattle bag of leftover pieces.

All I saw was darkness and suspicion. The great powers had won the war together but they weren't friends. The Soviets had lost the most and were angrily determined to make up for it. The British were clinging to an outsize notion of their own importance, and Roosevelt was only weeks from death. It was like a formal dinner party for starving children: a brief mutual sizing-up followed by a barely decorous rush for food that would degenerate into a panicked frenzy.

The bright moral and strategic clarity of the last war vanished, leaving us with a tarnished world of intrigue, proxy fights, and a queer black humor. Even the pretense of civility was owed to simple terror, to the horror that had appeared at the war's end. The new strategic language was all calculated risk, bloodthirsty audacity. The image of towering mushroom clouds swallowed all ideas of heroism; it made all the worries that had come before seem naive and quaintly Victorian.

It was, it turned out, exactly the kind of climate that a shrewd, pushy, ignorant person such as myself could turn to his advantage.

My other asset was that, as I discovered, I wasn't a nice person. Jerry Voorhis was a well-liked, Yale-educated incumbent Democrat and I was an underfunded rookie. I took liberties. I bribed, I pulled any strings I could, I begged favors, co-opted any press members who would return my calls and seemed open to a deal. I misrepresented Voorhis's record and made insinuations just short of slander.

And okay, yes, very well, Jerry Voorhis was not a Communist. But there were a range of things a person could do that were akin to Communism or trended toward it. Restrictions on commerce, price regulations; the relationship was—look, a campaign rally isn't a graduate philosophy seminar. I hardly had time to go into details, but I was pretty sure I was right on the basics.

And Communists were bad, weren't they? We were talking about Stalin and company here, so without knowing too much about it, even then I could say with certainty they weren't the greatest.

I fought Jerry Voorhis in all the ways I would have deplored in the abstract but that seemed reasonable in this particular instance—which is to say, when I wanted a thing very badly and felt that I should have it. Jerry Voorhis was perfectly competent and one of the nicer people I have ever met in politics. He just didn't know what I was going to be like. He was expecting a gentleman.

I never hid any of this from Pat. She knew that we had very little funding and only a few viable options. She believed I was doing it for the right reasons, that this was a small price to pay to get a decent man into Congress (or at least a man who was decent before the campaign and had very sincerely promised to become decent again once he got there).

I'm being diplomatic, because there's a more obvious reason why Pat didn't worry about my electoral scruples, which was that she didn't think it could possibly matter, because she didn't think anyone would vote for me.

I saw her point. Even with the benefit of youth, the Nixon face was never beautiful. And then what it turned into! Pear-shaped and heavy about the mouth. The brow and the jowls and the five o'clock shadow. It might at least have had a gritty bull-dog force if it weren't for the whoop-de-do swoop of the nose.

I once said I was an introvert in an extrovert's profession, but that was only a polite way of saying that people didn't especially like me. I was an abysmal public speaker. I did solemnity and righteous anger passably well, and I could manage an effortful smile telling a joke or bantering with the press, but for the rest of it I lapsed into a kind of rigid neutral glare, the outward shell of frantic self-consciousness and social panic. The only impression I made completely naturally was that of commonness. For better or worse, no one ever mistook me for a member of the elite.

What did I think I was doing? Why run at all?

I played football in college, and I was terrible. Our school was so small they had to let me on the team no matter how badly I played. I'd sit there on the bench but when we were far ahead or hopelessly behind, the crowd of students and alums would start chanting "Nixon! Nixon!" until the coaches sent me in and they'd all roar with laughter when I trotted onto the field. The ball would be snapped and I'd be knocked down by hits I never saw coming from college kids who had learned somewhere how to move like tigers. Why did I do it? I wanted to belong to something, be the all-American boy I never was and never could be, the loss that broke my heart before I quite knew I had one. So fuck them if they tried to keep me out. Let them try.

Much later I understood that I wasn't expected to win at all. Anyone who knew anything considered Voorhis unbeatable, and the Republicans needed somebody to run against him purely for form's sake. In fact, I was the only one involved in the race naive enough to think it was going to be any kind of contest.

No one took a poll during the congressional campaign. We simply made our speeches and tried our little ploys, and when the day came, they counted and we sat and waited for the numbers: 49,994 for him, 65,886 for me. I was terrible at football, but this was a game I could win.

Pat and I sat together in the Huntington Hotel in Pasadena toward the end of our third party of the night, blurry from champagne, numbed with celebration and fatigue. I'd played the piano; someone's pants had been thrown at the ceiling and still hung from the chandelier.

"What am I doing?" I asked her. "Remind me why we did this."

"We're getting on," she told me. "Going somewhere. We couldn't stay here. Is it that scary?"

"I'm just worried. Being a lawyer made sense. I don't know what this is."

"It's going to be interesting," she said. "We'll make it up as we go along. And whatever you say out there, I'm going to know it's not really you, all right? I'll know."

"All right."

"We won this. We whipped them good. Nixon's the one," she said.

It had been our campaign slogan: "Nixon's the One."

Is it possible some people simply aren't designed to win? That there are people who would be better off losing every day of their lives? That if you're the wrong sort of person, winning just breaks something in you?

I won but I wasn't like Pat. Because—and why this should be I'll never know—I never did a thing that wasn't somehow touched with selfish, furtive hunger, with a private, annihilating need for recognition. Because I'm like a child in a fairy tale cursed from birth, and there has never been anything I can put my hand to without tainting it, no triumph so great or solemn that it doesn't turn spoiled and ridiculous. Because, sooner or later, the darkness always gets in.

CHAPTER THREE

AUGUST 1948

"NO ONE RECRUITED me. I had become convinced that the society in which we live, Western civilization, had reached a crisis, of which the First World War was the military expression, and that it was doomed to collapse or revert to barbarism. I did not understand the causes of the crisis or know what to do about it. But I felt that, as an intelligent man, I must do something."

I was sitting in a large conference room in the Commodore Hotel in New York listening to a man named David Whittaker Chambers explain how he'd become a Communist spy. This was one of my congressional appointments, the House Un-American Activities Committee, set up a decade ago to hunt for Fascist fifth columnists during the Second World War.

David Whittaker Chambers was a pale and lumpish man with an enormous head, a scholar and translator and senior editor at *Time* magazine. He had a high-flown academic style of speech composed of long, precise, mesmerizingly dull sentences, perhaps because he'd been giving this same testimony for years to various military and civilian agencies without any result. As he spoke, he listed to one side like a slowly sinking ship. It gave the effect of a man on the brink of succumbing to a soporific drug.

I shifted in my seat, conscious of wasted time and wasted opportunities. This was congressional busywork. I paid a dogged sort of attention but I knew by then that all signs pointed to my being a one-term congressman destined for a quick trip home to Whittier. I should be making speeches on the House floor, I thought. I should be seizing the headlines.

When you get to Washington you feel triumphant. You've won an election and a place in the political elite. And then you realize that everyone else there won an election too, because that is how people get to Washington. And that Washington itself is a new and different game, and the skills that won you that election have nothing to do with the skills you need now. There are four hundred and thirty-five people in the United States House of Representatives, and they're not all going to be president, and in two years many of them will be going home, never to return. Whatever act you came up with in the provinces to fool Ma and Pa Voter isn't going to matter to the people here. They've all seen it.

It's very seldom mentioned, but I have very nearly the best academic record among United States presidents (due credit to Clinton and Wilson). It's true that I was smarter than the kids around me and I worked very hard. I think it's okay for me to say this. When I arrived in Washington I still, at the age of thirty-three, genuinely believed that people cared.

Maybe it's true that nobody likes a know-it-all, and maybe it isn't. It comes down to the same thing because, as it turned out, nobody liked Dick Nixon. I needed to project an image of confidence and connections and money, the things that draw powerful people and wealthy backers. I needed to be anyone but the desperate, lonely striver who worked his way up from his parents' grocery store. That was an inspiring story back home, but it played very poorly in the drawing rooms of the nation's capital.

Four or five nights out of the week, Pat and I would play the new game. We would climb in a taxi and go to that night's reception, testimonial dinner, cocktail party, anywhere we were even halfway welcome. We would chat up lobbyists and staffers and I'd sweat through the latest in a succession of midpriced rental tuxedos.

And at the end of each long, boozy evening I'd find myself in the wood-paneled anteroom of a well-to-do Georgetown home bidding good night to the slightly baffled hostess who was straining to remember how she'd come to invite this strange, doggedly earnest couple, Richard Nixon and his anxious, vaguely heartbroken wife.

Once in a while I'd see Jack. I was making my political debut at the exact same moment as the rookie congressman from Massachusetts who turned out to be the most prodigiously attractive politician of our generation. It was one thing to play politics badly; it was quite another to do it while being treated to the sight of a man playing the game as few others ever have. Jack was the one who taught me to truly crave political office. I wanted to hold a room spellbound, I wanted to change laws, I wanted to stand in front of a crowd of people who were shouting my name in righteousness or exultation and smile and drink it all in, the way he did. And later, every one of those things would happen for me. It's just the meaning that was changed, like light through a distorting lens. Tragedy for him; farce for me.

I'm the last man to heap further pieties on his legacy, but it was a particular thing to have known Jack Kennedy as a creature of raw potential. Before I met him, I didn't understand what a politician could be: someone in whom charisma, sex, intellect, and historical moment all came together. I'd ride home in the taxi and think about Kennedy and the way people's eyes tracked him at a party, the way even my own unwilling heart lurched when he looked at me and smiled. Even the unconscious cells of your body wanted him to like you.

At the age of thirty-one he was an object lesson in what nascent political talent looked like. I could see it; political strategists could see it. Most of all, my wife could see it. Being married, it turned out, only made every bit of this worse. It wasn't as if I were a stranger to social humiliation. I'd always shrugged it off. *Nixon can take it,* I told myself and I could have lived through it again except now there was Pat. From the start she'd told me she wasn't a political wife but she would do her duty, and she did. She laughed at jokes and stopped at two drinks and scraped up party invitations and lunch dates, but it wasn't working.

And what was completely unforgivable was, we both knew it. Pat could see Kennedy, and she could see me, and she could tell the difference. If I had been alone at these events, I might have shrugged off the tiny slights and disappointments, watched my petty private dreams become thin and strained. I might have said to myself, *Well, it doesn't matter so much. There will be other parties.*

But I didn't even have the solace of knowing that my petty private agonies were private. Pat saw every detail of it, and I saw her seeing it. It was like gazing into an ugly, sneering hall of mirrors. Someone who could see every vain and rotten and false detail of your life, who watched you flinch at every little slight, who saw you at your weakest and did not forgive.

Riding home with Pat in the back of a taxi, I stared at the side of her face as she looked out the window. *This is what marriage is,* I thought. *They're watching you drown and you're watching them watch you. You see them hating themselves for being trapped with you.*

And the next day I sat on the House Un-American Activities

panel and tried to focus on what a bizarre, pudgy little man named Whittaker Chambers was saying.

"In 1937 I repudiated Marx's doctrines and Lenin's tactics," Chambers told us. His voice was nearly inaudible in the crowded hearing room. "I resolved to break with the Communist Party at whatever risk to my life or other tragedy to myself or my family."

If nothing else, it was starting to become one of our more entertaining testimonials. He clearly thought he'd been involved in something genuinely sinister.

"Mr. Chambers," Chief Investigator Stripling said, hiding a smile, "in your statement you stated that you yourself had served the . . . underground, chiefly in Washington, DC."

I worried that we were egging him on a little too much but Chambers rose to the bait, replying at his leaden pace, "Even in countries where the Communist Party is legal, an underground party exists side by side with the open party. The apparatus in Washington was an organization or group of that underground."

He'd bought a revolver to protect himself. He'd slept by day, kept vigil by night, but the Communists hadn't come. I pictured them, assassins with goatees and berets and jazz records. Spies among us, our friends and neighbors harboring deviant beliefs regarding political economics. The filthy beatniks were inside the universities, the media, the federal government! Beware!

But then . . . Chambers wasn't just laying out for us in plain, forceful language the historic drama of our time—he was offering us a part in it. I began to see the power in the narrative. I'd implied before that certain people were Communists; I'd said it about Jerry Voorhis the way I'd said everything else I could possibly think of, but I hadn't quite grasped the scope or the urgency of it all. If I were being honest, I didn't entirely understand what a Communist was or what they were doing over there in Russia. None of us did. We saw the outside of it, foreign countries with unpronounceable names succumbing one after the other without warning in the dead of night. An international organization with an implacable hunger for power, for secrets, and for new recruits.

The atmosphere in the chamber was gradually electrifying. I looked around to see who was catching it, who really understood the potential. Chambers was good with details. He and his contacts met in a violin studio. There were seven men who ran underground Communist cells under the direction of a sinister individual, a former petty officer in the Austrian army, a man who still had not been properly identified. I found myself hoping he had an eye patch or was missing an arm, but it would work however we needed it to. Chambers was offering me a lifeline; I just had to think ahead, farther and faster than the competition.

And then the name of Alger Hiss surfaced, a man who worked in the State Department. As Chambers told the story, he'd known Hiss in the 1930s. They were friends, close friends, and Communist spies. Chambers left the party in 1937 and tried to convince Hiss to resign as well but failed. After that they parted ways, and for all he knew, Hiss was still operating, if we could just catch him. How hard could it be?

"'From Stettin in the Baltic to Trieste in the Adriatic, an iron curtain has descended across the Continent.'" I read Churchill's speech aloud while Pat listened. "'Behind that line lie all the capitals of the ancient states of Central and Eastern Europe. Warsaw, Berlin, Prague, Vienna, Budapest, Belgrade, Bucharest and Sofia.' You see it's got something, right? It's powerful."

"It's a good speech, I'll give it that."

"We need this," I told her. "I can't keep trying to win elections the way I did last time. It won't work twice, you know that."

"Do you believe it? The Soviet menace?" she asked. "I'm not saying it matters, but do you?"

"You read the papers, Pat. What they've done in Eastern Europe isn't a theory. They're a pretty rough bunch. I could make my reputation on this."

"Okay. I can see that," Pat said. She frowned, thinking it through. "Although—not to be a purist about it—what if this Alger Hiss is innocent?"

"He's not. There's too much detail. Well enough for a hearing anyway."

"And you're not going to lose?"

"Not a chance."

"All right. I see it. But Dick, you see what you're doing, don't you? You're trying to make people afraid. You're using them. And I know it's politics, and I'm not going to moralize at you, but this kind of thing can go very wrong."

"It's just until I get a foothold. You know it's not easy for us." It was the closest I'd ever come to mentioning those long late-night taxi rides, both of us breathing the air of failure until we couldn't even look at each other. The absolute indifference of the press, the looming deadline of the upcoming elections. Last time had been a surprise, a fluke, and we both knew it.

"And so you're going to say there are spies in the government."

"There are. You should have heard the testimony today."

"And our friends and neighbors?" she asked. "You're going to tell people their friends and neighbors might be spies too. That seriously doesn't worry you?"

"People aren't crazy."

"What about me? Did you ever think of that? I fit the profile."

"What profile?"

"I went to college. My people are poor, and I own jazz records. Maybe I believe capitalism really is awful. Maybe I believe people should just help each other, and this whole thing you call America is a scam for rich people, and I have a secret pact with Moscow to bring it down. What about that?"

"Then you can tell me. Calm down," I said. "This isn't about you and me, it's just politics. Okay? Just let me do this."

"Then be careful, that's all. You're a crusader now. This isn't the kind of thing you can screw up. Not and be safe."

"Don't worry. No one starts wars anymore. Not with the bomb."

CHAPTER FOUR

AUGUST 1948

"ARE YOU Mr. Alger Hiss?" Stripling asked.

"Yes; I am."

"Please stand and be sworn. Do you solemnly swear that the testimony you are about to give will be the truth, the whole truth, and nothing but the truth, so help you God?"

"I do."

"Be seated."

I could see we had a very different witness in Alger Hiss. This wasn't the doughy, mush-mouthed Chambers we were up against. Hiss was tall, thin, prim, and patrician in manner. He'd gone to Johns Hopkins and, inevitably, Harvard Law School. He was cut from the same cloth as Jerry Voorhis—a high-minded liberal reformer.

The hearing room was more than a third full this time. The usual clerks and interns and hangers-on, but also a few reporters who could already smell blood in the water. A very tall man stood leaning against the back wall. Another lawyer? I couldn't tell.

Alger Hiss didn't seem at all shaken at being called in front of the House Un-American Activities Committee. He took the stand and faced the committee with the poise of an Olympic fencer. He told us how he'd worked for Justice Oliver Wendell Holmes and served as secretary-general at the United Nations charter conference. He told us very plainly that he had never met anyone named Whittaker Chambers, that he was not and never had been a Communist, and that the whole business was absurd and confusing.

He played to the crowd. Here was an honest American singled out for Kafkaesque persecution by an utter stranger who claimed to have lived with him and been his close friend and who alleged that together they'd stolen U.S. government secrets and given them to the Soviet Union. Hiss was politely, firmly, innocently baffled.

What the hell was this? I was ready for a conspirator out of a melodrama. I expected evasion, fear, bluster, righteous anger, something I could beat down and break. But this?

I realized with a sick dread that I might really have gotten the wrong man. I'd been swept up in this grand idea that now seemed incredibly thin and, arguably, a little childish. Was I actually going to try to convince the world this guy was a Soviet secret agent? Where was my evidence? It was like accusing him of being a leprechaun. As proof, I had only the word of weird Mr. Chambers with his slurred speech and his sleepy demeanor and his foul breath, and I began to wonder why I'd staked my career on this guy's fairy story of ultimate evil.

I couldn't just apologize and walk away. I had grandstanded for the press and vowed to bring a dangerous conspiracy to light. Hiss was my star attraction and there was no way out but to try to convict him. And Hiss knew it; he saw that it was him or me, that one of us was going to be ruined over this. I could tell from the way he faced up to me on the stand. He hadn't come looking for this fight, but he obviously had every intention of destroying me.

I thought about whether Hiss might be innocent, but I had a terrible feeling that it was too late for that. The decision had been made. At thirty-five I knew this much about myself, that if I had to choose between ruining my career and convicting Hiss, I would go ahead and convict him. And if he was innocent, maybe I would do something for him later? Of course I would. Once I was in the Senate, I would fix everything.

The following day we brought Chambers back in to explain himself. I demanded, coaxed, begged him to give some solid evidence to support his story. He knew Hiss. He gave a detailed and intimate portrait of Hiss's life in the 1930s in a quiet, spare little apartment on a dead-end street in a Washington suburb. He had an eye for the telling detail and he seemed to nurse some private grievance. He described Hiss's wife, another Communist, as "a short, highly nervous, little woman with a habit of blushing red when she is excited or angry, fiery red." Her son Timmy by an earlier partner was "a puny little boy, also rather nervous."

The Hisses were struggling, decent, overeducated civil servants; Chambers was a persistent lodger and hanger-on and, possibly, a friend. Chambers's self-portrait was unsentimental, unsparing, and uncomfortably pathetic. He had been a struggling writer who couldn't pay his bills. He received the Hisses' car as a gift, and they forgave him his unpaid rent. Finally he told us in unambiguous language that Hiss was a Communist and a true believer. Hiss and Chambers stole United States government secrets together until Chambers had a change of heart. He'd seen something that changed his mind, something disturbing he refused to divulge. He pleaded with Hiss to leave the Communist Party, and when Hiss wouldn't, Chambers ended their friendship forever.

When Hiss returned eight days later, he corroborated the domestic details with cool exactness. He was candid and quietly dignified as we rummaged through his personal history. He and his wife were still together. Timmy had grown up, served in the navy; he'd run off somewhere but was in touch through a psychiatrist. Hiss didn't know a Whittaker Chambers or anyone of this description. The hearing room was shifting uncomfortably—people had come for a story, a drama, and they were getting something a little more human and disappointing. Someone here was acting in bad faith—someone besides myself, that is—but who?

Finally, after long deliberation, Hiss gave us something. That morning, he said, a name occurred to him, a lodger from 1933. A failed writer, he said, a man with bad teeth who had neglected to pay his rent. He had disappeared from their lives in 1935. He wrote the name on a pad of paper in front of him— *George Crosley.* We agreed that the following day both men would appear together and meet face to face. And we would learn whether this was an international Communist conspiracy, or a dumpy, delusional middle-aged man.

The next morning the hearing room was packed. The story had been building in the papers all week, the spy syndicate, the accusation, all hinging on the conundrum of the missing friend, and now we'd learn the truth. I could do only so much to stage-manage this. Chambers (or George Crosley, or whoever) would simply have to make the charges stick and my political career would live or die accordingly.

Hiss arrived and pointedly did not look at Chambers. He took his time through the opening questions, speaking slowly and clearly. He coolly requested we call the Harvard Club to tell them he'd be late for an appointment. Chambers sat quietly across the room until the time came, and we called him to the front.

"Mr. Hiss," I said, "the man standing here is Mr. Whittaker

Chambers. I ask you now if you have ever known that man before."

Alerted, Hiss stood and approached by a few steps, gunslinger taut. "May I ask him to speak? Will you ask him to say something?"

Hiss examined Chambers, who complied with a childlike docility. He answered biographical questions, read from a copy of *Newsweek* to demonstrate his speaking voice. Hiss had him open his mouth so he could inspect his teeth, strangely decayed. He sat down and cross-examined him until he reluctantly identified him as a man he had known casually under the name George Crosley.

All the while, Chambers spoke to Hiss as he would to an intimate friend, gently and with a certain violence—an intimate friend whose reputation he was going to ruin.

Hiss got out of his chair and advanced on Chambers and had to be restrained. He seemed pushed past the point of endurance. Chambers watched Hiss with a look that was both wounded and nakedly hungry, like he was gazing at a lost love.

The terrible thing was that I thought I understood them; the story made perfect sense with or without the spying. They'd been friends back when they were also people struggling to make their mark, people like me, just as talented, just as intelligent, only a millimeter less fortunate. Moving from one slightly too shabby apartment to the next; begging favors, falling behind on rent. They had shared some secret, too shameful or fearful for their friendship to sustain.

Hiss had made himself into a very different man than the one Chambers had known. He was a rising star now, brilliant and respected. That memory of a closeness between the vulnerable, awkward people they'd been was still with them, a delicate, embarrassing bond unwillingly shared. I was slowly, publicly dragging him out of that lie and he'd rather perjure himself before a grand jury than admit to being the man who was friends with Chambers long ago in a walk-up apartment on P Street. I was spending taxpayer money excavating the ruins of a friendship that had ended a decade ago just so I could stay alive politically, and Hiss knew it.

Hiss made his closing remarks while glaring at me with a sad contempt. I didn't even have the heart to glare back. Instead, I looked past him to see the tall, dark-suited man again standing at the back of the hearing room. He'd been there all day. Not watching Hiss at all. He'd been watching me.

CHAPTER FIVE

AUGUST 1948

OVER THE NEXT few days Hiss showed the world how he was going to beat me. He was blazingly articulate, dignified, and kept a sharp eye on the mood of the room. He knew this wasn't a legal trial but a testing of the political waters. He didn't need to prove anything, only stay in the ring long enough for the press to get bored. I sat with Pat every night, going over the facts, talking about the performance, looking for the angle.

Another long afternoon ended with yet another round of yes-you-did-no-I-didn't, and I followed the crowd out into the Commodore's lobby, which was full of reporters and assorted hangers-on. I was shuffling through, nodding to well-wishers, when I saw Alger Hiss in angry conversation with a small, dark-haired woman. She laughed and he turned to go, brushing right past me.

I'd expected him to be holding forth to reporters, taking advantage of the day's rhetorical gains, as he'd done on previous days. Instead he was almost shoving his way through the crowd, his features rigid in what looked for all the world like panic. I watched him cut through the mob, walking straight-backed and serious. On an impulse, I fell in behind him.

"Mr. Nixon? Mr. Nixon?" a man called after me. Tall, with a long face; it was the man who'd stood at the back of the hearing room. A reporter? I quickened my pace, keeping Hiss in view. I followed him out the door, expecting to see him hail a cab, but instead he rounded the corner and turned uptown. I knew he lived in far-off downtown. Where was he going?

There were a hundred reasonable answers—a doctor's appointment, a drink with friends. I should have let him go but I couldn't. I wanted to know what sort of person had been glaring at me across a room. I wanted to know, once and for all, if I was persecuting an honest man or a traitor.

He stopped abruptly, so much so that a large woman behind him almost walked into him. He studied a window display with what seemed like unnatural attentiveness. What was he looking at? Flustered, I stopped where I was and did the same a block behind him. A women's shoe store, as luck would have it. How did they walk in those things? I glanced ahead just as he glanced back, and our eyes seemed to meet, but his face registered no recognition. In another minute he moved on. I passed the window he'd been looking at—a florist?

We went on like that for half an hour. Every four or five blocks he'd stop for a moment. Once he turned left and I hurried to follow. Three more turns and he'd circled the block. It was my first time following anyone, but were all people so suspicious?

We ducked and dodged through the late-afternoon crowd of gray-suited men and he led me five, then ten, then twenty blocks up Lexington Avenue, past the long, curving Buicks and Chevys of that year, past the elegant young men who'd gotten all those law jobs I'd applied for. I sweated through my shirt in the August heat. Plenty of time to think about what I'd say if he picked me out of the crowd. Should I feign an attack of conscience? Probably not. He was a lawyer and knew perfectly well how to make a circus out of it the following day.

Any real political operator would have had a private investigator do this. Jack Kennedy would have, Kennedy who was no doubt in the Hamptons while I straggled up Lexington Avenue in an ill-considered gamble for political gain. I already knew I was making a fool of myself. If I could just resolve what exactly Hiss was, at least I'd know which kind of fool.

Hiss *was* odd, damn it. His brittle demeanor, his strange, rigid unwillingness to acknowledge a man who obviously knew him well. And now this paranoia. He was under terrible pressure, anyone could see that, but what was its nature? A Soviet contact, a mistress, a hidden illness?

The shadows were getting longer as the sun went down over the Hudson, the moment when the north–south avenues were half in darkness, and the east–west streets became, briefly, tunnels of golden light. At Seventy-First Street he stopped, his long spindly shadow in front of him. He glanced back once before turning into a side street, and for a moment I was sure he'd seen me. It wouldn't have been hard; I was puffing, red-faced, and squarely in the middle of the sidewalk. But he missed me or else he covered seeing me extraordinarily well.

I rushed to the spot where he'd turned and then hesitated, evening pedestrians streaming past me. He could be standing just around the corner, ready to confront me. No way to tell. I nerved myself and stepped into the side street just in time to see Hiss's tall dark figure turning into a distant doorway. I hurried after him, trying to keep a fixed sense of which door it was.

It was an unremarkable building, brick, six stories. A sign above the lintel called it THE WEXFORD. I peered in at a tiny lobby: linoleum floor, stairwell, and a dark lift. Apartments or office building? I slipped inside and heard Hiss's footsteps moving upward and out of reach. Was I really doing this? I had come this far. I pulled my shoes off and gingerly scrambled up the slippery marble steps in my frayed socks, past identical floors of identical hallways, doors receding in the distance. The footsteps stopped on the fifth floor and I stopped on the stairwell beneath, panting. I smelled pencil shavings, mimeograph liquid, old cigarettes. Whatever the mystery was, I was close to it.

It occurred to me fleetingly and too late that there might be actual danger here. If Chambers was right, there were people in the United States in 1948 who were sworn to a foreign power and ready to act against Americans. What if Hiss really was a secret agent? Would he kill to keep his secrets? He might. He could be executed for treason if caught. Communists were murderers and assassins, everyone knew that. I thought of the Czech foreign minister who had leaped or been pushed from a lavatory window out into the early-morning air, pictured vividly the few agonizing moments before he struck the pale stone streets of Prague.

I moved up a few more steps to look down the corridor. Hiss had stopped and was opening the last door on the left. It swung shut behind him. I crept close enough to read the number 519 on the door, cheap wood with a frosted-glass window sealing the mystery behind. I could hear Hiss moving around inside. Shuffling papers, typing. What now? The other offices seemed to belong to accountants, notaries, mail-order firms. The fourth floor was the same.

I walked away and came back and nothing had changed. I could feel in my gut just how bad an idea this was but couldn't tear myself away now that I was so close. I thought about what I could do if I had proof of treason. Who could ignore me then?

The phone rang, and I heard Hiss pick up and begin speaking quickly, angrily, like a man at the end of his patience. I was leaning in closer trying to make out the words when he hung up and his footsteps came rapidly toward the door. I froze in em-

barrassment, stood there in the bare hallway as the doorknob
rattled and the door swung open. I stepped back to avoid being
hit in the face. What could he possibly think when he saw me?
Words rose to my lips—an apology or a protest or an accusation, I'll never know. Then the door began to swing closed and
I saw Hiss's narrow back. He was striding angrily away from
me toward the stairs. I stared after him, flooded with adrenaline
and animated by a strange idea. The door was still open; the answer to all my questions was just inside.

What I did next came from no conscious plan—my natural
inborn genius for bad decision-making came to the fore and I
made an uncharacteristically athletic and completely soundless
leap forward, then lunged sideways through the closing door
and into the unlit office beyond. The door swung to and clicked
shut behind me. After that instant of frantic motion, the world
became utterly still.

I stood in a small office consisting of one room with a single
window fogged with dust that looked out onto an air shaft.
I stood in the pale gray light, breathing hard from the sudden exertion, waiting for the moment Alger Hiss would come
back. It was so perfectly possible—a forgotten wallet, a scrap
of paper, anything at all. There would be nowhere to hide and
no possible way to explain, but it was too late to think of that
now.

And what had I found? It didn't look like a lawyer's office. A
professor's, perhaps, an antiquarian of a dozen disciplines.

A chipped wooden desk overflowing with papers; four high,
overfull bookshelves crammed with old books, binders, and
what seemed like small statuary; two gray metal filing cabinets.
The walls were covered in papers of every description: maps,
star charts, gravestone rubbings labeled with names of various
New England towns.

The window was shut tight. It was still warm from the day's heat. I breathed in the smells of old books and the sweat of a stranger working long hours in a tiny space. I carried a book to the window where I could read the title. *An Englishman's Solitary Walk Through the Ural Mountain Regions and the Dire Events There Witnessed.* In succession I pulled down a heavily annotated copy of *Bradford's History of Plimoth Plantation, A Speculative Glossary of Early Etruscan,* and the more recent *Burgess Shale Anomalies: An Alarmist View,* which bore the stamp of the Peabody Museum at Harvard. I leafed through that one, looking at fanciful reconstructions of animals with five eyes and disturbing symmetries. On the desk, mimeographs of scholarly works on geology, linguistics, paleontology. What kind of spy was Alger Hiss, exactly?

Finally, rummaging in the drawers, I discovered a notebook marked *January–August 1948.* A diary. The handwriting within was barely legible, and it grew more ragged as the account went on.

IT IS WITH THE GREATEST TREPIDATION THAT I NOW SET DOWN THE DISTURBING EVENTS OF THE PAST THREE YEARS AND OF MY VISIT TO THE PLACE KNOWN AS THE PAWTUXET FARM. BUT I QUESTION WHETHER THE WORLD SHOULD KNOW OF THIS. PERHAPS THE VEIL OF BENEVOLENT ILLUSION THAT CLOUDS OUR COMMON UNDERSTANDING OF THE UNIVERSE SHOULD REMAIN UNDISTURBED, FOR HAVING SEEN THESE AWFUL SIGHTS I SHALL NEVER AGAIN SLEEP UNTROUBLED.

What was he getting at? More philosophical meanderings followed, none of which seemed too relevant. I turned the pages, looking for incriminating passages... SINCE EARLIEST CHILDHOOD I HAVE BEEN SUSCEPTIBLE TO MORBID TENDENCIES OF THE MIND... Was he a psychiatric case? That would explain a lot. THE DOCUMENTS PROVIDED PROVED SUSCEPTIBLE TO THE CRYPTOGRAPHIC METHODS OF THE ANCIENTS BUT THE PHRASES I LABORIOUSLY REVEALED CREATED IN ME A

NAMELESS DISCOMFORT, A FOREBODING OF . . . Jesus, this guy and his discomforts. Was he a spy or wasn't he? I skipped ahead.

MY NEWFOUND PARTNERS SUPPLIED ME WITH PROMISING INFORMATION, BUT COULD THEY BE TRUSTED? THE SMILING WOMAN IN PARTICULAR SEEMED CAPABLE OF ANY VIOLENCE OR SUBTERFUGE IN PURSUIT OF HER OWN INTERESTS, WHATEVER THEY WERE. I HAD EMBARKED DOWN A DARK AND DANGEROUS PATH IN SEARCH OF THE TRUTH BUT I COULDN'T STOP. ALL THOUGHT OF A SOCIALIST FUTURE HAD CEASED TO CONCERN ME. I DID MY ERRANDS AS USUAL BUT THE ABOMINABLE TRUTH HINTED AT IN THAT GENTLEMAN FARMER'S WRITINGS WERE A MORE PRESSING CONCERN. COULD THE TWO LETTERS TRULY BE IN THE SAME HAND, A CENTURY AND A HALF APART? WHAT STRANGE MATERIALS HAD ARRIVED UNDER COVER OF DARKNESS ON A BURMESE SLOOP? AND WHY HAD THE DEPARTMENT OF DEFENSE ISSUED A QUARANTINE ORDER?

Better! But it wasn't a smoking gun. And his weird obsession with old letters didn't add to the picture of a master conspirator.

I PROCEEDED TO THE CENTRAL BUILDING OF WHICH THE LETTERS HAD SPOKEN, THIS ONE STONE RATHER THAN WOOD OR METAL. I CREPT INSIDE IN SEARCH OF THE SOURCE OF THOSE AWFUL CRIES, STILL FEEBLY HOPING WHITTAKER HAD BEEN WRONG. I DON'T MIND SAYING MY HAND TREMBLED AS IT HELD THE FLASHLIGHT. THE DOOR SEEMED TO HAVE BEEN DAMAGED BY AN INDESCRIBABLE . . .

Enough already! I turned over more pages. Photographs of State Department documents. Cargo manifests coming through Boston Harbor. Aerial surveillance photographs showing a row of long white buildings in desert terrain, time-stamped a few months ago. Numerous documents in Cyrillic characters, meaningless to me. I picked up the last few pages.

I WAS STUNNED. I NOW MUST QUESTION EVERYTHING THAT HAS GONE BEFORE. DID THE SOVIETS EVEN CARE ABOUT THE INFORMATION I SUP-

PLIED THEM WITH? DID MOSCOW ORCHESTRATE THIS HIDEOUS JOURNEY? OR HAS [a name here was crossed out] FORCED ME TO RISK MY REPUTATION AND PERHAPS MY FUCKING SANITY FOR HER OWN...

Finally. I had no idea what the rest of it meant, but crazy Alger Hiss was a damned Communist. I glanced around, unwilling to leave the treasure-house just yet. I copied down a phone number I saw written on a scrap of paper. I searched for a few more minutes until I discovered a spare key to the office in the back of a drawer.

As long as he didn't know I'd broken in, he'd leave everything where it was and ready for my return. The important thing was, there would be an absolute triumph in the press. I didn't even need to feel bad about it because Alger Hiss was a dirty Commie spy. Dick Nixon was a hero.

CHAPTER SIX

I TOLD PAT I was feeling confident, that it was only a matter of time, and that I'd be working late again that night. In a few days, she'd see me win a clean victory.

I daydreamed through the next day's hearing while the rest of the committee questioned Hiss and he countered masterfully, the perfect image of an honest man beset and outraged at a baseless campaign of persecution. I doodled on my notepad and looked at the crowd. The members of the press were turning against me. Let them. If my case looked weak now, it would make the truth that much more shocking.

When Hiss left at the end of the day, I trailed him far enough downtown to satisfy myself he was going home for the evening. A thought struck me—what if the Commies were following me? I circled a downtown block, looked in shop windows. What else does one do? I had a drink in a bar and left by a back way. It was close to eleven at night when I returned to the building on Seventy-First Street and climbed the stairs.

My footsteps sounded too loud in the silence of the fifth floor, and I forced myself not to hurry. I was carrying a camera and a small flashlight in my briefcase to document what hard evidence I could, and tomorrow I'd claim to have received an anonymous tip from a concerned citizen. The next time I was here I'd have federal agents with me.

I turned the key and, relieved, slipped out of the hall and into the darkened office, but I knew immediately something was wrong. I smelled fresh paint and dust; my footsteps pinged too loud and sharp. What was this? When I raised the flashlight, the beam lit bare walls. I stared. I turned all the way around in place, as if the desk and chair and shelving were going to leap out from wherever they'd hidden. I put one hand on the cool white wall. This was badly wrong, but how? Was it the wrong office? The wrong building?

I heard footsteps coming steadily and purposefully down the hallway, and I froze. Then I snapped the flashlight off and stood waiting in the darkness. A key turned in the lock. It had to be Hiss. He'd known all along; he'd watched me come and he'd trapped me. I glanced at the window and thought of climbing out in a lunatic escape attempt, but there wasn't time even for that. Would he laugh? Arrest me? What was he planning? With a titanic effort I composed myself and turned toward the door.

It opened and two men stood there, silhouetted, and looked in at me with frank and unhurried curiosity. One was short and one tall, like a pair of comedians. The big man was a head taller and carried a steel briefcase. The smaller of them had a pistol raised.

"Please take two steps backward," the small man said in a light European accent I couldn't place. East German? I took two long steps back and the windowsill nudged me just above the knees. The gunman stepped inside, the large man following. He closed the door. I held up my hands in a placating gesture. I tried and failed to stutter out my last words.

"Is not to worry," the second man said. Russian. He switched on the overhead light. Under the bright bulb, he was a heap of a man with a nose that had been broken a few times; he wore a suit of gray wool, wrinkled and elephantine. He took off his hat and set the briefcase down as if commencing a day at the office. I could see dusty outlines on the wall where the furniture had been yesterday.

The other man was younger than I'd first thought, in his midtwenties at most. Hair combed straight back but balding already, and he looked like he hadn't been getting much sleep. Something about the bad fit of his suit made me tag him as a student.

"What's your name?" the small man said, studying me.

"Richard Nixon," I told him. I'd never been held at gunpoint before, and it was surprisingly awkward. I felt like a host receiving unexpected guests. I had no eye for firearms but the pistol was a small semiautomatic, not at all showy. The room was small and I was sure he would hit me if he fired.

"Hello, Richard. I'm Gregor, and this is Arkady." He glanced up at the big man, who nodded. I made a guess that Gregor was in command here.

"Are you the police?" I asked.

"We're not the police," he said. I waited for him to go on. I tried sitting down on the windowsill, but it was too narrow. I stumbled and straightened up again. They watched the performance.

"And what brings Richard Nixon to this part of town at such a late hour?" Gregor asked. He leaned against the empty wall.

"I'm investigating," I said, "a crime."

"A crime!" Gregor said, brow knit with mock concern. "And what kind of crime is that?"

"It's a very important case. A Soviet spy." I glanced up at the Russian, but he said nothing, just looked over at his partner.

"A Commie spy, is that it? Very exciting," Gregor said.

"Are you . . . Communists?" I asked.

"No," Gregor said.

"I am, actually," Arkady said, putting his hands in his pockets. "Sorry. Greggy is socialist pussy. But we work on him."

"What did you find, Mr. Nixon?" said Gregor. "In your investigations. I'd like to know." His accent nagged at me; he sounded as if he'd lived in half a dozen countries before his teens. His pink skin didn't sweat.

"Just evidence," I said. "Different kinds of evidence. Was found. Look, I don't know who you are but you can't hold me here." I stepped away from the wall. The big man took his hands out of his pockets, and abruptly the room felt even smaller. Gregor stood well back, his gun out of my reach.

"Seems very serious," he said. "Are you a policeman, Nixon? Federal agent, maybe? Counterintelligence?" He sounded like he was maybe about finished with this conversation and what I'd thought was going to be a long interrogation was just pre-execution banter.

"You don't have to do this," I said. It would be so lovely to be able to say I did something brave here. Laughed at their threats; spat in their faces. If I were that kind of person, post–World War II American history would have been a very different story. "Please . . . I'm a United States congressman, for Christ's sake. I can tell you things. I'll do anything."

"Really?" the Russian said. "You are Congress?" He seemed genuinely a little starstruck.

"California," I said. "The Twelfth District. Richard Milhous Nixon."

"Holy shit," Gregor said.

"Is not what I was told, Gregor," said the taller man. "Private detective, you said. This is the big shit we are in now."

"Shut up. I'm trying to think."

"Congressman we can't just dump in mudflat. Is not quite the same."

47

"Shut up, please," Gregor said, then turned to me. "Nixon! Did you take an oath?"

"A what?" I said.

"An oath of office. You took one?"

"Yes. Yes, of course."

"How did it run? Exact words, as much as you can remember."

"Well, it was . . . just a minute." I've always been proud of my memory. "It was—'I do solemnly swear . . . that I will support and defend the Constitution of the United States against all enemies, foreign and domestic.' Let me think . . . I've forgotten the middle . . . the ending is 'I will well and faithfully discharge the duties of the office on which I am about to enter. So help me God.'"

"You hear it, Arkady? You understand?"

"A little. What is it you are thinking?"

"He's federally sworn. A compact."

"I have theory background, yes, I get that far—"

"This is the asset we've waited for. We've got the blood of the Elect here, and your field kit. From this we can stage a strategic incursion."

"Bullshit. How?"

"You weren't in the meetings. I'll walk you through. You're finally going to see what the Nth Directorate does," he said. His lips were trembling a little.

"I think I make a call to the embassy if you don't mind."

"I am in authority here, Colonel, not you. You just do your part," Gregor said. He tucked his gun into an armpit holster and stripped off his jacket. "And you just stay where you are, Mr. Nixon. We're about to make history."

Gregor put the briefcase on the floor between us. It had a dull, scratched metal finish, a heavy industrial look, and two locks. Each man took out a key and set it in a lock, then paused. Gregor quietly counted, "One, two," and they turned the keys simultaneously to open it.

Arkady pawed through the contents and picked out two envelopes covered with emphatic Cyrillic script in various sizes, some of it in red. "We verify first. No mistakes," Arkady said.

"Very well." They each tore open an envelope and shook out a pen and a thick piece of card stock. Each wrote out a long string of characters on the card, evidently working from memory, then they swapped cards and studied the results against what was on the backs.

"Accepted," Arkady said after a moment. "You?"

"Yes. I will be primary, you will administer. Get us a proper seal, threefold. This will be one of the exarchs. Tolerances are here." He tossed Arkady another envelope. Arkady opened it, studied the contents, then took a measuring tape and a felt-tip pen and began marking precise points on one wall.

Meanwhile Gregor opened a metal box full of small glass bottles. He dug around in the briefcase, removed a miniature scale, and began measuring out little samples of powder and depositing them in a ceramic bowl. He poured in a few drops of clear liquid, spat into the dark mixture, and crushed all of it together using the butt of his gun as a pestle. A chalky smell filled the room and he coughed.

"Is what?" asked Arkady.

"Someone said bone. Comes from one of the dig sites."

Arkady took the bowl and a small brush and began connecting the dots he'd made on the wall, forming odd angles and curves.

"I want you to know I'll be alerting the authorities," I told them. "I will expect a full accounting."

"He does not know a thing, this one," said Arkady.

"Stay quiet, this will be easy," Gregor told me. "It's all standard procedure. Arkady, you know the axes go the other way on this continent?"

"Just waiting on an entity code."

"'Novosibirsk L three four oh nine.'" Gregor read this from a small piece of card stock, then tore it in half twice.

"Female, then."

"It's the Raven Mother. We gamed it out. Mother of millions. Optimal spread for urban deployment, and she'll—"

"I know what she does," Arkady said. "I read the file. Xenomorph exarch. This is wise, Greggy? She is hard to stop."

"Activation phase," Gregor said. This part, it turned out, was quite lengthy and in Russian. They took turns reading aloud from a numbered set of note cards, dropping each one on the floor when they were finished. I heard my name twice, mixed in with the rest of it. Gregor kept an eye on me, I suppose so he could stop me in case I tried to move. I studied what Arkady had drawn on the wall. It looked like a geometric proof or an unfamiliar set of constellations. Near the center he had filled in a large black circle. It glistened, refusing to dry.

At one point, they stopped, counted off, and, to my astonishment, launched into a rhythmic chant while shuffling through a complicated set of steps and hand movements. It wasn't a dance exactly, but it seemed like the product of a long technical rehearsal. When they finished I wondered what time it was. One o'clock? Later? I was feeling tired. The room seemed darker, although the bare bulb still shone.

"Are you ready?" Gregor said. "We'll have six minutes from when I initiate."

"I am still within my rights to object," Arkady said.

"Do you exercise that right, my friend? You'd best tell me now."

"I do not."

Gregor took out a metal flask, shook it for five seconds, then uncapped it. "Counting six minutes from now." He sniffed the mixture, made a face, and chugged the contents. He shivered despite the heat of the room. "Get him ready."

"What is he doing?" I asked Arkady. He ignored me. Gregor took his shoes off and kicked them to one corner. One of his socks had a hole in the heel.

"I would like you to touch that circle on the wall," Gregor said. He pointed to one part of the diagram.

"Why?"

"It is not important."

"I'm not going to," I said. I don't know why. It seemed obscurely humiliating like a bully's trick. I wasn't going to touch anything.

"It is only a formality."

"Do it, please." Arkady looked at me grimly.

"I don't—" I began, but there was a flash of light and then I was on one knee, the side of my face gone numb. It came to me that Arkady had just hit me. He was already hauling me forward by my wrist. I stumbled to my feet, trying to make a fist, but my nerves weren't connecting quite right. I glanced at the wall. The circle seemed bigger. Almost a foot across.

"Initializing host," Arkady said. There was a flash of cool on my palm, then a stinging, and my palm was bleeding.

What was this? I'd heard the Soviets had their own interrogation methods, that their foreign intelligence service dated back to 1917 or maybe earlier. That they'd do anything to get what they wanted.

"You'll get nothing from me!" One of them chuckled.

"Just touch the circle, please."

"No!"

"Touch it!"

"I don't want to!" There was a breeze moving through the

room now. A moment ago I'd been prepared to tell them any-thing, but for some reason I didn't want to touch the circle. I fought but Arkady was heroically strong. He twisted my arm, locked the elbow, and dragged me across the room.

"What's the matter? He should be immobilized by now." Gregor sounded panicked.

"He resists. I don't understand it either."

"Cuff him!"

"No handcuffs! I have only the murder stuff."

"Is this—I don't understand; am I being tortured?"

"How long?" Arkady said.

There was a ringing in my ears, perhaps from the blow.

"Shouldn't be long," Gregor said. "Just hold him."

"I've got a few drops on it now but it does nothing. He must be an outlier."

"Fuck! You hear that? We are at the final stage," Gregor said. And I did hear something, the sound of a woman laughing, an older woman. It sounded far away, elsewhere in the building maybe.

"I don't understand," I whispered.

"It's a new world, little congressman. There's going to be a new war. The last war. We'll see you at the ascension, Mr. Nixon. Get his hand in, Arkady."

Arkady's full weight was on me, crushing me against the wall, and I could see only a little slice of the room around his midsection. He rotated a little and I saw where my blood had been smeared on the wall and the floor. The circle was much larger now. Gregor must have added to it, although I hadn't seen him do it.

"When do we move to minimum safe distance?" Arkady said. "I am not liking to be here for the, what do you call, emergence."

"Get it done."

Arkady tensed again for the effort. I looked at the circle, and the blackness took on an impossible depth. I had the terrible impression it was no longer a circle but a dark hole tunneling into the wall.

"No!" Without understanding why, I was seized with a terror I hadn't felt since childhood. I thrashed, twisted. I managed to stomp hard on one of Arkady's cheap shoes and he yelped. I got my left arm free and clawed feebly at his face. I would have done anything to a human body just to be spared touching that circle. His grip loosened and I lurched back, arm free, gasping for air in the close room. The three of us looked at one another.

The hole in the wall was expanding, slowly. Beyond I saw stars and a bulky shape silhouetted against them. The air that came through was shockingly cold. Something on the far side moved, just a shadow. I couldn't understand the scale. It looked huge.

"It's going to be hungry," Gregor said, maybe to himself. He glanced from one to the other of us, making a calculation, just a whisper of thought. He reached toward his pistol, but in the same second Arkady was already moving, swinging one tree-trunk arm in a thunderous open-hand slap. Gregor staggered, fumbling the gun from its holster.

Arkady drove forward, using his bulk, almost falling into the smaller man. He had a hand on Gregor's sleeve, trying to control the gun. I scrambled across the room.

"You fucking idiot to pull this," Arkady said, oddly calm. Gregor strained against him, fired the pistol at nothing. Arkady swung him into the wall; the impact was like a man hitting the ground from four stories up. The gun fell to the floor and spun.

"We cannot abort." Gregor began talking very quickly. "She sees me now. The blood is his but she sees me —"

"You want to shoot me, Gregor? You think I don't know what you pull?" Arkady said. He muscled the smaller man toward the hole. Gregor clawed at Arkady and then froze, and his face cleared in blank terror.

"I felt it. It touched me," he said. Then, *"Ich bin bereit... Ich bin ganz..."* His shirt had torn and I saw a tattoo on his forearm, an eight-pointed star, like a black radiant sun.

"Pick up the gun!" Arkady snarled, one hand now around Gregor's throat. I realized he was talking to me. I grabbed it, checked the safety like I'd been taught.

"Stop this!" I shouted. "You're both under arrest!" Neither of them seemed to hear me.

"Shoot him now," Arkady said. "Do not wait."

"I can't." I held the gun close to Gregor's face, trying to make him look at it. I was intensely aware that I had never pointed a gun at a live human being, not even in the war. How had Gregor done this so casually?

"The king will come," Gregor spluttered. He was almost blue but seemed as strong as ever. Arkady was losing his grip. "The king of America. The blank throne." In one motion he pulled free and plunged his arm through the hole, impossibly deep, almost to the shoulder.

"Y'gsth——"

My body went slack, and in a moment when I didn't care what happened because obviously none of this was happening in the world as I understood it, I put the barrel against Gregor's chest and pulled the trigger. I lost, I think, a few seconds after that, and then I was sitting against the wall. I must have dropped the gun and fallen backward. Arkady was holding it now. He fired four more times into Gregor's body, a slow line down the torso. The body twitched. It would not lie still. I heard a faint crackling.

The big man stopped, waiting, pistol still pointed. He looked at me and pulled the trigger once more, and it gave a dry click.

"No more bullets, okay?" he said. "No more shooting. Is done."

I nodded. My ears were ringing but I didn't hear any sirens. The hole was a blank circle again.

"Is he . . ." I asked.

"I do not think so. We do not have the tools here to finish."

"What was happening to him?"

"I hear of such things but I do not believe until now. Grafts and injections, no one lived. Gregor was one in ten thousand."

"What did he say, just at the end?"

"Not here. Fuck. What a goatfuck tonight."

"Is he—dead?" I asked again.

"If he is not, then we are sure not killing him now."

"Is it . . . is that hell? Was that the devil?"

"I have heard it called an angel, or the last czar, or leviathan-grade bioweapons ordnance. It has a name for itself I cannot pronounce. Is not good place to talk here, or breathe even. I think it would be good to have a drink right now."

We found a dive bar a couple of blocks south on Lexington. The terrifying scuffle of a few minutes ago was fresh on my raw skin. I felt bruised and sore and my hand was swollen. Arkady ordered us each several shots of slightly cloudy vodka.

"You are really from California?" he asked.

"What? Yes," I said.

"What part?" His English was better than I'd thought at first, far less accented.

"Southern. Southern California."

"Ha!" he barked, abruptly, some private joke. "You see many movie stars?"

"Well, once in a while, I suppose," I said, thinking of the time I saw Cary Grant two cars ahead of me in a traffic jam.

"I'd like to fuck one of them one time."

"That . . . that'd be pretty fine," I said.

I held up my hand. There was a raw burn across the ball of my thumb. "I can't feel it now. Is it poisoned?" I asked.

"More like anesthetic. Thing is like wasp. Then it lays eggs."

"What?" I tried to see my hand better but it was too dark. "Jesus. I think I need to go to the restroom."

"You would know if they were there. Size of Ping-Pong balls. And I would have cut hand off at this point."

"Great. Thanks, though. For letting me go. Eventually."

"I have done enough shitty things, I am thinking. And Gregor was going to take me too, I am very sure of it. But I will say, I should not have tried to feed you to that thing."

"Cheers, then."

"Za vas."

We drank.

"What happened there? How did you know he was going to . . ." I made a gun out of one hand. Thinking back, he'd reacted impossibly fast.

"Richard, how old do you think I am?"

I looked him over. He had a couple of really nice scars and he'd spent a lot of time outdoors. "Fifty?" I said, guessing ten years more than that.

He shrugged.

"All right, fifty. So I been in the Soviet Union since I was nineteen, Soviet intelligence since—"

"Wait, you're a spy?"

"What the fuck you think I am? Since whenever. Point is, how many purges you think I go through? Mission fucked, he wants to burn me. I've done it myself to other guys. More than fucking once. I know what it looks like."

He gestured for another shot of vodka, and downed it.

"I know who you are, Mr. Nixon, the guy trying to catch Alger Hiss. You make a lot of speeches. You really that angry about it? All the Commie spies."

"Maybe I'm a little madder about it now, yes."

"I cannot blame you there. Was a bad thing, tonight."

"He is a spy, right? Hiss? That's what this is all about? Just tell me. I don't even know what I saw."

"Maybe nothing, huh? Maybe you just forget about this crazy stuff, yes? Hiss does nothing for no one but himself. I tell you what, Mr. Nixon. Probably best you go home. You go out looking for spies, maybe you find other things sometimes. You know this now. Is not for amateurs. Think of it as bad dream. Wake up tomorrow and forget."

"But . . . but I have to know what happened. What all this was."

He stood, put some money on the bar.

"I am sorry for it all. You not a bad guy. You need it, I help you out sometime maybe." He extended a hand. I shook it.

"Do not follow me. I see how you follow Hiss, it is pathetic." He took his hat from the bar and left.

I waited fifteen minutes. I started to shake a little and ordered another shot of vodka. I'd heard about American covert operations in Europe. I knew we'd tried to plant dozens of sleeper agents behind the Iron Curtain. Hardened men, partisans who'd fought the Nazis, nationalists who'd then stayed behind when the Communists took control after the war. In short, men and women a thousand times tougher than I'd ever be. We tried to get them into the government or the police, anywhere they could inform for us or sway a key election or just stay in one place until we needed them, but that dreamed-of resistance movement never quite found its moment. They went dark, dead or turned or scared into submission, every single one of them. I wondered now how they'd died or what they'd been shown to change their minds. I wondered if they'd acted any better than I had.

When I left the bar, it was maybe five a.m., still warm and humid, an August night shading into early morning. My hotel was on Central Park South. I walked the whole distance, not even feeling drunk. I sat on a park bench and watched the very tops of the higher buildings fading into view.

What was I doing? I was a stage actor pretending to be a politician, a spy hunter, a tough guy. Now that I'd met the tough guys, I knew I wasn't one, not even close. And I'd seen something else.

I was thirty-five and I'd thought I was playing political poker and it turned out I'd been playing in some other game I didn't even know about. Like I'd been holding a hand of kings and then the people around the table started putting down more kings, a king with a squid's face, a naked king with goat's horns holding up a bough of holly. A Russian king with an insect's voice. I knew the look on my face because I'd seen it on other people's faces, that moment when the cocky junior-league card-sharp who thinks he's been running the show all night looks around the table and finally figures out who the sucker is.

CHAPTER SEVEN

I WOKE UP still in the clothes I'd worn to yesterday's hearing. I looked out my hotel window into bright sunlight and smelled the faint scent of gunpowder on my jacket. It had happened. Now what was I supposed to do about it? Gregor was dead. Arkady had saved my life, or I had saved his.

I took the train down to Washington, and Pat picked me up at the station.

"Did you find any spies?" A sour edge in her voice.

"Not yet, dear," I said.

"Well, I'm sure you'll get them."

"You don't have to say that," I told her. I closed my eyes on the way home, pretended to nap. Some instinct told me to lock away what I remembered, to keep those strange blurred moments of struggle shading into inexplicable horror in a separate part of myself. Over the next few days, the strangeness faded and I began to doubt what had happened. The rest of the world continued as it had. I was a nobody with no connections and I was going to disappear from the world.

I went back to work. The hearings had moved to Washington, DC, and the political press was watching. Chambers described in detail the Hiss household, its decor, the family's quirks, and odd bits of personal trivia. When Hiss took the stand, he dismissed Chambers as a passing acquaintance, a parasite, and a mediocrity. I glared at him helplessly. I had seen the man's diary, and in theory all I had to do was wait for a slipup or a sign of weakness, but he had nerves like a gunfighter. He toyed with me, and gave up nothing. All that fall he kept it going. Prominent politicians were coming out in support of Hiss, and my grandstanding opportunity was turning into a national embarrassment.

One night I had dinner with my family in front of the television set and we watched American planes landing in Tempelhof Airport to bring food to cheering, blockaded Berliners. No one had to say anything; it was obvious. When I pointed the finger at Hiss I'd thrown a pebble down a hillside, and now it was part of an avalanche. For once I'd guessed right about where history was going, but my opportunity to be the Cold War's first great hero was slipping away. It was probably gone already.

I excused myself and went for a nighttime walk in the suburban streets, the air still warm with late-summer heat. I tried to see a way out of the trap I'd put myself in. Hiss was a spy, I knew it, but I couldn't say anything about the diary, and I couldn't prove it any other way.

What I did next was the kind of irrevocable step that you take without thinking or knowing why until years after. I was angry and unhappy, and on some profound level I didn't care about what I might be sacrificing, my reputation or my country or my marriage or the sanctity of my oath of office. I didn't give a shit, and I didn't even know it. Not until the moment I watched myself throw it all on the fire and let it burn.

I stopped at a public telephone and dialed the number I'd copied from the piece of scrap paper in Hiss's office. I held my breath as it rang. I still only half believed in what I remembered from that night. A woman answered.

"Hello? Who is this, please?" she said.

"It's Alger Hiss calling." I couldn't say my own name, could I?

"Just a moment, please," she said. Then, farther off, "He says he's Alger Hiss." I heard a click as the phone was transferred, then a familiar voice.

"Mr. Nixon! It is good to hear from you. You are well, yes? I see you in papers all the time now. How is trial?"

"It's not a trial, it's a hearing. Hello, Arkady. How did you know it was me?"

"Who else? The hearing goes well, Mr. Nixon? You catching the spies yet?"

"Not really, Arkady."

"Well, then. How can I help you?"

"Do you know . . . do you know where I got this number?"

"Of course I do, Richard. Why do you call me? No spies here, I promise you."

"Where are you, Arkady?"

"Russian embassy, of course. In my job as cultural attaché. I am arranging Kandinsky show here in Washington, you must come. You need tickets? This is why you call?"

"Thank you, Arkady. But . . . that night you said . . . well, if I needed something."

"Of course, of course. Just tell me and we talk about it. Man to man."

"Well—you know our mutual friend? The one who I had . . . come to visit. I had the sense that maybe . . . maybe we could talk about him more. Maybe you and he were . . . not so friendly?" I realized I was trying to talk like a spy when I had never met a spy. Except Arkady.

"What you want, Dick?" he asked. And that was the question. What I wanted.

"I guess I want to talk."

"We can, yes. But you are sure about this?"

"Of course."

"Very well. You know the Grant Memorial?"

"Yes."

"Perhaps you go there around midnight tomorrow. Wait for sound of owl then begin walking north. Four blocks. You see a man with white hair carrying copy of *Middlemarch* and you follow him. He get into parked car, you get into car three cars behind him. Say the name *Annabelle* to driver. If someone follow you, they die, understand?"

"All right. Yes."

"No! Don't act like asshole. No one cares what you do. Just come meet me tomorrow, one o'clock at my office."

The next day I told myself it was just to see what happened. Just to see how far this game would lead. It was just a conversation, nothing more. Just talk.

In spite of what Arkady said, I took a taxi from work to a crowded department store, walked in circles for half an hour before guiltily buying a set of earrings for Pat, then left by a different exit and hailed a taxi. We had driven for a few minutes before I realized the driver was shaking with laughter.

"Now I am chauffeur, eh?" Arkady said. He turned to look at me. In daylight he looked uglier. Lined face, worn overcoat, thinning jet-black hair.

"You followed me?"

"You try and do the spy thing, I think, *All right, does not kid around*. We do not wait. I am going to introduce you to a person, you talk to them, we see what happens."

I tried to look calm and confident, as if I often let Russian spies drive me through the streets of the capital. I touched the revolver in my pocket. I'd bought it at a pawnshop earlier. It was heavy and loaded, but it still felt like a stage prop.

After perhaps twenty minutes, we pulled up at the loading dock of a brick office building. He left the motor running and turned in his seat to give me a long look. He had a wide, fleshy peasant face. Up close, he looked sixty at least, older than the government he served. Old enough to have survived the NKVD purges of the 1930s. Old enough to see straight through a thirty-five-year-old social-climbing congressman who fancied he was a spy hunter.

"She's in room eight, Dick," he said. I stepped out into the cool air and the city noises. The taxi glided away and I was left alone on the loading dock, useless gun heavy in my pocket, looking at a gray steel door with a metal handle. I stood outside for a few moments waiting for a cue that didn't come. The door wasn't locked.

Room 8 was halfway down an anonymous corridor, thin gray carpeting and fragile-looking drywall, door numbers painted in sky blue. I could hear a radio playing rinky-dink jazz elsewhere in the building; a man and a woman arguing. I stopped outside the door to room 8. All I could think about now was having a gun in my pocket. I tried to come up with something to say if I was searched. Maybe lots of congressmen carry guns.

I took a breath, knocked. No one answered. I tried the door-knob and it turned easily. It was a surprisingly large office, anonymous modern furnishings. A woman sat behind a desk, apparently expecting me, in an olive-green suit made out of some cheap polyester. It was the woman I had seen Hiss arguing with the night I followed him.

"Hello, Mr. Nixon," she said with only the faintest accent. She stood and we shook hands. "How pleasant to see you again. You may call me Tatiana."

"Hello," I said as we both sat down. "Are you—you're not Russian?"

"Only when I want to be." Her black hair was tied back neatly, and her lipstick was immaculate, but she smelled intensely of stale foreign tobacco.

"So what happens now?"

"What do you want to happen?" She looked at me for a long nervous unblinking moment.

"I want . . ." I found I had forgotten to take a breath. I made myself say it out loud. "Well, you know who I am, I guess. Arkady must have told you. We met under, well, odd circumstances. But I was led to—well, it seemed like you'd talk to me about Alger Hiss."

"If Mr. Hiss were in our employ, why would we give him to you, of all people? Richard Nixon, the anti-Communist crusader? The man who hates us? You do, don't you?"

"I don't know. It's not so simple. We're in opposition, yes. It's my job to protect my country." I cleared my throat. "I wasn't sure you cared about Hiss."

"Even if Alger Hiss is innocent, he'll be watched the rest of his life. He'd be awfully hard to make use of."

"Well, yes. I'd thought ahead that far."

"You want to convict Hiss, but that's not all you want, is it?" She paused to let me speak, but I had nothing to say. She went on with something like a hypnotist's odd cadence. "Richard Nixon, I represent a nation of a hundred million people. We are a new civilization on this earth. Forget about Alger Hiss for now. We're doing extraordinary things, things you can't imagine. We're not evil; we're not even your enemies. We can transform your life. Now, tell me: What can I do for you? What do you want?"

She leaned toward me as she spoke. She had an odd, charming, sloppy, lopsided smile and a way of giving you her whole attention that was hard to resist. It was, I later learned, the spy's craft to know there are people who go through life feeling that those closest to them can't hear them no matter how loud they shout, people just waiting to be asked to spill the whole damned list. Or was it only training? In the end I told her everything. I told her I wanted a Senate seat. That I wanted Pat to respect me and be happy. I wanted everything I'd been shut out of because of where I went to school, because I didn't talk right, because my parents were poor. I told her what happened at the Wexford building. I told her I wanted to be president of the United States and that I wanted to know why there was a tiny part of me that didn't care what happened to anyone as long as I got what I wanted.

And I thought of all the smug people who had laughed at me for playing it straight, for being the hardworking student sweating through the nights to keep up with his classmates, the navy man, the small-town lawyer grinding through divorce cases to make ends meet. I'd worked hard for what people like Kennedy got for nothing. And I decided: No more. I was tired of being a schmuck. I'd get what I had coming and I wouldn't play fair. By hook or by crook.

Was this how they'd gotten Hiss? Somehow, I thought not. Whatever had happened, he'd probably put up more of a fight. It was ten minutes' work for them to turn Richard Nixon.

"Why would we give Hiss to you?" she asked again.

"I thought . . ." I said. There was a long breathless pause, because this was the moment I'd never really admitted to myself would come. When I spoke again it was with a stranger's voice. "Maybe I could do something for you as well."

"You are in luck, Mr. Nixon," she said brightly, a smiling nurse jollying a needle-shy patient through an injection. "We often deal in cases like yours. Mr. Alger Hiss is an exceedingly bright man who had a few too many ideas. We would be happy to see his credibility undermined. You seem like a man who could make that happen." For a moment I had the impression

I was speaking to someone else entirely, a person of great age, impossibly regal. A flash of some other room, gold and dark wood, and then it was gone.

"I can do it; I just need evidence he spied. Enough to go on TV and make that claim, that's all," I said. "But what do you want in return?"

"Favors to be named later," she said.

"What if I don't want to do the favor?"

She smiled. "We are betting that you will," she said, and she stood up. The interview, it seemed, was over.

"But—how does this work?" I asked her as I was leaving. "How will I know?"

"We'll find you. It's one of the things we do."

I found myself out in the hallway. I barely knew what had happened. Outside, the sun was going down, and for a moment I was a new person, a strange new man in an unknown city hailing a cab. Was it really this easy to change your whole life? And then I got a cab, and the driver asked me for an address, and we drove back to where I lived, and I was the same person again, almost, but knowing that something had shifted forever inside me and I wouldn't be able to take it back.

That night Pat asked me where I had been. I told her I'd been working.

"You smell funny. Cheap cigarettes. Have you been drinking?"

"No, dear."

"You know you can tell me anything. Don't you, Dick?"

"Of course, dear. There's just nothing to tell."

"Welcome to the Watergate Hotel, Mr. and Mrs. Nixon," a young man said, gesturing us through wide double doors. Pat held on to my arm, still wobbling a little on new heels.

The ballroom beyond positively hummed to itself, full of a mix of journalists, high-level administration types, staffers, socialites, celebrities. Handsome silver-haired white men in tuxedos and beautiful women in satin dresses. One of them smiled at me and I blushed. Everyone smiled at me now. The room was hot; the windows fogged. Outside it was winter. December 23, 1948.

A few months earlier, I would never have been invited. But then I had found, tucked into my morning newspaper, a manila folder showing the exact location of a cache of microfilm concealed in a pumpkin patch near Alger Hiss's home. Hundreds of stolen State Department documents, incontrovertible proof of the threat posed by American officials secretly in the employ of the Soviet Union. Explain that, Mr. Hiss. He'd tried, and maybe I'd get him only for perjury, but I was going to win and everyone knew it.

"Is it true you've caught that awful Mr. Hiss?" a helmet-haired senator's wife asked me.

"Almost," I said.

"My husband is very concerned about the Communist threat, isn't that right, Dick?" Pat said.

"Yes. Yes, of course," I said.

I towed Pat onward through the crowd, looking for our host so I could say hello and be congratulated.

"I didn't think it was going to be like this," Pat whispered to me. Her grin looked a little less friendly. For a person with her arm through mine, she was making an astonishing effort not to have any physical contact with me.

"We got lucky for once. Can't we just enjoy this?" I'd spent hours wondering if I should tell her the truth. Each time, I promised myself I'd do it tomorrow.

"I don't like the way this happened. All these people I wanted to like us, and suddenly now they do, and it's almost worse."

"Can we please enjoy this?" I asked her again. "I won. I won the case."

"Don't be smug," she said. "What if we just enjoy it in a mean-spirited way?"

"Deal," I told her. "Just do the mean part on the inside."

It wasn't as fun as I'd thought it was going to be; even I had to admit it. They liked me now that I'd had a success, but I'd spent too long hating them to value what they had to say to me. I'd seen what they were like to people they couldn't use.

I excused myself to the drinks table or to another guest maybe forty times, until the moment when there wasn't any other place I could bear to walk to next, and I simply kept going, past the restroom and up a set of cordoned-off marble steps to the cool quiet of the second floor. Let them drag me back if they wanted to; I needed a moment alone. The second floor was dark and solemn. Hiss might once have been invited to a reception like this, but now, instead, he was making plans for a legal defense and worrying about staying out of prison. What did I care? He'd been a spy, hadn't he?

I stepped out onto the balcony in my tuxedo, let the snow fall on my face for a moment, muscles slack. Downstairs the party was still in full swing.

"Congratulations, Mr. Nixon," I heard behind me. I turned, smiling my party smile, and then I realized it was Tatiana, wearing a strapless green ball gown, her hair up, a drink in her hand.

"You can't be here," I said.

"Why not? I have an invitation. I am a respected member of the Soviet cultural delegation."

"It's not in very good taste. You should leave. Our business is done."

"I don't work for you, Dick," she said. She looked directly at me in a way I didn't like. "I didn't vote for you. In fact, you owe me a favor."

"How did you know the microfilm would be in the pumpkin patch?"

"Alger told me it was there. I keep very close track of my American contacts, Mr. Nixon. Especially the interesting ones. I believe you'll be a senator soon. They've asked you to run. Helen Gahagan Douglas's seat."

"How do you know that?" I said, squirming a little. I wondered if anyone could see us.

"Oh, goodness, maybe there are Russian spies in the United States government, wouldn't that be awful?" she said. "You're going to be an influential man soon, Mr. Nixon. How do you like it?"

"Christ," I said, sweating. "Would you please go? I feel bad enough as it is."

"Don't be stupid. And stop glancing around like that. There's no one here. And no one would suspect anything. You look like a guilty husband." It was true; I could barely pay attention to what she was saying. "You feel bad about what you did?" she continued. "I don't believe it. Your whole life you tried to succeed, and you got what for it? Hack lawyer, then hack politician. And now you see you can be more than that. Slip your skin, walk between the walls. Break rules."

"Betray my country."

"Don't be dramatic. You're sorry about the deal you made, I know. Your feelings, yes. 'I'm a traitor to my country!'" she said in a growly woe-is-me voice, the first of many Richard Nixon impressions I would witness over the years, and not the worst. "Do you care about it that much? Flag, Star-Spangled Banner? Christmastime and apple pie? I do not think you do."

"There's more to it than that."

"Is there? I know you, Dick; you don't care about all this, not deep down. Who are you betraying? What did these people ever do for you? Who's pulling for Dick Nixon here? We are. We got you Mr. Chambers and Mr. Hiss, and we'll get you more. Lots more."

"No. I won't do it." I was drunk and tired and sounded pitiful, I knew.

"Oh, Dick. You already are doing it." She might have been hiding a smile. "You're one of us now, Dick. It's not so bad, is it? There are more of us than you think."

"How many? And who are you really? And what was all that nonsense Hiss wrote about in his diary? That night—"

"Is not good ask so many questions," she said, pouting and putting on a heavy Russian accent.

"Dick?" I heard Pat's voice float up the stairs. "Are you up there?"

"Go now," Tatiana said, and she raised her glass and gave me a twinkly toast. "Enjoy bourgeois party and loving wife. I will be seeing you later."

"I'll be there in just a minute, Pat," I called, glaring at Tatiana.

Pat stared at me curiously as I descended the steps.

"What were you doing up there? We need to go."

"Just getting some air, dear."

"Get our coats. I'll meet you by the door," she said. "Are you sure you're okay?"

"I'm fine."

I thought of the last thing Hiss had said to me as he exited the courtroom, knowing his mistake, knowing he'd overreached and that they'd closed in. "Of course I'm guilty," he said, clutching my arm and whispering. "I'm as guilty as you are. I'm trying to get out!"

But you can't get out, can you? The thought came to me clear and unbidden. And now there is nothing that is not a lie.

CHAPTER EIGHT

JUNE 1950

"MR. NIXON? Mr. Nixon?" A man hurried to meet me as I was walking back to my office in the Capitol but I didn't bother stopping. Senators didn't have to stop.

"Mr. Nixon? My name is Howard Hunt. I'm with the CIA. Could I have a word?" The man approaching was tall, bony-faced, a few years younger than I was but with an awkward gravity. A lobbyist? Then I realized I'd seen him before. It was the man from the hotel lobby that I'd walked away from many months ago, the night I followed Alger Hiss.

"Walk with me to my office. What the hell is CIA?" I asked.

"Central Intelligence Agency, sir, the new umbrella. We were CIG for a bit. OSS, Foreign Documents, all of it got folded in together. I'm in counterespionage."

We walked on to my office, and he chattered away. An English major at Brown University, then a failed novelist, he'd been recruited in the postwar intelligence boom. He reminded me, for some reason, of a young priest.

"Now, how can I help you?" I asked as we sat in my office. It was after seven, and the building had emptied out.

He opened a briefcase on his lap, shuffled through his papers for a few seconds, then looked up at me searchingly. "Mr. Nixon," he said, "how much do you know about the international Communist conspiracy?"

How could they know? was my first thought. I tried to freeze a neutral expression onto my face.

"It's a concern to us all," I said after a moment. "A grave concern."

I felt the explanations welling up behind my lips. *It was only a conversation. No one got hurt. I just wanted to be famous.*

"I know you brought in Alger Hiss. I don't think he was acting alone, and, well, it's just that I've made some rather odd discoveries lately. About his research. Very curious indeed."

I'd lose everything. Richard Nixon would be a villain and a laughingstock.

Or...I looked him over. *Wait.* No wedding ring, and his shave was sloppy. Socks matched, but the shoes weren't shined. A bachelor? Maybe he wouldn't be missed. The gun was in my desk. Or I could use the heavy glass ashtray. *Jesus fucking Christ.* It was just a conversation.

"There's a great deal of chatter coming out of Eastern Europe these days." Hunt continued talking, oblivious. "All sorts of nastiness got churned up in the last war, too much to pick through, really, but I do find the occasional bits and pieces. Have a look at this? I'm going to assume you have security clearance."

I nodded. And then, with wild relief, I thought of Arkady. He'd know what to do. He'd pay this nobody a visit. Those strangler's hands would fix everything; tomorrow, I'd wake up safe in my own bed, life would go on, and no one would be the wiser. Dear old ugly Russian!

I wasn't even listening to what Hunt was saying. He passed me two photographs. What was this about?

They were two pictures of the same man. In the first, he was clothed, a doughy, mustachioed, bald man in a cheap wool suit lying on a flowery bedspread, obviously dead. Mouth open; his hat had fallen off and rolled away. He'd taken his shoes off before dying.

"W-what killed him?" I asked. Why was he showing me this? A warning?

"Choked. Smothered, actually."

The second photo showed him naked on a gurney, sad middle-aged flab. Almost six feet tall; he must have been a powerful man once. A scar on his hairy upper thigh, very likely a bayonet wound from the First World War. There was a pale gray tattoo on his left wrist, an eight-pointed star. Gregor's black sun.

Whoever had taken the first photograph had felt motivated to arrange the dead man's personal effects on the bedspread next to him. A needle and thread. A shaving kit, well used but in good condition. A vain man or a man with a habit of cleanliness and order instilled early. Clothing well maintained but worn out. Liquor in a glass bottle, unlabeled. Boys' adventure novels.

"Who was he?"

"Italian passport, but it's trash. We think his name was Helmut Berdych, a Nazi, survivor of the Berlin siege, trying to sell off intelligence materials."

"To us?" I asked. Was I not in trouble? I tried to follow along, beginning to feel relieved.

"This is a hotel room in Warsaw. Our man found him only a few minutes after he'd met with his contact in the opposition. He was, we believe, a schmuck. Nazi middle management in a research division selling the contents of his department's wastepaper baskets. But the market for Nazi assets wasn't so good in 1946. This was what we found with him."

He handed me a stack of documents. Most of the writing was in Russian. There were a few photos—a blurry picture of a concrete building in Berlin bombed to almost nothing, white with plaster dust, two children playing in the rubble. Gaps in the foundation had been circled, black openings into a foul sub-basement. The kinds of things they did below street level in Berlin. And then stationery of the Third Reich, swastika surmounted by eagle, part terror and part kitsch. Scrawled notes of some random Sturmbannführer: *Rabenmutter.*

"What is it?" I asked.

"Research results. Nazi lunatic fringe, we think, the kind of people who sent Ernst Schäfer to Tibet to look into mystical gods. You know Schäfer, the ornithologist?"

"Of course," I said, knowing nothing. *Birds,* I thought. *Raven Mother.* Hiss was an ornithologist too, I remembered; it was part of how we had caught him.

"The thing is, we think the information may have been intended for Alger Hiss. I believe he was stealing secrets from the United States, yes, but also from behind the Iron Curtain. His papers are still missing."

"Well, we took care of him, didn't we?" I said through numb lips.

"Mr. Nixon," he said, "I believe we are in very grave danger, the extent of which I scarcely know how to estimate. What is the Soviet Union, do you think? What is it really?"

I shook my head. In many ways, I still had very few answers to that question. What were they doing over there? What came to mind was nonsense. It was Europe, but then it was Asia. It was nine million square miles, I had read, more than twice the size of America, and I knew almost nothing else. I pictured a snowy plain under a gray sky. More snow was falling; bearded men and beautiful women wore fur hats. They drank and schemed while organ music piped fiendishly and the Kremlin loomed into the heavens behind them, a glowing red hammer and sickle surmounting the scene.

"They're the enemy, I know that much."

"Do you know the term *naukograd?* " he asked.

"I don't speak Russian."

"It means 'secret science city.' A part of the new Soviet in-dustrial push, an entire metropolis devoted to a given research question. They're not on maps; some of them are underground. Blacked-out science cities, off in the frozen tundra. Dozens. Hundreds, even."

I felt cold; my stomach seemed to drop. A country without religion and without limits. A scientific state of which we understood almost nothing. Hunt fixed me with an unsettling sepulchral stare.

"It is my belief that the Soviet Union is at work on a far greater threat than we imagine. I'd like your cooperation, Mr. Nixon. I need more men like you to be aware of the threat they represent. And it's not just them. Hiss was . . . well, I'd better not speak of it."

"Of course," I said.

"Don't forget, Mr. Nixon."

The next afternoon, I went to a congressional security brief-ing where we viewed classified footage in flickering black-and-white. A plain-faced woman with her hair done up in a messy bun sat at a kitchen table with some household objects before her: a saltshaker, a box of matches. She bent over the table, face pinched with concentration, and made strenuous passes with her hands. The saltshaker moved a fraction of an inch. She redoubled her efforts and it moved again. A voiceover told us she'd driven a tank for the Red Army before her abilities were discovered, and they were even now being duplicated by Soviet scientists. What kind of dreamland were they building over there? What was this new world?

CHAPTER NINE

JANUARY 1951

UPTOWN THEATER, *Cyrano de Bergerac, 1:00 p.m., Wednesday — your old friends.*

They'd written the message on a small plate underneath a piece of carrot cake served in the Senate cafeteria. They could have just sent me a postcard for all it mattered, but I guess they wanted me to know they could reach me anywhere. Because they wanted to show they knew I liked carrot cake and would always finish it. Fucking spies.

I glared at the cafeteria workers, daring one to look up at me or betray just the slightest nervous tell. In vain. And what was I supposed to do with the plate when I was done? Was that nail polish? I picked at it with a fingernail but it wouldn't come off. Was there some obvious exit strategy that wasn't occurring to me? I slipped it into a coat pocket. Yet another thing I'd have to throw into a large body of water and forget. On Wednesday, I told my secretary I was taking a long lunch, and she smiled and nodded as if every single thing were right with the world. I left the Capitol, smiled and waved and nodded at people I knew from television. I lived in a different universe now. No more Nixon the anxious striver; I was a crusader and a young star of the political world. I had won.

Even Pat had to admit it. Or I imagined her admitting it in a long flowery speech, explaining how she understood the pressures I was under and the sacrifices I had made and that it wasn't a perfect fucking world, was it. In my imagination she admitted it all the time. We had not spoken recently.

I ducked into a taxi and had it take me to a shopping mall, where I purchased dark glasses, and then I walked half a mile to the movie theater. Once or twice I circled a block to see if I could spot whoever they might have had following me. It is a terrible truth of the spy trade that, just like adultery, it lends itself inescapably to cliché.

When I arrived, they were sitting together in the back row. I don't know how they'd contrived to have the rest of the theater empty, but they had. Arkady gestured to the seat in front of them, and I sat for a few moments before twisting awkwardly around to glare at them.

"Why are we meeting here?" I asked. "Don't you have an office?"

"I do not know about this movie," Arkady said. "Hero is badass but does not make good choices."

"He's in love," Tatiana told him. "He wants it to be pure and chaste. It's how he keeps his self-respect despite having a big nose."

"Because the ladies don't like big nose? This is attitude problem for them. He looks fine. Needs better hat."

"It is different for the French. Russia, it is no problem. We are an advanced society. Hello, Richard."

"It wasn't easy for me to get away," I told them.

"But you manage it. That is good. We are impressed," Tatiana said.

"What do you people want?"

"We have something we'd like you to do."

"I don't work for you."

"Of course not!" she said, mock horrified. "We are not capitalist bosses in a historically obsolete system of economic slavery. We work together. We are comrades." Was she being sarcastic? Was she even a Communist at all? Her Communist Barbie demeanor was like a jamming system for normal nonverbal signals. Maybe this was what it took to survive as a woman in the KGB. I glanced at Arkady.

"I mean, I can decide not to do this," I said.

"We'll see, won't we? Aren't you curious what we want?"

"Just tell me."

"All right. You remember our friend Alger Hiss," she said. "I think you'll recall he was very interested in a place in Massachusetts called Pawtuxet Farm. We would like you to go and see what's there. Simple."

"I don't have time. I have a very full schedule."

"You will add this to your busy schedule. We have confidence in you."

"You can do it. You are Tricky Dick, yes?" Arkady said. I was, by that time. A souvenir of the Senate race.

"Why do you want me to go?"

"We believe there is a government facility there and that it is interesting to us. And perhaps to you as well. I want you to learn what is happening and who is responsible. Where does the money come from? This sort of thing. A little history."

"I won't spy for you," I told them. "You can't fuck with me the way you think. I'm a senator now. I'll have you deported."

Tatiana sighed.

"Dick, in what we do, it is usual for people to make things pleasant and not cause a fuss. Great spies are polite and easy to get along with and that is by far my personal preference. But I can also make things unpleasant. Do you think we can't ruin you? It happens all the time. Tricky Dick Nixon the Commie senator will be a great embarrassment to your country. The entire world will laugh at you. Arkady and I will get the Order of Lenin."

"Already got," Arkady said.

"Then you get a second one."

"I would like that, yes."

"You think Hiss has it bad right now?" Tatiana said. I turned away. "You get it a thousand times worse. For treason, you go to jail for life, or maybe you get killed, who knows? But it doesn't stop there. You become a historic figure. You are Benedict Arnold. And your daughters are, what, three and almost six now? They grow up as the traitor's kids. How do you think they'll do at school? They change their names but doesn't do any good, does it? You know how kids are. And Pat, what about her life? She finds out you lied, you're nothing to her. And to the world she is the traitor's whore. Or on the other hand..."

I heard her shift in her seat behind me. Her hair brushed my neck, and I felt her breath in my ear. "We could do this the other way. I can be nice to you." She leaned her head against mine. "Has anyone ever been nice to you, Richard Nixon?"

I wanted to turn. I gripped the seat in front of me. I wanted to kiss her. I knew it was a trick. This was spy craft, the rote professional manipulation of lonely and unhappy people, the thing she did for a living. But I felt it. I hated Pat for it. She was starving me to death when I had a right to be happy. What made it okay for Pat to do that? Shouldn't I just get what I want?

Up on the screen, Cyrano was laughing at some sad-sack aristocrat whose girl didn't love him. I thought of a letter I'd written a long time ago, when I was a boy. They would laugh at me about it later, historians and journalists, but it wasn't my idea. It was a school assignment to write something in the voice of a pet dog. I wrote,

WHILE GOING THROUGH THE WOODS ONE OF THE BOYS TRIPED AND FELL ON ME. I LOST MY TEMPER AND BIT HIM. HE KIKED ME IN THE SIDE AND WE STARTED ON. WHILE WE WERE WALK- ING I SAW A BLACK ROUND THING IN A TREE. I HIT IT WITH MY PAW. A SWARM OF BLACK THING CAME OUT OF IT. I FELT A PAIN ALL OVER. I STARTED TO RUN AND AS BOTH OF MY EYES WERE SWELLED SHUT I FELL INTO A POND. WHEN I GOT HOME I WAS VERY SORE. I WISH YOU WOULD COME HOME RIGHT NOW.

    YOUR GOOD DOG,

    RICHARD

I thought of that phrase, the *swarm of black thing*. It had chased me all the way from Orange County, and now was I a good dog or wasn't I? Wasn't I? And was anyone going to come home? None of the historians ever said.

I heard Arkady moving in his chair uncomfortably. He might be a Stalingrad veteran but he didn't want to watch this. He knew how these things were done but he didn't like it. Maybe he had feelings for Tatiana. I saw suddenly, clearly, what I looked like to Arkady. I knew that I hadn't humiliated myself entirely at this point, but if I wanted to finish the job, this would be the way to do it. I stood up and faced them.

"Forget it," I said. "I mean, I'll do it, sure. Just forget about that stuff, okay? I'll do it but then I'm out. I'm not a spy." Ta- tiana's look was as unreadable as ever. She'd already seen every dodge, every rationalization an intelligence asset could give. She was just letting me say what I needed to say before I cooper- ated.

"Pawtuxet Farm, then," she said. "You are on train to Boston tomorrow, nine in the morning. Don't worry, you will not be alone up there. We will join you later."

"Easy job, nobody get hurt," Arkady said. "Not like last time. And take this." He handed me a packet of papers. Alger Hiss's notes. "To read on train."

CHAPTER TEN

FEBRUARY 1951

A LONG, LONG February train ride north from Washington, DC. There were fewer highways in this pre-Eisenhower world, and to go by car would have meant meandering along a hundred poorly maintained roads and byways in a country that was already beginning to look a bit stranger to me than it used to. The nation was still a disconnected patchwork of odd little plots of land, towns and farms and cities, some seldom visited and little changed since the nineteenth century. A whole day's travel on the train, myself and salesmen, families, men obviously out of work, chattering college students. We rattled and swayed past stubbled snow-drowned farmland, past small-town railway platforms and the neglected back lots behind brick warehouses and factories, and through cities, Baltimore and Newark. In New York City, I ate lunch in the echoing din of the vaulted crystal palace of the old Penn Station. Then onward north, the landscape growing whiter as we moved past New Haven to Boston. Traveling north was like moving slowly into the past, into a world of clannish towns and families in decaying colonial farmhouses out there surviving the winter. I looked out at the countryside and wondered what lay ahead to the darkening north.

My name is Alger Hiss. It is with the greatest trepidation that I now set down the disturbing events of the past three years . . . I imagined him in his dingy little office, typing out his confession by night after a day of lying to me before the public, chronicling his private secret war. Yes, he'd been a Communist all along, although it turned out there were different kinds of Communists. There were the pitiless master manipulators of the steppes, and then there was the school-masterish Mr. Hiss, a principled, rather prudish lawyer who thought working-class people were treated unjustly in the West and who'd decided to risk his freedom and reputation to do something about it.

He wasn't naive. He'd been at the Yalta Conference, where, in the aftermath of the Second World War, England, America, and the Soviet Union met to decide the fate of a broad swath of the entire world. He'd been in the room with Stalin. He'd read the Long Telegram, America's first formulated idea of the Soviets' policy of intimidation and fear. He'd seen dirty tricks on both sides, and he'd chosen.

He planned his treason carefully around a modest, austere family life and his promising career. He quietly photographed State Department documents and passed them on, day by day, patiently and professionally. The diary reported his moments of disquiet and doubt. Anxiety about being caught, and about what would happen to his wife and stepson. He didn't care for Stalin and his aggressive policies but considered them a necessary compromise. In his public life, he went from success to success, and the work was steady. It might have gone on for decades.

The change came when his old handler was retired and his replacement arrived.

A young woman, dark-haired, who speaks fluent English, one of the new breed from the Leningrad academy, born and raised in the Soviet tradition. No peasant girl, an intellectual. We met and talked late into the night discussing Dostoyevsky and Lermontov, the nature of good and evil societies. I have seldom met a more challenging thinker. In our work she began pressing me for information on specific government programs not mentioned in the news and not funded through regular channels.

Were she and Hiss lovers? There was no mention. Certainly, as the days went on, Hiss spent less and less time with his family as Tatiana—it could only have been her—pressed him to take greater and greater risks. Soon Hiss was rummaging through trash bins, forging credentials, and amassing dossiers on military research programs that would never appear on an official budget.

As the diary reached 1947, Hiss became more and more fixated on the facility called Pawtuxet Farm. Whatever was happening there had, it seemed, been happening for some time.

During the war, there had been an American program labeled Blue Ox. All Hiss knew was that it began in 1939 and involved recruitment of civilian professors from the faculty of a number of colleges and universities as well as a few dubious independent scholars. The program lacked the decisive effect of the Manhattan Project—in fact, it showed no results whatsoever on paper—but it remained active year after year. After much searching, Hiss worked out a location for the facility in Pawtuxet, Massachusetts.

Hiss nursed dark suspicions that he wouldn't quite specify, but he quoted figures on the purchase of exotic chemicals and the rate of psychiatric breakdowns among the project's personnel. I knew we were in an arms race and that the pace of research was only accelerating, but he seemed to believe we had a nuclear testing site in rural Massachusetts. It didn't make sense.

Was this the next triumph in the arms race? I knew there was a black budget for military research; I'd voted on the 1947 National Security Act myself. But people weren't telling me things. I didn't have real friends in Washington, or at least not the right ones. If there was a success to be made here, it occurred to me I should be a part of it. Was I going to be left behind, outflanked by a Washington clique I had no access to? Why not get a jump on the bastards before they even saw Dick Nixon coming?

As Hiss and Tatiana grew closer, Hiss's investigation branched off in another direction. He became suspicious of his own masters in the Soviet hierarchy.

Tatiana has told me of what she witnessed in the Ural Mountains. The walking shapes, the secret fires (nuclear?) that burn there ceaselessly. She tells me that she believes the USSR has a similar, perhaps more advanced program. I have begun to suspect a truth more dark and terrible than I can commit to paper at this time.

He began a separate investigation into the Russians. Certain military units were detailed for specialized duty and then vanished from the normal border postings into Russia's trackless interior. Truckloads of political prisoners were taken from the gulags and then disappeared from civilization forever. A salt mine in Ukraine was decommissioned, but trucks still came and went. Circled and reprinted in larger Cyrillic characters was the phrase *Проект Кощей.* (Later, with a worn used dictionary, I painstakingly puzzled this out into Proyekta Koshcheya. Project Koschei.)

Tatiana, it seemed to me, was a master manipulator, and Hiss had met his match in her. As far as I could tell, she'd made him her stalking horse in an internal political rivalry. She'd played on his native paranoid streak and driven him into his own little private, paranoid cave. Was this what I was going to end up like? A whiny, self-absorbed neurasthenic prophesying doom for all?

I spent the night in Boston at a cheap hotel near the railway station. I sat at the fake-wood-grain desk in my room as snow fell outside and continued reading the diary under a bare bulb, trying to shut out the clattering of the elevator and the shouted drunken conversations outside my window.

I rented a car and made my way north and west, over the border to New Hampshire, along narrow roads that ran for miles and miles through pine forests. I stopped at Lowell to consult maps and ask directions, a succession of lefts and rights at the odd-sounding town names the indigenous world had left us—Mascuppic and Musquash. I found Pawtuxet just as the midafternoon sun tipped over toward evening and the buildings' shadows seemed to lean into the street. I drove past a small village green with surly hangers-on trampling the snow into dirt; a church with a stunted-looking steeple; a market; a one-story motel.

I tramped through the snow of the parking lot to the front desk and was given a curiously appointed room, Victorian wallpaper and a towering chest of drawers in dark wood.

I sat down to read while I waited for the others. Did Hiss stay at this motel too? I found myself wishing he were here to talk to.

I read the last pages of his diary in the dimming light that filtered through a yellowing shade. The works of which I have obtained evidence defy belief, and yet the sober testimony of these trusted and brilliant sources cannot be entirely ignored. It has become necessary to begin researching on my own. And, if required, conducting my own experiments.

This was where Hiss revealed a surprising breadth of scholarship for a civil servant. He read monographs couched in arcane academic phraseology. Some concerned the recent rediscovery of works of a pre-Indo-European civilization in the Ural Mountains; others followed North African trade routes in the eighteenth century. He copied out long passages in Greek from medieval alchemical texts.

At the same time, his record of events became, if anything, even more overheated and elliptical. A passage read, I have obtained (with what trouble and expense I shall not record here) that true mixture of which the Syrian wrote. I believe his original text contained certain code words whose true meaning I have lately divined. The Baltimore night holds terrors I have not imagined, and I sleep perhaps one night in three. Was this a Middle East arms connection? Nuclear materials denoted by code words routed through Syria?

It was around this time that I myself started to be a feature in the diary, and I saw the hearings take shape from his point of view. I was a hired gun from the government's secret committees, and Chambers was a fat pathetic tool making moon-eyes at him from across the room. I remembered his contempt for me in the hearings. I also remembered his icy cool and his genial manner most days, joking with the press and making light of himself as a hunted man. I'd seen more bravery than I thought.

There was no further mention of a Syrian, only more cryptic library visits, until this, just two days before I broke into his office.

At last I have tangible proof of what has henceforth been discussed in whispers. I have both spoken with the dead and looked at the horror that will walk this earth ten thousand millennia hence.

And then a single word set apart in a paragraph on its own.

CROATOAN.

I must learn why they died and why the others lived.

He seemed to have suffered a psychotic break. Or did he just have a night like the one I'd had? Either way, it's no wonder the Reds were eager to be rid of him.

There was a knock at the door.

"Is Romanian whore you ordered!" Arkady bellowed.

"Just a minute!"

"She cannot wait for you! She has many clients!"

I opened the door.

"Shouldn't you keep your voice down?"

"Relax, is Ukrainian accent. Locals suspect nothing."

Just after sundown we set off, balding tires slewing sideways across a wide patch of ice as I pulled out of the motel parking lot. Tatiana gave directions and we followed a narrow paved road that led straight off into the unlit void between Massachusetts towns. The forest was black around me and came up almost to the border of the asphalt. The lights of town were lost behind us.

"Not so fast here, we are close," she said. I slowed down but saw nothing other than trees on either side. But soon the road's shoulders widened and a hurricane fence appeared, running parallel to the road and topped with barbed wire.

"Stop."

I backed up to where the fence started and parked on the narrow shoulder. With the engine off, the night was silent, just wind and the creaking of the trees. The air smelled like pine sap and cold.

"You'll go in alone," Tatiana said in a whisper.

"What? You two aren't going in?"

"It is not permitted for me to be captured by a foreign state," Arkady said flatly. "Nor Tatiana."

"But you guys are the spies."

"Think of yourself, Richard," he said. "If you are caught with two Russian nationals, what lies will you tell them? You are best off alone."

I shone my flashlight through the fencing and saw only more trees. The fence extended along the road for what might have been miles. Up ahead there was a padlocked gate.

With the spies watching me, I thought for a moment what to do, shuddering in the wool coat and scarf Pat had bought me when we'd moved east. I'd told her I would be at a conference for a few days. What was she doing now? Being safe and warm and disliking me.

I walked up to the gate and tested the padlock, and it was indeed locked. Maybe the metal was brittle in the cold? I didn't know.

"What you do now?" Arkady called.

"I'm looking for a rock!" But there didn't seem to be any rocks.

"Just a moment." Tatiana got out of the car, walked to the lock, and held it in her hand for a moment. She shifted her feet a little.

"You do not see this," Arkady said, coming up behind me.

"See what?" I said just as Tatiana gave the lock a quick hard jerk. There was a snap and a ringing sound, and something metal flew off and hit the pavement. The gate swung open.

"How did you do that?" I said.

"Do what?" She slipped the lock into her coat pocket. "Go on, then. We circle back on the hour. Good luck."

I shrugged and stepped through. I could always turn back if it got any worse. I glanced behind me to see them silhouetted in the headlights, Tatiana shaking her hand as if it stung.

The path leading from the gateway vanished almost immediately. I turned off the flashlight, but it was shockingly dark, and after almost plowing into a tree, I kept the flashlight on. The cold bit through the thin leather of my shoes. The snow was only an inch or two deep, but wet. After a hundred feet or so I reached a second fence, identical to the first. A sign was fixed to it with twists of wire, and I shone the light on it. U.S. ARMY PROPERTY. NO TRESPASSING. VIOLATORS WILL BE PROSECUTED. It was old, rusted through in places, and the wires looked like they'd crumble at a touch.

I walked a few more minutes without finding a break. I stumbled over a raised stone and almost fell across what turned out to be a long rectangle of low stones. I traced out a foundation, no telling how old. I stopped when I heard an engine, faint and far off, and saw the dim glow of headlights inside the fence's perimeter. Indistinct voices drifted across the wintry space. Tires on a gravel road. Now that my eyes had adjusted to the dark, I saw the silhouette of a building in the cleared space beyond the wire fence. It was a compound of some kind.

I was cold and wet and was probably going to freeze to death at this rate. I had never been the kind of boy who climbed trees, even such as we had in dusty Yorba Linda, but I chose a tree, laid one hand on a low branch, and got a face full of snow. I heaved myself up and slowly, painfully, ascended, smearing sap across my expensive congressional-grade overcoat and getting a startling amount of snow down my collar. I crawled out on a thick branch that stretched over the fence, hung a moment, and then dropped heavily onto the frozen ground.

What now? I got up and stood there for a while in the dark, watching the small cluster of lights in the center of the cleared compound. Nothing much seemed to be happening there; I heard a few sleepy footfalls.

I walked along the inside of the fence until I found a gravel path and followed it toward the lights. I tried to stay quiet; I was just about invisible, and as no one was expecting a wave of congressmen to come pouring over the fence, as far as I knew, I pressed the advantage. The facility was settling in for the night. There were three or four low Quonset huts with barred windows and darkened interiors, and I peered through the windows. One was obviously a dormitory. In the next, a window looked into a room with an examination table, shelves of instruments, and labeled glass bottles. An infirmary or an autopsy lab. The table held sturdy restraints. Another window showed a room of metal bookshelves and filing cabinets crammed close together and seeming to fill almost the whole space. I skulked from one hut to the next with no clear idea what I was looking for.

I thought of Alger Hiss's words: The surveillance images at first seemed to show distorted human forms and cloudy architectural vistas. But on further study I marked the correspondences with certain ancient texts I had encountered and with images copied from the deeper regions of the Lascaux cave complex, areas that were purposely collapsed by the original explorers. I have become convinced that these are images of real phenomena, evidence of a terrible militarization of an obscene and dangerous antiquarian knowledge.

A two-story farmhouse stood in the center of things. Lights were on on the second floor, and figures moved about inside. Looking upward as I walked, I stumbled down a flight of stone steps and into the doorway of a cellar, closed off by rusty metal bars, stingingly cold. The flashlight revealed nothing behind them but more stone steps leading farther down, and then—a shape that looked oddly like a bare foot. I looked again and saw nothing.

I turned to go and found myself staring straight into a blinding white light.

"Sir?" a young man's voice called. "Sir? You ain't supposed to be in there."

I half lifted my arms in surrender.

"Don't move," he called. "Look away, okay? Please, I—I don't want to see your face." He sounded terrified.

"All right, all right. I can explain," I gabbled, absolutely certain I could not. Where exactly would an explanation begin?

"Are you—you're not one of them? From the diggings?"

"No. I'm Senator Richard Nixon."

"Dick Nixon?"

"Yes . . . yes. That's me," I said.

"Well, I'll be. Senator Nixon himself. I'm a hell of an admirer, sir."

"Thanks, thanks. That's me. Just inspecting the facilities."

"I wasn't told you'd be on base, sir. It's an honor. You okay? You lost, maybe?"

I nodded. "Maybe a little. What's your name, son?"

"Miller, sir. I thought maybe you was one of the things— well, I ain't meant to say but I'm sure you know. Come on back to the farmhouse."

I was hustled into the light and warmth of the main house and shook hands with a Colonel McAllister, Army Corps of Engineers, who didn't seem particularly surprised to get a congressional visit at this hour. I tried to place his age but it was hard. He might have been a harried, weathered forty-five or a rugged, enduring sixty. His skin hung unusually loose on his face.

"Look, I understand why you're here, Senator."

"Ah, well, I'm glad of that."

"You're with, what, Armed Services? Intelligence?"

"Ah, no. Just routine oversight."

"Jesus, all right. You ain't puissant, are you?"

"What?"

"Forget it, forget it."

"Well," I said, "we've got a right to know what you're up to. It's only common sense. Just here to see the taxpayers' money is being put to good use."

He ran a hand through thinning hair. "Money, Jesus. You'd think we were—well, listen, forget it. Senator, we're keeping America safe best way we know how. I understand the situation's serious. But we've got attrition rates, we've got material we just don't know what to do with yet. It'll take time."

"How much time, do you think?" I said. What did he mean?

"We got the material, we're going to see results. You'll see."

I was shown to guest quarters in what looked like a New England bed-and-breakfast and fell asleep reading excerpts from Bradford's history of the colonies, some battle or other in King Philip's War. As ever Captain John Morton had fought his way to the very thick of the fraye and was the first to enter that dredful space beneath the Pawtuxet hillside. Fourteen men followed after, white men and Naragansett, and for a space of nearly an hour there was silence untill Morton emerged alone nor he wd not speke of what he witnesed therein . . .

I was awakened just before dawn by a frantic lowing among the cattle that lasted maybe fifteen minutes, and I didn't sleep again after that.

In daylight nothing looked quite so worrisome. The temperature climbed above freezing just long enough for a miserable bout of rain, which rang off rectangular buildings of corrugated metal slumped in a desultory arrangement on a piece of farmland. They looked temporary but had clearly been there over a decade.

Miller took me on a walking tour of what might have been the world's shabbiest research institute. A library, rows of bookshelves and a sharp musty smell, books with pages swelling from the damp. I looked at a few, a mix of early American history, theology, and the latest in behavioral psychology. A few were written in dense Gothic script I couldn't decipher.

The next building was divided into classrooms and offices. In one office, a group of four Germans looked up from a heated discussion over coffee. In the next room, a darkly bearded man angrily moved to block my view of a blackboard and waved us on. The room after that was quite large, almost a third of the building's floor area, and empty except for a wall-size map of Europe and Asia densely inscribed with notes and studded with pushpins.

The next building was a storehouse of architectural debris: chunks of pillars, gargoyles, weathered stone blocks crowded together. Mixed in were odder items—a field artillery piece that might have seen action in the Franco-Prussian War, tapestries, carved wooden furniture. The next building stood entirely empty except for large scorch marks on the concrete floor.

Miller told me the areas of the base I was advised not to go near: four bunkers standing in a precise row and a blunt gray concrete pyramid surrounded by a low moat with water at the bottom that hadn't frozen. A cooling tower? In one far corner there was a small cemetery marked with old, old granite stones. Pawtuxet Farm looked small and snowbound and sad.

I was, frankly, a little bored. What was happening here? I'd seen plenty of books in Arabic script, so I conjectured it was a kind of applied anthropology center for political hot spots.

The only unusual thing about it was the level of everyday unease on display. No one seemed to be getting much sleep. I passed a lavatory and heard the sound of vomiting. There were no women at all on the base, or at least none that I saw.

I went back to the stone steps once but there was nothing to indicate they ever saw any use. I looked up to see a figure watching me from the farmhouse's upper floor; it stared at me for long moments until I walked off, and the curtains closed.

That night in McAllister's office, I played the only card I could think of to play.

"Colonel, about these results—"

"What is it, Nixon? Is the general not satisfied?"

"Frankly, there's talk of suspending funding."

"You can't possibly—" He seemed, all at once, terrified.

"That's right, Colonel. If we don't see results soon —"

"You Washington people really don't know the situation." He had turned a startling yellowish white. "There's things we've started here that you'd best not stop."

"Well, Colonel, I'm not seeing the results I'd hoped for."

"Results." He giggled to himself and shook his head. "You'd see some results if you shut this place down, that's for damn sure."

"Well, I've come all the way up here, I'm going to need something to put in my report. To the general."

An orderly poked his head in. "Sir? Sorry to bust in. There's been an arrival."

"What've we got? American?"

"Yes, sir."

The colonel rose and shrugged his coat on.

"Well, come on, Mr. Nixon. This is what you wanted."

I hurried after him, out into the cold and bright stars, followed him between buildings at a half trot, and then I was back in the map room. Seven or eight uniformed men stood uncomfortably against the walls. The only light was what spilled in from the hallway. The room was as empty as before except for a folding chair in the very center of it where a man sat, his face in shadow. Everyone spoke in whispers in the semidarkness.

I took my hat off without knowing why. There was something sad and solemn in the occasion.

The man in the chair stirred.

"Sir? I've—I think there's something wrong with my eyes, sir," he said. The voice had a thin, whistling quality that made it a little unpleasant, as if something were wrong with his mouth.

"You're okay, son," McAllister said. "Now, listen, I'm with the military and I have a few questions for you. What can you see right now?"

"I—I don't understand. Where's the captain? The flight plan—" the man said. He sounded young.

"You're back in the States now. You're home."

"Where am I? You're—did we crash or something? Am I in a hospital? I don't like this."

"This isn't working," somebody growled.

"What was the flight plan?"

"I don't know. We were over water. The Adriatic. Then east, Turkey. Just trying to bait 'em. I do ECM—jamming and stuff."

One of the uniformed men began sketching on the map.

"Try the words," said a second voice.

"Proctor, you do it," McAllister snapped. Rustle of a piece of paper changing hands. Proctor squinted in the dim light.

"'By the Ninth'—what does this say?" He started again, louder. "'By the Ninth Article, Section Seven, of the United States Constitution, I do compel and require you to answer all questions put to you by order of a duly sworn representative of the executive branch. By such articles of the ruling covenant as shall not be mentioned in this place.'"

"Now, tell me, son, what can you see?" McAllister said.

"There's a—a hill, I think. And a house in the distance. There's a sun but it don't look right, it's orange. How can that be? I don't like this at all."

"Is there anyone else with you?"

"There's a—in the distance. A man getting closer. And he's—why does he look like that? Is he all right?" he said. "I—I still can't remember what happened. How did we get off course? My memory..."

His voice got more and more whispery, then trailed off into nothing.

"Hit the lights," Proctor said. The fluorescents flickered on and we all blinked as at the end of a play. The chair was empty.

"Waste of time," McAllister said. He walked slowly to the center of the room and put his hand on the chair wonderingly. The others filed out, grumbling. I heard two men arguing in German, their voices fading into the night.

"Blue Ox initiative. One of our less successful nights," McAllister said finally.

"I don't understand. Who was in the chair?"

"Tentative ID, Tech Sergeant John Bowman. ECM specialist, crewed on a modified C Ninety-Seven out of Wiesbaden last year. Four hours out they realized he wasn't on the plane anymore. We've had him a couple of times now. He never knows shit."

"Where—where did he go?"

McAllister sighed. He looked tired. "One of the mandates for Blue Ox is intelligence gathering," he said. "But we've still got nothing behind the Iron Curtain.

"Ever since the last of the Romanovs bled out, it's been batshit in there. For forty-five years, from the Polish border to the Sea of Japan, it's been open season. We don't even have good maps of the place. At the end of World War Two we had all those guys in place, ready to stick it to the Sovs, be our eyes on the ground. Tough guys who'd fought the Nazis. And the NKVD rolled 'em right up, every one.

"We did what we could, started picking up German POWs who got let out of the gulags and repatriated. Bits and pieces. Railway lines, airfields, mines. A couple whole cities we didn't know about. You can think of this as the logical next step. There's more than one way out of the Soviet Union. So you tell the big man we're making progress."

"Big man?"

"Ike. None of this happens without him."

I lay awake the rest of the night, watching the cold light filter back through the curtains. I had never spent much time in New England and the cold was new to me, and the pitiless trackless forests. I wondered that anyone had thought to try to live here. I wondered about the Pilgrims making their way here, grim and God-haunted, scraping at the iron soil, and about what they would or wouldn't do to survive. Were they in any sense American? What did that actually mean?

Pat didn't meet me at the station, so I had to get home myself, and it was ten p.m. when the taxi let me off half a block short of our brownstone. The street was blocked by a couple of shiny town cars, and two dark-suited men flanked the door of my house. I stayed in the shadow of an elm tree, watching them.

I'd been discovered, that much was certain. Followed by U.S. counterintelligence to one of my meetings. Perhaps Pat had grown worried about me, had had me followed by a private detective who had stumbled on the truth. Or maybe Arkady and Tatiana had traded me away exactly like they had Alger Hiss.

I shouldn't have been surprised. If people had betrayed me, it was because I'd betrayed them first. The only oddity was that I hadn't expected it. I'd wandered along in my own little bubble of deception, taking no more precautions than a child skipping school. As if it weren't real. But now the black cars were outside my house, and men in dark suits were at the door.

I had no better idea than to run away. Turn the corner of our block and keep going. Back to the train station, where I'd buy a ticket west, and vanish. Who could find me? I saw myself reaching San Francisco, where I'd make my way to the dockyards, join the merchant marine, ship out for foreign ports. I could slip my skin and be a different man, and Dick Nixon would cease to be. In two months I could be in Shanghai, Tokyo, Jakarta. I stood in the freezing night watching that house where Pat was waiting inside, looking at the doorway, which was more terrifying than anything beneath the ground in Pawtuxet.

I thought of the alternative to running. Standing on the threshold and meeting all of their gazes.

Mr. Nixon, we'd like to ask you a few questions, they'd say, but everyone in the room would already know. The policeman's gentle hand on my shoulder, maybe a young man barely out of his teens, more puzzled than hurt that a man his country looked up to could be caught in such a position, a thing he could never in his life picture doing. And Pat, withdrawn, visibly preparing herself to live with the knowledge that she'd picked the wrong man. Then the storm of publicity: "Crusading Congressman Tied to KGB Spy Ring." Whatever Hiss had lived through, I'd have it a thousand times worse. And who knew what further punishments would come? I'd learned in Pawtuxet that my government was a stranger thing than anyone knew.

It's hard to describe the thought process that led to my stepping out from behind the elm and walking unsteadily toward the door. The far-distant chance that Pat would at least understand, that I'd be taken away knowing I had one person still behind me. Fear of the double humiliation of being caught running away. The idea that I could salvage a little bit of the situation if I faced my accusers and went willingly.

The two men watched me climb the seven steps to my own door. One of them said, "He's waiting for you, sir," and opened the door.

Inside I faced a strange scene. Pat rose from where she'd been sitting on the living-room sofa, stiff with formality, and called, "Dick," in a voice much too loud.

"We have a visitor!" she practically screamed. She stumbled against the coffee table, which rattled with five or six cups of tea. A dark-suited man stood by the wall, tea-less.

A man seated in the easy chair facing away from the door twisted around to look up at me, then stood. He had a wide, froggy face with a generous crooked mouth and dark blue eyes that peered from below an enormously capacious brow, giving his head a top-heavy appearance. His ears stuck out comically and the whole effect would have been cartoonish if it weren't for the impression of danger, of a cold shrewdness applied to every interaction.

I recognized him, of course, as the president of Columbia University, former governor of the U.S. occupation zone in Germany, and former chief of staff of the army, the architect of Operation Overlord as well as the Blue Ox program. Dwight D. Eisenhower.

PART TWO

CHAPTER ELEVEN

FEBRUARY 1951

I HAD THE momentary urge to salute, which I quelled at the last instant and turned into something between a rather stiff offer of a handshake and a low-angled *sieg heil*. He sat back down, just as if my living room were his private office.

"Now, listen, Mr. Nixon," he said, "I'm sorry to barge in on you after your long trip."

"Oh, it's no trouble," I said, as if I regularly held open houses for world leaders. What was happening to the world? I glanced at Pat. How long had she been attempting to make small talk with the savior of Western civilization? I sat down next to her on the flowered sofa. I wondered how much trouble I was in, and with whom.

"You were—where again? Boston?"

"That's right, sir. Massachusetts. Euro trade conference."

"Any fun?"

"Boring stuff, sir." I couldn't help staring. After I'd spent months currying favor with senior senators and State Department officials, the most important man in America—in American history?—was planted immovably in my living room.

"No sightseeing? No side trips?" he said. Eisenhower's skin had a waxy pale look, as if he had been annealed by the heat and pressure of surviving in the crucible of twentieth-century history. He was unreadable, the man who had funded Pawtuxet.

"Well, sir, there was a kind of side trip. Fact-finding." I was at that moment when you begin to tell a lie and have to decide how much of the truth to reveal, knowing that you don't have time to think it through but that whatever comes out of your mouth is what you're going to have to stick to. I trailed off and shot a meaningful glance toward Pat. I was trying to telegraph to Eisenhower both *Classified information, not for civilians* and *I was not at all freaked out by your terrifying occult secrets.*

"Never mind, never mind. You've been doing very interesting work. With Communists. I meant to tell you that."

"Thank you, sir."

"Can't be too careful. About time somebody stood up to those people. Got some real answers."

"Yes, sir."

"Except not McCarthy, you know? Takes it a bit far. And there's — you know —" He mimed swigging from a bottle.

"Right. Right. Doesn't know when to stop." Stop drinking? Stop persecuting Communists? There was no clarifying. Even I didn't know what I was saying.

"But not you. A real go-getter, that's what they might call you."

"Thank you, sir."

"You're really going places, that's the plain fact." He sipped his tea, unhurried, the center of the universe.

"I hope so, sir," I said. I glanced at Pat, who gave me a shaky nod. Going places. Good?

"Now, I hope you're ready for it," he said abruptly. "People can give you a hard time in the press when you've got a high profile. You're not hiding anything? No skeletons in the closet for Dick Nixon?"

"No, sir. Not me," I answered. "I'm a straight shooter."

"Well, I'll take you at your word. Dick Nixon is a straight

shooter, that's what they all say." He had an easy, folksy smile. On a prettier man it might have looked slick or ingratiating but on him it was endearing. It was one of those gifts fate gives a person who goes into politics, a single trick that makes him likable to millions.

"Exactly."

"Welp, I'll be toddling along now. Past my bedtime." He stood, and I walked him to the door. His attaché opened the door for him.

"Th-thanks for coming over, sir," I said. Behind him, Pat winced, but he only grinned again.

"You'll be hearing from me soon enough."

One dark-suited man—a federal agent of some kind, I assumed—went first, to alert the others, then Eisenhower, then two other agents. We stood in the door watching the entourage finish their choreography, scouting lines of sight and then, agent by agent, folding themselves into the shiny cars, which pulled away down the snowy lane and headed back toward the corridors of power and influence, fleeing the scene of our quaint little living room.

We went inside to clear the tea things.

"Well," said Pat. "Is there something you want to tell me?"

"I didn't know that was going to happen."

"I just sat with him for three hours. I really need to pee," she said. "He never peed once. How is that possible?"

"I don't know. I don't know." We sat on the couch together, and then she bounced up again, poured me a tumbler of whiskey, and sat back down.

"So you're going to be vice president?" she said. "That's what this means, right? Or I am, conceivably. One of us."

"I guess that's what it has to be. Did we—did we pass?"

"I don't know. If he ran next year, would he win? He would,

wouldn't he?" she said. She got up again. "He will. And you're going to be vice president."

"We're going to need new clothes," I said.

"Right. We are."

"And servants. Does this mean servants?" I said. "Can we have servants?"

"I don't know. Possibly."

"God. What else?"

"You're going to have to give speeches," she said. "And go to parties. Like now, except——"

"Except we'll actually be invited," I said. I might have giggled a little. We both did.

"And then you'd be president."

"Oh God, Pat. I know things haven't been that great for us. I know——"

"I just spent three hours with General Eisenhower, Dick. We talked about gardening and bridge and Shakespeare. I had to remember the plot of *Twelfth Night*. And about sports. Are the Steelers a sports team? We may have been talking about actual——"

"It's okay. I don't know either. But you really helped."

"I just want you to tell me you're a good man. Can you do that? That's what I need to know. Because you can't do this without me. And I need to know that. And you'd better not lie to me."

"I am, Pat. I know it doesn't always seem like it. I know I'm not always doing the right thing. Exactly. But I'm trying to figure it out. I really am."

It's what I said. At the time I was thinking only *I'll figure out a way to make it true later.*

CHAPTER TWELVE

A COUPLE OF days after that I found a note in my jacket pocket. I called Pat to tell her I'd be working late and drove to a parking garage in midtown and waited for them to walk up, which they did, holding hands, laughing, and chatting like a married couple. They let themselves into the backseat, immediately drenching the car with the Russian atmosphere of tobacco, sweat, cheap aftershave.

"Drive us, please," Arkady said. "How much time do you have?"

"I can be out until ten."

"Plenty of time for a drink, then," he said. "I direct you."

"We're impressed," Tatiana said once we were under way. "Eisenhower likes you. I think you have his attention."

"To watch you fuck up this way and receive enormous reward, it is touching," Arkady added. "American system is perhaps not so different from Russian after all."

"Did you bug my house?"

"Of course we have listening devices there. You are one of us, Dick."

"What did you find inside Pawtuxet Farm?" Tatiana asked. "I want to hear your thoughts." I hesitated. It wasn't really treason until I told them about it. I stalled, took the car around in a pointless circle just to see if anyone was following, even though it was dark and I wouldn't have been able to tell.

"Stop pretending to be spy," Arkady said. "No one follows."

"You read Hiss's diary," I said. "The place is what he thought it was."

"Yes? Go on."

"Americans are working on—I don't know what you call it. Biological weapons. Spiritualism. I saw a kind of séance. And cells and hospital beds and people doing research. Germans, some of them. I wasn't allowed to see all of it. I talked to the base commander, who didn't seem all there. Is this what you want? Do you need numbers? What do you want?"

"That is good enough for now. What did you think of it?" Tatiana asked. "You can tell us."

"Is not for report," Arkady said.

"What I think is none of your business."

We reached one of their apparently infinite supply of nameless dive bars. Arkady and I sat in a corner booth while Tatiana went to get the drinks.

"You do it and we do it," Arkady said. "We maintain parity. Is Cold War doctrine, I know. I read your Defense Department policy sheets."

"How do you—"

"I'm a spy. When we steal stuff, that is what we steal. And unlike most congressmen, I actually read them. And since you and I are fighting a war against each other, I do you the courtesy of explaining there are rules you evidently do not know."

Tatiana returned with a small tray of vodka shots.

"Shouldn't we drink something a bit less Russian?" I asked.

"You want Pat to smell it?" Tatiana said. "Didn't you ever drink when you were a teenager?"

"I was trying to get into college."

"Happy graduation." She and Arkady downed theirs first.

"America got atomic bomb," Arkady went on. "Good for you. You drop the bomb and war ends. But now what? Is freaky situation. Who is enemy? Who is friend? Who is tough, who is not? Rules are all different.

"We got plenty tanks and men and all that but what do we get for it? You are top dog, we are chumps. If you decide to blow up Moscow, all we do is watch the plane go past and get a melancholy feeling.

"But you're not so special. You got bomb first, but we get it sooner or later. Maybe we got it already and don't tell you. You don't even know. But when we do, rules of the game change, but they are not complex.

"We can attack with great force but we cannot defend. The winner is one who goes first, if they are fast enough to strike the crippling blow. It's the smart play. Nobody wants to attack but nobody wants to lose either. Every day, everybody wakes up knowing this and thinking, *Is today the day? Is today the day everybody just fucking goes for it, takes their pants off and shits on the table?* And what triggers that? Some new device, maybe, the next thing after the bomb, changes the rules again. Maybe something different from the bomb. So that is why we are spies. We try to figure out what you've got and when it becomes that day."

"It's more complicated than that," I said.

"Yeah, yeah. Proxy wars, second strikes, limited war. Why does everyone think I'm an idiot?"

"Because you're old and you've had your nose broken what looks like seven times."

"The kind of shit I do, bloody nose is like first prize. Second prize not nearly as good. I hand out a lot of those, asshole, I can remind you. But not lately. Now mostly I sit in cars and watch and do this thing we do now. Thinking war. Lying war. Cold War.

"So, Dick, I am not Soviet director of intelligence. I am mostly here to get shot at. But even I see that if Soviet asset is given job of U.S. vice president, it is interesting situation."

"Arkady, please. Let me out of this. It's too big now."

"It is big, yes. At present the Kremlin knows you only as Flamingo. They know nothing of who you are or what you may become. If I tell them more, they get perhaps too excited. They overreach, yes? Eisenhower gets a poison dart, and you are in the top spot."

"Oh Jesus. You can't let them do that."

"Do not worry. I do not tell them. Why? Perhaps because I know you are crap spy. I wish it is your wife we hired. Your older daughter, maybe; I think six-year-old girl might do better for this."

"All right, all right. But I want out of this."

"We're not here to ruin your life."

"What are you going to do with me? Because you can't expect me to—well, I'm not a puppet. Understand? I'm not the KGB."

"I do not mean to be impolite but you are already a KGB asset," Arkady said. "So now it is only a question of your duties." He signaled for another round.

"Don't exaggerate," Tatiana told him. "Dick, we did not send you to Pawtuxet Farm to get us information we already have. We sent you so you would know what we know. Arkady and I work a long time together in Russia. We see a great deal. We are Soviet intelligence, yes, but that is not a simple thing.

"Arkady has told you of the Romanovs, what he sees there. Yes? And you see for yourself. That's only the first part," Tatiana said. "So listen to me. When I am little girl, my father works in a factory, very poor. Engine parts. I was in school in Kiev. I remember not much of it. Dirty air, dead cat in the street. In school there are tests, history and foreign language and mathematics. I do very well, I score first in my region. I am prodigy. Also, I am pretty.

"A man, a party official, notices me. He speaks to my father, who can do nothing. And I say okay, why not. I want only to leave that place. I go to Leningrad with him but it does not last long. But another man gives me idea to go to school. Spy school, yes? They teach this now. I learn to shoot, to take apart locks, to speak English, German, French, Hebrew. I learn many things. How to handle informants, pass messages, all these things. Make a man or woman fall in love with me." She looked at me steadily.

"I graduate, I go to Moscow and begin work. The war comes. I am in Poland, then I am in Berlin. Lots of work for a person like me. It's a big world now. Go out every night and sleep till noon. Champagne and dancing and photographing documents with horrors in them. I am twenty-six years old then, thinking every day I am vanquishing demons, risking life.

"When Germany breaks, I have four passports and I speak six languages. What do I do? I could be Italian, I could be American, or British. I could even be German." She said it crisply, swapping accents as she went, a South Carolinian accent for America, her British one a film-star version of the upper classes. Maybe it was just a party trick, a one-off; maybe it wasn't. I wondered what, if anything, of her demeanor wasn't a conscious performance. It was perhaps the most frightening thing I ever saw her do; it was as if her mastery of espionage made her a kind of animate mask, as if human speech were no more than insect chirps or birdcalls to be mimicked.

"I could have disappeared but I went back to Moscow, the city that made me. Who else really knew what I was worth? It was 1946 and there were more meetings, more parties. We should be happy, everything going so well, we got Hungary, Poland, Czechoslovakia. Yugoslavia, more or less. Osterreich, sure. But no, everyone drinking and shit scared, because you got the nuclear bombs. Who will save us?

"And maybe we'll get the bomb. Other projects. People will try anything when annihilation coming. It is only that the Manhattan Project finished first. We got some Germans, but did we get the right ones? But there are other options, maybe. Europe is a rummage sale now, crackpot ideas and mystic frauds the Reich poured money into. More than one way to blow up the world.

"I meet a man. GRU colonel. He has a wife but he likes me better. I learn there are shadow regiments, not on the books. There are weapons. He tells me there are people in the Kremlin who fear what is happening, but then there are others who try to find uses for these things. They try to summon them or to— well, make them. They manage to kill a lot of people but they are trying. You see the result in Gregor, I think.

"I meet Arkady. We are partners, we go out into steppes, places you never heard of. Follow stories. Voices in the forest. Missing children. Radiation burns where none should be. Cattle death. A woman says she meet the devil on the road outside Kirov."

"That one I believe still," Arkady said.

"We agree to disagree, okay?"

"Two years we are out there." Now Arkady took over. "Bad roads. Moskvitch, you know this car? Piece of shit. Take trains. Fly when we can. Out there is nothing for hundreds of miles. Then a factory stamping out wheels or farm machinery. This is the part you never understand. Old Russia dying out and children like Tatiana—sorry—don't remember. Children on these collectives all watching each other, speaking from script. And we see things. And we tell the party. And the science cities spring up. *Naukograds.* Bone city, digging city, city for magic. Places where there is no name. Stalin will do anything he likes. And he needs a result.

"One of these times we get a little too close. It is hard to tell. And so maybe we leave a few bodies out there. We get ourselves transferred to embassy here. And here it's easy. Steal the bomb. Bomb plans, bomb materials. Anything bomb. Easy by comparison. Commies every place, right? Just like you are saying in the speeches.

"But even here it's not all bomb, is it? Even in America it is rotten."

"Hiss told you this?" I asked.

"He dug for me," Tatiana said. "Why do you think I ran Hiss like I did? We need to know what is happening. Hiss over-reached, of course he did. He was a Baltimore intellectual. Not trained, just a civil servant with a notebook, a camera, and a library card. The Russian intelligence service is an institution hundreds of years old. I was trained by agents whose teachers operated against Bismarck and infiltrated the court of Queen Victoria. Hiss, he is so sloppy that even you catch him. They take his memories by now; probably he believes he was an innocent fellow traveler.

"But then you come. The crusader, the coming man. Young and capable and smart. And look at you now. We like you very much, Mr. Nixon," said Tatiana.

"Yes, we do," Arkady said.

"But no," she said, lighting a cigarette. "We do not let you go."

"What do you want from me?"

"We will never be allies. We are not friends. But you have

seen what you have seen, haven't you? And not just at Paw-tuxet," Tatiana said.

"I don't like this. You said yourself I'm not properly trained."

"Trained, who is trained?" Arkady said. "No one we trust, at any rate."

"What happens if I say no?"

"There is any number of things that could happen," he said, "because you have made yourself very vulnerable by entering public life. We do not have to look hard to find the next ambitious man, eager to be the one who brought the famous Mr. Nixon down. For instance, you would not like for people to know you are in the company of such an attractive Russian lady without Pat's knowledge."

"Pat's not part of this. She is not."

"Ideally, she does not come into this," Arkady said. "Pat has a happy life, hears none of this. She is one of the civilians like you used to be. But is why you must do this. We can threaten you, but that is not the reason you do this. There are things to be afraid of much worse than us. Eisenhower himself."

"So now we come to Eisenhower. Not entirely what he seems," Tatiana told me. "Believe me, we have ways of detecting things."

"He's . . . what? Not human? The devil?"

She shook her head. "Not like that. But he has touched a power he should not have. Like Gregor did. Maybe worse."

"Could be they make him hybrid," Arkady added. "Or he has a being inside him. Spirit from Pawtuxet. Or maybe he got it in Europe. You Americans got up to plenty of tricks over there."

"I want you to learn what he is hiding. Okay?" Tatiana said. "I do not trust this one."

"He's Dwight D. Eisenhower. He ran the show in the Second World War. He's a legend. What exactly do you suspect him of?"

Arkady said, "He reads wrong, I know this. Maybe he did something to himself to do all he had to? Agreed to something he should not have? Maybe not his fault. But we should know. He has a secret. I would be very curious to know whether he is genuinely alive."

"What do you mean?"

"The colonel told me once that the Cold War isn't about East against West," Tatiana said. She seemed to be remembering something, reciting verbatim words she had heard. "You have seen strange things, and I do not care if they are Russian or American. And when it comes to such things, we are not KGB. Not after the things we've seen. Do you understand? Not Russia, not America. I do not understand who is in power now. The Kremlin itself is a scene of horrors I would rather not describe. The real war is the living against the dead."

CHAPTER THIRTEEN

FALL 1952

PEOPLE TALK ABOUT 1968 as Richard Nixon's greatest year, when I took the presidency in one of the most improbable political comebacks in history. Or maybe the greatest was 1972, the year I won a second term and took my historic trip to China. But I'm not sure anything ever mattered as much to me as the months of July through November of 1952, the late summer and autumn when I learned how to be a spy, and I ran for vice president, and I fell at least partly in love with Tatiana.

I would leave the venetian blinds in my office open to a certain level, and Arkady would know to meet me. Or he would leave me a message, a laundry notice, perhaps, with a prearranged set of numbers contained in it. Through what sleight of documentation I don't know, Arkady managed to obtain for himself a legitimate-looking taxi, and he'd pick me up at a discreet distance from the Capitol.

We would meet for drinks and talk about curious rumors floating in from all over the globe. We could never quite see the full picture but we knew that underneath the elegant black-and-white chessboard of nuclear strike and counterstrike there was another conflict playing out. In Southeast Asian conflicts, bodies of men and women with hooves, with solid black eyes, with half-developed wings were found. A house-size lumbering form was photographed moving among the trees of a Florida swamp.

Chunks of the defense and intelligence budgets dropped out of view with even greater frequency than one usually expected, and the little we could trace ended up at university presses and with crackpot mystics and in shell companies whose origins we could never discover.

I lost sight at times of whether I was cooperating or being blackmailed. Like bullying older siblings, Arkady and Tatiana kept me in my place with alternating warmth and threats, smug in the knowledge that I would never dare to appeal to a higher authority. On nights when it was just me and Arkady and we were particularly drunk, we would give up on passing secrets and do spy training. We'd split up and then meet in an all-night grocery pretending to be strangers; we'd slip each other messages, give signs and countersigns, then vanish into the night. I'd tail him through the city streets and he'd disappear from view and then appear out of nowhere a few minutes later to clap me on the shoulder. When we reversed roles, I was never able to shake him, even on moonless nights.

As the months passed, I noticed that Tatiana grew paler and distinctly haggard. I wondered what her duties were when she was not terrorizing me, who her other agents were; people whom I'd met, perhaps, and never suspected? Once, coming out of the Capitol building, I saw her in the street. Dressed as a businesswoman or executive secretary, stylish and aloof in dark glasses. I tailed her, trying on Arkady's skills, until she reached the Supreme Court building, and I watched her enter by an unmarked metal door. On a whim I tried the handle. Locked.

"Alger Hiss was the least of it. There is risk, a grave risk, of active foreign intelligence sources within the United States government," Agent Hunt said. "Worse than we'd ever admit to the public. I'm talking deep cover, gentlemen. Men and women who have waited years for this opportunity to inform on us. Isn't that right, Mr. Nixon?"

"Yes, quite right," I said. "Do you have plans in place to find these bastards out?" He was staring at me with unnatural intensity. Spend too long as a spy and everything starts to look like a secret message.

"We have methods, yes. Signals intelligence. Defectors from Soviet intelligence. We correlate small pieces of data, for years if necessary, and they don't even know we're observing them. And then we act."

"What kind of people are these?" asked a gray-haired senator, a hatchet-faced statesman of the Midwest. "What could possibly make a person act this way?"

"There are various answers, but typically it comes down to mundane motives of the lowest sort. Greed and ambition. A childish need to feel important. Many of these people are broken by other means, intimidated or blackmailed, and are simply too cowardly to resist. A very few really believe in what they are doing. Soviet intelligence knows how to handle each of these types and runs them all with immaculate perfection. Sooner or later we will get them, each and every one."

True, all of it, but I could have told him more than that if I'd known how to explain. The exact weird mixture of desire, fear, ambition, and selfishness that pushes you privately across an invisible line, past whatever it was you used to think was so important and sacred. And when you cross the line, it vacuum-seals behind you, and it's as hard as steel, and there's no way to go back.

And why should you want to? I would have asked Agent Hunt. Why did people ask you to play a game when the deck was stacked against you from the beginning? Why shouldn't I lie to their faces and steal the food off their plates? What did I owe to any of them?

*   *   *

The spy hunt was in full cry, that much was clear. I went back to my office and shifted the potted plant in the window from the left corner to the right. I let Pat know I'd be working late, left the building, drove to the high school, pulled into the parking lot behind it, and walked the length of the football field to the back fence, where Tatiana was waiting in a long, dark coat, smoking as usual.

"Yes? What is it?" she said. I wondered if I'd interrupted her plans.

"Does anybody else know that we're talking?"

"Arkady is the only one. I am sure there are analysts in Moscow who would like to know who you are but they will not know for sure. That at least I can promise."

"But how do you know? You could be tortured."

"It is possible. I have much protection, though. Friends. And I know a great many things about people. If they want to burn me, you are not the only one at risk."

"Okay," I said. "But I'm a spy, right?"

"Sort of. I'm not sure what you think of as a spy, but yes, okay."

"Well? Where's my protection? How do I do this?"

"You have a point, Dick. We pull you into this too fast, I think. I talk to Arkady, we make arrangements."

"Okay, okay. Thank you," I said.

"Is that all?" Tatiana said.

"Well. I just . . . I just wanted to talk, maybe."

"We are not friends, Dick," she said again, and not for the last time. "Is common mistake. You will hear from Arkady."

She turned and walked along the length of the end zone and into the darkness. I waited for a car or anything to start but there was nothing. A disappearing act.

I hurried home to a reheated dinner that Pat watched me eat.

"Are you happy, Dick?" she asked. She'd ask me that at odd times during the week, at dinner, before bed, driving home.

I stared at her across the dinner table, confounded. I wanted to say, *I have a terrible secret.* I wanted to say, *I think the twentieth century is going very badly wrong.*

"Of course, honey," I said. Pat was perfect. I was a liar. I hated Pat.

"You look worried. The campaign's going all right, isn't it?"

It was. We were going to win by a landslide. As she very well knew.

"Great," I said. "Couldn't be better."

I had no idea what she was thinking at that moment. Possibly that she was married to the most boring man in creation.

Save me, idiot, I thought, so loud it felt like I was screaming it. She cleared the dishes. As the years passed, the one thing I'd never forgive her for was not catching me sooner.

I didn't see Eisenhower again in person for a long time. Not until the convention the following year, where the Republican Party took only thirty-five minutes to approve him as the nominee. I was in my underwear when I got the call summoning me to his hotel suite. In a rumpled suit, I barged in and mistakenly called him "chief" and generally behaved like a nervous boor as I was introduced to his wife, Mamie, and said something too loudly about ideals. It was a blur of whiskey and handshakes, and Pat heard the news on television. Nothing about it seemed quite clear or real, even after his bone-dry claw of a hand hoisted mine overhead and he called me his running mate in front of thousands and perhaps millions of human beings. And my job became making him the most important man in the world, although after the convention, he once again ignored me entirely.

In September an article accused me of taking donations from a group of rich people. Which, on its face, struck me as slightly comical—from who else was a presidential candidate meant to receive money? But the charges were beginning to stick. Articles appeared in the national press. Pat and I were shouted at while checking in to our hotel, while eating in restaurants. Men and women threw pennies at me.

Worse, they were heckling Eisenhower. And Eisenhower? Maddeningly, he released a statement that read *I believe Dick Nixon to be an honest man. I am confident he will place all the facts before the American people, fairly and squarely.* He seemed to wink at me from the page of the *New York Times,* challenging me to wonder what he knew about me. Thomas Dewey, smirking, beetle-browed Thomas Dewey, the three-time presidential loser, called me to suggest I resign from the ticket. Was he relaying a message from Eisenhower? He wouldn't say. Was Eisenhower testing me? Was he simply an egregious asshole?

Panicked reflex: I called the number, long distance, from a pay phone outside a Portland hotel. I was told to take a long walk late the following night. I excused myself to Pat. I walked uphill in the waning heat of the Indian summer, not caring about the direction, past seedy bargain stores and brownstones, losing my way under the yellowing trees. Someone shouted at me on a street corner and I ignored it, walking until a black limousine pulled up beside me; Tatiana making her usual entrance. She beckoned me inside.

"Why did you call me? Why the fuck do I fly to Portland?" she said. She looked even more tired than usual.

"Because I don't know what to do. I could lose because of this."

"And you want the KGB to help you? I thought you were good at this—isn't that what you said, Senator Nixon?"

A policeman pulled up next to us and I slouched down uselessly. Tatiana politely ignored it.

"Do you think Eisenhower knows—well, about us? I don't understand why he won't help."

"I don't know what you think 'us' is, Dick. But Eisenhower, I think he knows a great deal more than he says. But who can say for a man who has seen what he has seen?"

"Then what do I do?"

She lit a cigarette and thought.

"Why are you asking us? You must have people for that."

"Nobody I trust." And it was true. How could I trust any of them? They certainly couldn't trust me. The Russians were the only ones who could.

"I am not an American politician, although I have stayed alive for quite some time in Moscow. But in Moscow, it wouldn't be this way. Would happen behind the scenes. Probably you are quietly killed and then Stalin makes a speech. Not this schoolyard shit."

"But what about Eisenhower? Why doesn't he back me?"

"He is afraid for your weakness. Has he chosen the wrong guy? You caught Hiss, you acted like you were a tough guy, but he suspects now you are just sneaky bitch. I think he insults you on purpose. He asks you to fight for yourself."

"Do you know yet what's wrong with him? I thought you were investigating that."

"I get a little from our people from the Reich. The Nazis who went east. The military types, they respect him, you know? He was smart, he outplayed them. But then we have a few others, the fringe ones. Bavarian shaman and a couple vets of the Tibet expedition, Ernst Schäfer's people. Eisenhower scares the shit out of them."

*   *   *

The Checkers speech is a joke now, if it's remembered at all. In the moment it was something else; it was bizarre and electric. No one had thought of this before, a candidate getting on TV and sitting down to talk things out. It was Pat's idea. Who else would have thought of just telling people the truth?

She sat next to me in the TV studio on the corner of Hollywood and Vine. It was the set of *The Colgate Comedy Hour* and *This Is Your Life,* and it smelled of foundation powder and the burning of hot lights. I had slept for four hours the previous night. At the last minute they set up a little fake office for me and I sat down to face people as if I were a school principal or a regional manager. I would go on at nine thirty, after Milton Berle was finished.

Behind me, hastily arranged curtains and bookshelves. The cameraman looked no older than twenty-two, a skinny kid staring at me blank-faced, waiting for the farce to begin. I tried to look into the camera rather than at his eyes. I tried to picture a person on the other side of the lens. All I could see was a cheap wise guy watching in a half-empty bar, knowing an asshole when he saw one. The camera swung around, irised in on me where I sat behind the host's desk, and I was live on television. Afterward I learned there were sixty million viewers. Eisenhower watched; my own mother watched.

I didn't have a script, just an impulse. You start with "My fellow Americans" and you go from there. "I come before you tonight as a candidate for the vice presidency and as a man whose honesty and integrity have been questioned."

Humility and folksiness, bathos and nasty innuendo. I caricatured my own working-class origins, maybe the one truly admirable thing about me, turning it into gross sentimentality. I smeared my opponent for employing his wife on staff. I relied, as always, on being a slightly worse person than my opponents expected.

It seemed, though, that the production was plagued by odd technical misfires. The temperature in the television studio dropped precipitously, then rose to a stifling level. Strange audio blips, voices whispering and then shouting in my ears, until my own speech seemed garbled and hollow. Voices that were completely absent from the recorded audio. In some moments I saw peculiar figures occupying the studio audience seats, cloaked figures, bizarre even for Los Angeles. I never heard another person acknowledge them.

Whatever she thought of me, Pat knew her role, which was to sit and smile. We were onstage again, *The Dark Tower* once more. I used everything I could. I had the line about her cloth coat. I told them I wasn't a quitter and neither was Pat, and I ad-libbed something about her Irish background. She sat and smiled politely into the camera while radiating the knowledge that I had turned her into a political prop right along with the family dog.

The temperature rose, became feverishly hot. As the half hour closed, I stumbled to the finish with a final burst of irony, a resolve to fight "the crooks and the Communists and those that defend them" until my last breath. And then the finishing blow, a plea to viewers to write the Republican Party directly. Let Eisenhower answer that one if he could.

"And remember, folks," I told them, "Eisenhower is a great man. Believe me. He's a great man, a great man..." I repeated it, trailing off, as they cut to commercial. I staggered toward the camera lens, zombie-like, utterly spent.

Pat and I got drunk as the news came in: It was a triumph. They'd bought it. At ten minutes to midnight a telegram arrived from none other than Dwight D. Eisenhower. It read *Good enough.*

"Ho-kay. Tatiana and I talk, we think maybe Nixon deserves a little more respect." It was a spy-training night, definitely. We were drinking in the kitchen of a sordid little suburban safe house; on the linoleum counter, a bottle of vodka sat steaming with cold, the liquor pure and clear and foreign. Pat and I never drank it at home.

"Thank you. I think it's about time, to be honest."

"The man is a TV star now, we say. You know they came after you there in the studio? You notice anything strange?"

"Noises, I guess. And the temperature."

"Tatiana felt it too. *V'yedma*—witch or some shit. We investigate. But meanwhile we decide to get you a little something."

"A little something?"

"Sure, you spy now, we think you're ready."

"Fuck you guys, you know? You're asking me to risk my fucking life—"

"Okay, a little quieter. Raising voice now."

"—asking me to steal from the United States government and you give me this shit, talk down to me. I'm a senator, okay? Not your little flunky." I sat back.

"Okay, you got point. You're not flunky. Not flunky."

"That's—that's right."

"But you need a couple things we got for you. Okay? Like you asked. We got, first, this." He handed me a matchbox. Red and blue, a trio of dancing girls. "Is tiny camera, okay? Got a couple packs of film. Photograph anything you need. Low light okay."

"All right. What else?"

"Hold out hands." I did and he gave me the smallest pistol I had ever seen, scaled for a child. He poured a dozen pill-size

miniature bullets into my other hand. I worked my finger behind the trigger guard and it felt light as a paper cutout.

"Does it work?" I asked.

He shrugged. "Close range only; is useless otherwise. Get
here or here." He touched his heart and then his head. "Do
you really need to shoot anybody? If potential vice president
is shooting people, it is not a good mission at that point. But
maybe you feel better to have it."

"Thanks, I don't."

"You want cyanide pill?"

"No."

"You sure?"

"I'm okay."

"Nobody wants these. I got like fifty."

"Anything else?"

"Also this." He handed me a thick envelope. I unsealed it and
poured the contents onto the table and caught my breath. Passports. Dark reds, blues, greens like the hides of exotic animals,
all embossed with gold.

He ticked them off. "Canada, South Africa, Palestine. Two
from United States, two from UK. Not cheap. You ever need
to disappear, this is how you go. And these." He set down, with
a blunt click, two small gold bars glowing with bright mystery,
heavy with their potential. "I get you special suitcase, false bottom, nobody ever know."

I grinned, speechless. I didn't know how to thank him, but
he clapped me on the shoulder.

"See? You're a secret agent. One of us. Happy now?"

I was. It felt right. I pictured what it must look like to
an omniscient observer, the two immense networks of intelligence gathering. Fathomless, overlapping, reciprocal, and
interpenetrating organizations built on secrecy and compul-

sion and shame. Like a clandestine empire of the passive-aggressive.

I didn't know why it should have been like this, but for the first time since I started public life, I felt safe. Who was Richard Nixon anyway? Whoever he was, I could get rid of him if I had to, throw him away and lose myself. I drove home, the passports lying on the passenger seat where I could glance at them, like million-dollar bills, like the Count of Monte Cristo's treasure chest.

I pulled into the driveway and reluctantly slid the pile into my briefcase. As I stepped into the familiar smells of home, I saw it for the flimsy thing it was. I could live here but I'd always be ready to board a flight, to open a briefcase and shuffle identities and passports until I was lost in them. I wanted to step into the mirror maze and never come back.

CHAPTER FOURTEEN

WHAT IS IT like to be made vice president?

On one level it's a nearly hallucinatory degree of success. I was barely forty years old, and a shaky, sixty-three-year-old heartbeat from the leadership of the entire Western world.

It was also like throwing up in convention-hall bathrooms before giving speeches, and after. It was sitting through dinners with men and women with whom I had nothing in common. Spending an enormous amount of time on trains. Promising things and agreeing to things as advised by people I had barely met, on very little sleep. Huge sums of money were changing hands and everything happening on the grandest scale imaginable while still in most moments remaining pointless and usually outright seedy. I pretended to learn to fly-fish; I watched sporting events. In Maine I was assaulted by a lobster; it seized my lapel in a threatening manner. I tasted local foods and admired factories, farms, department stores, hotels, and (unless I'm misremembering) several empty plots of land.

In the end, we beat Adlai Stevenson and John Sparkman— no, we annihilated the pair of them by an absurd margin, giving up only a couple of states in the Southeast.

It was like being given what was almost the nation's highest honor by a man you held in infinite esteem and regarded with perhaps a certain amount of terrified suspicion, a man who disliked you and clearly wanted nothing to do with you, who would scowl and change the subject at the mention of your name. And then being given a very important and very nasty job by that person, and despised for it, almost as much as you despised yourself.

This isn't a plea for pity. It can't be. Eisenhower and his advisers knew how I'd won my first few elections and they wanted more of the same: dirty tricks, innuendo, and scare tactics carried on at a safe distance from Dwight's presidential bid.

I could have stood on my integrity and refused, but, well, the historical record is what it is. I wanted everything he was offering, wanted it with a panicked desperation, and I decided I would have it. I had already done worse for a great deal less reward.

I endorsed Senator McCarthy's efforts while stopping just short of McCarthyite excess and avoiding his uncomfortable, nakedly self-destructive presence. I pretended to like him and then carefully leaked my distaste for him to a reporter at the *New York Times*. I had an intuition and a timing for this kind of manipulative nastiness. I didn't care what I did to McCarthy, of course, no one did, but that was the least of it. I blamed Adlai Stevenson for the course of the Korean War and for tolerating a potential Communist insurgency. I said ridiculous and frankly childish things. I called him Sidesaddle Adlai for his leftist positions, with the leering implication that he was somehow female. Senseless, pandering, inciting statements that only stupid people would enjoy. I, Richard M. Nixon, did these things, and much worse. I was good at it as a congressman, even better as a national candidate.

It was not a talent I understood. It's not how I spoke to my brothers or parents or schoolmates. It's not how I acted in the navy. But in front of groups, in front of reporters, I knew how to get the effect I needed. I had an ignoble knack for meanness. Reporters would get out their notepads and scribble, nodding, knowing they had a quote. A talent perhaps learned in the early days of my childhood in some quiet moment of observation when I was very young, untraceable. I've said my mother was a Quaker and a saint; I've always said it. But then there was a night deep in October 1952 when I woke to the trace of a memory: One night when I was eight and found her alone in the sitting room. The wind was off the Santa Ana Mountains, dry, hot, and I couldn't sleep. I stood in the doorway of the room and watched her talking to nothing in a singsong language. She sensed I was there and looked at me and I knew at once that she was teaching me what a secret was, a memory contained between the two of us and only we two. That there was more than one side to me. No matter how pure I seemed, righteous all the way through, there was always another me that couldn't be put down, a sly one, a clever one, a lying one, a vicious one. I could be elected president of the whole goddamned United States but I'd always be Tricky Dick.

Of course Pat was there for every meal, every speech, every standing ovation, every sneering put-down. Alone, we scarcely spoke. Onstage she was perfection but I always watched her watching me and registering all of it in the tiniest hardening of her lips, the tiniest expression of the eyes, going vague for an instant, going elsewhere. In some moments, I saw what might have been suppressed laughter. I imagined a minuscule spasm of amusement at a renewed recognition of the striving, gutless wonder she'd married. At the realization this guy was actually winning the vice presidency.

On the day of the inauguration, after the swearing-in, she spent the afternoon alone in her room preparing, and when she emerged it was as someone I scarcely recognized. I stared.

Her hair had been reengineered into something complicated, mounded and waved and clipped. She wore a white silk blouse and a jeweled brooch at her throat. This was the Pat the world knew later, the president's wife, glazed over and sealed into history. This was Pat telling me she understood that our marriage was her job now. This was her telling me that I'd lost her.

CHAPTER FIFTEEN

FEBRUARY 1953

PEOPLE TALK ABOUT Eisenhower's golden age, the bright era and the wise, blandly all-American figure at the center of it, his oddly hieratic grin beaming a beneficent influence throughout the country. Nostalgia for the wholesomeness and boom economy has long since passed into cliché and there's only so much I want to go into. I suppose in a sense the clichés were true for plenty of people. They had lovely cars, television sets and kitchens, oral contraceptives, Teflon and FORTRAN. Rock and roll and credit cards and white-out and Barbies and the bloody Mary. A mood of confidence, of joy and astonishment, at their own wealth and daring.

Or so I'm told, and I'm certainly glad some people were happy. I'm reading it in a book, because how the fuck should I know? It all happened without me. What is the vice presidency? The Constitution dictates only two duties: casting the deciding vote if the Senate is deadlocked and replacing the president if he dies or is impeached. Apart from waiting for those two things to happen, you made the rest up and were duly forgotten by history. The exception being Aaron Burr, who shot someone, decisively lowering the bar for the rest of us.

What I remember is small pieces of the world: the West Wing, the insides of planes and hotel lobbies and conference rooms. My life was dinners with Pat and the children; airplane flights; placeholder meetings with foreign dignitaries during which I nodded and reminded them I had no power to make an agreement but would speak to the president. Stomach-turning formal breakfasts, speeches to party elders and tradesmen. I opened factories in Detroit and Akron, breathing the various stinks of canneries, slaughterhouses, or rubber plants and bestowing that vice presidential combination of glamour, flattery, and the tacit reminder that they didn't quite rate a visit from the top guy.

The rest of the time I was part of the consuming desperate purpose of the Eisenhower gang: the war. Not just the proxy war in Korea but the omnipresent, glacially vast global war with Communism. There were moments when it felt like Whittaker Chambers and I had dreamed up the Cold War in a conference room at the Commodore Hotel, but by 1953 we were all in the dream and it had changed and accelerated beyond all recognition, supercharged by the postwar boom in prosperity and science.

In October 1952 we exploded a thermonuclear bomb a thousand times more powerful than the atom bomb. The numbers had stopped meaning anything, but men from Strategic Air Command screened the footage for us, a smear of red clouds and fire like the Last Judgment. The bomb annihilated the island on which it had been built and made a temporary crater in the Pacific waters a mile wide and a hundred and fifty-two feet deep. We made this for you, they said, then they stood back to see what we would do with it. The Soviets exploded their own hydrogen bomb less than a year later.

Every month, it seemed, the solemn young men of Strategic Air Command briefed me on the latest wonder. The B-47 Stratojet that could fly for thirty-five hundred miles without refueling; the USS *Nautilus,* a nuclear-powered submarine that could travel under the ocean for thirteen hundred miles without needing to surface. I was born into a world that had just seen the first cars and airplanes, and Eisenhower could remember a world where the cavalry charge was still state-of-the-military-art. In a decade, conventional weaponry had all but ceased to matter, and the airborne nuclear war was the only thing that counted. Thousands of years of military doctrine had been made obsolete and we were looking at a clean sheet of paper. And this wasn't even counting what I'd seen at Pawtuxet and on East Seventy-First Street in the Wexford building.

Who better than Eisenhower to lead us into the new age? But then, who was Eisenhower? I saw so little of him and what I did see was almost too bland to be believed, a tediously wholesome middle manager who liked nothing more than to get business done and return to the golf course or go on a card-playing weekend with his buddies, a crew of portly, glad-handing businessmen.

What did I know about him? Apart from his military record, I knew almost nothing. His name meant, literally, "iron-hewer," and his family had been in the United States since the eighteenth century. He smelled like dry grass, like dust, like Texas, like the Great Plains. And, for reasons never made clear, he'd appointed me his vice president.

The American side of the Cold War began to assume its real form in Eisenhower's mind and in his weekly planning sessions. We crowded into the Oval Office, myself, John Foster Dulles, a gang of uniforms from the Pentagon, and, in their spectacles and expensive suits, the men from the RAND Corporation, the strategy-and-policy think tank whose reach was breathtakingly wide. Cold-blooded intellectuals of the eastern elite.

At one level, the logic was relatively straightforward. In 1949, the United States' first-wave attack plan consisted of a fleet of planes loaded with a hundred and thirty-three atomic bombs, the idea being that they would destroy about seventy cities and 40 percent of the Soviet Union's industrial capacity. There was a general feeling that the Truman administration had been a trifle tentative, and we were determined to roughhouse a little bit if we had to. This year's plan featured a robust seven hundred and fifty-five bombs, all of which could be dropped within a couple of hours.

The basic tenets of Eisenhower's strategic policy were spelled out in a typewritten document handed around the inner circle, the notorious NSC 162/2, a report to the National Security Council. The Soviets were actively expansionist, determined to conquer or disrupt Western capitalist democracies. The document modestly stated that given the current state of affairs, "a prolonged period of tension might ensue, during which each side increases its armaments, reaches atomic plenty and seeks to improve its relative power position." But, good news, the Soviets could likely be kept in their place if we Americans showed ourselves ready to play. And, buried in section 39.b.(1), the heart of the Eisenhower doctrine: "In the event of hostilities, the United States will consider nuclear weapons to be as available for use as other munitions." We were ready to go, with "massive retaliation" the scenario of choice.

Thorny issues remained, however, such as the strong incentive to make the first strike. Clearly, the first player to move held an enormous advantage as long as its forces could reliably take out the opposition's nuclear arsenal at one go and didn't mind gratuitously murdering tens of millions. The idea of a preventive or prophylactic war still occasionally came up for debate, although Eisenhower was firmly against it.

On a brisk day in March we were in the Oval Office reviewing a new RAND report, mulling over the issue of just how much damage we would have to do to effectively dissolve the USSR and turn it into nothing but a group of ragged comrades with a common language and fur hats. I looked at the assembled faces and wondered who knew what. Who had been to Pawtuxet and had Blue Ox clearance apart from Eisenhower himself? Why weren't we talking about it?

Eisenhower read the key passages aloud to the group while pacing the Oval Office's perimeter. "'Just what it takes to destroy a society is uncertain... The destruction of hundreds of cities in the space of hours is possible...we simply do not have any human experience with the loss of ten or a hundred major cities in one night.'" He paused, struck by some vivid mental image, then called on me like a gruff professor. "Well, Dick? What do you think? What's it going to take to put them down?"

"Sir, with respect, it doesn't matter."

"Well, why the hell not?"

"According to your policy, we're not striking first, not in an all-out attack. We're only going nuclear if they do."

"Go on," he said.

"And it's well documented that a Soviet first strike would knock out most of our bombers. If our nuclear arsenal dies on the ground, there's no counterstrike. So if we don't strike first, we don't strike at all." I was addressing the room as I spoke, and they all shrugged. Everyone had gotten this far. "If I can figure that out, you certainly can, which leads to another conclusion."

"Which is?"

"If we're talking about this, there must be another dimension to the strategic landscape," I said. "You must know something I don't."

"Again, I'm fascinated."

"Is there a new anti-air-defense technology I haven't been briefed on?" I knew there wasn't. And submarine-mounted nuclear missiles were a decade away. "Is there something . . . else?"

"Else?"

"Some other technology. Altogether separate from nuclear devices." I'd started this without thinking and I could feel my face getting red.

"Like what, Dick? Cosmic rays? Moon men?" He stood over me, a teacher singling out an unruly student for mockery.

"No—nothing like that."

"You must have something in mind."

I patted my forehead with a handkerchief. Eisenhower wasn't sweating, but he never seemed to perspire.

"Sir." I took a deep breath. "Sir, I know there were other programs. Like the Manhattan Project, but ones that went in other directions. Project Blue Ox." A couple of the RAND guys flinched, but everyone else either had not heard of it or was too well trained to show anything.

"I've heard the name," Eisenhower said. "But I'm not familiar with the details. Remind me?"

"I'm not—I'm not sure everyone's cleared for it, sir."

"I hereby clear you all for Project Blue Ox," he said to the room, making a mocking magician's pass with one outsize hand. "Well, Dick?"

"I know you funded it. I've been to the Pawtuxet Farm." At that, there was a long silence.

"And what did you see there?" he said finally.

"I saw the farm."

"And there you saw . . . chickens? Ducks?"

"Germans. Old buildings. A man who—who vanished."

"Have you ever seen anything like that before?"

I could feel that I was blushing but I didn't say anything. I wasn't going to tell the president that I'd been forced into a ritual occult summoning by a pair of Russians.

"Have you?" he said again.

I muttered, "Never."

"I see. And what did you think of what you saw?"

"A sort of a trick? I didn't understand it. It seemed like he was . . . well, a ghost." The generals were all smirking now, old comrades, I supposed, who knew the president's routines of old.

"Well, if we're done considering ghost-based strategic technologies, gentlemen, I believe we'll close for the day." Dismissed, we filed out. I expected to hear his voice call me back at any moment but it never came.

Every hour, I thought I'd hear from the Russians. They were only waiting for their chance to issue some impossible order or maybe just to bring the hammer down, turn everything they had over to the media and end the charade. I sweated and sometimes all I could hear was my own inner voice saying, *Liar, liar, liar,* as I wondered if the next thing to come out of my mouth would sound crazy or not.

I could have struck at them first, and I thought about it a hundred times. They were two little spies, and I was the vice president. With a little work I might have gotten the Kremlin suspicious of them, had them discredited as corrupt or even mentally unstable. And I could do worse. The CIA was a new thing and it was still the Wild West in American intelligence, without oversight or clear rules of engagement. And the two Russians were, in the end, the sworn enemies of my country.

But I felt the cold knife at my throat. They'd been in this game longer than I had. They had photographs, perhaps recordings; who knew what kind of insurance measures they'd taken?

I lay awake thinking of how much I didn't know. For all the vodka shots and gunpoint camaraderie we'd shared, Arkady and Tatiana were spies, which is to say, liars. Anything or nothing they said could be true. I had a lot more to lose than they did.

Or was that just an excuse? I'd waited for eight weeks and then that afternoon following the meeting where I'd brought up Blue Ox, almost without thinking, I found myself dialing the old fake number I'd been given for a fake laundry service and I told the guy who answered the phone I wanted my fake shirts back by fake Tuesday.

Soon Arkady would pull up in his disguise as a White House driver in the black monolith town car, swooping in with a little extra snap, maybe. I'd climb in the backseat, into the smell of sweet tobacco, leather, Russian sweat. He'd reach over and we'd clasp hands and then we'd drive a few minutes in silence and I'd be in the mirror world again, barreling along in a black car at night, family and office and loyalty forgotten, remembering what it felt like to be myself.

CHAPTER SIXTEEN

MARCH 1953

DWIGHT D. EISENHOWER had lied, indisputably and straight to my face. I wanted to know how and why, and it was possible I didn't care whether I wanted it for the Soviets or myself or, perhaps, America. I wanted to know more than I did and I lingered late in the evenings, alert but not sure what to look for.

I knew he kept secrets; of course he did, he was the commander in chief, there were any number of eyes-only briefings, but that didn't explain the general air of unease that settled over the West Wing after twilight. I'd hear footsteps overhead on the second floor, wander up to investigate, and find only empty offices. There were nights when I left and looked back, without knowing why, to see a light moving from window to window, warm and flickering, just for a few seconds before it winked out, leaving me standing alone in the dark in the scent of roses. At other times I thought I heard the sound of singing, a keening tenor chant just on the edge of hearing. Did it mean anything? If Eisenhower liked to sing, was that a strange thing in a president? I didn't even know what counted as strange for a Presbyterian. Or what was strange at all, given the monthly and weekly miracles disclosed by the Strategic Air Command.

I stayed late in the West Wing more nights than not and acquired a reputation as an obsessive worker or an aggressive climber, depending. One evening in early March, well after midnight, I smelled what seemed like incense. I went from door to door, first floor and second floor, but it seemed to have no source, or else the source was everywhere. It grew stronger outside the Oval Office and as I stood there, I distinctly heard voices.

How much can a vice president get away with? I reached for the forbidden doorknob and, slowly, put pressure on it, and it turned. I hesitated, then thought of how Eisenhower had lied to me. He'd brought this on himself. I was, I argued, carrying out a patriotic duty.

I eased the door inward as far as I dared. The furniture of the Oval Office had been pushed to the curved walls. There was Eisenhower, motionless, bent over a small stack of papers. He'd been chain-smoking and the smoke drifted up past the two great flags that stand behind the chief executive's desk.

He remained there for a long minute, then he harrumphed a little, straightened, and walked very deliberately around to the front of his desk. He turned to face something I couldn't see and then he said, clearly, "Well, on we go."

A voice answered, "Yes, sir." I recognized the high-pitched voice of the secretary of defense. Somebody Wilson. I could barely hear him. He sounded like a man talking in his sleep.

"Are we recording?" the president asked.

"Yes, sir."

"Let's get through this. No questions, you understand? And not a word to the Joint Chiefs." Eisenhower took a deep breath, cleared his throat, and took up a long knife from the desk. "Am I on the spot we marked?"

"Looks like it, sir."

"Commencing tactical incantation. This is attempt four," Eisenhower began. He rolled up one sleeve and drew the knife — I saw now it was a worn-looking bayonet — across the top of his forearm in a quick jerk. He stood a moment and watched it bleed until he was satisfied. He shook it out and I heard the blood spatter. I risked leaning a little farther into the room and saw that he was standing before a portable bulletin board on which was pinned a large map of Korea. It was dotted with blood now. The president held up a page and read from it.

"'Eighty-Sixth Engineer Searchlight Company.'"

He repeated the blood-spattering gesture and spoke again, very quickly and quietly, tonelessly.

"'Let their fates pass from them. Let them go unobserved. Let them strike fiercely in the night. Seven Hundred and Second Ordnance Maintenance Battalion. Let their fates pass from them. Let them go unobserved. Let them strike fiercely in the night. First Psychological Warfare Leaflet Company. Let their fates pass from them. Let them go unobserved. Let them strike fiercely in the night.'"

Each line was the same except for the unit name. By the time he reached "'Fourth Chemical Company of the Twenty-Third Chemical Battalion,'" the flow of blood had just about stopped. He let the page he was holding fall to the floor.

"Right, then," he said. "We'll do the heavy stuff now. Authorization code one, one, Charlie, uniform, victor. Presiding, Dwight David Eisenhower."

"Authorized," the secretary answered. "You are to proceed."

"I do so. Phase one, confirm target First Deputy Chairman Lavrenty Beria."

"Confirmed."

"I hereby offer him my ill will, malice, and condemnation in the full power of my office as president. Let all manner of mischief befall him. Let the Black Lady of the Woods prey on him by night. Conclude." I noticed he was sweating, unusually.

"I witness."

"Phase two, then. Confirm target General Secretary Iosif Vissarionovich Stalin. Jesus, that's a mouthful." His voice shook a little.

"Confirmed, sir."

"Proceeding. Let Abaddon-class entity designated Twelve Sierra, name redacted, visit him in its accustomed manner. Let the following authorized agents of the United States military inflict their harm: entity Fortuno, entity Mentalis, entity—" He stopped in a fit of coughing, bent over for a moment.

"Is there—"

Eisenhower spat on the floor. "And entity Pariah are granted full scope and discretion in the matter. Conclude."

"Conclude."

Eisenhower straightened, crossed to the fireplace opposite, and slowly and deliberately put the typewritten pages on the fire as Wilson bent over the wastebasket and puked his guts out.

"All right there, Wilson?" Eisenhower said, rolling down his sleeve and moving to his desk. "You can go. I'll see to it you won't remember this tomorrow. Not a thing."

"Thank you, sir. I'd really very much appreciate that."

I'd been absorbed in the scene and realized a moment too late that Wilson was walking straight to the door. Before I could move, he opened it and walked sightlessly past me, leaving the door wide open. In the abrupt, ringing silence, I looked down the length of the Oval Office at President Eisenhower.

"Hello, Dick," he said.

"Mr. President."

"This is a surprise visit. Is anything wrong?"

"I thought I heard a noise," I said.

"A noise." He thought a little while. "A suspicious noise?"

"Well, odd, maybe. Talking."

Slowly he shook his head.

"You're sure it wasn't a radio? This new music kids listen to. They say it's just terrible." He looked me in the eye as if daring me to argue. *Call my bluff,* he seemed to say. He wasn't a large man—an inch shorter than I was—but for a moment he seemed to loom over the desk from an unfathomable height.

"Maybe . . . maybe you're right, sir. I'm sorry to intrude."

"Wait, wait! While I have you here," he said, and the momentary impression of great height was gone. "Something I've got to show you. Really terrific." He fumbled in the desk drawer.

"Mr. President?"

"Ha!" He found what he was looking for and came around the desk to meet me. He was holding a deck of cards. I noticed once again how enormous his hands were. Pillowed in one palm, the deck looked as tiny as a matchbox.

"It's a really great trick." He shuffled the deck automatically; the cards cascaded from one hand to the other. "Do you like card tricks?"

Did I? I couldn't recall anyone ever showing me one. I shrugged at him like a sulky adolescent.

"All right, here we go. First take a look at the deck." He handed it to me to inspect.

"Completely ordinary," I said, returning it to him.

"All right. Now you pick one." He fanned the deck out one-handed, facedown, and I chose one: the king of clubs. "Give it back." It was one of the longer conversations I'd had with him since the inauguration. He shuffled the cards and fanned them again, watching me intently.

"Okay, now pick another." I did. It was the king of clubs again but evidently from a slightly different deck. This one had a demented little grin, and instead of gazing off to the side, it stared straight out. It looked, annoyingly, a little like my younger brother Arthur. I handed it back.

"It's a nice trick, Mr. President."

"Nearest thing to being a general, isn't it? Misdirection. Pop up where you're least expected. Now go again." He was a little too pleased at having a captive audience. I picked another king of clubs, but this time it had a larger mustache, a squarer head. It looked oddly familiar. Stalin.

"Once more. Last time. Watch my hands as I shuffle. This time for real." I watched cards pour from one platter-size hand to the other. I've never been good at figuring this stuff out. He fanned out the cards.

"All right," I said. But as I reached for a card, he drew the deck back.

"First I want you to remember something."

"Remember what?"

He turned the deck over so I could see that it was all kings, the entire deck. Or were they kings? The one at the far left was more than familiar. Washington. Then Adams? Then Jefferson. I looked for Eisenhower's face—the thirty-fourth president, there in the middle. Was I next? I looked for my face but the cards that followed were all in shadow.

"Remember to stay out of my office." He flexed the entire deck then let it go so it spat toward me, cards scattering straight into my face. I stumbled back and blinked, just for a moment, and the room was dark.

What the hell? I took another step back and banged into a desk that hadn't been there a moment ago. My eyes adjusted and I saw I was standing in my own office, down the long hallway and around the corner. Had I fainted? Been hypnotized? I stepped into the corridor. I really was there. The building was dark. The Oval Office was locked; the West Wing was silent. Somewhere in the building a radio came on, and a voice told me that Joseph Stalin was dead.

CHAPTER SEVENTEEN

MARCH 1953

THE FOLLOWING DAY I was going to signal that I had news when I took a call from a Mr. Lermontov at the Russian embassy—Arkady's signal to me. He picked me up an hour later. We drove for a few minutes, then parked to check for a tail.

"I'm sorry about Stalin," I said.

"Is not that asshole." He started the car again, then gave me a look. "Is you. You okay, boss?"

I glanced over at him. He was back to watching the road, impassive. Arkady had fought at Stalingrad. Arkady had returned fire at Wehrmacht troops from behind the stacked frozen bodies of his own dead. What registers as "not okay" if you're Arkady?

"Why did you ask if I'm okay?" I said. "Is something wrong?"

"You're drinking too much. Your tradecraft is for shit."

"You're saying I'm a drunk? Or a lousy spy?"

"You're a smart person. So then you don't check your angles, you show up forty seconds late, I wonder why. I'm left circling the block like chump just waiting to get made. If a CIA guy rumbles you, who do you think has to clean that up?"

"You haven't actually done that. Have you?"

"You're fucking up, Dick. Vice president and you're spinning out. What's the problem?"

I felt the walls of the car around me, and I felt like no one could hear me, and I thought, *What will happen to me if I tell the truth for once? Just say it out loud.* It came in a rush.

"I'm . . . I'm unhappy in my marriage. I can't talk to her about any of this. I come home and kiss her on the cheek, I tell her some story about working late. I look at her and she looks at me, and it's like we both know and we can't say. Jesus. I'm in hell."

Arkady turned the wheel, pulled us off the main drag.

"Where are we going?"

"Don't worry. Nobody going to know you here."

A few blocks north, shops and apartment buildings gave way to warehouses and faceless industrial brick. He seemed to know the territory and found us a bar, an unmarked storefront with the door standing open, dark wood inside. It might have looked the same a hundred years ago.

We drank out of bottles labeled in Cyrillic.

He considered me. "You fucking Tatiana?"

"No! No, I'm not fucking Tatiana. Jesus."

"Okay. So we don't got that to deal with. You gonna be okay."

"What am I going to do, man? I'm fucked. Sooner or later I'll get caught. Or, Jesus, one of you guys will get the order to rat me out. Photos go to the CIA and I go to jail."

"Why you always have to imagine the worst thing?"

"You killed, what, two agents domestically in the U.S. in 1950. Another one three months ago. You know how many agents we've lost over on your side?"

"I do. I know also what happens to them. It is not my fault your country's intelligence service sucks. We had the atomic bomb since 1946, guys didn't even figure that out until '49."

"Wait, you guys had the bomb in '46?"

"Our guys know how to keep their mouths shut. We test in . . ." He trailed off, mumbled in Russian. "In remote place. Very remote."

"How come we heard about it in '49?"

"Honest? What you guys picked up is not a test exactly. We had a little problem at one of the blacked-out research cities in Kazakhstan. *Naukograd,* archaeological division. A dig site. In Moscow we get code from them. Priority signal. Codes can mean different things, you see. In Moscow we got big chart, what all the codes mean; what we do in response depends on the site. One code means, maybe, 'We need supplies.' Or 'Medical help.' Some are good. 'We make discovery.' 'Hey, prototype works as planned, it is hovertanks for all comrades.'

"This code, not a good one. Chart says it is very bad. Chart says do not trust anyone emerging from this site. We shoot down helicopters coming out. We drop gas. After three days, no more come out, but sounds are heard. Chart says to be very afraid. We drop bomb."

"Did . . . Jesus, did it work?"

Arkady shrugged.

"We wait a couple years then send a guy. We do this four or five times since then. Russia is big place, you know? But you get me off track. I have thing to tell you. A problem. You remember the man named Gregor?"

"Of course."

"It is not exactly true that he is dead."

"But I shot him. You shot him."

"Even at the time I tell you I do not know for sure. What we did that night was to summon a great beast, a *chudovishche.* A thing of the steppes. A first-strike option, one of the early developments. Never tried, of course, never had the ingredients. It would have heavily compromised life in the northeastern United States, at least."

"My God."

"Yes, yes. All is well that ends well, yes? But what happened to Gregor is not understood. Cleanup team was well briefed but what they found there killed them dead for real. Gregor was not found."

"Why didn't you tell me?"

"Because I am not working for you—when the fuck do you learn this? Because you do not need to know. Because I tell you what I tell you. You know how long I work with Gregor? A lot longer than with you."

"Sorry."

"Okay."

"Where is he now?"

"He knows how to disappear, as we often must. Was in Prague, I think. Guatemala certainly. I hear things through the network, jobs that look funny. Hijacking here, sabotage there. Bodies are left behind in odd condition. Ones who survive, they also are not well."

"Are you going to—take care of him?"

"Gregor is our man. You worry about yours."

CHAPTER EIGHTEEN

MARCH 1954

IT'S EASY FOR a vice president to fill up the days, to fill up a year, given that there's no end to the minutiae, meetings the president would rather not take, positions that need defending that he'd rather not defend. In the cosmology of the Eisenhower administration, I was the lurking shadow to Eisenhower's Sun King, a darkly goblinish servitor dispatched to loom in senators' doorways and remind them where their votes were going to go. They knew I was willing to be nasty about it; that was the Nixon brand, after all, if anything was. I was sent to put down Joseph McCarthy for doing exactly what I'd done, just a little bit more stupidly and shabbily.

Stalin was gone, then his bloodthirsty henchman Beria. The Korean War came to a close. The CIA backed a successful coup in Iran to keep the Soviets out. A new man emerged in the Kremlin, the foul-mouthed, belligerent Ukrainian peasant named Khrushchev.

The longer it goes on, the more spying becomes a habit of mind. I made space for it in my day, gave my excuses to Pat without thinking. Mentally tracked schedules in the West Wing, looking for the little windows when I'd be alone and unobserved. Who was I spying for? Not the Soviets. For myself, for the lonely three-person cabal of Arkady, Tatiana, and me. For the sake of the mystery.

I don't know why I forced the issue that particular night. I had stayed late; word had come of a ruinous defeat for the French in Indochina at a place called Dien Bien Phu, and although we had supplied their effort, it hardly seemed of material interest that the French had lost another relic of the colonial era. But a strangely doom-laden aura hung over the event; there was an odd coda in the aftermath report—lights in the jungle and ugly silhouettes. In fact, we'd offered to nuke the site off the map, but the French had decorously declined.

Nonetheless, I felt a new urgency. Presidents and vice presidents looked down at me from the walls of the West Wing. This wasn't my house. Had any of them felt like this? Intruders in a strange, ancient structure? I padded along the plush carpet listening at each door. Senior staff. Chief of staff, situation room.

I thought of a dream I had had when I was eight after memorizing the whole long list of presidents for a school prize. In the dream there was a long dark hallway lined with marble statues that stretched on down the years, and these were statues of the presidents.

I walked along the hallway in my pajamas, passing under the gaze of each one. It started with Woodrow Wilson, president when I was born. I passed Taft, Roosevelt, and went across the century mark to William McKinley, rotund and scowling.

I looked down the line, seeing how each one was different. One seemed to laugh; others seemed deeply serious. But each one an infinitely noble, infinitely complex individual. An exalted lineage of the great.

I kept walking, feeling compelled. Harrison, Cleveland, Arthur. The statues were growing larger and less human, like crude pagan idols. Lincoln towered above me, a skeletal giant. The light dimmed, and past James Madison I could barely make out the statues' awful faces. Washington himself was hidden in darkness but I knew he was there and that if I saw his face it would drive me mad with fear. *I cannot tell a lie,* he seemed to say, still holding the fatal ax. And in the dream I prayed that he would please, please lie, for if he spoke, what terrifying truth might he reveal? I woke, gasping, in my attic room, to the news that Warren G. Harding had been elected.

Now I tried the door to the Oval Office. It was unlocked again, and it opened noiselessly. The Oval Office is thirty-five feet long, twenty-nine feet wide, the seat of power in the Western world. Low cabinetry and bric-a-brac along the walls, low couches and coffee tables. A landscape painting, a horse and rider. The president's desk is at the far end but most of the room is open space, dominated by the great seal, the eagle clutching arrows and olive branch. A room for discussion, state visions. What else? Stepping inside was like stepping onto a great stage. I heard a low hum almost below the threshold of perception, or perhaps I imagined that. Or maybe it was due to the fact that I was quite drunk.

The door swung shut behind me. My feet made no sound on the carpet. In the dark, I felt bodiless. I drifted through the space toward that massive desk, like a castle rampart. I would get Eisenhower. I would stare him down. Whatever he was doing, whatever he was, I would drag it into the light.

Tricky Dick it would be. I tried the desk drawers. Locked, each one. I felt for secret compartments, buttons. Nothing but smooth wood. I sat in the deep leather chair and leaned back. What was I looking for anyway?

I spun in the chair, looked out at the gardens, invisible by night. Dimly seen, my beetle-browed reflection looked back at me. The world outside was incalculably strange and huge. In Korea the sun had already risen over two armies, and there was nothing I could do about it. I hadn't been given a secret key to control the government, and there was no inner circle, unless it was the domelike skull of Eisenhower himself.

I spun again, the world revolving around me, feeling more relaxed than I had in months. I was in the White House! For whatever reason. In 1960 I'd run for president and win and then I'd rule over half the world. President Nixon. Why not? Hail Caesar, hail the great Trickus Dickus. Hail King Nick.

I spun yet again and flashed past a pale figure that loomed over me across the desk, skeletal and macrocephalic. I yelped and jammed my feet on the carpet as the figure resolved into Dwight Eisenhower in shirtsleeves.

"Hello, Dick. Back again, I see. In my office."

I had had, at that moment, enough of Dwight Eisenhower. I was a little too drunk to be terrified, and a little too terrified to care about what I was saying.

"Mr. President, what am I doing here?"

"Now, I would have gotten around to asking that myself in a moment. Looking for ghosts, perhaps?"

"Not what am I doing in your office. Why am I vice president? Why did you ask me to do this? Respectfully, sir. You came to my house. You drank tea with me. Then you gave me the second-highest office in the entire world. You could have picked anybody in America. Philanthropists. Millionaires. War heroes."

"You think I wanted a war hero? I wanted Kennedy flashing his grin all over the place? An all-American?"

"With respect, I'm as good a man as Kennedy."

"You're a climbing little rat. The way you went after Hiss, the way you got on TV and spilled your guts, the way you begged for it. You're bent, Dick. You were by a long way the sorriest son of a bitch I could get for the job."

I don't think I realized until that moment how much I admired Eisenhower. How much I valued his opinion of me, knowing that he was better than I was and that secretly he must despise me.

"Don't worry about it, Dick. I picked you for a good reason."

"What was it, then? If that's what you think of me."

"Dick, it's just you and me in here, isn't it? Just a couple of presidents. So I'm going to say a few things that stay between us. Executive branch only."

"Yes, sir."

"You figured it out. The nuclear policy makes sense only if we have something else up our sleeve, isn't that what you guessed? If you really were guessing, and I don't think you were."

"I'm not sure what you mean."

"There are things out there that will live through a nuclear hit and remain deployment-ready. There are things that even the Reds are afraid of. We're developing second-strike capability, and it isn't nuclear at all."

"I — I know, sir."

"What if, Nixon, there are rooms underneath the White House? Strange rooms? What if even Ulysses S. Grant, the Butcher himself, sealed them off for fear of the terrible things that were done there? Because he saw what was left of Lincoln by the time they killed him. What if there are worse things in the world than nuclear weapons?

"I could have had Kennedy for the asking. I picked you because I knew the next president would have to be a little shit of a human being. The things that were done in those rooms? I did them. I killed Stalin. I did a lot worse."

I was backing away by this time. "Sir? What does that mean?"

"You're a liar, Dick, and I'm morally certain you're also something worse. You want me to take a guess? I think Hiss went down a little easier than he should have. I think you got help."

It's often been said that I don't have a gift for ingenuous speech. There is no gesture, no words that are not filtered through a moment's calculation. And maybe there was never a time when I didn't feel like I was maintaining an elaborate false identity, that I was born into a deep-cover operation. To become a Russian intelligence asset was only to confirm what I always knew. At least I could put a name to the unspeakable secret inside myself. But Eisenhower had spoken it.

"No," I whispered. "That never happened." I wasn't brave. I would do anything to keep the truth from getting out. I drew the revolver from my pocket and pointed it at him.

"Oh my. Oh my," Dwight said. He looked intense, impatient. "What happens now?"

"It's not true," I said. His look was cold as he leaned forward over the desk, the calculating stare of a man who'd gotten the drop on the entire Wehrmacht.

"What's your plan? Are you going to shoot the president?" he said.

I realized in a sudden panic that I couldn't see his hands; he'd gotten them under the desk. He could have a gun there, or anything.

"Keep still," I said. He couldn't rush me from where he was.

"You're a finger twitch from the presidency. Don't you want it? How badly?"

I never found out. His right hand whipped up in a curious gesture, fingers half closed. I told myself to fire but there was a thunderclap, and my right hand felt as numb as if it had been amputated, and the gun thudded onto the carpet. How had he touched me? Had I hit him? I didn't even know if I'd managed to fire. My right arm hung limp. He spread his arms to show me a clean shirtfront, no hole, no spreading stain. He looked a little surprised himself.

"Well, this was hardly presidential," he said after a moment. "Damned awkward, actually." I started to apologize but he cut me off.

"I'll give you this one, Dick. Maybe every vice president should get one free shot at the big chair. Good for morale."

"You authorized funding for Blue Ox," I said. "We both know it. You lied to me."

"Yes, I did. I did a lot more than that. And if you were at Pawtuxet Farm, you didn't get there on your own. Now, how much of this do you want to talk about?"

"All of it, sir." I said it quickly, for the first time that evening not having to think about the answer. "You have to tell me what's going on. I'm the vice president. I have a right."

"Yes," he said, "I suppose you do. A long time ago Bill Taft trusted me, and one of these days I'll have to trust somebody or it will all be for nothing."

"What will be for nothing? Sir?"

He shook his head, for once looking every one of his sixty-four years.

"All of it. Lincoln, Taft, what they did. The H-bomb, the RAND Corporation, the king of Persia, the whole long con of it all. Go to bed, Nick. When it's your turn I'll make sure you have what you need."

"You take care, sir," I said, which was, I think, the only time I ever made him laugh.

After that I didn't sneak into his office again although I couldn't help but see that he was working on something. I'd pass his office and see huge blueprints spread out on the desk; they were always carefully locked away when he wasn't using them. I'd hear him talking to another man at night, wrangling over longitude and latitude. And I knew that whatever he was doing absorbed a massive appropriation from the Department of Defense's black budget.

I'd seen it only once, only for an instant. He'd stood in the center of the oval room late at night, the curtains pulled back, and for a moment I saw what he did: the landscape outside was full of incandescent lines that ran north and south and east and west, out past the horizon. At this scale it was impossible to tell for sure, but the lines seemed to curve just slightly, as if we were seeing the tiniest portion of an unthinkably big, utterly invisible design.

CHAPTER NINETEEN

AUGUST 1956

THE STATE DINING Room buzzed with suppressed aggression and shone with the best silver and the most attractive members of the waitstaff. We were hosting a Soviet delegation and wanted to foster goodwill and demonstrate courtesy in the most viciously showboating manner our economy could support. It made for a glittering evening, one of the finest of the Cold War, the peak of its frigid glamour.

The Soviets filed in two by two with an extra swagger in their step. The Warsaw Pact had been signed the previous year, formally aligning the Eastern Bloc against us. They'd scored one victory after another, brutal interventions in Poland and Hungary and Syria. Guy Burgess and Donald Maclean had lately turned up in Moscow, confirming the suspicion that Soviet intelligence had well and truly eaten their British counterparts for lunch. And Khrushchev was finding his feet on the international stage with a theatrical flair. "History is on our side," he'd just told us. "We will bury you."

We, of course, had come to play. We'd held on to Iran and the trump card of nuclear superiority. We had developed a defensive nuclear missile to knock out incoming bombers and had ICBMs with a truly impressive kill radius if you didn't think too hard about the fact that you were setting off nuclear explosions in your own atmosphere. Our bomber teams were drilling like

Olympic athletes at midair refueling, staggered taxi and takeoff formations, anything to sweat a few more seconds off our response time. Our nuclear submarine was up and running. We had, moreover, built Disneyland.

Cocktails were served in the Red Room and I lingered there. Pat was in good form, chatting up the crowd of visitors, the men puffy and frighteningly pale and nervously drunk, the women bitter and imperious. They were all survivors. There was a charge in the air, though. They'd been let out for recess. It felt like they wanted to get into trouble.

Eisenhower worked the opposite side of the room. Since the night I'd tried to shoot him, he'd accorded me a little more status, unless I was imagining it; maybe it was just a more respectful form of neglect.

It was a tradition that everyone got a handshake with President Eisenhower, and that let me slip into the dining room to get an advance look at the vice presidential table, the losers' bracket of the status-conscious delegation. Tonight it was a Sergei Ivanov to my right and an Irena Ivanov to my left. I consulted my note cards—the two were embassy figures rotated in to advance American understanding of traditional Russian culture and to monitor and maintain ideological correctness among the permanent staff.

I slipped back into the smoky crimson of the Red Room, and I had joined Pat when I was accosted by a half-familiar voice speaking in the smooth, only slightly exotic accent of the Russian diplomatic corps.

"Mr. Vice President? It is a signal honor to meet you. I am Sergei Ivanov." I turned to look into the middle depths of an extremely large, exquisitely made tuxedo shirt. Arkady had still managed to rumple it somehow.

"This must be your lovely wife," the old monster said. He

kissed Pat's hand in a deadpan caricature of European manners. "And this is my niece Irena, gracing our embassy as a cultural ambassador." It was Tatiana, in low-cut black. I said nothing. Worlds were colliding and only I could hear the thunder.

"Very pleased," she said in a Muscovite warble, as if she'd painstakingly memorized the phrase. Her color was unnaturally high and she looked a wide-eyed twenty-five. She curtsied unsteadily in her own pitch-perfect interpretation of a stock embassy character, a newcomer out of her linguistic depth, drinking much too fast to kill the nervousness. She was, I hoped, only pretending to be drunk.

Pat and Tatiana shook hands and smiled, showing teeth. I shook hands with Tatiana myself. She smelled of her Russian cigarettes, the ones I had come home smelling of too many times.

"A pleasure to meet you," Pat said. "We'll see you inside."

I took her arm and walked her into the dining room for our ritual entrance. She was escorted on the opposite side by a slightly aggressive-looking cadet.

"Dick, do you know those people?" she asked me.

"I might have met them at one of these functions. He certainly seemed to know me."

"The daughter is very pretty," she said.

"Niece," I said. "It's on the note cards. She'll be a bore but we'll manage."

Pat was seated across from me, Tatiana and Arkady to my left and right, respectively. Eisenhower stood and gave a short speech, barely audible to us over the distance to the head table. A string quartet went into its act, and the salad was served.

"What part of the Soviet Union do you come from, Irena?" Pat said.

Tatiana mumbled something too fast for me to catch.

"Famous for its grain production levels," I said too loudly. "You must be proud."

"Not since locusts. Twenty years," she answered, making a mournful pout. "We know great suffering." Arkady choked a little.

"Tell me, Miss Irena," Pat said, "what does a cultural ambassador do?"

"I come of an ancient people," Tatiana began, and she launched into an extended set speech about traditional dances. She kept up a kabuki flirtation with me, touching her hair, glancing at me and shyly looking away, her hand brushing against mine. I edged as far away as I could, almost into the folds of Arkady's massive tuxedo jacket.

Pat watched and listened. Maybe she smelled the cigarettes; maybe she just saw I was in a situation I wasn't happy about. She'd sensed—I knew it—that a door to a secret world had cracked open, and she was hungrily sniffing the air. I wanted, very badly, to tell her we were sitting with my best friends. That I'd known them for eight years, that we were investigating a vast occult conspiracy.

After an hour of terrifying brinksmanship, Tatiana looked at my wife. "Mrs. Nixon, I feel a little unwell. Would you escort me to the—how do you say it?"

"Of course, dear," Pat said. They left, Tatiana leaning heavily on Pat's arm. Tatiana looked tiny next to my wife.

"So this is famous White House," Arkady said, grinning like a loon. His accent returned the moment they had gone. "Is nice. A little bourgeois, maybe. Your wife is nice lady, no?"

"You asshole! Why the fuck are you trying to ruin my life?"

"Relax," he said. "No one is ruin anything. Tatiana is bored, that is all. Relax and have fun."

"And why didn't you tell me you speak perfect English? Why

the fuck do you talk like this all the time?" I said. "You sound like fucking Boris and Natasha."

"Is easier I talk this way."

Pat returned and sat heavily in her chair, Tatiana following. I could tell something was wrong. In a few short minutes the KGB agent had managed to get my wife drunker than I'd ever seen her.

We all stayed at the table for a while after that. The candles burned lower and most of the guests cleared out to the Green Room. We were nearly alone.

"But Mr. Ivanov," Pat was saying to Arkady, "do you really believe in all of it? In dialectical materialism and the workers' paradise? Do you truly?"

"What do I believe?" he said. In the last half hour he'd slipped back into his regular pidgin English, but Pat didn't seem to notice. "I tell you story. In 1917 I am Cheka, you understand? Bolshevik police. I am eighteen-year-old dumb fucking asshole who thought it would be cool to carry a gun."

Pat nodded, rapt. This was the world she was normally kept from. Tatiana watched as well, and I wondered if she knew where this was going.

"So one night—we got the czar now, yes? We are doing so great, good for us. We got him in this house outside Yekaterinburg. But White Guard on its way—czar's people, yes?—and they got Cossacks. Nobody sure what's to happen.

"We stand around in the snow in the dark and one guy starts joking they are going to do it tonight. Kill them all. Asshole, but I think he is right maybe. Two in the morning, a dozen guys go into the house, Yurovsky in command. Watchmaker, he used to be.

"I hear all kinds of yelling inside, the whole family woken up. Goes on for an hour and they move to basement. We hear how they are cranky, is no place to sit and so on. No doubt now what is to come, so we all listen at the basement window waiting for it. Yurovsky reads an official statement. I think it cannot be real because somebody would stop it or maybe the world would turn inside out. *'Chto,'* says the czar. Man who fixes watches is now shooting him? He does not believe it either.

"I hear each man had assignment to shoot a person but instead they go all at once. Five minutes of shooting, then it stops, then starts again. How many times they shoot these people?"

I looked around. The room was empty except for the four of us. I wondered why Arkady had chosen tonight to show his face and then tell this, to spill his guts. Pat would remember them forever now.

"Afterwards nothing is conducted well. Bodies brought out but no one thought of stretchers. Put in blankets. We drive them a few miles but the truck gets stuck in trees so we find carts. Other people are with us now and I don't know who they are. Some are taking things from the bodies.

"The sun is coming up and one guy says a child escaped the basement during the shooting, other man says bullshit, no one knows for sure. White Guard is near, hunting us, so we throw bodies in a mine but then orders say take them out of the mine, so we do and drive on. It's noon almost. We stop, dig a pit, throw bodies in again, and that is how the empire ends. Sun comes up the next day, whole country is a new thing."

"You're a monarchist?" Pat said. You might have thought she was meeting a prince in a story. "I thought they shot people for talking like that."

"Do not worry for me, Mrs. Vice President, I am real Commie. Forty years I am secret police. Cheka, OGPU, NKVD. Nth Directorate, yes?" Tatiana stood up, evidently ready to physically restrain him, but he glared her down.

"I clean up weird shit, Mrs. Nixon. I see collective farms a hundred miles out in the steppes go bad, and no one knows why. Farms burned and tracks lead into the snow. Farms where they speak with only one voice, or where they look like they turned to birds. I see dead men walking in the frost. I see the salt mine they dig too far, and the things that fly out. I see the kids at Dyatlov Pass and what happened to them. Irena and me and Gregor, we see a hundred fucked-up things we swear not to tell."

"Yes, Sergei, you swore," Tatiana said. "And why do you tell it now?" Tatiana and I exchanged glances. If Arkady was spilling his own secrets, was he going to spill ours while he was at it?

"I make point, dearest niece. I think there was something in the Romanovs to keep this from happening. Because that night when we threw them into the mine, they tell us to pull them out again. Why? I go back in. Mine is filled partly with water but I have seen the last czar die and I am feeling nothing. There was a person there in the mine. Not one of us, see? Big eyes, round, wide apart, watching us, just a little man living in the mine where no one should be. He sees how we have murdered these emperors and empresses, old men and children. He knows we have done this."

"You can't blame yourself, Arkady—Sergei, excuse me," I said. "You weren't going to stop what was happening."

"I know," he said. "And you know, Nicholas Romanov was good-for-nothing, real son of a bitch. But what I wish for, what I wait for, maybe, is the true czar. A true king, yes? Who will show me that? We must drink, yes?"

"Is time we go," Tatiana said, all but lifting him out of the chair as he emptied the last of the vodka into the remaining glassware on the table.

"Last toast!" He raised his glass, and his voice echoed through the darkened White House. "To the old gods and the lady vice president and let me think of the words—do not worry, it is British toast, no Commies. Yes, I think of it. 'That we may work in righteousness and lay the foundation of making the Earth a Common Treasury for All, both Rich and Poor.' Anything else makes you an asshole. *Za vas!*"

CHAPTER TWENTY

NOVEMBER 1957

TOWARD THE END of 1957 the Cold War had begun changing again, a new war even less intelligible than the previous ones had been. A space war.

Notionally, we had the lead. We had U-2 spy planes flying seventy thousand feet up, in theory too high to show up on radar. From there we could count their missile-production facilities, their Bison-class long-range bombers, anything we could recognize in a blurry photograph.

There were drawbacks, in that violating Soviet airspace was an act of war. And the crews flying certain routes suffered a mysteriously high attrition rate. Psychiatric, at first. Multiple incidents where pilots destroyed their own photographic records before landing. Written reports produced less and less actionable intelligence and instead described unexpected mountain ranges, disturbing geometries, and giant forms or lapsed into single words and phrases, such as *writhe* and *oh God, the dance*. It got worse as time went on. Here and there, planes would land and we would open them to find only bones inside, as dusty as if a thousand years had passed inside the cockpit.

In August of that year the Soviets had tested a long-range ballistic missile that could strike a target six thousand miles away. Europe, Khrushchev asserted, could become a "veritable cemetery" if he wished it.

As if that weren't enough, in October the Russians had put themselves even further ahead. Nine hundred kilometers above us, they announced, invisible yet radiant, Sputnik spun and shimmered and made its soundless bleat every half a second or so. A month later, its sequel would bear the corpse of a dog over our heads, like the terrifying banner of a barbarian nation.

One night, I found Eisenhower waiting in my office, listening to the beeps on the radio, the keening little moon. He'd been drinking, but mostly he looked tired.

"Dick," he said, "I know you have questions."

"I'm going to be president in two years. I think it's time you told me what you're planning. And what happened that night when I shot at you?" I asked. "Why didn't it work? And what are you?"

"Well," he said, "to take the last question first, I'm the president of the United States. I swore an oath to uphold the Constitution. You could say I'm a party to a very old contract with some very odd terms. When you swear the oath, it . . . takes you a certain way. Taft could have explained it better, he was the technician."

"Presidents aren't bulletproof. McKinley was shot. Lincoln was shot."

"It works differently for everyone, no one knows why. Lincoln swore the oath and it didn't seem to do anything. Chester A. Arthur's laugh could break the bones in a man's hand. FDR's gifts killed him and he never knew why. As far as I'm aware, I am the most powerful chief executive of the past hundred and fifty years."

"What about, you know, George Washington? Was he . . . powerful?"

He nodded. "There are no first-person accounts of Washington operating at full strength. I don't think it was a survivable

167

event. Perhaps in the British military archives, but we've been denied access. If I'm being honest, we're not clear on whether he's entirely dead.

"We're ignorant, Dick. We live on the tiny fringes of a habitable moment. There are great beasts, Nixon. There are ones under the earth who watch us; there are things in the deep oceans we can't even get a look at. There are things that wait in the future and lurk in the deep past, Dick. We just don't know."

"What are you planning? I saw it once for a moment, but it was too big."

"My legacy, Dick. A strategic architecture for the twentieth century. When you come into your own, you'll see it for what it is."

"But when will I? Why did you make me vice president if you don't want to tell me anything?"

"If you must know, I didn't want to," he said. "I did it because Calvin Coolidge told me to."

"Coolidge?"

"Coolidge, who learned from William Howard Taft, who was the smartest person, I believe, ever to hold the office. The line broke, you understand? Whatever the founders knew, we lost it when the Union broke, or maybe before. No one would know anything if it weren't for Taft. He passed it on to Coolidge, who passed it on to me."

"What about Truman?"

"He didn't know anything. Not every president teaches his vice. Maybe FDR didn't think Truman could be trusted. And Dick, that raises the question I'm trying to figure out. Because I have the same problem FDR did, but worse. You could be the greatest since Washington, is what they told me. The greatest or the worst."

CHAPTER TWENTY-ONE

NOVEMBER 1957

THE SUPERNATURAL STRATEGIC initiative of the Eisenhower administration ended on November 25, 1957, with what was described publicly as a minor stroke that left Eisenhower weakened but still very much in command.

The night before there was another state dinner, again for the Russian delegation, but one with a very different atmosphere. The Russians laughed too loud and drank vodka they'd brought themselves and acted as rudely as they dared under our roof. It was their turn to gloat.

At cocktails I was startled but not quite surprised to see two familiar guests. I hadn't seen Tatiana or Arkady since the reception in August of 1956. Arkady was plainly a risk factor at this point. When they asked for meetings, I told them to wait or ignored the requests altogether. I was never sure what Eisenhower might or might not know about me. And then, it was possible that I didn't need them anymore. I enjoyed having secrets, and maybe—to put the worst face on it—I'd been offered better secrets with a better deal. Why be the secret traitor when you could secretly be the future greatest president of all time? For the most part, I'd stopped thinking of them.

But there they were. Arkady had maybe slumped a little further into his big man's slouch, and a little more of his hair had been swept off. He was nearly sixty. Tatiana remained in an eerie stasis, raven-black hair and blue-veined skin, only a little more gaunt and pale. She was reprising her fake-drunk routine with a couple of married senators.

There was a tap on my shoulder.

"Mr. Vice President? Can I speak to you a moment?" It was Howard Hunt of the CIA. He had aged noticeably, the lines in his long face deepening. I had had word of him over the years, a sort of roving meddler for American intelligence—a fixed election in Guatemala, then covert duty in Japan and Uruguay. Occasionally the reports would come in with darker messages written in Hunt's feverish prose. An urgent, unexplained request to have defoliant chemicals shipped to Uruguay. A plea for us to ask the Vatican for an assist after a hushed-up incident in the Nagasaki suburbs. He had a way of finding unusual trouble spots, or else he was drawn to them.

"Howard. How are you?"

He walked me into the hallway, away from the guests. He seemed a little breathless. "Listen. This is a sensitive matter, but I can trust you, can't I?" In his formal wear he looked more than ever like the functionary of some grim church.

"Of course." I hesitated. I'd forgotten how much he knew about the Hiss affair.

"Sir, there's intelligence—reliable, in my estimation—that there is a security issue on the grounds. The case has been building but I now believe there's a hostile asset that's been operating undercover on a long-term basis inside the White House itself."

"In the White House?" I repeated, stupidly. Was he watching my face for a reaction?

"There have been rumors for years in the service, a case on the back burner. Data that correlates a little too well. Too many things going wrong. There's every indication of a breach at the top."

"Who?" I managed to say.

"I have only guesses. But the handlers must be here; it's almost the whole Russian delegation. We've been tracking a huge spike in coded message traffic. There's an operation tonight, I'm sure of it."

Wait, was it a trick? Was this how they got you? I tried to catch Arkady's eye, then stopped myself. "When I think about what those dirty Russians could be getting up to in our nation's capital, it makes me sick," I said with all the vehemence I could muster.

He looked distraught, and I wished I could help him. The worst part about having a secret isn't the secret as such, it's making the puppet version of yourself, acting the way you think a person who doesn't know the thing you know would act while at the same time you hold the white-hot coal in your mouth, gingerly, desperate not to burn yourself, unwilling to let the truth out yet desperate to let it out.

"We'll get the bastard. I'll give this my personal attention, Howard. Anything you need. I won't let you down."

"Thank you, sir."

I returned to the party and looked around at the crowd of guests, State Department officials, cabinet ministers . . . were there other moles? How many?

Tatiana brushed against me, stumbled, and excused herself.

"Let me get that for you," she slurred. She reached out to fix my lapel, then jammed her hand into the pocket of my jacket. The handoff was so clumsy, I realized all at once that she actually *was* drunk. Smashed. She lolloped back to her seat, leaving me to slip into the bathroom and pull out the scrawled note. *Blue Room. One hour. Old business.* I tore it up and flushed it away as they called us for dinner.

At the table, the Russians talked about the future as they ate, about going to the moon and beyond. Arkady's laugh boomed. He told stories of the Russian front to his embassy cronies, ignoring his hosts. Two places away, Tatiana smiled up at me from the ruins of her lobster thermidor, although given how much she smoked, I didn't know how she could taste it. Mine tasted like ashes, the little of it I could get down.

"Are you all right, Dick?" Pat said. I realized I hadn't spoken for ten minutes. The table around me, the vice president's table, had gone dead.

"Just not feeling well. I'll be right back."

"Okay." She looked at me, concerned.

I went into the marble entrance hall and then wandered through the multicolored rooms, like chambers in a palace in the Land of Oz. It wasn't so often that I got to walk alone through the White House. I wondered if this would be my last night in office. If they really were on my trail, I was about to become the center of the worst scandal in presidential history. It didn't seem real. It couldn't be. I hadn't even spoken to the Russians in a year, and we'd been careful. Hadn't we?

I walked into the Blue Room to find Tatiana waiting, backlit. The room was another of the White House's stylistic follies, done in monumental Egyptian fashion, all gold and lapis lazuli, a hushed temple to unnamed gods. Two obsidian caryatids held a pair of candelabra aloft, their candles smoking. I looked around for Arkady but we were alone.

"Hi, Richard. It's been a long time for us," she said.

"It's been a difficult year, Tatiana," I said. "I'm busy. How are things?"

"I have bad news."

"I know," I said. "They know there's a mole inside the executive branch. This man Hunt is going to find me."

"That's not possible," she said. "Not unless you . . ."

"I didn't tell anyone! Not even Pat. I thought this was you. Revenge because I wasn't in contact."

"It's not me. It could have been, but it's not. I didn't." She put a hand on my chest and kept it there. It was unpleasantly like a scene I'd desperately wanted for a long time. What was the point of being a spy if I couldn't be James Bond?

"Listen," she said. "I have to tell you—"

"Dick? Are you all right?"

Tatiana was gone even before Pat stopped speaking. Some spy trick Arkady had never covered in our drunken nights out.

"I'm in here."

"I thought I heard you talking to someone," Pat said, coming in.

"The embassy woman. She's drunk," I told her. "She's gone now. Come on, we'll go back."

There are times when it's great to be a spy. When you're carrying around a secret, a part of you no one can reach, your own secret room. You could be a husband or a father but unbeknownst to anyone you're also fighting a large, important war. You know you're bigger than all of the people around you. There's nothing anyone can do to you that you can't burn away along with your latest passport.

And don't get me wrong, you were an absolute genius to create that room. But then there are nights like this, when it feels like that safe secret room you created for yourself is filling up with an invisible toxic gas. And you're banging on the window trying to get somebody's attention because you just now remembered you forgot to tell anyone about your hiding place. And maybe no one else knows about the idea of having rooms, maybe you were the only one ever to think of that. Too late now.

*   *   *

We'd reached the ballroom phase of the evening. Eisenhower had turned in, then Pat, leaving me to play host for as long as it took. I drifted with the crowd of happy Communists who sang songs at the exquisitely tuned piano and drank while I waited for what was coming. Around four in the morning, it came.

"Sir? Could I borrow you for a moment?" Hunt tugged my sleeve. I followed him down the service stairs.

"I saw two handlers slip away. The older Russian man and the drunk woman. I think they must have been making a drop. Let's check the library first."

It wasn't much of a library; gift books that had wound up here over the years, antique first editions. Eisenhower wasn't a reader. We began gently ransacking the small room, feeling under couch cushions, running fingers along the undersides of coffee tables.

How long would it take Hunt to figure this out? Minutes? Years? The odd thing was that I liked him. I remembered a conversation I'd had with Arkady on one of our bar crawls.

"Have you ever killed a friend, Arkady?" I'd asked.

"Do I kill a friend?" he'd said. "No. Or . . . I do not think of us as friends, but he did. Gave him ride to airport once, he got the wrong impression."

"Was it . . . worse, I guess? Than killing a stranger?"

Arkady reflected. "He was not a bad guy, he was a double agent, but it happens sometimes. No real choice but to . . ." He made a motion with his hands that I think must have been tightening a garrote, then shrugged. "But maybe better that I did it than someone else. Why ask me? Wait, did you kill a friend? You planning to?"

"Maybe," I'd said, and I shook my head.

"Tell you what," he'd said. "You need to, I help you, understand? I help you do this thing. It happens quick, happens clean, we go have a fucking drink. All over. Who's this friend?"

In the library, I wondered if Arkady was close by. I circled left, trying to face away from Hunt so he wouldn't see my hands shake. *It's all too obvious,* I thought. I wondered what he'd say if he knew I was the man he was looking for. Would he shoot me? Arrest me? Start crying? I couldn't begin to imagine.

"Got them! Dick! Come here!" I heard Howard call from the sitting room next door. Inside, he was holding a pistol on Arkady and Tatiana as they sat on a rather ugly Victorian couch.

"Look at this," he said. "Sneaking around."

"What's going on?" I asked.

"I am Sergei. We have met before," Arkady said. "My niece was not feeling well."

"Howard, this is Sergei and . . ."

"Irena," Tatiana said. "Is an honor to meet you. There are things I must explain."

"You're not allowed in this room," he told her. To me he said, "This old guy's been the DC station chief for years."

"I make complaint," Arkady said. "Mr. Vice President, I am guest in this house."

"Quiet," Tatiana said to him. "Mr. Hunt, I would like you to look in that room over there. I think you will find a more pressing problem." There was a doorway leading to a bathroom. Hunt shuffled over and looked inside, then stepped in.

"Oh my good Lord," we heard him say. He backed out, his shoes tracking something dark onto the floor, mumbling, "It must have come out of him. It must have come out of him."

"Did you find any spies, Mr. Hunt?" Tatiana said. She looked as though she'd tasted something bad. I stared past Hunt at what lay on the floor, a body, maybe of a Secret Service agent. Most of what was identifiable was his suit. Something was scattered around it. Black feathers. There was a strange burned smell, like scorched caramel.

"You are experienced man, Mr. Hunt," Arkady said. "You can see that is not our work."

"What was it?" he asked. "I saw this before——"

"In Uruguay, yes. There is serious problem here, yes?"

Hunt nodded, ashen.

"Then perhaps we work together for now. I believe your president is in danger," Arkady said.

The lights were on in the Oval Office. Hunt and Tatiana and Arkady went in first. Standing in a corridor that was inexplicably coated with dirt and leaves, I heard the rising tones of an argument.

"Mr. President," I heard Hunt say.

I walked into the room. Predawn November light was just starting to creep in through the trees and across the lawn, silhouetting Eisenhower, who stood with his back to the windows, the dome of his broad forehead faintly illuminated, the rest of his face in shadow.

"You shouldn't be here," Eisenhower said.

I thought he was speaking to me until I saw the little man. Eisenhower stared down at him, and he looked almost doll-like in that presence, but it was still Gregor.

"How did you do it, thing?" Eisenhower said. "How did you pass the borders?"

"You're making a mistake, Mr. President. I'm much more than you think I am," Gregor said. He ignored the others in the room, his hands in his pockets, his eyes locked on the chief executive, who stared back.

"You can stand down, Mr. President," Hunt called. He cocked his gun. "We're here now. You should go to safety."

"That's right, we're here," I said. I drew the pistol from my jacket pocket, the tiny one Arkady had given me years ago, and pointed it at the man I'd met nine years before in New York.

"Don't move, please, any of you," Eisenhower said. "Our guest here is clearly more than he seems. He poses a certain amount of danger. But he is in violation of a treaty, and he should remember that. He can be destroyed here." Nonsensically, I remembered a line from the Constitution about presidential authority: "He shall have Power, by and with the Advice and Consent of the Senate, to make Treaties."

"Would you care to test that theory?" the little man said. He took his hands from his pockets. "I've come a long way to try."

Eisenhower looked at me. "Dick, it's a bit late to begin your training, but I want you to watch what happens. This is going to be a field test of American strategic capabilities. We'll see what the oath can really do."

"The results won't be what you expect," Gregor said. "You've got a wolf in the fold, Mr. President. I should know; I'm carrying his blood. Didn't your vice ever tell you?"

"What? Dick, what does he——" Eisenhower began, but before he could finish the question, I pulled the trigger and shot Gregor. There was a brittle pop, and his body twitched. I shot him three more times as Arkady sprang forward, hefting a bust of James Madison in one hand; Tatiana had drawn from somewhere an engraved silver dagger. Suddenly Gregor inhaled, and then shrieked. The sound was shrill and yet thunderous, impossibly loud, not at all human, like the braking of a massive industrial steam engine. We staggered back as the sound came to an end. Hunt was on the floor. And then Eisenhower held up a hand.

"There's a lot of strange things out in the steppes, I'll grant you," Eisenhower said into the silence. He talked like a Kansas schoolteacher, but somehow the room was held. Gregor didn't move. "And after 1917 they started coming back, didn't they? There's the Great Worm in Tunguska, and what's at Arkhangel'sk, and the pine men, and that which you tried to put down with the bomb in '49."

There was, oddly, a cold wind blowing, a lot colder than a Washington November. I smelled, of all things, snow. Snow was weeks away. And the windows were closed. The Oval Office doesn't have any corners, but somehow darkness began creeping in. Eisenhower coughed and spat something onto his desk that bounced away. A pin.

"The men and women who founded this country were very odd indeed. You remember them as naive idealists in funny hats, but they were hard people. They believed in the devil and they believed in spirits and there were things they found here that made a lot of sense to them. Those first years, a lot of them died but a few didn't."

The wind picked up and it got darker. I heard creaking pines and there was a scratching at the window.

"Why is it so cold?" Hunt muttered.

Eisenhower, I saw, was shaking. He gave a wet cough and spat out another pin. His face was a pale mask, brows and black eyes. His crooked ears looked not comical but alien, or as if he'd been taken apart and put together slightly wrong.

"Devils in the forest. You could have another name for it. The Black Stranger. The people who started this country made a deal, and they drove a very hard bargain."

In the dark it wasn't Eisenhower's face at all now. It must have been a trick of shadows that made it seem like the walls weren't there, that it was just forest. And I saw a face looking at me through the trees, bobbing slightly, as if it belonged to someone walking toward me from an impossible distance beyond the walls.

"Do you know where you're standing, Ambassador?" I heard Eisenhower say. "This room burned in 1928. There are rooms in that wing that are still burning."

The being in the darkness began to run and for a moment I was alone in a primeval forest in the night. I knew in my bones that there wasn't a building or a human face for a thousand miles. A heavy footstep crunched in the snow behind me and I screamed as the panic became unbearable.

Abruptly it was bright again, morning now, and I was back in the Oval Office. There was no trace of the stranger, but Eisenhower was sprawled forward on his desk. I ran to him. He looked at me, then at Hunt. He mumbled a few distorted words that I'm pretty sure were "Get that son of a bitch Nixon out of my office."

The next twenty hours or so may have been my first term as president; I've never been quite sure. Eisenhower was unconscious but not officially incapacitated and no one bothered to sign anything to the effect that I was in charge.

"There is some impairment in speech and motor control but I believe he'll recover. Were you there when it happened? Was there a particular stress involved?"

"N . . . no. Not at all. I was working in another room."

Eisenhower still knew me, more or less. He evinced a complete grasp of domestic policy and international relations. He seemed to have lost only that knowledge of which he was sole possessor, the key to America's grand strategy of supernatural geopolitics, along with any awareness that there was such a thing.

The old discipline of American magic died with Eisenhower's stroke. Knowledge saved and passed on for two hundred years had disappeared in an instant. I could only guess at what had been lost. Ritual initiation. Modes of attack and defense. Eisenhower claimed to have killed Stalin—how? And there must have been a history, a secret chronicle of the greatest empire the world has ever known.

Taft had pieced it together once, Eisenhower had said. But from what? I went back to the meager White House library, but it was useless. The knowledge was gone.

CHAPTER TWENTY-TWO

SEPTEMBER 1960

"MR. KENNEDY, I apologize for intruding, I know it's against protocol. I wish to explain to you why I must be allowed to win this election.

"I believe—I am quite certain—that we are engaged in a shadow war against the Soviet Union, on a level beyond what the public has knowledge of. I believe the Soviets have weaponized monstrous entities from the Precambrian era and occult forces beyond the comprehension of our present-day science that may soon eclipse the striking power of our conventional and nuclear capabilities, if they have not already done so. These have already been deployed in the European and Southeast Asian theaters, to terrifying effect.

"Furthermore, it is—excuse me, I'd like to finish. Furthermore, I believe that our own nation is also—thank you for your continued attention—engaged in its own occult arms race, which may or may not be firmly under our control. I'm the only man capable of—excuse me, sir—of comprehending . . . of . . . there is nothing funny about this. Nothing funny at all. If you'd seen the things I have, you'd understand that the walls of our everyday reality are perilously—perilously—

"Very well. Very well, if that's your response, I will see you in the television studio for our scheduled debate. And may the best man win. I assure you, it will not be you."

Kennedy didn't know anything, and what this told me is that he could not be allowed to be president. But what did Jack Kennedy have? He'd been to Harvard and he was freakishly handsome. He had coasted on his family's money into a lazy career in the Senate while I strove and scrapped for power. He was exactly the man I'd been training to beat in my fifteen years in politics. I was going to take him apart, like I'd taken apart Jerry Voorhis and Alger Hiss.

Two years ago I was the heir apparent. I'd played it almost perfectly. I spent eight years in the White House as vice president during what was little short of a golden age. Eisenhower's plan wasn't finished, but he had done so much. The interstate highway system stretched across the nation, projecting a new utopia of motion, dynamism, thrilling euphoria. It was as if Americans finally understood what the twentieth century was for, and we, Dwight D. Eisenhower and Dick Nixon, had built it for them, together.

And we had also built a heroic drama. An encroaching shadow. The previous year I'd gone to Moscow to face down its evil vizier, Khrushchev. We'd debated the merits of our respective worldviews in front of the camera. Never mind what the cameras didn't seem to pick up—the hissing, buzzing sound that intruded whenever Khrushchev spoke. The insistent voice in my mind that told me to run, that panicked me, the entire time I stood inside the monumental architecture of their great city; the sense I had that something inside the Kremlin was deeply wrong. I'd smiled for the cameras and pretended a gentlemanly rivalry.

Yes, Eisenhower had turned on me. Our late-night talks were forgotten. He barely knew me; I was only the populist shit-stain and political hatchet man that he'd recruited in order to win the

1952 election and then sidelined. I was a necessary evil, and the fact that I did the nasty jobs he assigned only confirmed his impression of what I was good at.

They said I had the flu the night of the debate. I remember very little of my state of mind that evening. Just images.

I remember shaking hands with Howard Smith, the moderator. Then the studio man called out, "Thirty seconds to air," and I hurried to my lectern.

I had a momentary, confused impression that a bird, or maybe several, had gotten into the studio. The sound of wing beats kept coming back, but my eye could never quite follow where it was. It was almost impossible not to look.

"Twenty seconds."

Handsome Kennedy smiled at me with his irresistible grin and even in that moment I felt drawn to him, felt a little gleeful that it was just me and him up there—everyone's seeing me up here with Jack! Although the grin was also slightly knowing, like maybe he understood something about these goddamn birds that I didn't. Like once again there was a sucker in the room and it wasn't Howard Smith and it certainly wasn't Jack Kennedy.

"Ten."

A last-minute glance at Pat, waiting backstage along with my campaign staff, wearing a look of well-intentioned, sympathetic, supportive concern that a loved one puts on to convey the earnest belief that you're about to humiliate yourself in public.

The hell with that. Yes, Jack wanted the title, badly. He wanted me thrown out. But he'd never competed at this level and he knew it. They counted us down and then we were on the air. The first presidential debate on live television.

"Good evening," the moderator began. "The television and radio stations of the United States and their affiliated stations are proud to provide the facilities . . ." I tuned him out for a moment. Why was it so incredibly hot in here? Why did Kennedy want to go to the moon so fucking badly? Why couldn't I focus?

"According to rules set by the candidates themselves, each man shall make an opening statement of approximately eight minutes' duration." What was going on with his droning intonation? He sounded hypnotized. Which was ridiculous; no one was hypnotized.

Kennedy talked first but I wasn't listening, just going over my own stuff in my head. The opening statement was easy. I was coming off an eight-year golden age; Kennedy was a Democrat and basically Harry Truman. Done and done.

The first question went to JFK, about his youth and inexperience. I almost smirked but cut it off. Pat was signaling to me. She kept touching her face like there was something wrong with mine. Didn't she realize that I couldn't see my own face? I risked a glance around the room, but there was no mirror. Why wasn't there a mirror?

"Mr. Nixon, would you like to comment on that statement?" I had no fucking idea what the statement was. No. I glanced over at Kennedy. It was really quite hot, but he didn't seem to be feeling it.

Question to me. "Now, Mr. Vice President, your campaign stresses the value of your eight-year experience, and the question arises as to whether that experience was as an observer or as a participant or as an initiator of policy-making." What were they getting at? That I was no Eisenhower? *The arcane secrets of the presidency are hidden from you, aren't they, Mr. Nixon?* Of course not. I have plumbed their depths, I said. Or words to that effect. I tried to look right into the camera.

The hour seemed to stretch on, telescoping into two, five, ten. Didn't everybody know 1958 was a recession year? I seemed to see a translucent form now, dimly phosphorescent, a slow wafting tendril like that of an enormous sea anemone probing the television studio. Then another. I tried not to flinch as they drew closer. Did no one else see this? It was outrageous, and I planned to lodge a protest.

By this time I was hearing phantom laughter every time I spoke, and the studio smelled of lemons, the same lemons that fell on my father's farm and rotted and burst. It smelled of dust and sickrooms, and I didn't understand how my mother could be operating the camera and my two dead brothers the boom mikes. And I hadn't prepared note cards for any of this.

Kennedy was still smiling, handsome as ever, so fucking handsome, and in a fleeting moment of clarity, in and around my explanation of the inner workings of the Soviet economy, I realized what that handsomeness was. I realized that maybe the camera showed me too clearly, that it showed my face too clearly, and everyone could see I had witnessed things I didn't want to think about. I'd put these things in a place inside myself, a dark shape against the sun. Kennedy didn't have a place like that, and that's what everyone loved about him. He just beamed at you.

I glanced over at my supporters, a knot of people gathered off camera. Brows all furrowed except one, Pat's. Was she smiling? A wicked little smile I'd never seen before.

I saw Eisenhower's face in the audience, his eyes pleading, trapped somewhere far off. I saw Alger Hiss. I saw my father, young and healthy, a sack of lemons on the seat beside him. I gripped the sides of the lectern, bore down on every word. I deserved this victory. I was the man who knew the real world, the man who'd bled for it. The country needed a man who knew the darkness inside it and the darkness beyond. It was me. I was going to save everything.

CHAPTER TWENTY-THREE

OCTOBER 1962

I WAS READING in the news about Kennedy and the Cubans and how he'd saved the day again when my secretary gave me a message about my dry-cleaning, a fanciful mix-up about suits and handkerchiefs, and a number to call back. It was an old signal out of our playbook, but I remembered it. Handler-to-agent priority sign, *We need to talk,* the numbers translating to a place and time.

Pat and the kids were out, and the press people just weren't that hungry for Nixon stories, but I still made the time for a countersurveillance regimen that took up an hour of my afternoon: driving up and down West Hollywood and parking on a side street before walking to the diner on La Brea. I would be late but I wanted to show up clean. I was relieved, frankly. If anyone could get my career back on track it was Tatiana and her contacts. I'd almost stopped thinking of it as a betrayal; it was just how I did things.

When I got there she had nestled herself in a booth in the far back corner and was nursing a coffee; she wore a pale trench coat and scarf, despite the weather, and sunglasses. She gestured for me to sit.

"Sit down, Mr. Nixon," she said, and coughed into her napkin. I sat down opposite her.

"Sorry I'm late," I said. "I wasn't followed."

"I know. You do a good job."

"Are you feeling all right?" I asked. Closer in I was a little shocked by how bad she looked: too much makeup, hands shaking, squinting at me.

"Just a cold," she said. "Is the air travel, too much."

"Where did you go?"

"Havana. Is bright in here, yes? Too much sunlight." It was four in the afternoon and the sun was starting to go down behind the hills. It wasn't bright at all.

The waitress brought me coffee and I ordered an omelet without thinking. Tatiana watched her until she was almost back to her station before saying anything to me.

"What have you got for me, Tatiana? What's the plan?"

"Is no plan. Not for you anyway. American assignment is concluded now."

"What do you mean, concluded?"

" 'Principal agent is no longer positioned to provide quality intelligence. Does not merit further expense or attention at this time.' "

"Now, just wait—there's a lot I can do. The California governor's race is coming up. I have a really good chance there."

She smiled at that, an odd smile. I imagined that this was something closer to what her natural smile had been, before she put in her hours in the mirror in a Leningrad dormitory. For a moment I felt a flash of her vulnerability. Of how physically small she was and how much effort she had to put out for the likes of me.

"Is a good thing about you, the ambition. But you are no longer active agent for us. Your status is revised to sleeper. They do not lose your file, if that is what you are hoping."

"No . . . no. But what about you? Us? Arkady?"

"Is not strictly relevant but American posting is finished for myself and Agent Arkady. We return to Moscow. Finished. Done." She made a sweeping-away gesture.

"What? Why?"

"Recalled for debrief and reeducation. I am too long in United States, much risk of ideological weakening. Catching flight in two days." She broke off with an ugly round of coughing. She spat in her napkin, and the waitress looked up.

"You're leaving?"

"Don't be sentimental, Dick."

"I'm a little surprised, that's all. It's been fourteen years. Where will you go afterward? A new assignment?"

She shook her head, took out a cigarette but didn't light it.

"I don't know. If I knew I could not tell you anyway. My case goes under review. I am gone a long time from home office. Stalin was still alive when I left Russia. The people who hired me have been shot. The people who shot them have been shot. I must go and meet the new Kremlin and find out what they wish of me."

"It's a purge, isn't it. You could be killed. Or sent to Siberia."

She gave me a level look. "I am Russian intelligence. I survive a long time in this job."

"You don't have to go."

"Of course I do."

"You don't! You could stay here. Defect. You and Arkady. It would be so easy. I know all the right people. I don't understand why you didn't do it years ago."

"That is what you would do, yes? People like you, it is natural."

"Like me? What people?"

"I work with many people like you. People who are afraid, who are greedy, who do whatever they want to spare themselves. You lie to your wife. You spy on your country. It is easy to make those people behave as I want them to. You think you are a spy, but you are only a liar and a coward."

She lit her cigarette, finally. I cleared my throat.

"You've got to know by now that I love you," I told her. "If you stay in the U.S. — we could get married. You could get citizenship." I said it before I could think it through. Would I really divorce Pat? Some days it was all I thought about. Some days it seemed like it would be the act of an insane person. My whole life would be gone. But otherwise Tatiana was going to leave. And probably get killed. Was she telling the truth?

She looked at me for a long time.

"I do a real job on you, Nixon, I see that now. I'm even a little sorry for it." She stood up to go, belted her coat.

"Don't go," I said.

She stopped for only a moment. "Business is concluded, Nixon."

"Will I ever see you again?" I asked.

She shrugged. "People live a long time. I hope you enjoy your life, Mr. Nixon."

CHAPTER TWENTY-FOUR

NOVEMBER 1962

"WELL, MR. BROWN, it's been a hell of a fight and I'd like to formally extend my congratulations to you. Governor Brown, I should say. I'll have to get used to that. Yes, and to you. And your family. Good-bye now."

I shrugged Pat's hand off my shoulder. We were both a little drunk. It was after two in the morning.

"I think I'd like to be alone."

"Aren't you coming down?" she said. She was still dressed for the victory party, holding her purse. We'd arranged a massive celebration for an assured victory, before I'd lost by about three hundred thousand votes out of six million.

"Forget it. The press corps are going to be waiting. You know I can't face them."

"You have to. And everyone else is there too. The people who worked for you. You should talk to them."

"I'd really rather just stay up here for a while, okay? I'll have dinner, then I'll be down."

"Well, we'll be waiting for you when you're ready."

She left. When I told the family I was running for governor, I'd gotten only half a sentence in before she stood up from the dinner table.

"What he means is, here we go again," she'd said, and she walked out and slammed the door, leaving me to stumble on through prepared remarks, lying to my own children about the budget crisis, about the nation's second largest economy. I should have just told them, *Daddy wants this and no one is going to take it away from him,* and left it at that.

Afterward she'd been good, she'd smiled and she'd been charming; she'd done everything right. It was just that I knew she was waiting for this to stop and for the joke to be over. Coming in as the overwhelming favorite, I'd lost the closest presidential election in history. Then, instead of riding off into the sunset, I'd stayed around to lose the race for the California governorship. Pat was done. Everyone was done.

There was a knock on the hotel-room door. I opened it to a small, slightly stooped man in uniform.

"Room service!" he croaked. I'd forgotten.

"Where should I put it?" he asked.

"Just near the bed," I said. I stepped aside to let him wheel it in while I fumbled with the check. I calculated the tip, wrote it down, then saw that it had already been included. Crossed it out.

"Whenever you're ready, Mr. Nixon," he said.

"Yes, thank you." I signed hastily and handed it back to him. I wanted to be alone. My political career had just ended.

"Hell of a race, Mr. Nixon," the waiter said. Something nagged me about his voice.

"It sure was."

"Probably the Cuban thing nixed it for you. Weird energy there."

"Most likely," I said. Some people liked to string out their moments with the former vice president, padding the stories they'd tell later. He stood there, swaying a bit in front of the tray, which was neatly laid out with condiments, silverware, cloth napkin, metal-covered dish. I wanted nothing more than to lie in bed and eat my hamburger.

"Is everything to your liking, Mr. Nixon?" he said. He had a slightly smug, goblinish air to his lined face.

"Of course, yes."

He kept standing there, expecting something. I fumbled for a tip just to get rid of him.

"We've met before," he said.

"Have we? Were you with us in '60?"

"Oh, before that. I'm a real early Nixon man. You know, I'd feel better if you made sure it's what you ordered, sir. Just hotel policy."

I stepped over to the tray and lifted the lid. Something black and glossy lay there, limp on a bed of lettuce, smelling of rot. A dead bird.

"What the hell is this?" I turned back to him.

"It took you long enough," he said. Gregor—I now saw—had aged badly. His encounter with Eisenhower had taken something from him, and the last six years looked like five times that. The smirk was the same.

"You can't be here," I told him. I thought of the KGB pistol Arkady had given me. I kept it with me for some reason. I'd never fired it again.

"It takes a lot out of me, I agree. But it'll be worth it."

"What do you want?" I asked.

"Just to see you. It's been a long time. You've done well, present circumstances excepted. You're all they talk about at Moscow Central."

"Are you even Russian?"

"Yup. I went to Exeter. This is a nice room." He opened up the bar, closed it again. He didn't seem in any kind of hurry. I edged over to my suitcase.

"What do you mean, I'm all they talk about?"

"Well, Kennedy's just a joke, isn't he? Why'd you let him in power? You and Eisenhower have a plan going, but I can't figure it out." He was looking out the window now, making a show of unconcern. I fished the gun out of my suitcase, dropped it into my pants pocket. I wondered how many times I would have to shoot him if it came to that.

"We're not doing anything. I just lost."

"Ike's as smart as they come, and you with your bloodline— no. Maybe I should ask your wife. Or you want me to ask your girlfriend? We can ask her anything we want. We've got her in a cell in Moscow now."

"I think you'd better go, Gregor."

"Is that a tough-guy act? That's funny, with you breaking so easily back in New York that time. But if you feel like going toe to toe again, we can do that."

"Please just leave," I said. I remembered how strong he'd been before. Even Arkady had barely managed him.

"Not until you've had your chicken," he said. He pointed to the bird on the tray. It was stirring a little, struggling to get up. I stared at it, only for a moment, but when I looked back, Gregor was gone.

In his place, in his clothes, was a creature that looked like it belonged in a children's book, and it might have been cute there. A children's book where the main character was a black bird shaped roughly like a man, a thing that stood upright, and wore a bellhop's uniform, and had wings poking through the waiter's sleeves in place of arms and an enormous shiny black head with a beak that stuck out a full two feet, and the perfectly round unblinking eyes of a bird on either side of its head.

It looked at me and screamed, the raucous high scream of a bird but coming out of the lungs of a man.

I screamed too, I think. I think I lost control of my body entirely for a short period. I fired the gun. I sprinted away, banged into the cabinet holding the television set, and staggered into the hallway. Then I ran the way you run in a nightmare, rubber-legged, gibbering, veering into walls, the screaming behind me so loud it seemed to follow me down the hall, only inches away from my ear.

I ran past the bank of elevators and face-first into the door to the fire stairs and then I ran down them, seven flights, one after another, panting with fear. It was only at the last flight that I willed myself to look back. I saw that I was alone. I couldn't say when the noise had stopped but the echoes seemed to ring off the walls without ever quite dying away. I looked down to find the gun still in one hand, the metal dish cover in the other. I threw the cover down, stuck the gun in my pocket. I didn't know where anything—my wallet, my hotel key—was or where exactly I was. I shouldered through the exit door into a crowded room.

There was a moment of quiet and then a blinding flash and men's voices. "Mr. Nixon!," "Mr. Vice President!," and, more quietly, "He looks wrecked."

"Mr. Nixon?" It was Herbert Klein, my press secretary. "I think I'm done here, but, um, would you like to say a few words?"

"Yes . . . yes, thank you," I said.

"Good morning, gentlemen," I began. I resisted, with all my strength, the urge to look behind me. I was safe as long as I stood here talking.

Fortunately it turned out I had things to say. About my political opponents, about Governor Brown, about the press corps. All these fucking gentlemen who had never seen a man turn into a crow. Who had never seen the Oval Office turn into a haunted forest and then back into an office again. They stared at me. Klein was on the sidelines, a hand raised tentatively, not sure how to cut me off.

Why should I care? I didn't. In 1962 I was already a joke, the man who didn't know when to leave the party. Nothing like what came later, obviously. But a joke.

I'd lost and lost again and had just been chased by a man-size crow. And possibly been dumped by the love of my life. So who was I doing all this for? It was time to take the hint, drop my parting witticism, make a mocking bow, and leave.

"You won't have Nixon to kick around anymore, because, gentlemen, this is my last press conference," I told them. And at the same time I was talking to Tatiana and Arkady, who couldn't hear, and to Gregor. To Eisenhower. To Pat, standing at the back of the room, arms crossed, mouth a straight line. She seemed to be taking a grim, amused satisfaction in it all and I remembered seeing the same look during our first days in Washington, mirroring back at me the bleak knowledge that she'd tied herself to a man not quite good enough.

It didn't matter anymore. I was tired of trying to figure it out or fix it. Your good dog, Richard.

CHAPTER TWENTY-FIVE

FEBRUARY 1963

WITH THE MOVERS gone we lingered, listening to our footsteps echo off empty walls, but at last, just before noon, the four of us got in the car and pulled ourselves away. Pat and I had had a fight last night. I was packing a few last things and at the bottom of my closet, for some reason, I'd kept a stack of poor Alger Hiss's work, rubbings from some old graves in Pawtuxet. Pat had picked them up and asked what they were and I'd snapped at her and grabbed them away. I told her they were classified and she glared at me and called me a liar. We'd done this before. Later that night I burned the papers, all of them. Never again. Why keep them?

But as we rounded the corner at the end of our block everything lifted a little. We beat the traffic out of the city and made good time, driving northeast with the late-afternoon sun curling down behind us. The highway cut through a barrier ridge into the glowing red interior, the ruddy pastels of the rocky desert like a Warner Brothers cartoon, holding the heat in a radioactive orange smear of dusk. The sun set behind us; ahead, the sky purpled and dimmed.

Pat was silent. I knew she was thinking about what she'd seen. She knew there was something wrong, but she didn't know what, or even if she could ask. The girls in back, fifteen and seventeen, stared out, mesmerized, as we slipped through the vast invisible membrane. We were leaving Los Angeles for good.

It was 1963 and we were crossing the entire breadth of the United States from west to east, Los Angeles to New York. Politics was over for me. Ambition was over. The Russians were gone, not a word since Tatiana walked away. Swallowed whole back into the dark, vengeful dream they'd come from. I'd accepted a partnership in a law firm in New York City. I was going to be a rich lawyer with a statesman's pedigree, a modest and respectable success until the end of my days. I'd write about foreign policy on op-ed pages; I'd give speeches. I was going to live in one single world, unconcerned with the KGB or hidden horrors. I'd live without darkness and without secrets.

We stopped at a highway diner outside of Barstow, and a few travelers recognized me—men smiled and waved, a simple nice-to-see-you. I shook hands and signed a place mat for a young couple. Nobody had to do any voting. After that, the rustle and buzz of recognition died down and people left us alone. It would happen less and less often in the days to come. Afterward we walked out into the warm night and the gasoline fumes blurred the air and I realized I was happy inside myself in a way I couldn't remember being since those very first few days in Washington.

We kept going, past one motel after another, each adorned with neon suns and palm trees, each time thinking we'd go just another ten or twenty miles. I could just drive away from it, I realized, and when I knew that, I didn't want to stop. Something toxic was draining out of us.

The motel we finally chose was like a warm sandbar in an ocean of dark. I'd forgotten how much darkness there was between cities, how quiet and profound the world was. Like the world I was born into in 1913, before cars and highways and streetlights were everywhere. I suppose there must have been things out there under the sand, deep down in the cool clay, or roaming the sands, bodiless, spirits of the terrible lizards that came before us. All the things I was told about. But they stayed quiet. They were vast and I was small, just a former vice president.

The next day we skirted Las Vegas. Our car glided across the knife edge of the Hoover Dam. Tricia bent over a book; Julie pressed her face to the window wide-eyed, asking questions.

By lunchtime, the desert heat was blinding. We pulled into a diner in our cream-colored 1959 roadster with red vinyl seats. I was sweating in my wool suit, but the light was glowing like liquid vanilla fire. I was sick of darkness. I turned to look at Pat, with her blond hair and yellow-and-white summer dress; her mouth was expressionless under cat's-eye sunglasses. For a second I didn't recognize her, and for that second we could have been any family. A man mopping the floor in the diner glanced up at me—did he wink? I couldn't tell, and it didn't matter. We ordered shakes and hamburgers and got a free toy, a flying saucer.

We drove on in great slow loops through the red desert rocks, through Eisenhower's highway system. I'd failed, I realized, but I was still alive. I was out of politics, and out of the occult. No lies, no lies anymore, no more people with animal heads or blurry photographs or secret signs between agents, no shadows and no dark underbelly to the world. All the long afternoon, it was like the light was flooding my senses, telling me, *There is only this existence and no other.*

Over the next two days we followed Interstate 15 through forest and desert, past the great slumbering presence below the Grand Canyon to the south, and then took I-70 to climb the plateau to Denver. Then the long slide down and into the plains, day after day waiting for Des Moines to rise out of the fields.

The last time I'd crossed the country by car as a private citizen was in 1947, and I had begun to realize we were in a different place and time. I'd been inside the political bubble for so long, talking down to people from lecterns, locked inside the White House or hopping from hotel to hotel. Now, like a time traveler, I'd popped back in and was staring gobsmacked at the clothes and cars and people. It was 1963 and it was the future. Clean lines, brave people, nervous, excited, hopeful, angry. People under thirty talked in a rhythm I couldn't quite catch. The Depression and World War II were what old people talked about. Ike and I had built a world that we didn't belong in.

The highways, I realized, were Ike's plan and his victory. I'd never understood quite how big it was or what a change it made. Even the landscape looked newly washed, like after a rainstorm. Ike had wrought a runic inscription right across the country that cut through the hidden places of the vast interior and let the air and light and traffic come in. Nothing like it since Rome first paved Europe.

The country, I knew, was haunted, but whatever powers there were felt the encroachment, the mighty world-shifting nudge of modernity. The things that lived in the in-between places, strange survivors of long-vanished primeval forests. Tribal taboos and ancient curses of millennial standing were swept away. The frailer enigmas died out; the stronger ones grumbled and shambled deeper into the swamps and valleys. Eisenhower's binding held, and the long grief-stricken century smiled. The world was changing, maybe all the way down to its rotten taproot, maybe forever.

*   *   *

The phone rang at four in the morning. I pulled myself out of a confused dream about Yorba Linda: Awake in my bed, I had heard my mother singing. I'd crept downstairs. She was at the kitchen table, facing away from me. "Mother?" She'd turned, and just for an instant, I saw her face, a terrible crow's face like Gregor's.

I couldn't remember where I was. Was this the White House? Was this the first strike? Where was Eisenhower? Where were the missile codes? Then I remembered—I was in my apartment in New York. I wasn't going to have any launch codes ever again.

I picked up the phone anyway.

"Hello?"

"Dick?"

"Yes, who is this?'

"It's Jack."

"I'm sorry, who?"

"Jack Kennedy. The president."

"Jack, oh God, sorry, Mr. President. I was asleep."

"It's all right, Dick."

"How did you get this number?"

"Who is it?" Pat asked, rolling over and turning on the light.

"It's Jack Kennedy," I said.

"What?" she said. She sat up. I made an impatient gesture meant to convey that I was trying to have a conversation with the president. She turned the light back off. I dragged the phone into the bathroom, trailing the cord behind. I sat on the toilet in my nightshirt.

"How can I help you, Jack? Er, Mr. President."

"Dick, the last time we talked—just by ourselves—I was a little rude."

"It's okay."

"No, really, I'm sorry. You know it was — it was a weird time. We were both a little tense, and when you came in, you looked a bit —"

"Crazy, I know."

"I mean, we were about to debate on TV. I thought it was a crazy trick. Psyching me out. They warned me about you, you know."

"I guess it must have seemed pretty strange."

"Heh," he said. There was a little bit of silence. Then: "Dick . . . do you ever feel like a phony?"

"Well, sometimes, Mr. President. Sometimes I do."

"I feel like that all the time now. Like there are things about my health and, well, my personal life that I couldn't tell any-body ever. Like I don't belong in this job."

"I guess everybody feels like that sometimes, Mr. President."

"Maybe you should have won, Dick," he said. "I really think about that sometimes." There was another pause, and I heard him breathing. I imagined him in the Oval Office, the lights off, breathing into the same black phone we used to use.

"Dick, you worked in the West Wing for a long time, didn't you?"

"Eight years," I said.

"Did you ever see anything — well, I don't know how to say this — strange? In the Oval Office? Not animals, but shadows that look like animals that are someplace you can't find? I know this sounds —"

"Crazy, I know. I . . . did see things."

"And then like someone's crying but you can't find them? I walked all over the house but I couldn't find anything. I can still hear them late at night. And once I thought I saw a woman and she turned around and —"

"Jack, I think we should probably talk about this in person."

There was a long silence, and then: "I'd appreciate that. I just haven't known whom to talk to."

"It's all right," I told him. "I've been there. There's a lot I can tell you."

"Look, I'll be gone for a couple of days, Dallas, but if you could come to Washington when I get back?"

"I'll meet you there."

"Thanks, Dick. We'll have a real talk then. And I'm very sorry, about before."

"It's okay. Really. See you soon."

PART THREE

CHAPTER TWENTY-SIX

MAY 1966

FOR MOST OF you, the ones born in 1970 or after, this is where my life starts, the accelerating disaster you read about in the history textbooks. At a tiki-themed fund-raising event at a New York hotel not far from the Commodore, I began to run for president for the second time.

I'd lived in New York for three years and in most ways I had come to resemble an ordinary citizen. For three years, I hadn't even thought about the boom-and-bust drama of the electoral cycle. I'd cashed out, gotten an ordinary, unheroic job. All the rest of it faded remarkably fast. The glamour of power, the sense of a calling beyond myself, the idea that it had to be me making the decisions. And of course the memories of what I'd seen faded too. The sight of Eisenhower chanting in the Oval Office, of space folding, of horrors in the Pennsylvania Avenue night were—not unreal, but I could put them somewhere else in my head.

I told Pat most of this, as much as I could. I told her it was over and I was different, this time for sure. I told her the stress of governing had made me imagine some strange things, and I might have been out of my head for a while, but I was fine now; in fact, I was happy. I promised, solemnly and openly, that it was done. She didn't leave me, but there was always that space of reserve I'd come to recognize, the stance of a woman living on intimate terms with a man she can't entirely trust. We had dinner together every night; we explored the city. Once we happened to walk past the Wexford building on East Seventy-First, and by an effort of will I didn't even look up.

I did go through the motions of being a former vice president. For a fee I gave speeches at college graduations, talked about political and inspiration themes, looked down from the lectern at the increasingly shaggy undergraduates of the mid-1960s. They in turn looked up with a declining sense of interest and it was obvious that they, too, were less and less sure of where I belonged in history, which vice president I'd been exactly and when and what I had done or not done.

Why should they have known anything? They had only just been born when I met Whittaker Chambers, when the impulse caught me one summer evening to follow Alger Hiss uptown to his strange little office. The Eisenhower administration was just a long vague halcyon era of their middle childhoods. The Russian menace and the Cold War were immutable facts of the world they lived in.

Somehow they remembered the little, wrong things about me. That people had thrown rocks at me in South America. That I gave a speech on television about a dog. The image of me sweating and fidgeting on the debate stage. And they remembered—every last one of them, without even knowing why—that my nickname was Tricky Dick.

The party was just a midterm election fund-raiser but it was already a boozy, sequined arena for the small set of people positioning themselves for the Republican primaries in '68. The Democrats were weak, there was going to be a Republican resurgence, and everyone wanted it to be about them. The crowd was a mix of wealthy people, career politicians, press, and the hard-to-classify but well-connected riffraff that fill in the gaps.

It was not a triumphant return. Everyone recognized me, of course, and I smiled and shook hands and played the elder statesman at fifty-three. But I caught murmurs in my wake: *Can you believe he's still around? What's he doing here?*

People have long since forgotten the ludicrous improbability of my return to presidential politics. But you have to remember, I'd spent eight years in Eisenhower's shadow, his dubious little hatchet man, eight years in a White House that ushered in a golden age. Then, handed this legacy, teed up as no politician ever was, I bungled it for the Republicans.

Remember, I didn't even bungle it properly; I lost it by the thinnest margin American history had ever seen. If I'd lost by a respectable amount, I might have walked away clean and decent, bowing to a mightier political talent. But I managed a graceless, mean loss that left doubt in everyone's mind and a bad taste in everyone's mouth. And then there was the governor's race and the hysterical concession speech and political *Selbstmord*. With my particular genius I had turned eight triumphant years in the White House into a story about failure. Not until the year 2000, from where I hid in foreign parts, did I witness a closer race and an electoral loss of equivalent unforgettable nastiness.

But here I was. Because Pat had been bored and irritable and drinking that night, and with the children off at college, I was the only other person in the apartment and the target of her moodiness. And I wanted to see the new front-runners, the presidential-candidates-in-waiting. I'd read about them but I wanted to see them in the flesh. Did any of them know what Eisenhower knew? Had he truly been the last of the presidential initiates?

There were three of them and they were easy to spot because they were American politicians. They had large square heads, beautiful hair, and sharply etched features. There was the movie star, Ronald Reagan, who carried himself like an Olympic athlete, who was gorgeous and kind and blandly ambitious with a lizardlike hindbrain that sensed opportunity and danger. George Romney, millionaire and governor of Michigan and apparent simpleton, whose one trick seemed to be canting his shoulders like a gangster and fixing you with eyes of an eerily vivid blue. And Nelson Rockefeller, prodigiously wealthy, with the life and education of a young American prince.

They milled around, trying to stay visible but not stand out too much. They were waiting to be called to the office, to emerge as the obvious choice to run for president in 1968.

They were also easy to spot because they avoided me with an almost visceral disgust and terror. I watched their panicked entourages herd them away as I drifted toward them. Part of it was the timeless and instinctual revulsion that arises on the cellular level between a pack of ignorant bullies and someone who at least tried to get good grades in college. But mostly it was just the feeling that failure was contagious and that I carried it like a plague.

I stared at them with tactless directness and tried to see anything other than confidence and charm. I tried to see darkness, nervousness, any hint that any of them had stared down horror, heard unpleasant secrets he could never convey to a living soul. I got nothing.

A waiter came through the crowd wheeling an oversize novelty cake, a vast cream-colored totem head, and as the crowd collapsed in again behind it, I saw something I didn't want to see. A large man in a tuxedo standing apart from the crowd, scanning the room. I didn't literally drop my drink, but I paled and swayed so badly that an especially alert Supreme Court clerk gently reached out and took my drink from me. I barely noticed.

My body knew what to do before I did. In a moment I was peering at him from behind an arrangement of tropical flowers. I looked more closely. It was him, wasn't it? Wasn't it? Yes and no.

Arkady had aged, but in a peculiar way. Instead of bending him, time had straightened him; he looked three inches taller. He'd lost his sad-sack slouch along with twenty or thirty pounds. His face had lost a little of its soft Slavic humor; it had graven itself into more seriousness, had squared its jaw and looked windward.

Maybe I should have been relieved to see an old friend I'd thought lost, but in reality, I felt nothing but dread. For three years I'd felt I'd cheated the past, been through all that strange darkness and gotten out clean. When Arkady and Tatiana left the country, they took my secrets with them forever. And when I lost the governor's race, it was as if my ill-gotten gains had ceased to be, and that was that. I'd made my pact with the devil and escaped with my skin intact and at least a piece of my soul, a fair bargain and no hard feelings, right?

No, it wasn't, and deep down I knew that. The moment I broke into Alger Hiss's office, I'd stepped off the straight and virtuous path. I'd been rewarded for it well beyond my wildest dreams, and I had no business pretending that didn't happen.

And here it was, a big fat Russian reminder in a tuxedo. The accursed city had been drowned in the depths of the ocean. But now, after a thousand years, the waters were drawing back and the haunted streets and nightmare statues were emerging from the depths again.

I wasn't going down without a fight. It was still possible he hadn't seen me. Keeping the enormous cake between us I avoided him the way the rest of the party avoided me. When he moved, I moved to keep away from him, and Rockefeller,

Reagan, and Romney moved to get away from me. Their entourages followed in turn, so together, Arkady and I stirred the circular ballroom with a slow anxious rhythm. I inched us toward the coat check. A few more minutes and I could make my excuses, collect my things, and sprint off into the night, and everything would be back to normal.

Behind me I heard a glass drop; glass shattered and there was a little scream of delight. I turned back too late and saw now that I would never get out. Arkady had seen me and successfully reversed course to cut me off.

"Dick!" he called loudly, unnerving a pack of Reaganites. "Dick, you motherfucker!" He grinned maniacally at me as he battered his way through the crowd, shoulder-checked Nancy's security detail, and strode to where I stood pinned against a column.

He clapped an arm around me, outwardly friendly but hard enough to make it clear to me I was caught.

"Dick, my friend," he whispered, "I think it is best we visit the bar for a moment."

He steered me to the open bar, plainly showing I was in his custody.

"You are surprised; is not an unusual reaction. Do not worry, I am not here for murdering of any sort. I am your friend, a legitimate diplomatic representative of our great workers' republic."

"It's good to see you. I just didn't think—"

"You thought I would be purged due to the wisdom of our party elders. Is not so unlikely. But that is not what happened."

"Is there a way we could be more discreet about this?"

A matronly party elder was staring at the former vice president and his Communist buddy.

"No. I have reason to be here. But first we drink a little, like old times. How is Pat and kids? How is boring life? You are rich capitalist now."

"I'm—I'm fine. Really. Being a lawyer is different. Arkady, what happened? Are you okay?"

"I'm fine. Long story. Three, four years now, right? We go back to Moscow, Tatiana and me. Aeroflot, Chicago to New York to Oslo. Drinking, mostly not talking. Party men meet us at airport. Then off to questioning."

"Her too?"

"They take me off for strip search, I thought was just for a minute, but after that I do not see her again. I am sorry, Dick. I came out of this so maybe she is okay somewhere."

"Are you—" I glanced around, tried to hush my voice in the party din. "Are you still KGB?"

"Jesus, you still suck at this. So bad."

"Are you?" I asked, turning to look at him.

"I don't know. Are you?"

"Did you—tell them about that?"

He shrugged, fatalistic. "At first they ask about you. When they stop, it is how I know you lost election. Sorry. More interested in Eisenhower and American defenses. I tell them about the highways."

"You told them the plan?"

"Was an interrogation. I give them a little something, Dick. And I felt bad; I don't wish to be unkind, but it was not that great of an interrogation. These kids try to mess with me, set little traps. Change details and ask me to verify. A little yelling and screaming. But they are simply not that good. Commie types, they punch like philosophy majors. Almost I take pity on them. But no, I do not tell them about you."

"And they let you go?"

He shook his head. "The Kremlin has become strange.

Offices and bureaucrats who speak odd languages. And many new subbasements. A few I have glimpsed inside. Fires that do not consume. Statues of silver that speak and sing. And in the tomb of Lenin, he does not sleep.

"In the end, so that I may serve the motherland, I am considered for corrective labor camp, a little uranium mining in Kazakhstan, perhaps. I believe our friend Gregor intervenes. The Nth Directorate gets hold of me, sends me to Baikonur. You know it?"

"The space program."

"Kosmograd, yes. It has changed since I am there last. Rockets, yes, but also I am shown stone gate, and through it I see stars. Strange machines and metal towers that rose towards the heavens, and today one cannot even see where the highest ones end.

"I was there with a Science Pioneer Detachment, twenty spies and criminals and political malcontents. I am oldest man by far, most not even twenty-five. We are informed we will receive experimental surgeries. Tissue-grafting procedure. I must report that morale for Pioneer troops was not high. Much belated talk of the pleasures of uranium mining and other missed opportunities. The surgical unit was enormous, like an airplane hangar. Shielded trucks delivered the materials and medical personnel wear heavy leaded clothing.

"We are taken one by one. I lie awake and think of Czar Nicholas, of Anastasia, and think maybe this is justice. I am nearly the last; perhaps I benefit by the surgeons' experience. Many die, many survive but are not fit to be seen. I am fortunate exception."

"My God, Arkady."

"Those who survive such things are much valued. I am reassigned to field but perhaps a little disenchanted with Soviet policy at this time."

"Arkady, listen," I said. "Listen, it was nice to see you again. Really, really great, but I'm through with all that—you know, stuff. I'm in a different place right now and I don't—"

He put one hand on my shoulder to stop me. He had always been strong, but now it was like a girder had descended on me. "Dick, I am not come to talk about your feelings, although, yes, always interested to hear. I wish to do you a favor and bring you to a man I have lately become acquainted with. He is standing close by."

My shoulder was going numb. I saw the man waiting for me across the room, like a dark heavy stone in the frothy sea of blond hair and jewelry.

The strange thing was, I knew him. He was older and fatter now, with a kind of permanently delighted twinkle, as if he'd stumbled on a piece of good news that meant nothing to anyone but him and that he'd decided to keep to himself, forever. But I knew his face. I'd seen it in the war.

In 1944 I was a naval passenger control officer for the South Pacific Air Transport Command. On behalf of my unit, I traded favors, used whatever leverage my position and rank gave me in a very complicated game of supply, demand, and priority played very fiercely among competing sections of a vast and deeply corrupt but surprisingly functional bureaucracy.

My view of the war was the traffic of objects and people through the transportation network. I filled out itineraries and requisition forms as we leapfrogged north and west from the Solomon Islands to the Philippines. I scheduled flights and re-fuelings for marines and wounded soldiers and VIPs. I watched the planes take off and land and helped load and unload crates of pineapples and bandages and spare tires and footwear and type-writers.

I knew where we were stalled; I knew about the islands that

wouldn't be taken, that week after week ate fresh men and supplies and sent back the dead, wounded, and exhausted. One of the islands was called Peleliu.

And I knew about things that weren't officially supposed to be there because they belonged to something too weird or secret to talk about. Crates and entire planeloads of matériel that had been redacted. Experimental devices bound for field-testing; high-level cryptographers and intelligence analysts; civilian specialists. I'd send the CO a questioning look and he'd give a tired wave of the hand or a curdled, indifferent shrug. The people who had set up the system also created exceptions to it for their own reasons.

I knew there were code breakers being delivered to freshly captured cryptographic materials. A few celebrity entertainers made their visits to the troops incognito. I'd heard rumors of the Manhattan Project and the thing that was silently being transferred to within striking distance of the Japanese mainland.

Sometimes I couldn't even guess. Two men from the Corps of Engineers transported two old, roughly rectangular stones wrapped in newspaper to the front lines. I was instructed to give them a plane to themselves. There were crates of dirt; an enormous tank of seawater. A basalt obelisk traveling by itself. Some of it, I now understood, emanating from the farm at Pawtuxet.

And once, a pale, dark-haired teenager in a white shirt and a sweater-vest despite the heat, flanked by four marines. Slender, bespectacled, and oddly beautiful. They walked him through checkpoints more like a piece of experimental ordnance than a soldier. Whenever they stopped he would pull out a tiny, worn book barely the size of his hand and page through it rapidly. We passed him up to the front, to Peleliu.

They passed him back two days later along with the planeload of exhausted soldiers. He sat as unruffled as if he were riding the subway, maybe on the way to a chess tournament at the local YMCA. The other passengers on the crowded plane had made a collective decision not to go within ten feet of him. I later heard rumors about what had happened on the island. That they'd let Henry walk into the jungle on his own, that they'd heard voices bellowing and chanting in languages neither English nor Japanese, that they hadn't even found all of the dead. Firsthand I knew only that air traffic was being routed to give the island's interior the widest possible clearance. This was Henry at twenty-one.

CHAPTER TWENTY-SEVEN

AUGUST 1966

"RICHARD NIXON, THIS is Henry Kissinger," Arkady told me, and I found myself shaking hands with a bland, spectacled little man. I've asked myself many times since if it was really a man at all.

I'd heard rumors of the wunderkind of foreign policy, genius of Bavaria and the Upper West Side. Heinz Alfred Kissinger, called Henry, refugee, bright star of Harvard and the RAND Corporation. I'd been curious to meet him, a man in politics who was famous for being smart. In person, he was thickset, alert, but somehow sly. He had something in common with Eisenhower, that sense of a calculating intelligence kept well out of sight.

"Pleased to meet you," I said.

"I am very much looking forward to your presidency," he said in that German accent with a tenor lilt. He looked up at me shyly.

"I'm sorry?"

"Henry has very interesting ideas about you," Arkady said. "He's done a lot of thinking about what's happening in the world right now."

"Indeed I have, Mr. Nixon. I will come to the point: the current outlook is most unfavorable for the West. It is evident that in the next few years the United States will become quite overmatched, disrupting the carefully achieved balance of power and precipitating a catastrophic clash of forces well beyond what has previously been imagined." He spoke, like always, as if to a lecture hall.

"There isn't really a missile gap," I said. "That was all—"

"A canard of the Kennedy administration, yes," he said. "But there are strategic elements apart from the nuclear. I would think you of all people would realize what I am speaking of, Mr. Nixon. From your talks with President Eisenhower."

"You know Eisenhower?"

"I have met with him on multiple occasions, yes. He was most forthcoming on certain matters, although others remain—how do I say—obscure. This much is clear, however: The doctrine of mutual assured destruction can continue only as long as no new, disruptive technology appears on one side and not the other. Since Eisenhower's infirmity and your unfortunate electoral, er, moment, we have no one in the leadership echelon prepared to appreciate fully the dimensions of this conflict. Not Romney. Not Reagan. No one but yourself." His voice had a hypnotist's gently persuasive rise and fall and carried with strangely perfect clarity in the crowded hall.

"I'm not a part of this."

"I wonder," he said. "But you know what I'm speaking of, don't you? You have seen things. Long ago, yes? Very long ago, I think. A thing spoke with your brother's voice."

"You can't know that."

"Notwithstanding," he said quickly, and I wondered if the others had even heard him. Or if I had imagined it. "I was Rockefeller's adviser for years and he seemed a promising figure, but I see that you are the man I was looking for. I am here to make you president."

There was a long silence, under which I heard Reagan's stage-trained voice talking about the deficit and the workingman. Arkady watched me expectantly and I held my features still, as if I'd ever been able to hide anything from him.

There are the rare, rare moments when you've lost a thing

you treasured and made your peace with that loss; your life is going to go on without it, a diminished place, but you've figured out how to twist yourself around just right to love and appreciate that new thing you've become—and then you're given another chance at the thing you wanted so badly. And you have to choose—are you the old person you remember, or the new person you taught yourself how to be?

"You've made a mistake," I told him. "I no longer have political aspirations, Dr. Kissinger." Caesar refusing the laurels, only not remotely as convincing. But I was still ready to pretend. I turned to go, half staggered, but Arkady simply stood in my way and corralled me while Kissinger spoke.

"I haven't been clear, Mr. Nixon," Kissinger went on. "Mr. Eisenhower's schemes for America's strategic architecture have gone badly awry. You are needed. Your loss in 1960 was a disaster for America's supernatural armaments preparedness. What Eisenhower began has languished, it has spoiled, whereas the Soviets have embraced this arena of possibility with an enthusiasm I find most exhilarating. Your old acquaintance Gregor, or whatever consciousness now goes by that name, has thrived in the Soviet command structure.

"Long-range missiles with hybrid thermonuclear and necromantic payloads. Grafted and crossbred infantry divisions. Strategic alliances with folkloric, extraplanar, and subterranean entities. Field deployment of weaponized paleofauna. Large-scale saturation of target areas with invasive fungal and floral xeno organisms. Megadeaths and mega-undeaths. This is the Cold War now. An American president must be found who, whatever his other qualifications, is prepared to maintain our competitiveness in this area. I'm afraid that that person is you."

"It's not me," I told him. "What did Eisenhower tell you? It was supposed to be me but it's not. He never trained me. It's no one."

"I know," he said. "Eisenhower was a soldier who fell in his country's defense, and his knowledge is gone. But what was lost can be recovered. As Taft did, so can we. You are the one, Mr. Nixon. He chose you, and no one else."

Arkady looked at me expectantly. A man who had heard the Romanovs' death agonies and lived the fifty years that followed wasn't about to be fooled by any coy foot-shuffling when it came to political maneuvering. He'd sensed from the very beginning that there was a part of me that would do anything to win and that it would never, ever go away.

"But you're forgetting that even if I wanted to do it, I'm done politically. They finished me," I told him. "I'm unelectable. Really, you want one of them." Romney and Reagan and Rockefeller worked the room and secured funding and made sure that everyone knew that, if the time came, they would humbly answer the call and serve their country. I knew the call wasn't coming. Phone disconnected, hacked off at the root.

"As to that, Mr. Nixon, I believe that you can and will be president. But I must have your answer."

"I'm going to have to speak to my wife."

"Yes. Speak to her," Kissinger said.

I thought about what I'd built for myself and my family. We were safe and prosperous and had the chance to live normal lives now, comfortable in our modest place in a great nation's history. Who could complain? Who would ask for more than that? More than the vice presidency in the golden 1950s. What kind of person wouldn't be satisfied at that point? Only a foolish or pathological self-obsession would drive a man to climb farther.

It wasn't possible, and if it was possible, it was almost certainly undemocratic. Nobody wanted me to be president except me, and Henry, and Arkady (who was Russian KGB, which presumably affected his eligibility as a voter). But what's the point in pretending I said anything other than yes? That was as much convincing as it took. Yes, please. God, yes. Make it me.

I'd gone to the reception to get away from the apartment. It was a gorgeous, incomprehensibly expensive residence on Central Park East. I could look out the front windows into the closest thing Manhattan offered to total darkness.

Pat was still awake. It was past eleven and I could smell her cigarette smoke, which meant she was drinking in the front room. Marriage. I leaned in the doorway.

"Hi, dear."

"How was the reception?" she said. She was in a dressing gown and pajamas. When she was drinking she cultivated a kind of Hepburn oddball sophistication.

"It was—it was interesting. I had a strange conversation."

"What, did they ask you to run for president again?"

"No! N-no," I told her. "I mean, why would you say that?"

"Oh, Dick. I'm not stupid. I see the look on your face. You went to a Republican function and you hung around the drinks table waiting for people to recognize you."

"People recognize me. I was vice president."

"For eight years. And then you were almost president, and then you weren't. You're not going to be. Have a drink."

"What if I were, Pat? What if there's someone who believes I can be?"

"We all believe in you. Nixon together!" Pat started to say but giggled halfway through it.

"Dr. Kissinger does."

"Is that a psychiatrist?"

"The Harvard academic," I told her. "He thinks I should run. He has backers. Real money."

She looked a lot more sober now.

"I would be horrified if I thought this was at all serious. Are you drunk?"

"No," I said. A little.

"Are you lying to me?"

"No!" Was I? About the backers, yes. Maybe it didn't matter.

"Dick, think about this. Please. We were just starting to have a life here. I know we haven't been, well, close, but this is just craziness. After all that's happened. They can't take you back." It was awful, but it was almost good to see how heartbroken she was. At least it was a reaction.

"Pat, I think it might be serious. What if——"

"But you promised."

"What if there was a reason I had to run?" I said, sitting down opposite her.

"A reason?"

"An important one. A thing you don't know about, but it's really important." I tried to put it into my voice like politicians do. A great cause. A heroic destiny. Surely I could sell this.

"You always give reasons; that's what you do. Taking the nation forward or something. Don't talk like that in here."

"No, a real reason, an important secret reason I couldn't possibly tell anyone. But it's why I have to do this. Why I've done all of this."

"I don't care if it's secret."

"It's a state secret and you'd think I was crazy if I told you."

Pat sat and stared at me while cars honked outside on Fifth Avenue. I was going as far as I could. Daring myself to go farther, but I couldn't.

"I'm going to bed," Pat said. I stepped aside as she went into the hall. "Do what you want. You always do anyway."

"Are we going to get divorced?" I called after her.

"No, we're not getting divorced, idiot. Shut up." She came toward me until she stood closer to me than she had in years. "We're not getting divorced. I'll help you do this thing."

"Thank you."

"But other than that, I do what I want. I don't talk to you if I don't want to. I sit where I want to on the campaign plane. I eat my meals separately. I sleep separately. Is that clear?"

"Yes, dear."

She glared at me a moment.

"This would be easier if you would tell me what the fuck your stupid secret is. If it's an affair, just tell me. I can't think what else it would be."

"It's not. I don't know how to explain it, but it's not."

"I think this is the worst idea I've ever heard."

"I know," I said.

"Well, good luck."

I went to sleep thinking of the last thing Henry had said to me: "I will do this for you. I will make you the greatest president the Republic has known but there is one thing you must agree to."

"What is it?" I asked.

"There is a pact we must seal, you and I, if I am to lend my powers to yours. I cannot be president, you understand? I am Bavarian-born, ineligible. But I can partake of your presidency. A little blood, a few words, and it is done."

I nodded, hardly listening.

CHAPTER TWENTY-EIGHT

JULY 1967

THE AIR OF the Miami Beach Convention Center was hot and still and tense. There was a murmur, nonplussed and restless, as I arrived at the lectern. They knew they'd voted for me on the first ballot, but they weren't exactly sure why—it was a confused moment in their memories. But here I was at the microphone, confirmed and present. Old Nick had returned.

"Mr. Chairman, delegates to this convention, my fellow Americans. Sixteen years ago I stood before this convention to accept your nomination as the running mate of one of the greatest Americans of our time—of any time—Dwight D. Eisenhower.

"Eight years ago, I had the highest honor of accepting your nomination for president of the United States. Tonight, I again proudly accept that nomination for president of the United States.

"But I have news for you. This time there is a difference. This time we are going to win." It was, basically, the worst thing I could have said. A reminder of how badly it had gone the last time. A reminder that nominating me was a horrible idea.

Well, I could have said something worse. I could have said, *In the entire course of my public life I have never done anything remotely this terrible. I have tricked you all in monstrous fashion. Standing before you now, I am the likely death of democracy and the rise of a sorcerous tyranny.* Certainly that's what I was thinking to myself as I began my address to the 1968 Republican National Convention in Miami to accept the party's nomination for president.

I congratulated Governors Romney, Reagan, and Rockefeller on a hard fight and said that I counted on them for their support, all the while thinking of the moment I came through the door of the hotel suite where they were meeting to divvy up power.

"Dick," Reagan had called to me.

"Come on in," said George. They'd sounded puzzled and looked up at me with patronizing smiles, a little sad that this aging prodigy, the one-time icon of the party's future, was pretending he was welcome.

"Just thought I'd look in on the young bucks," I'd said. "You all know Dr. Kissinger?" I asked. He stood in the doorway and made an awkward half bow before I gestured him in.

"Of course, Dick. Take a seat." Rockefeller stood, courtly in manner but, I could see, terribly uncomfortable. I sat, and Henry stood behind me. I tried to ignore the terrible feeling of being an uninvited, pitied guest.

"Go on with what you were doing, really," I said. "I won't be any trouble."

Reagan cleared his throat. "Now, George was just pointing out some of the problems we'll have in the South if we give this to Nelson—"

"I don't expect to be given anything for free," Rockefeller interrupted.

"Please, I think you all forget the crucial demographic here," Henry broke in. "You forget the silent majority. I think that is the phrase."

"Henry means the middle class," I said. "The conservative

middle class who aren't grabbing the mainstream press coverage the way the hippies are."

"The silent majority," Henry intoned. And then, bafflingly, he began to sing.

"What is he doing?" Reagan asked. It wasn't a pleasant song—a high, soft chant. Part of it sounded as if it had been recorded and played backward. Part of it sounded as if more than one person might be singing. The air in the room seemed to solidify into a clear, hard substance that prevented any of us from moving until the music was done. I remember Ronald Reagan's anguished, confused stare as the song explained to him in words he would never remember why he would not become president in 1969.

My speech in Miami wasn't a long or good one. Cheap metaphors and easy shots. I declared war on the loan sharks and Mafiosi and drug dealers. I talked about the face of a child. "Tonight . . . I see the face of a child" were my exact words. Pat's face, though, is the one I remember. Shocked and smiling, the doll's face smiling as the world broke.

We all remember the Chicago riots and the shooting of Robert Kennedy but that was earlier. It shook out to a three-way race, me, the Democrat Hubert Humphrey, and right-wing Southern firebrand George Wallace. History records it as a wrenching, divisive violent election cycle.

I remember it as a numb, angry, sour blur of days and weeks hurrying from place to place. After the Democratic Convention I was ahead by double digits. I didn't debate either of the other candidates—why bother? Why bother doing any of it?

In October the numbers shifted again, the weight of inarticulate discontent slowly and measurably turning back to Humphrey, like an unstoppably vast sleeping animal shifting as it dreamed.

There was a darkness overseas and only I could prevent it. I spent four hours thinking of that darkness while I recorded dialogue for a comic variety show. "Sock it to me?" "Sock it to me?" "Sock it to me!" They thought it was hilarious.

But this was my fourth time in a real presidential campaign: 1952, 1956, 1960, and now 1968. I ran a series of expertly managed press and media events choreographed around a candidate in a paroxysm of terror and urgent loneliness. I knew on some level—we all did—that everyone would learn from this and that we would leave the world a far more Nixonian place.

Pat campaigned for me, shaking hands on the rope line for hours every day. I knew she hated smiling and grandstanding and shouted conversations. I wondered why she was there, hour after hour. Did she think I was going to be a good president? Did she like me after all?

We were in danger, I knew that much. A handful of times, I saw—or maybe I didn't—a misshapen figure watching me from the back of the crowd. It might have been Gregor; it might have been no one. I would look again and it would be an ordinary man, somebody silhouetted wrong against a second person, somebody leaning at an odd angle, someone in a hat. And once, another time, I saw my brother Arthur watching me from an upper-story window as I spoke to reporters. Saw him distinctly, mind you. I stopped speaking and looked, maybe four seconds of silence and eye contact. At the very end, he gave a negative shake of his head and then one of my press secretaries jostled me and the window was empty again.

I asked Henry about it, and he said only that we would know when the time came. That the enemy would not hide its face. Henry wasn't officially part of the campaign at all. He wasn't on the schedule, or on the buses and planes. He arrived at all hours to give his odd little instructions, usually words or phrases to include in the next day's speech. At times I wondered if the other people in the campaign could see him. He'd stand looking over Pat's shoulder; I'd spot him in crowds peering quizzically up at me through his thick glasses.

We slept on buses, trains, in hotels, but what I remember were the airplane rides by night, the DC-3s that would shake and pop and vault into the air. Then the lights would dim, and I would settle deeper into my seat with a coat draped over me and try to sleep. In the darkness, I felt the least like Nixon that I ever would again. You couldn't see my absurd-looking face, the caricature that had fixed me in the world, in history.

Months passed and it seemed impossible that the world wasn't seeing through this. Could this possibly be how a world power worked? A grim farce at the heart of it? Kissinger was managing the whole thing with some subtle sorcery, from my campaign speech to my cameo on *Laugh-In* to election night itself, when my campaign volunteers and smiling, bewildered Spiro Agnew and even Pat seemed on some level pleased. I had, I realized, lost track of whether I was a centrist Republican stalwart, a right-wing anti-Communist demagogue, a mole for Soviet intelligence, the proxy candidate for a Bavarian sorcerer, or the West's last hope against an onrushing tide of insane chthonic forces. No one seemed to notice that Tricky Dick was himself a trick.

In the few genuinely spontaneous public moments, I found there was a strange angry charge in the world. The middle twentieth century was a terrible, menacing environment and it seemed as if on some level that truth had penetrated. As Garry Wills would later write, "As I stood, bewildered like most reporters, in the insane din of that Wallace rally...I realized at last what had not sunk in at Miami's riot, or

Chicago's. I realized this is a nation that might do anything. Even elect Nixon."

We were doing what we had to do. There were terrible and vast forces outside our control that necessitated a Nixon presidency. I knew that, but I also knew a few other things by then. I knew that I was getting what I most wanted in the world. I was getting my heart's desire, a gift out of all proportion to merit or fairness. But I knew on what terms I was getting it. I was winning it all, but in such a way as to ensure it would never mean anything. So maybe people don't change after all.

PART FOUR

CHAPTER TWENTY-NINE

JANUARY 1969

THE SOUTHEAST WENT to Wallace and Texas went to Humphrey. I won Ohio, Florida, Illinois, and then California. One by one the great names fell and it was decided. I was going to have it.

But when I took the oath, would I become someone different? How was it going to feel? What would I know that I hadn't known before? Would I feel a new power? Eisenhower had known something, but Kennedy hadn't, and Truman hadn't. Probably not Johnson either, but he was far too cunning to guess at.

The time came. White-haired Chief Justice Earl Warren spoke the words into the cold morning air and I answered him, clearly and precisely.

"I, Richard Milhous Nixon, do solemnly swear . . . that I will faithfully execute the office . . . of president of the United States."

This was it, I thought, right at the moment. I was saying it. I tried to feel every bit of it as it happened, to feel myself changing from civilian into the thirty-seventh president. To become, finally, something other than shitty Tricky Dick.

"And will to the best of my ability . . . preserve, protect, and defend . . ."

Nobody was ever going to fuck with me again. I was president! I tried to feel what Eisenhower felt, to take on that power.

Eisenhower folded space, shrugged off bullets. Eisenhower was going to save the world. And now there was no Eisenhower. It would have to be me. *This time it's going to be different,* I told my-self. A brand-new Nixon.

"...the Constitution of the United States..."

It was almost over. It was ending. I was changing. Wasn't I?

"...so help me God."

I looked out at an entire planet staring back at me. I'd just become the most important person in the world, and not just to myself. There they all were. I wanted to rise into the air, the immanent Nixon, and stare fire from my eyes down at them. I waited for it to happen.

I walked off the stage as the exact same person I'd been when I walked onto it. Only a little bit surprised at how much I'd gotten my hopes up. At that, and at how, when the oath was concluded, the chief justice whispered a single word, so low that only I could hear: "Good-bye."

Afterward, the inaugural parade, in which Pat and I rode down Pennsylvania Avenue while protesters threw rocks, sticks, garbage, and firecrackers at us. Called me a liar and a vil-lain. I hear they held their own ceremony and inaugurated a pig in my place, proclaimed me an impostor. Pat was composed and angry; the Secret Service was polite, worried, and apologetic; all I could think was *Of course I am. But how did they know?*

CHAPTER THIRTY

JANUARY 1969

WHEN THE FAIRY-TALE round of dinners and dances and toasts and cheering concluded, at one thirty in the morning, Pat and I moved into our new house. The chief of the housekeeping staff walked us to the door but wouldn't follow us inside, not after midnight. A staff tradition, she explained, glancing nervously up at the empty windows.

The doors closed behind us. We'd been there dozens of times, but never like this. The entrance hall is two stories high with white columns. Our footsteps pinged off it and echoed. The house was cold and empty. Pat led the way as we stumbled from room to room, neither of us speaking. Eight years gone. All of a sudden, tears were running down my cheeks and dripping onto the lapel of my inaugural suit.

George Washington himself oversaw the laying of the first stones, a hundred and seventy-five years ago, and now we lived here. The entrance hall was shining checkered marble. Here was the State Dining Room again. I remembered how much I'd resented sitting in the back. Now I'd sit at the head table with everyone looking up at me.

We had a ballroom that seemed to stretch on for blocks, an inland sea of pale hardwood floor. I sat down at the Steinway grand piano and sent "Moon River" tinkling through the halls of government, liquid and immaculately pitched, as if the instrument had been tuned that morning and every morning. There was a map room, and a library, archipelagos of sitting rooms and pantries, doors disclosing new rooms with others visible beyond them rambling onward through archways and interior windows. We spilled from one to another, each a little jewel box or tiny world. James Polk's Red Room dripped with baroque imperial opulence; low, crimson divans begged to be lounged on in depraved, melancholy attitudes. I had no idea how strict Puritan ideals had allowed this room to come into being — perhaps Benjamin Franklin had inspired it? A side deal with the Marquis de Lafayette? I struck a Napoleonic pose and almost got a smile from Pat.

I staggered upstairs, through a yellow oval chamber — why always ovals? — and onto the Truman Balcony, looking south onto Pennsylvania Avenue and the real world.

When Pat wandered off I tried out the armchairs in every room. Struck attitudes at windows as if weighing the fate of the universe. This wasn't just the White House; people would call it the Nixon White House, a moment in history. No matter how I'd gotten here, I had the chance to make it great. What wouldn't they say about the Nixon White House by the time we were done? Whatever was past, I could still be the man who saved the twentieth century, who saved the world. There was still time.

I came through a doorway and saw Pat again. She never liked to show her real smile; she thought it made a mess of her face, and she used to turn away when she absolutely couldn't help grinning, but I'd see the corner of it and know it was there. But she'd long since taken absolute control over her face, and she knew how to smile the way she wanted to.

But now she was facing away from me. She was standing perfectly erect and hugging a pillow taken from one of the four-poster beds. She might have been happy, just trying to hold herself together and have the moment. Was she so happy she was trying to convince herself it was all real? I doubted it. She looked like someone unutterably weary who had forgotten how to find her way into sleep and was trying to figure it out again.

However, shortly before dawn, there was one final formality to observe. I went to a storage room just two floors below the ground, the lowest place on the White House grounds. A small room, metal shelves with folded towels, linens, table-cloths. Henry was waiting. He had a small table set up.

"It's time, Mr. President."

"I'm here."

"The last ritual. They have sworn you in but we have a little more to do. I apologize for what comes next; there will be some pain." He took off his jacket, rolled up his sleeves.

"What is it we're doing?"

"We weaponize the chief executive, yes? We must begin. You will be missed soon enough."

He arranged several candles on the table and lit them and turned off the overhead light. He spoke rapidly under his breath, intent on his work, punching certain consonants, but I didn't understand any of it. After some minutes he looked back up at me. "You must take off your jacket and shirt, Mr. President."

"What? Why?"

"It is what I need if I am to help you. You must be marked. Your—er, your flesh." He unrolled a cloth bundle containing needles, scalpels, typewritten notes.

"I'm going to get a tattoo?"

"Your back, yes." The candles were making the air uncomfortably warm. "Sit, please."

"Wait, what are you putting on me?"

He showed it to me, a photocopy of a slightly blurred daguerreotype of a man's naked back. The man was lying down, his head not shown. "What you see here is not generally available. It was taken by one of the men who prepared Lincoln's body for burial."

"This is a photograph of . . ."

A version of the presidential seal, covering almost his entire back. The seal, but not. The eagle was primitive, more lizard than bird, the staring eye just a dot, crude wings raised rampant toward strange stars. Tiny stick figures arranged around the periphery. No one, Henry explained, knew who had tattooed Abraham Lincoln.

"It is for the presidency, sir."

I took off my tie, my jacket, my shirt. It was close in the room, and we were neither of us small men. Henry sprinkled dried herbs into a glass ashtray and set them alight.

"You will perhaps wish to close your eyes," Henry said.

Henry chanted again as he worked, first in what I guessed was Old High German, then something harsh and unrecognizable. Through it all his hands moved, swift and cool and sure, and I wondered where he had learned the craft of it. It took maybe half an hour, a burning prickling across my back, my arms, my shoulders.

He sang and I realized I knew the song, my mother's song. And I remembered now what had happened when she sang it. We smelled it on the wind, something like rotten meat, and then we heard it running—fast! Right at the house, right to the eaves, and it stopped. She kept singing, and I think maybe it listened. The next morning footprints circled the house, over and over, then went away toward the reservoir. We kicked dirt over them as the sun came up but I remember how small they were—a child's footprints, or a small woman's.

I never learned what it was, or whether the song kept it away or brought it to us, or why. And did she learn the words in California, or in Ohio, or in another place? I'll never know. A saint, I realized now, but of what dark church?

I came to myself as Kissinger's song grew louder and more rhythmic, punctuated with cries of *"Iä! Iä!"* I opened my eyes for a moment to see Kissinger chanting, his eyes closed, shirt sweated through. After a few minutes he stopped, panting, opened his eyes and focused, and he was Henry again, Harvard political consultant.

"It has worked," he said at last.

He marked my forehead with something cold, then a sudden and frightfully incongruous touch of dry lips between two older men who were past their most attractive years, and it was done.

"We are together in this, you and I," he said. "I gamble on you, and you do likewise. We are friends, yes? Against all of them."

Afterward I examined myself in the long wide mirror of the palatial bathroom upstairs. The markings were runic characters and odd curving geometries. They extended down my arms and up my neck almost to the collar line. I would never dress informally in public again and it was a good thing Pat and I slept apart these days. I craned my neck to see what was on my back. A great circle and that awful rearing figure, face crude as a child's drawing, wings outstretched, eyes to the stars.

I was fifty-eight, sore and bloody; I had been elected vice president and then president. For the first time I felt changed.

The next morning I walked the colonnade that led to the West Wing, not even feeling the January cold. A guard stood at attention and I saw, peripherally, one watchful Secret Service agent hand me off to another. I had, I remembered, a job to do. Maybe the swearing-in hadn't done the trick by itself, but there was still a great deal to explore. Doors that opened only to the sworn president? Hidden messages that appeared only to my eyes? My nerves buzzed with it.

The West Wing is just a bunch of slightly cramped offices, except for the Oval Office itself, which is marvelous. I tried to remember the last time I'd been in there completely alone. Not since the night I'd shot at Eisenhower, maybe. I let myself in, closed the door, and inhaled, smelled the freshly cleaned carpets. I'd be president for four whole years, at the very least. I had time.

I walked around the room, making sure it was all in place. The new desk, the two low couches, the coffee table with the flowers on it. It was all mine. Nobody could kick me out of here. I sat at the desk and surveyed the room where the fate of the world might be decided. Checks and balances, yes, but who was kidding whom? This was where they kept the red phone.

Okay, but there was more to it than that, wasn't there? Shouldn't I have magical powers now? I remembered Eisenhower standing at the desk, standing on this spot, glaring at the little man in front of him. He'd brought his hand down as if tearing away a curtain between us, and it had shredded the world outside. I made the same motion and only disturbed the chilled air of the West Wing.

I looked at the portraits around the room. The presidents who could have told me something were all dead. Truman lived, but they'd never told him. Nor Johnson. Herbert Hoover was six years dead and took his secrets to the grave. Who else? The Supreme Court? I was sworn in by Chief Justice Earl Warren, but he'd given no hint.

I had to admit it to myself: I didn't feel any different. Why should I? The United States of America is logically the least magical place in the world. Planned by committee, not even a country, just a legal umbrella for fifty associated provinces, an elaborate polling system for creating other larger and more permanent committees. No mysteries; no demons; one God at the most.

Sure, it had its own folklore and tall tales, but it wasn't the same. Its rulers weren't descended from men and women who spoke with birds and rode dragons. Johnny Appleseed and Paul Bunyan were hayseeds, folksy also-rans compared to the madness in the ancient royal blood going back to the Druids, to Byzantium, to Mithraic cults. Eisenhower claimed to have spoken with a member of the house of Windsor who'd told him, in confidence, that the royal family had a cordial agreement with an adult kraken whose tentacles spanned tens of miles of open ocean and who had plucked Messerschmitts from the air over the Channel. Where was my damned kraken?

I paced the room, round and around, already getting sick of it. Clock, window, horse statue, desk, dresser, bookshelf, door, bookshelf, fireplace. There was the presidential seal, a pattern of colored carpet fibers I'd walked over a thousand times. What the hell was it? An eagle, wings extended, ringed by fifty stars. It had a shield on its chest, a spray of radiance coming up from behind it. Thirteen clouds, thirteen stars, a scroll that read *E Pluribus Unum,* "from the many, one." In its right claw, an olive branch. In its left, a bundle of thirteen arrows, nastily barbed. Peace on the right, war on the left. Thirteen for the thirteen colonies, I got that. It was still a weird collection of stuff for a bird of prey to be carrying around. What was the lesson here? Why couldn't I read it? What's the matter, Dick? Come on, Tricky Dick. Show us a trick.

I couldn't feel a thing. I got down on my hands and knees.

I prayed to no one in particular. More begging than praying. I thought of Eisenhower's grandiose posturing. Eisenhower spoke Latin. He called lightning; his thunder rattled the White House walls. He folded time, he spoke to the man in the woods in his own language. Eisenhower was born in Texas, raised in Kansas, the real America, not a flat little housing development in Orange County. What was I doing here?

There was a tapping on the door, and I had a moment of panic at being caught in the Oval Office before remembering.

"Come in," I called out, and Kissinger came shuffling in.

"It is only me," he said. "I came to see how you are. Big day, yes?"

"Yes, it is," I said.

"Today we begin! We must locate and destroy this man Gregor, whom I believe to be operating in Southeast Asia. Aggressive measures will be necessary. With your approval, of course."

"Well . . . yes, I suppose, but it's a delicate business. Isn't it?"

"I suggest you do not concern yourself with such matters."

"What matters?"

"Your policy agenda—forgive me, Mr. President, but it does not matter. I will handle such things."

"But I have plans—"

"Mr. President, I need you to do what only you can do. Find these secrets Eisenhower possessed. There is a power here but it lies dormant. It must be found if we are to begin an offensive infrastructure. Little else matters."

"But—"

"The rest of it I will take care of."

"I'm the president, Henry."

"Of course you are," he said. "We will discuss such things at Monday's staff meeting, which I have scheduled. Your secretary will keep you informed."

I thought about the other presidents. It was impossible not to; their portraits and busts frowned and grinned at me from every corner of the place, reminding me that I would never have Eisenhower's broad easy smile or Teddy Roosevelt's boyish violent charm and that I should learn to ride a horse. At times their faces seemed to speak. *You'll never be what I was,* said Washington to all of us. And jug-eared Eisenhower, whose voice I could still hear: *I'll be gone soon, Dick, and only you will remember what we hoped to accomplish.*

I'm sure the American people would like to hear me say I'm sorry I obstructed justice, sanctioned domestic spying and intimidation tactics against my political enemies, bribed and lied and bullied, and was a lousy president. Sad Nixon, confessional Nixon. Sorry.

Do I maintain my innocence? It's complicated. It's a difficult word to use in the face of what I've seen and done, and there are many ways you can be innocent. Of wrongdoing, of bad intention, or of facts about the world.

But whatever happened later, I'll argue before any court there has ever been or will be that I hoped I would be a good president. Even I, even Nixon, daydreamed then about what I'd do now that I'd made it. Eisenhower gave us the golden age of America. Kennedy brought us the New Frontier, a bold era of science and social reform. And then Johnson's Great Society reforms of civil rights and Medicare, which was a messy and expensive and angry business, but it mattered, anyone could see that. What would they call the great wave of Nixonian reforms?

There's a diary entry left over from late on my first night as president that reads (I had time for only a few fragmentary thoughts):

COMPASSIONATE, BOLD, NEW, COURAGEOUS . . . ZEST FOR THE JOB (NOT LONELY BUT AWESOME). GOALS—REORGANIZED GOVT. IDEA MAGNET . . .

MRS. RN — GLAMOUR, DIGNITY . . .

OPEN CHANNELS, FOR DISSENT . . . PROGRESS — PARTICIPATION, TRUST-WORTHY, OPEN-MINDED.

MOST POWERFUL OFFICE. EACH DAY A CHANCE TO DO SOMETHING MEMORABLE FOR SOMEONE. NEED TO BE GOOD TO DO GOOD . . . THE NA-TION MUST BE BETTER IN SPIRIT AT THE END OF TERM. NEED FOR JOY, SERENITY, CONFIDENCE, INSPIRATION.

That's what went into the presidential archives anyway. There were a few extra pages, and I remember writing, *I will discover the secret mystical force locked within the presidential residence and/or West Wing thereof. I will become Eisenhower. Oh God and Jesus, what am I going to do now?* And there were several pages after that, the kind of thing that is, I suppose, why the Oval Office has a working fireplace.

CHAPTER THIRTY-ONE

FEBRUARY 1969

FOR ANYONE INTERESTED in the policy decisions of my first hundred days, or thousand, or the whole two thousand–odd mornings, afternoons, evenings, and regrettable midnights, I refer you to any of the estimable scholarly works on the subject or the public record. It may not surprise you to learn that with the benefit of hindsight, I would do some of it a bit differently.

We were a Republican administration but the Democrats held both the House and Senate against me. I'd gotten a bare plurality, 43.4 percent of votes cast, less than a percentage point over the opposition. I'd lost Texas and New York, and it was a good thing I was born in California. These electoral numbers didn't look like a mandate; in fact, it was on the border of historical accident.

I'd campaigned on the slogan "Bring Us Together" and it already seemed like a bad joke. I checked the Gallup opinion polls almost daily, and on the day I took office there was a substantial bounce: Approve: 59 percent; Disapprove: 5 percent; No Opinion: 35 percent. Then again, people threw beer cans at my inaugural parade. They shrieked and jeered at me and burned pictures of me. The moment I swore that oath I became, basically, a powerless minor god; I was the grinning, capering effigy of everything that was wrong with their lives. I'd be burned at the stake, caricatured, my name uttered as a curse word. They would wear my face.

I sat down at the Wilson desk and, after some agonizing over the mot juste, wrote at the top of the page the heading **ENEMIES**. And then:

Communists. In the years since I'd been out of office the Soviets had replaced Khrushchev with a new general secretary, Brezhnev, who had rolled tanks through Prague six months ago to crush dissent.

Since I'd left office they'd increased their nuclear stockpile tenfold, matched us in ICBMs, greatly outmatched us in conventional forces. In the occult war they'd left us far behind: hybridization, extradimensional capability, exobacterial-weapons payloads, and those were only the ones Henry knew about. We were fighting a proxy war in Southeast Asia and political battles in Chile, Guatemala, Iran, Egypt, Libya, every region in the civilized world. The Soviets were digging in Antarctica.

Gregor. Malevolent and uncontrollable; evidently he changed his face at will and had intervened in a dozen proxy wars that we knew of.

China. A vast unknown. Communist, of course, but they had clashed with the Soviets. But then they were actively supplying the North Vietnamese.

Hippies. Campus radicals, antiwar protesters, beatniks...who were these people? The young men were like exotic bearded foreigners to me. Even Henry had only theories, but he believed they possessed a supernatural potential unknown to us. Harmless children? A malign occultist fifth column for the Soviets? Or something else entirely, a powerful force with no known motive? Well, one known motive: hatred of me. Enemies.

Hollywood. Everyone apart from John Wayne, evidently.

Musicians. Beloved of hippies, q.v.

The Media. The television news ran a continual apocalyptic montage of street violence and rampant inflation. The less said about the *New York Times,* the better.

The Intelligentsia. Whoever they were. Academics? Poets? Unclear.

And then, after a long pause:

Pat. I didn't like to think about it. She did what she needed to in the election but we were nearly strangers. We slept apart, sat apart on the campaign airplane and bus. In private, we barely spoke. But she watched me, and there were even times when I'd found my belongings disturbed as if they'd been searched. Maybe not an enemy. But not a friend. Wife.

And I had no powers. No fucking powers. All that madness outside, and I had four small sections of the Constitution to work with; three, really, given that the fourth was nothing but thirty-one bleak words: "The President, Vice President and all civil Officers of the United States, shall be removed from Office on Impeachment for, and Conviction of, Treason, Bribery, or other high Crimes and Misdemeanors." No help there.

What did I have? Yes, the unauthorized domestic wiretapping, coordinated smear campaigns, secret funds, physical surveillance, obstruction of federal agencies, blood rituals, and flagrant abuses of power, which is to say, the aforementioned Crimes and Misdemeanors. But apart from these, what?

The one thing I could count on? The thing that really might Bring Us Together: In June of that year, on my watch, America was going to change the world, change man's very relationship to the cosmos. It was going to make my presidency unique in all of history.

"Only a few short weeks ago, we shared the glory of man's first sight of the world as God sees it, as a single sphere reflecting light in the darkness," I'd announced in my inaugural address. In March there would be Apollo 9, the next in a planned series that was going to send us to the Earth's satellite. Three men put the lunar module through its paces with exacting care, and everything went perfectly. We were going to the moon. I assumed that this part could not be screwed up too badly. We'd been working on it for nine years now.

Week by week, the scaffolding at Cape Canaveral mounted. By day it steamed in the Florida heat, and in the bloodred moonlight, it shimmered. Altar to the god of prophecy.

If you want to know what it's like to become president, think about one of those horror movies, the kind where a happy family moves into an old house in which terrible crimes have been committed, only no one knows it. There's the first part, where there are home movies of everyone smiling and waving at the camera. People run all over the house and find the rooms they want to stay in. They hug and talk about the future and about how everything's going to be absolutely perfect. Maybe there was some trouble in the past, a secret affair or a failure at a job, but they've left that behind. A new beginning. What could possibly go wrong?

And then, for at least a little while, it really *is* perfect. The shadows of the past have been banished. The husband's new job is working out great. Everybody's happy. So far, so good.

Sooner or later, though, it always happens: the happy, perfect family starts to notice one or two little things, nothing terribly obvious but just a tiny bit odd.

I started a notebook where I kept track of anything out of the ordinary.

Like that the White House was supposed to be a residence but it looked and smelled like a hotel, and a lot of people had lived there but only for a short time. And it's great, and you can call it your home, but you know the staff is always thinking ahead to the next guest, and you know that more than a few people have died here; you're just not sure which rooms it happened in.

Like that the servants in the White House were oddly silent. I watched them move with exaggerated care, as if they were afraid of startling someone. They averted their eyes when I passed them. I wondered what Johnson had told them about me before he left.

Like that the door to the Lincoln Bedroom was stuck fast, and a tiny plaque informed me that it had been closed off for decades. People had been disappearing into the nondescript Victorian bedchamber and not returning ever since the late 1880s. The last man to enter did so in 1922, armed with camping gear, climbing equipment, two pistols, and a month's worth of provisions. Several months later he was heard crying out for assistance in the hallway near a third-floor closet, but when the walls were broken through, there was no trace of him, and then the voice went silent forever.

Like that no one has ever heard of or mentioned a North Wing at the White House.

Anyway, as the movie goes on, the father in the family gets crazier and more obsessive and secretive. But by this time the family is unable to leave the house. Perhaps it's financial, or perhaps it's because leaving will do no good, the strangeness will follow them forever. No matter how compelling the reason to go, they cannot leave.

Late one night I stood on the lawn and watched the house while Secret Service agents eyed me curiously. The mansion sat there, mute and hunched and squat and elephantine in the way its facade distended toward me. An Irish architect named James

Hoban had designed it. Washington ordered it built and supervised its construction but he never lived there.

Was the building itself dangerous? A day's research told me that two presidents and three First Ladies had died there. A son and a daughter, two fathers, and a mother. A press secretary. The kingdom of Hawaii's minister to the United States. Hardly enough for a mass grave, not over a span of a hundred seventy—odd years. No trail of bodies here. Ghost sightings were similarly paltry, given the possibilities. People saw Lincoln's ghost slouching around the place, which felt a little too predictable to me, like a madman claiming to be Napoleon. People saw Lincoln everywhere. It was just a house.

Except for the color, naturally. I remembered Melville's diatribe in *Moby-Dick* on the subject of the color white, how it was part of the peculiarly terrifying quality of the polar bear and the great white shark. I looked up his words: the *vague, nameless horror* of the white whale. He can't get over it. *And yet so mystical and well nigh ineffable was it, that I almost despair of putting it in a comprehensible form. It was the whiteness of the whale that above all things appalled me.*

I understood his feelings. The house was all colors and no color at once, the blind blankness of the End of Days, the white rays of an annihilating sun. They'd built a throneless palace for a country without a king—what other color could they have chosen? I looked up to the sky above the house and to the other grayish-white shape dominating the scene.

And of all these things the Albino whale was the symbol. Wonder ye then at the fiery hunt?

CHAPTER THIRTY-TWO

MARCH 1969

I WAITED TO enter last, just the way Eisenhower used to do. It used to enrage me as a piece of petty one-upmanship but now it seemed the only possible way to play it if you were the president. The opinion polling for the week had just come in: Approve: 62 percent; Disapprove: 10 percent; No Opinion: 27 percent. *Stay on top*, a little voice told me. *Keep them down.*

I came in to find them seated around the broad circular table I had had installed in one of the wide empty chambers below the White House. There's a surprising amount of space down there and after a while you get tired of being disappointed that there isn't a cavernous secret room with a circular table and a giant map with blinking lights on it that you can go to for discussions like this, so I had one built. It's sealed now, silent and cold and forgotten, the access stairway bricked up, my lost architectural legacy. Every president has left his own stamp on the White House. Rutherford B. Hayes installed the first telephone. Chester A. Arthur had Louis Tiffany redecorate the interior, his work now tragically lost. Truman gave us the Truman Balcony; Edith Wilson, the China Room. What I'm remembered for is giving the White House its second bowling alley. Not even the first one—Truman's was first. So I fucked that up too.

They were mostly military types at this meeting. Senators

with an interest in defense and intelligence. Melvin Laird, secretary of defense. William Rogers, secretary of state. Alexander Haig, a four-star general, advising on defense. Hard faces, gray suits, military insignia I'd never learned to read, racks of medals brought to the party. I tried to repress the instinctive helplessness and deference that a civilian feels toward senior people in the armed forces. They all knew, and I knew, that I'd gotten to be their commander in chief by winning a very dubiously certified popularity contest.

But there I was in the center seat. At the last minute, I'd added two cherry-red telephones that might plausibly have been linked to something interesting. In fact, they connected to a number that told the correct time.

"Gentlemen," I said, "I have asked you here so you can receive a briefing by our national security adviser, the distinguished Dr. Kissinger, formerly of Harvard University, the Council on Foreign Relations, and the RAND Corporation." (Translation: The dubious-popularity-contest winner is here to introduce you to his even more dubious friend, who is going to tell you your business.)

Most of the military guys looked frankly bored to be sent back to school at nine a.m. on a Monday. Kissinger stood in the corner like a talent-show competitor waiting to be introduced. He was doing a weird thing with his fingers, touching all the tips together in order, and I wanted to tell him to cut it out.

"Now—now, just a minute," someone said. Senator Kennedy. "Before we get started I'm going to need to talk about Operation Menu, and, yes, I know about it. We've got B Fifty-Twos over Cambodia now? Who authorized this?" There was a rising murmur behind him. He was not the only one here who wanted to talk about this. The bombings in Laos and Cambodia were intended to destroy ammunition supplies, although the fact that there were reports of Gregor's presence in the area was not incidental.

"I want you to understand," I went on, "that Dr. Kissinger has my full confidence in all such matters. Dr. Kissinger will inform you of a national security crisis of which you may not presently be aware. Dr. Kissinger? The floor is yours."

Sensing a challenge, the military men shifted in their seats, square heads swiveling back and forth in confusion, harrumphing into their little microphones.

Henry could not have looked more pleased, there in the center of the room, evidently unaware that my administration's credibility was resting on his wide flabby shoulders.

"Thank you, gentlemen," he said. "I wish to begin by reminding you that this meeting is classified top secret ultra, a new clearance level applying only to the people in this room. Also that there are lawyers at work developing new penalties that will be applied should you ever speak of what I am about to discuss. I trust we understand this? Good, then."

"Mr. Kissinger, really," one of the senators said.

"*Nein*—excuse me—I will ask you to please hold questions for the moment," he said. His singsong accent seemed borrowed from a German burlesque show: hissed sibilants, misplaced emphases, whip-cracked *t*'s and *k*'s. With his voice and his slight stoop, he was like a figure from a fairy tale, a quaint little tinker passing from town to town, peddling his magical wares. The setting seemed to fill itself in behind him: rustic houses and churches leaning in over narrow streets, peaked roofs shadowing the town at all hours. Little Heinz Alfred Kissinger playing barefoot on the cobblestones, collecting firewood, learning Latin and Greek from Papa Kissinger's modest library. One day, perhaps, discovering an old volume carelessly left out, beginning to read the forbidden words, the words to his horrible songs. And then comes National Socialism, and the war, and an American soldier—Eisenhower?—who sees Kissinger's value, and then the long chain of deeds and ambition that brought him here. Was that how it happened?

"You are all familiar with the small trickle of anomalous intelligence that arrives from various fronts of our prolonged global rivalry. Fringe reports that may strike you as impossible or the product of battle fatigue. Accounts of anomalous biological samples. Friendly units destroyed or subverted en masse without explanation. Sickening and dying, perhaps? Wounds of unidentifiable source, without visible origin. Does this sound familiar? You have many of you been in the field yourselves. Seen things that cannot be perhaps explained away so easily." Why was he smiling? No one could tell why he was smiling.

"You will accept it when I offer as plausible that just as the Manhattan Project was developed in secret, so were other equally destructive avenues of research. You all know the Third Reich had its paranormal inquiries, yes? In our country these took place under the rubric of Blue Ox, officially disavowed and forbidden under classified UN agreement of 1946. Yes? No? You do not."

"Mr. Kissinger—" Kennedy again.

"Doctor."

"Doctor, then. I've gotta ask you what this little talk is about. How much of this do you really expect us to believe?"

"I am not speaking on matters of faith, Senator Kennedy. I am here to demonstrate to you that recent shifts in the Soviet high command reflect a heightened commitment to this strategic modality, the deployment of weaponized supernatural forces.

"Our principal opponent, the Soviet Union, has many forms of xeno-, exo-, and cryptobiological ordnance to draw upon. Some that emanate from the distant Precambrian past, and some from the far-distant apocalyptic future. Those that lie sleeping, and those that do not sleep and are ever vigilant."

"Mr. Kissinger!" It was Alexander Haig. "You are asking a great deal of us right now. Most of us are military men. Many of us are scientifically trained."

"It is Dr. Kissinger, please. And I understand, and do bear with me as I come to the point."

"Please do."

"If I may? We display the film now. It is ready, yes?" He nodded, and a waiting projector I hadn't noticed was pushed to the center of the room and threw a small square of color on the far wall.

The image was of a small room with a window looking into another room or cell. An observation area, I realized, with one-way glass through which one could see a small test chamber. On our side of the glass, two young technicians in white shirts and military haircuts looked into the other room.

The test chamber had two occupants. The young man had a cocky, nervous, eager manner, like a star athlete fresh from high school waiting to show the college coaches what he could do, knowing they'd never seen anything like him. He had a couple of electrodes taped to him, wires leading to a small box on a table. An older man stood over him. It was Colonel McAllister.

"You know what we're asking you to do, son?" the colonel said.

"Yes, sir." He nodded crisply.

"You know what Blue Ox is."

"They told me it's some kind of weapons research program, sir. Like the A-bomb? I've got a master's in aeronautical engineering; they said that was a plus."

"Good man. I can see you'll do fine. First thing we do is a little test of your eyesight, okay?"

"Fine, sir, but it's been tested, on day one. I'm twenty-ten; they say you can't do any better."

"That's all right, son, that's real good, but we've got to follow procedure. So you're going to read what's on this paper here." He opened a folder liberally stamped with classified warnings and brought out a single typewritten sheet of paper.

"Kinda funny writing. Is that . . . do I say it '*Yogso*——' "

"Well, Jesus, son, not yet!" The colonel cut him off. For some reason the two techs watching were half out of their seats, but we couldn't hear what they were saying; there was no microphone. "Wait till I give the goddamn word."

"Sorry, sir."

"Just count ten seconds after I shut the door and then start. I'm going to be in the next room, right next door, okay?" the colonel said, backing away. "We'll be watching over the closed circuit. We'll see the whole thing."

None of the text was in English. Standing behind the one-way glass, McAllister and the techs watched the young man read it, slowly and clearly, stumbling over the unfamiliar syllables. In a couple of places the audio cut right out, although his mouth kept moving. The two technicians flinched in unison at a few key passages. During one of those, the glass window rippled a little, as if bowed inward by a change in air pressure. After two minutes the boy finished and lifted his head expectantly.

"That all right?" he said, not sure where to look. The colonel pressed the intercom button.

"That's just fine, son. Real good. We'll be in in a second."

Here there was a rushing sound like a jet engine revving, cutting in and out. The recruit didn't seem to hear, just waited, staring forward curiously. I couldn't see the techs anymore, or the colonel. The camera lurched as someone nudged the tripod.

"Sir—" the recruit said just as an alarm klaxon began far off in the distance. "Sir, what's happening?"

There was a loud bang as something heavy hit the metal door of the test room.

"Sir?" The bang came again. "You locked out, sir?"

The recruit reached for the doorknob but the film skipped, and then, without warning, it was over, leaving only an after-image of its final frame, the door standing open and what was visible on the other side. In the darkness, Henry spoke.

"What you have seen here is film recovered from the Paw-tuxet Farm facility several years after it ceased to become oper-ational."

Henry paused, perhaps waiting for a question that didn't come.

"The Soviet program, which has been in place much longer, has met with considerably more success. We have limited information about their progress but I would like to share with you a few slides. As you know, on March fifteenth, there was an altercation across the Sino-Soviet border at the Ussuri River—"

"We know." Haig spoke now, interrupting, shaking off the mood. "We all have access to the relevant briefing materials. The matter's closed."

"There are a few items I did not think should be shared but which I now present to you," Henry said, grinning as if with-holding intelligence from the Defense Department were a cute idea of his. "These photographs came off one of the KH satel-lites."

There was a pause while a slide projector was set up. He showed us a view of a forested hillside with a road cutting across it, a line of vehicles ascending, and then the same scene appar-ently following a mudslide or fire.

"The effect recorded happened inside a four-hour window during the conflict. The Chinese attributed it to a chemical agent but I have other theories based on firsthand accounts of the event."

The blurry image of a horned humanoid figure against the tree line, the scale disturbingly ambiguous.

"But the important thing is the Soviet division present at the scene, the Thirty-First Army Engineers."

Another slide: a group of men and women standing at attention outdoors while a line of enormous military trucks passed behind them. A May Day parade. The people were notable only for being older and thinner than the typical Soviet paragons on display, more like the graduating class of a doctoral program in medieval history. They stared straight ahead, perhaps twenty of them, assembled behind their unit's banner, which showed a circle with a wobbly five-sided polygon within.

"What is that—is that a constellation?" somebody asked.

"That is correct," Henry said. "A configuration of stars, but a curious one indeed. If you were to wait another million years you might see it in the skies over the Southern Hemisphere. But I do not think you would enjoy the ambience." He chuckled, evidently at a private joke.

One final image. A bearded Caucasian man, shirtless and smiling, posed by a half-track next to two smaller Asian men flourishing AK-47s. The half-track was painted with the same unit insignia. The man was unmistakably the one who'd been shot five times in a shabby little office in Manhattan twenty-one years ago.

"Taken in Laos in the past year. Elements of the Thirty-First are deployed in the Southeast Asian theater, embedded with NVA divisions. I do not—quite—understand their capabilities. They might summon inhuman intelligences, or cooperate with them in some fashion, or perhaps they have been hybridized in that regard."

"Why the hell would the Russians do a thing like that?" Haig said. "Even supposing it's real. This is thin, Dr. Kissinger, awful thin."

"This Cold War involves far more horrific ideas than the nuclear bomb and radioactive fallout, General. It is only what we ourselves wished to do. But without Eisenhower to direct them, our domestic programs failed or destroyed themselves, yes? That is what took place."

"I don't believe it. Any of it. This is bullshit." This was John Mitchell, attorney general.

"John, let him finish," I told him.

"You can't seriously—is this a training exercise? I don't understand how we can be sitting here discussing this."

"To think so is not unusual," Kissinger said. "I quite understand. You do not know the world as I do. You do not picture a time of strange and mighty races that voyaged between the stars, or a tragic war that shattered and changed them and confined them to Earth. You have not seen certain tombs in the sub-Saharan regions, or certain caves in the mountains of Antarctica, or the stars above Grand Carcosa, as I have. I have a limited understanding of such matters myself but—"

"I'm leaving, Mr. President." Mitchell was on his feet now.

"John—"

"Respectfully, I'm not a scientist or a military man but I've heard enough."

"Please keep your seat, Mr. Mitchell," Henry said, but Mitchell was already walking away, and a few others had risen to join him.

Henry barked out a three-syllable word that afterward none

of us could remember and they all stopped, perplexed. He said it again, louder, then raised a hand for silence. And in the silence we began to hear something that sounded like a human voice, a panicked wail or scream that went on and on; we waited for it to take a breath, but it didn't.

"What sort of trick is this?" Haig growled.

"I don't know," I said. "Henry?"

"Let them see, Mr. President," Henry said. "Let them see who waits for them on the other side. Let them consider the strategic implications."

A cold wind blew a spattering of droplets into the room. The wailing sound grew—not as if it were getting louder but as if it were approaching or falling toward us from a direction none of us could see.

About half the people had already risen to their feet and were moving toward the door. There was a shadow being cast in the room now—we couldn't see where it was coming from but it, too, was growing. A big man pulled at the door handle with increasing urgency but it wouldn't open. Somebody in a uniform retched. I stayed in my seat. So did Haig. Kissinger waited calmly in the center of the room. Both of the red telephones began, impossibly, to ring.

"Stop it!" Haig said. Kissinger didn't answer. It didn't seem like the sound could get much closer without its being on top of us. I forced myself not to move.

"Stop it. I'm begging you!" Haig said.

"Stop it, Henry," I said.

The sound and the wind and all of it cut off abruptly.

"The meeting is over," I said. "I hope you will remember this demonstration. I may brief some of you individually beyond this. All I ask of you at this time is to be aware that we are responding to nontraditional strategic exigencies. And that you follow my and Dr. Kissinger's instructions when asked."

They filed out, one by one, until it was just me and Henry, who was bobbing in place and trying to suppress a smile.

"Henry, what the fuck was that?"

"You know? I did not think that it would go half so well," he said.

CHAPTER THIRTY-THREE

JUNE 1969

"**MR. PRESIDENT?**" **GARY** said. Gary was the man Strategic Air Command had assigned to follow me around. We were rehearsing. Since Kennedy's time, the presidency had included unannounced drills to train the chief executive to respond well in the event of a nuclear war.

" 'What is it?' " I said. I was reading from note cards.

"Pinnacle, sir."

" 'How many?' " I said.

"Multiple. A lot, sir. Well into boost phase."

" 'Origin and targets.' Pronto." I liked to throw in a little improv to keep things loose. Gary was more a by-the-book man.

"Forward bases all over the Russian subcontinent, sir. A couple to the UK, the rest over the poles to us. Analysts guess they've emptied the silos. What are your orders, Mr. President?

"Mr. President?

"Mr. President?"

Gary was another part of being president that took some getting used to. He was pale and small and slightly stooped, the way a taller man would be, with a prominent nose. He looked a little like a goblin. He bore the rank of captain but I suspected this was honorary. He didn't look fit for any duty other than this, but he was perfectly suited for his current job; it was as if they had tested a vast pool of candidates for discretion, tact, single-mindedness, patience, and immunity to cold, flu, jet lag, and boredom (and they probably had).

Gary's stoop could be attributed to the forty-five-pound weight he was handcuffed to, the reason why he was required to follow me around at all times. Gary carried what we called the nuclear football. It had no resemblance to a football; the name was the only surviving element of an Eisenhower-era nuclear-response plan called Dropkick, which, given the name, was probably best forgotten.

The nuclear standoff game had changed since Eisenhower's time. ICBMs and submarines were the order of the day as much as bombers equipped with multiple independently targetable reentry vehicles. Rapid-response and defensive technologies were destabilizing the simple logic of mutual assured destruction.

Therefore, Gary was literally not allowed to be more than thirty feet away from me. Most of his time was spent posted in the corridor outside the Oval Office or sharing the backseat of a limousine with myself, Pat, and Al Haig. Only a few months into his assignment, Gary had already seen a broad cross section of Nixonian life: Gastrointestinal episodes following lengthy fund-raising dinners. Frozen, silent car rides with Pat. Unresponsive teenage children. Furious arguments with Pat. Self-administered pep talks in bathrooms, greenrooms, helicopters. Restrained, dignified weeping. Gary and I were not friends.

When the war went hot Gary would be the person to tell me there was a problem. Presumably a bad problem. The nature of this problem would be explained to me carefully and clearly, insofar as anyone understood it.

Gary himself would be passing on information from a creaky,

semifunctional network of satellites called MiDAS, satellites that sat 22,326 miles over the equator. They used infrared to scan for the characteristic pattern of heat emitted by intercontinental ballistic missiles when they did their initial launch burn over the poles. Or so I was told by the RAND Corporation. This innovation would give us a full twenty-seven minutes to react to the news that most of the U.S. population was about to die in a nuclear fire. (Henry was working on something new, called Safeguard, that relied chiefly on the contents of a blunt concrete pyramid in North Dakota, the details of which he refused to disclose.)

It was common knowledge that the nuclear football contained a bulky, secure radiotelephone and a booklet with the various go codes that would activate America's nuclear arsenal. Also an illustrated escape plan that got me to the emergency command center, a bunker equipped with hardened communication lines and a staff of relieved but stricken-looking men and women already in the throes of shared survivors' guilt. These were the people with whom I could expect to spend either the next forty-eight hours or the next seventy years, depending. In the latter case, we would, incidentally, also be expected to repopulate the blank martyred planet Earth. There was also a mobile consolidated command center on monstrous tractor tires and an E-4B airborne operations center that would take off for an aerial view of the apocalypse.

Finally, the football contained the single integrated operational plan, the SIOP, the concentrated, distilled result of decades of strategic thinking. The twenty-seven minutes wasn't enough for me to decide where to send thousands of nuclear warheads; instead, I would choose from a list of prepared contingency plans, depending on whether this was a limited strike, an all-out nuclear launch, or a conventional attack large enough to merit a thermonuclear reply. All expressed through coded shorthand. Birds in the Air, for instance, translated to "Multiple incoming warheads from over the North Pole, evidently the product of a bold, enthusiastic new talent in the Kremlin's planning committee."

In most of these scenarios, life on Earth would change radically in the subsequent hours. Millions would die, perhaps billions, depending on my moral calculations or my particular mood. The SIOP was a sort of à la carte doomsday menu.

What was on the menu? We got one good whack at them, and there were set priorities of what to hit. Easiest call: Probably we should take out their nuclear capabilities—missile silos, bombers on the ground, submarine bays; men, machines, supply caches would vanish in a flash and a boom over the horizon. Or, item number two, we could get a little more daring, target the isolated air defenses and conventional forces they had off in the mountains and wheat fields of Soviet Russia. Third, for a more robust flavor, we could include the targets nearer civilian population centers. Fourth on the priority list were Soviet command elements, if I wanted to make it personal.

And number five was simply the fuck-you zone of black humor and megadeath, civilization-busting scenarios that even classified SAC memos described as "spasm or insensate war." Twenty-eight hundred world-class cities pretargeted for your pleasure; Europe, Russia, Asia, and the Middle East fully in play. This was the time to consider spraying Romania merely on the off chance something was there or taking out West German cities to keep the industrial base out of Russian hands. Pop quiz, hotshot. Oh, and extra credit if China's involved.

Since his successful demonstration to the military leadership Dr. Kissinger had made it his business to extensively revise and expand the number of possible contingencies.

New codes included Surf-and-Turf Frisco-Style, which meant "Multiple unidentified infantry divisions emerge from the surf north of San Francisco, humanoids threading through the redwoods and engaging local defenses." KC Shake-and-Bake was "Chthonic entity erupting onto major American city, toxic and/or mind-control emanations in evidence, accompanying soul desecration on massive scale."

The nuclear football now also contained waterproof matches, the skull of a tiny hominid, a small woodwind instrument, a scroll written in imperial Aramaic. A needle and thread, a packet of salt. Two cyanide pills, one for me and one for Pat (unless Gary wanted to partake). A chip of granite from the capstone of a sub-Saharan tomb at least thirty thousand years old. An alleged piece of the True Cross (won't know until we try it). Envelopes not unlike the ones I'd seen Arkady and Gregor shuffling long ago.

Last, a third-generation Xerox of a single typewritten page watermarked with EYES-ONLY—BLUE OX CLEARANCE.

Not all military elements will be vulnerable to nuclear weaponry or associated effects such as radioactivity, kinetic shock, and firestorms. Potentially nuclear-resistant entities, domestic and foreign, should be accounted for in any postconflict planning scenarios.

These include:

(a) Corn Men

(b) Entity code Raven Mother and attendant fragments/hybrids

(c) Exofauna of Baikonur region

(d) GRU command elements above the rank of colonel, who are reputed to be experimentally radiation-hardened by hybridization, grafting, and injection with tissue samples from various archaic and exoplanar fauna

    (e) Vladimir Ilyich Lenin

    (f) Unidentified Dyatlov Pass survivor

    (g) The British royal family

    (h) Little Hare, a Native American trickster god of the Southwestern United States

Of course, it wasn't all about me. The nuclear football was just the origin point of a long chain reaction, rippling out to bunkers and hangars and submarines and ending in sealed envelopes torn, codes checked, combinations dialed. Small groups of two, three, and four men exchanging glances, turning their keys in unison. And at the far end of the chain, ignition and blastoff.

Or maybe it was about me, the president, the piece of equipment I understood least of all. The exact same person who, sixty years ago, had stayed awake for hours after bedtime, pretending to read until I couldn't keep my eyes open, letting the desert moon shine on me until I fell asleep to silvery, light-drenched dreams. It was all part of me, faint mysterious memories that at times still surfaced of the low, garbled songs that floated up to me and the faint answer that echoed out of the lemon groves. The faces of my vanished brothers. The mysteries of what my mother saw as she stared out into the darkness from our front porch long after midnight, of why she had married at all, of why lying was as natural as breathing to her, and to me. Or why Gary and I weren't friends, but we weren't.

CHAPTER THIRTY-FOUR

JULY 1969

WE WERE PULLING troops out of Vietnam; everything was about airpower now. Five months into my first term as president and we seemed to be building momentum.

The day of the Apollo 11 launch was drawing near and I waited for a portent or a warning or any information to explain the sense of foreboding hanging over this, arguably humanity's greatest and most daring exploit. Earlier, I had toured the launch facilities, making a show of marveling at the manned missile looming and puffing smoke.

A week after that, I hosted one of the chief scientists at the White House. He was an older man but trim and polite. He wore a brown coat and kept a small, neat mustache. He peered around the Oval Office with its seal and flags. I couldn't help but think he must have been in rooms like it in Berlin before the fall, so perhaps he was not all that impressed.

"Thank you for seeing me, Mr. President. It is an honor."

His English was excellent.

"Thank you for your efforts in these historic times," I said. I tried not to think about the last world leader who'd handed him that line. "You had a concern about the Apollo mission?"

"I do not know to whom I can speak and who not, you understand?"

"It's just me and Haldeman here."

"As you say, Herr Nixon. When we were—in the other place—we spoke often of this work, to go to moon. Von Braun, he always wished to do this, and with the success he brought us, he was not argued with. Of course, it never came to be."

"Not until now."

"That is right, and even here for a long time I do not think it likely. I do the work, of course; in my position I have little choice. But now the time is perhaps here and I wish to say perhaps we should not go. Perhaps it is best not."

"We're not canceling the Apollo project." That morning my approval rating was 58 percent; disapproval was 22 percent, and those with no opinion, 20 percent. Eisenhower had done better even after having a heart attack and a stroke.

"I know. Such a coup for our people, for any nation, to be first on that strange far shore. And it is my life's work, yes. Please do not repeat what I tell you now. In the other place—"

"The Third Reich, you mean," snapped Haldeman.

"Yes. In the Reich, the Nazis cultivated all sorts of people. Scientists like myself, but also mystics and so-called philosophers, men without degrees, confidence men and frauds, to say it plainly. Anyone could enrapture the party officials with tales of dwarfs and Rheingold and a fabled age to come. They were given offices and budgets equal to our own.

"There was one, though. A professor of anthropology who'd been disgraced and then joined the party. He showed great interest in our work. He had, he told me, translated a great many writings of a mystic sect from the fourteenth century. He spoke of lunar travel as if it were a settled thing. He showed me maps of the dark area. He laughed at us.

"Of course I do not pay him any mind. But I spoke with the men of Apollo Eight when they returned. We have seen the Earth rise above it. We have seen it now, this dark side." It was true. That same month, Julie had married David Eisenhower, and there was already talk from Henry of a dynasty such as had not been seen since the pharaohs.

"Then surely——" I said.

"His maps, I still have them. Kept for a joke. But they are too good. Much too good. The strange appearance, the land formations, all too similar. It is as if they had——"

"Coincidence," I told him.

"But I wonder what we find there. What we send these men to."

"It's just rock. Surely you know that much better than I do. A dead world."

"Yes, we know things. Gray rocks and fine dust. Perhaps deep down we discover ice; that is all. I know. But this moon——it becomes more curious as we look at it. We see it there, so large in proportion to our planet, as in no other pairing we know. Its own world. Not a mere asteroid, as the ones circling Mars.

"We do not know its age. It stood in the sky over America's dawn, over the streets of Nero's Rome, over Babylon, Carcosa, the Black Forest of my ancestors, over cities whose names are lost. Over tribesmen who scarcely spoke, over the glaciers, over the great lizards before them. Before that, over the blank seas that teemed with forms of life we do not dream of. It has lain so close to us for so long, yet it is a stranger to us. It hides its face!"

"Have you spoken to this professor lately?"

"When the Allies came he was one of those who cut their own throats rather than continue. It seems as if he was sincere after all."

I was tired of searching the Oval Office but I had no other ideas. Kissinger warned of a major supernatural insurgency on its way, a power play of unprecedented proportions intended for mid-August.

So I took pictures down and gazed at the blank spaces, tapped on walls and floors. Stared into space; wrote in my journal. One day, a lazy warm afternoon, I'd felt absolutely certain I had gotten somewhere, located the final piece of the puzzle. I found myself in an unfamiliar suite on the third floor, opening door after door where there shouldn't have been any. I covered dozens of yards, so much distance that surely I should have been walking across the North Lawn and straight through the fountain to Pennsylvania Avenue. And then, impossibly, I heard Eisenhower's voice from the next room. Eisenhower, who'd died in March not knowing me, barked his military laugh and recited his familiar warning: "In the councils of government, we must guard against the acquisition of unwarranted influence, whether sought or unsought, by the Military. Industrial. Complex." His voice went on, growing louder and louder, until I came awake at an executive staff meeting. It was unclear whether anyone had noticed.

In May, the tenth Apollo mission had flown only nine miles from the lunar surface. I had had the astronauts sworn to secrecy and debriefed exhaustively. Nothing stirred there. A dead world, surely. We'd prepared for so long. And on July 16, 1969, we would go to the moon.

"We are going to the moon," I'd told everyone. "Kennedy said so, Johnson said so. I said it myself about a hundred times. America is going to the moon, and that's that."

Now we stared at the television, at an image of the Apollo 11 steaming and puffing on the pad.

"It is most likely a mistake. A trick of some kind," Kissinger said. "But I admit I do not understand its nature."

"How can the moon possibly be a trick?" I asked. "And why is this coming up only now? Is that going to be my opening move? Canceling the moon shot?"

"I think they plan this. I feel certain of it. Goad him from the start," Kissinger said. And I began suddenly to feel ill. Had Arkady said something about this? I was drinking a lot in those days.

"Why would they want us to go to the moon? The entire world is watching us. It's our moment of triumph. We do this, it's almost like we're going to another planet. We are the interplanetary world power."

"The moon . . ." Kissinger said, staring into space. "What is it? What's on it?"

"It's—well, it's a big dusty rock, basically. Isn't it? Doesn't have an atmosphere. Doesn't have water. So, dust. Craters."

"Craters, yes. I think I begin to see. Things flying through space. They hit the Earth, they burn up. But the moon, not so much. Things hit the moon, they stay there."

"They'd hit it pretty hard," I said.

"There are very tough things out there. Spores, they survive the vacuum of space. Every crater on the moon, something landed. What if something did survive? What if any number of things did?"

"But we're still protected . . . aren't we?"

"A great deal about this war depends on legal ambiguities, yes? Treaties, thrones, and dominions. Every place on Earth there is some kind of legal agreement. Even Antarctica, where no country is. But who rules the moon?"

I pressed the intercom.

"Rose? John Mitchell, please."

"I'll get him."

In a few moments, Mitchell answered his phone.

"Mitchell, who's got the moon? I mean, legally, what is it? Is it a country? Is it like international waters? Is there a legal category of unclaimed planetoid?"

"Sir. There is at present no legal treaty covering the moon."

"Thank you."

Kissinger looked a bit distant. "Sir, I believe this represents a serious problem."

"We're at eight thousand feet above lunar surface. Seven thousand. Six thousand. We are descending as per projections, velocity as expected."

"Roger that," came the voice from Houston's Mission Control. Kissinger and I sat listening.

"Open the private channel," I said.

"Mr. President?" I heard Buzz Aldrin say.

"I need your report, Buzz."

"Everything looks clear from this altitude. We are descending normally."

And then: "I see—but this is impossible—it appears to be a sort of a . . . well, a rock formation of regular outline."

"Mr. Aldrin, is it possible to halt your descent?"

"I am relaying. I'm not sure. It's becoming clearer. A ziggurat, I believe. Monolithic white stone. There are figures carved. Now coming into view—"

"Apollo," Mission Control broke in, "I believe your descent has slowed?"

"Executive order, sir. I'm seeing a city now. A vast city. Carvings visible from above. This is not possible. It is enormous. Castles carved into the crater wall, eternally in shadow. Armstrong, are you all right? He's having a fit of some kind."

"Go on, Aldrin."

"Five-sided symmetries, geometry—I can only call it obscene. Armstrong is speaking now . . . a language I don't recognize."

Kissinger took the phone's receiver from my nerveless hand.

"Mission Control? We will move to the Maya contingency, yes? Confirm, please."

"...Confirmed, Dr. Kissinger."

The crew manning the soundstage was extraordinarily skillful, and the production was extremely convincing, and if in moments the wires were visible, this was almost never spoken of. The astronauts, on their return, performed a very creditable show of triumph and euphoria. Dr. Kissinger spoke to them privately and the matter was not touched upon again.

CHAPTER THIRTY-FIVE

NOVEMBER 1969

PEOPLE WERE LIGHTING fires on campuses, fighting with police. Abroad, we were bombing Cambodia, and we'd gone public about it. It was the kind of thing that is frankly horrible to remember. Quite simply, a rigged popularity contest had made me undeniably responsible for incomprehensible violence.

"We are doing perfectly well in the polls, Mr. President," Henry said. And we were. I had a 67 percent approval rating, the highest I would ever see. Henry had earlier come up with a new formulation, the silent majority, a purportedly massive demographic that dared not speak its name, the counterweight to the vaunted counterculture. Whether these people existed or not, they were my base.

"Have you read what they print about us? In the *New York Times?*" I asked.

"I saw that there were quite a few letters in support of you."

"Don't you know I had those written?" I said. "I paid for them. Hundreds of them. We've got to walk this back somehow. Apologize. Say something."

"On the contrary. If we are to apprehend Gregor, sterner measures will be needed. The proposal we spoke of for a nuclear airburst over North Vietnam. It will take a demonstration of force to convince them."

"A lot of these things I don't object to, but really. Give this one up, would you?"

"I have explained the madman theory, Mr. President, it is your only card to play. As long as you are a rational actor, they will not fear you, but once they believe you are capable of anything, that changes. The minds that inhabit the Kremlin, well—at present, there is what I might call a 'madness gap.' Only give the word. Not even. Nod your head, and you'll be the president they talk about in a thousand years."

"Henry. It's been coming for some time now. I know our partnership has been an important one in both our lives but—"

"Mr. President—"

"I mean it, Henry. I'm asking for your resignation."

"I gave up a great deal to place you in this position, Mr. President. More than you can ever know," he said. "I am owed, you understand?" He had reddened slightly.

"Henry, I'm sorry. It's my decision."

"Mr. President, this is irresponsible. You are not prepared to lead in the world where the Soviets—"

There was a knock, and Pat poked her head in. "We're late, Dick."

"Just a minute, Mrs. Nixon," Henry said, and turned back to me. "I ask that before you do this, you meet me tomorrow at the Pentagon. I wish to show you something important. After that, you may do as you like. And I will tell Gregor he may have you."

He left, brushing past Pat.

"What's the matter with him?" she said.

"Nothing."

"Who's Gregor?"

"I have absolutely no idea," I said.

*   *   *

The next day, a page led me through the security labyrinth to a meeting room inside the Pentagon complex where Henry waited, smoking, with his world-weary but faintly impish demeanor intact.

"Mr. President, I wish to make plain how the chain of command will operate in time of emergency so that you will understand your role. If you will please follow me."

We walked. The section we were in didn't seem to see much use. The fluorescent lights overhead were dim and set at wide intervals, so that as we reached the midpoint between two of them, we walked for a moment in darkness.

He seemed to know his way perfectly. I glanced into one of the offices we passed but there was no one inside. The furniture was stacked in a corner. We kept going, and it seemed that none of the offices in this wing were in use, and perhaps never had been.

"The Pentagon contains seventeen miles of corridor," he said. "Did you know this?"

"Yes, Henry."

"Of course, that is only aboveground."

I glimpsed, far off down a side avenue, a man piloting a floor polisher. I wanted to call out to him, maybe just for reassurance, to get a friendly wave. We kept walking and he was lost in the dark behind us. Henry led me through a fire door and into a stairwell lit by bare bulbs.

"The upper levels were completed in the latter phase of the Second World War, but construction has continued on and off."

I peered down over the railing and saw the utility stairway spiraling down into darkness. He led the way, one flight after another of identical concrete steps and landings, each with an unmarked metal door. It was getting colder. Henry kept talking as we went.

"A much larger structure was initially planned. The original architects had some very interesting ideas."

From far off, I heard a man reciting a long list—names? numbers? towns?—and it seemed I was just about to understand the words when Dr. Kissinger stopped at the fourth landing and turned into a corridor identical to the ones above.

At the end of the corridor we reached a door that looked just like all the rest. Henry opened it and the sound leaped out at us and I saw an enormous room where dozens of men and women were at work at rows of terminals; on the wall in front of them was a map of the world. A few of them jumped to their feet but Henry gestured them down again.

"Where are we?"

"This is called the Deep Underground Command Center. You have seen the plans, yes?"

"Yes, but . . . the funding wasn't there."

"Really, Mr. President. Have we ever run short of money on this end of things?"

"I guess not."

"The funding was reinstated, simply from an unrecorded source. I see that it is maintained."

The room stretched on for at least a quarter mile, dozens of military personnel. I glanced at the man at the closest terminal and realized his skin looked odd, an unhealthy gray. His eyes bulged. I wondered how long he had been down there. How long since any of them had seen the sun. What had Henry done?

We walked farther on.

"Do you know how it is done, the nuclear attack and response?"

"In theory."

"It is most interesting to observe. It is beginning now. Sighting, I think, over Nova Scotia."

A lone little light went on at the far top right of the great map. A man in a headset perked up.

"Contact, sir."

"What have we got?" Henry asked him.

"Nothing on the schedule. Not one of ours."

Several more lights appeared.

"Multiple contacts, sir. This is way outside the norm. We're locking down."

"Is this a drill, sir?" another man asked. He looked nervously to Henry and then to me.

"What is it? A demonstration," Henry told him. Now the big board had dozens of contact lights, slow-burning pinpoints falling down across the pole. Henry waved his arms as if conducting an orchestra. "We can extrapolate a targeting pattern here. At this point it's military targets only, but right there at the edge? Just the hint of a second wave and I bet it's major-metropolitan-area stuff. I wonder what can have set them off."

"Do you give the go-ahead, Mr. President?"

"What?"

"The launch code. We must retaliate."

"I—I don't know." I had always known that in the clutch, I'd fumble this. I hadn't learned my lines.

"The president wishes to go ahead," Henry told the room. "Comprehensive scenario, you understand? We empty the silos. We need their command elements down. Transport, runways. No way to knock out the submarines, I'm afraid."

There was a hush, then they bent to their work, reciting code phrases, thwacking and chunking heavy plastic switches into place.

"It is working. Men are picking up the phone now. Two men

under the Nebraska plains are receiving instructions right now. Glancing at each other shyly, seriously. Going to their code-books. They will target Kiev. Men in a submarine in the North Atlantic, en route to Bangor, have stopped. They listen, then gather briefly in prayer. Twenty-seven thousand five hundred and fifty-two warheads in all. Like Samson in his blind despairing rage, we take this temple down.

"We will need an attack profile, yes? Something forceful yet nuanced. Proportional. Civilian targets with industrial value must be considered, I'm afraid."

Here and there in the background, staticky communication chatter cut in and out, urgent voices exchanging codes and countercodes. Somewhere a young man cried until his channel was silenced.

"There's a high-pressure system this week; the winds are blowing west but it's a blessing in disguise, at least they'll be sending their infantry into West Germany's irradiated sectors as they come toward us. I shouldn't worry for ourselves. This facility is well shielded and well supplied. We may dwell here for years to come in safety.

"SAC B Fifty-Twos are already en route to target, awaiting final confirmation. If we go dark they'll assume we've been hit and carry out their last instructions. This is the end of the world, Mr. President, at least as far as your species knows it. As for whatever else might rise in the nuclear winter ahead . . . it is not for me to say. There's a kind of relief in it, isn't there? Knowing it's all decided." Henry's words had a hypnotic spell on the room.

"Tell them to stop, Henry," I said.

"I will not," he said softly.

I felt weightless and numb. A cadaverous MP stood staring up at the world map, and I snatched the pistol from his belt and pointed it at Kissinger's forehead.

"Please, Henry," I said.

Across the chamber two military police aimed their rifles at me.

"Put your guns down, gentlemen," Henry said. "No one will be harmed here."

"Yes, sir." The two men lowered their weapons. I kept mine pointed at Henry's forehead. He took a step closer to me.

"Tell them to stop," I said. "You're destroying the world. You've made your point."

"You, Mr. President, may continue," he said. "Pull the trigger. Satisfy your curiosity, if you wish to see the result of shooting me. You will not be the first."

I lowered the gun.

At that moment, the lights on the massive screen vanished. A half dozen separate, musically discordant electronic tones ceased to sound. The room collectively exhaled. Henry smiled. He beamed.

"What about that, Mr. President? It seems to have been a false alarm after all," he said. "A glitch in the system. Makes you think, doesn't it? About how precious it all is, this little blue marble."

I looked again at the men and women at the machines and knew, finally, what they were. The pale skin, the livid fingernails, the stiffened moves. Not rotting but somehow preserved. Dwellers in the underworld, acolytes of the final god. The dead-hand system, I saw. The true silent majority.

"We ascend now," Henry said. "We may take the elevator this time." He gestured toward a set of brushed-steel doors. They closed behind us and we stood there, side by side.

"You're insane," I said.

"Not at all. I am only a minor sorcerer," he said after a moment. "Barely one thousand years old, but I am well able to access the Strategic Air Command's conventional command-and-control protocols. Is that understood?"

"Crazy."

"The aftermath of a thermonuclear exchange would be an uncomfortable time for me, but not a decisive one. And there are many things alive today that would welcome such a development."

I had the pistol fired before I could think, twice, into where I hoped the kidneys were. The air in the tiny elevator was acid with the smell of gunpowder and a sickly-sweet dust and tiny floating bits of tweed from Henry's jacket.

Henry shuddered slightly but that was all. He turned slowly toward me, his face close to mine. It seemed unnaturally large, like a grotesque idol's.

"The year 1976 will be the final one of the American Republic," he whispered. "Cut free from the Twenty-Second Amendment, you will be an immortal mage-president. Able to crush the rebel cult of the Supreme Court implanted by rogue initiate founders. You will subjugate the massed power of the four legislative bodies—House, Senate, Gestalt, and Hovering. You will sit on a white throne in a white house for all eternity, ruling the two hundred and forty-eight states of the Final Union. *E pluribus* Nixon, *eternum.*"

The elevator doors opened and he left, still trailing threads and dust, and lost himself in the empty halls of the Pentagon.

CHAPTER THIRTY-SIX

MAY 1970

BY THEN, ALL the headlines could talk about was the Nixon administration. Secretive, unpopular, indifferent to the will of the nation. Approval stood at 57 percent, disapproval at 32 percent, those with no opinion at 11 percent.

I suppose that's what it looked like. On the inside, I was trapped in the belly of an enormous beast, a conspiracy that had swallowed me up like a foolish boy in a fairy tale, the kind of story they tell kids to keep them from making stupid mistakes. I was the boy who followed the pretty lights too deep into the forest, never thinking about the path and the setting sun, and now I was in the dark and I had met the beast. *If you do not do as I say I shall come and eat you up.* Another boy would have known what to do, had a trick, a lucky pebble, a magic sword.

Yes, Mr. Beast, anything you like, said Dick Nixon, and oh, how I wish I could claim it wasn't me, that I never said it, but I had. I'd said yes and been eaten up just the same.

Where could I turn? Eisenhower always said Chief Justice Earl Warren was surely the wisest owl in the whole operation. He was Eisenhower's generation. Governor of California, vice presidential nominee, and now he wore the black robes. He had administered the oath of office to four presidents—Ike for his second term, then Kennedy, Johnson, and me. He'd looked each one in the eye and made him president.

Eisenhower had told me once about the justices' secretive order. How they danced and laughed and chanted by night and lights shone from the windows of the high court, but those who intruded found nothing but silence and dark corridors, and they would not have good luck thereafter. The judges served for life and told their secrets to no one and weren't to be called on except in times of direst necessity.

I set out for the Supreme Court building in full state; it was all of a mile and a half but I took a motorcade and a police escort. Surely they couldn't ignore the chief executive? The driver stopped in front of an empty lot. I rapped on the window separating us but he only shrugged as a Secret Service man opened the door.

I stepped out of the car. This was where the building should have been. I'd passed it a hundred times. But the pavement was cracked, the stones shattered and askew. The familiar set of broad steps led upward but it was all wrong; they were smooth and overgrown as if lost for a thousand years, a relic of an empire long gone. The monumental statues were worn down to faceless nubs and beyond those, the weathered stumps of eight pillars. The rest was gone as if swept away by a ruinous cataclysm centuries ago. Overhead, the midday sun looked orange and weak and uncomfortably large. Beyond, the city of the present day continued. Only I seemed to see all this.

I stood on the pavement while a crowd gathered and curious press snapped photos. Someone shouted questions.

"It has begun," Henry later told me. "The great separation of powers is at hand, and the court cannot see you directly, nor you them. The chief justice is a wily old barrister, and what you saw is a day that will come long after your time, when the sun fails at last, and the nation's capital will move to quite foreign shores indeed. But perhaps I shall live to see it after all."

*   *   *

On May 4, National Guardsmen fired live ammunition at student protesters, killing four and wounding nine. A crowd was already gathering at the Lincoln Memorial, and I found Kissinger waiting in my office.

"Do not speak of it," he said. "There is more happening than you can possibly understand. They're going to kill us if they can; better for us to see to them first."

"Who?"

"Rival magicians, perhaps. There have always been such, hiding deep in the unreclaimed South and the forests of Maine. I hunt them. They know the executive is growing stronger and they make common cause," he muttered. "They showed their hand at Woodstock. I believe they wish to destroy us."

This had gone far enough. Only an idiot would deceive himself about the presidency; I was the chief executive of a huge organization, the federal government, and parts of it killed. But this? If there was a line I would not cross, this might as well be it. Action must be taken. I held an impromptu screening of *Patton* and drank a considerable amount of whiskey.

Later that night I called Kissinger. There was no answer so I dialed the number a few dozen more times. But no, Kissinger was not the man to save me here. I called my valet Manolo at four thirty in the morning. "Have you ever been to the Lincoln Memorial at night? Get your clothes on, we'll go!"

I set out through the French windows onto the lawn, dew soaking my slippers.

I heard someone shout, "Searchlight is on the lawn."

"Where's my car?" I called to the Secret Service man who was sprinting along the colonnade in search of his superior. I moved as fast as I could, knowing Kissinger would try to catch me before I could break free. Knowing I'd be too afraid to move if I stopped to think.

"Where's my car!"

I heard the lawyer Krogh, one of Ehrlichman's people, stage-whisper to somebody in the war room, "My God! Searchlight has asked for a car."

"Searchlight wants a car!"

An intern was working late, or maybe early, a moonfaced undergraduate, prematurely balding. I recognized him and leaned through his doorway. "Do you have a car?"

"Yes, sir!"

"Then let's head to the parking lot. What's your name?"

His name was Lionel.

Gary found me somewhere along the way—I had to respect that he'd taken the football in preference to finding his shoes. We all crammed into the backseat of Lionel's VW. It took him two or three tries to get the car started. He was succumbing to the civilian nervousness that follows me around, the starstruck paralysis of people shoved onto a historic stage. But he managed, and we were off.

The sun was coming up when the four of us reached the steps below the Lincoln Memorial, the giant stone body staring from its plinth, one square-toed shoe projecting off the edge. There was a small camp of college students wrapped in blankets, a few of them awake, singing an indistinct melody.

These, then, were the ones Henry feared, the notional white witches.

"Hey! Help me..." I called out. "You have to help me." In the half-light I could have been anybody in a suit, a businessman coming off an all-night bender. Not a man walking into the teeth of the enemy.

"What's wrong, man?" a bearded kid with a kind voice called out. "You okay?"

"I need to talk to you. All of you."

"Sure, man, sure. It's a safe space. What's going on, man?" A couple of others roused themselves as I edged into the circle. Kids born in the 1950s, I realized. When half my life was over.

"But—it's me," I said. "It's Dick. Dick Nixon. The president."

The kids laughed. Did they think I was doing impressions? Then a blonde in a velvet cape narrowed her eyes at me. "I think it's really him." That got them. Two of them leaped to their feet, arms halfway lifted in an awkward movement that suggested an obscure martial art or sorcerous intent.

"Wait! I have to talk to you. I have to explain."

"What do you want here?" the girl said. Long blond hair and a tired face, but angry.

"What about Kent State, man?" someone behind me asked to shouts of agreement. People were shaking the sleepers awake now.

"I didn't know," I said. "I didn't want any of this. I never knew—" I'd expected them to be overawed but they were already shouting me down. My crowd sense was long out of date.

"There's no time! Do any of you know about black magic? I need your help." The angry voices stopped. I had finally managed to surprise them. "You can tell me. I need to know. I need to know right now!" I heard the hiss of a walkie-talkie. Men in black suits were advancing up the Mall at a stiff walk.

"Hey, chill out," the bearded kid said. He put a hand on my arm and then whispered in a voice too low for anyone else to hear, "We know who you are. Who you *really* are, dig? Who your mother was. We have our own agent in place. Peace, man."

"Oh, thank God. Thank God. You can't tell them I said this.

Nothing, all right? Tell them we talked about football. Sports. Lie to them. Just do that much." It was full daylight by then and the men in suits had reached the lowest steps and all at once I felt how tired I was. I was still drunk. I lunged at the student nearest me and seized his hands in mine. I thought, *This might be the last time I speak to a stranger free and unchaperoned.*

In the next day's papers it said I'd met with a student delegation that morning. They said I'd talked about football.

The next morning I told Rose to mark the schedule with five hours of staff time and to let absolutely no one in. There was no one waiting to tell me my own secrets. If there was a power in America, I was going to find it myself. Taft wasn't smarter than I was. Eisenhower wasn't. If I could do just the smallest bit of magic, a gust of wind, a spark, anything, I could follow that thread. The power was everywhere around me. It was merely a matter of rituals and forms, and I needed to stumble across only the tiniest piece of it to start figuring it out.

I began by reading the Constitution aloud, syllable for syllable, 7,591 words, including the amendments. I waited to see if it had any sort of effect. Then I read it aloud backward. I did the same for the Declaration of Independence. I poured a small whiskey, neat, and began on the Articles of Confederation.

I repeated the oath of office and said the Pledge of Allegiance. Magic wasn't about dignity, I decided. I sang "The Star-Spangled Banner." I sang "God Bless America" and "My Country, 'Tis of Thee," which has eight verses and is not an enchanting melody, but a small drink between verses improves it. The sun was low in the sky. "Yankee Doodle" has fifteen whole verses and it didn't do a damned thing.

"Dick?" It was Pat, standing in the doorway from the residence. How long had she been there?

"Hello, Pat."

"What are you doing?"

"I wasn't doing anything."

"You were singing."

"I was providing leadership to the free world, which is the thing I do in here every day. Which is why you should knock before coming in."

"I did knock. Someone—apparently not you—was singing 'Yankee Doodle' too loudly to hear me. Have you been drinking? I'm also wondering why you're wearing that flag as a cape." That I had put on around the tenth verse, a matter of thoroughness.

"Everything about this situation is classified."

"I think we need to have a talk."

"You know I'm busy, Pat."

"I heard about the students. It's terrible, and I don't think it's your fault. I just want you to tell me if you're all right."

"Am I all right?" I said.

"Just tell me that."

I could tell her, but she'd ask why.

"I'm the president," I said. "It's all we ever wanted. Don't ask me that again."

CHAPTER THIRTY-SEVEN

OCTOBER 1970

I'D GONE TO San Jose to yell in the faces of maybe two thousand protesters. Haldeman had told me to goad them, but I didn't need prompting. They were the nastier kind and I was in the mood for it. I gave them the jack-o'-lantern grin and the old signature V sign, guaranteed to set them off. Why not? Let it rip, fellows. Give me what I deserve. If you have debris hurled at you often enough, you can recognize the sound without even looking up. You don't need a Gallup poll when they're throwing vegetables, eggs, and, if they've really worked themselves up, stones. A medieval mob chasing down the heretic in chief.

We drove straight to the airport afterward, skipping the ceremonial dinner, standing up Ronnie Reagan. Pat seated herself a good three rows away and I leaned back to sleep in the semidarkness. I dreamed I lay in my childhood bed listening to that distant train whistle, my old ticket out. I didn't even know about airplanes then.

When we landed, I was met by a CIA man, an enormous blond who flashed his ID too fast to see.

"Sir? We have a situation." I nodded to Pat and the entourage and stepped toward the waiting limo. A situation sounded about right to me.

The motorcade left the airport, lights flashing, police motorcycles flanking the central limousine. It was a shell game; I was in the black town car that veered off halfway along the route to lose itself in the side streets until it reached a shaded driveway in front of a suburban ranch house. They explained on the way what was happening—a high-level defector had demanded my personal attention. She'd already offered enough verifiable intelligence to establish her value.

An older CIA man, white-haired with a brick-red face, opened the car door for me.

"Connors, sir. We're holding her until we can figure out what to do with her. She's refusing medical attention until she talks to you."

"You're sure she's not armed?"

"Nothing on her, and we got her a new set of clothes."

"And you're sure this is worth my time."

"According to our Kremlin watchers, yes. If she's the genuine article."

"How do we not know?"

"You'll see, sir. Dates of service look a little funny. But they hit her pretty hard in Budapest before we got her undercover. If this is a scam, she's showing a fuckload of commitment to the role."

A Secret Service agent opened the front door and called, "Searchlight coming in," to somebody I couldn't see. I stopped in the doorway and let my eyes adjust. The house was a rambling one-story construction. I could see what must have been the kitchen light on toward the back.

"She's in the kitchen," Connors said. "We had to cover the windows. Snipers. She wants to talk to you but—"

"Stay here," I said. "I'll call if I need you."

"Okay, sir."

The kitchen was in half-light, newspaper taped over the windows, sacks of newly bought groceries set up on the linoleum counter. A dark-haired woman sat at the kitchen table over a cup of tea. She was dressed in a man's white button-down shirt and gray slacks but I couldn't see her clearly until she looked up.

I saw what they meant about medical attention. On the left side of her head, most of her hair was gone, and bits of her scalp. The left half of her face was raw and scraped and burned in places.

"It's been a while, Dick. Did you still want to marry me?" she asked with her lopsided smirk. It really was her, the reason I was president, the reason I was never going to be truthful with anyone except her.

"Hi, Tatiana. Are you all right?" I stopped where I was. I wanted to take her hand, and I couldn't. I couldn't even move.

"I'm all right," she said.

"Does it hurt?" I said. I sat down across the table from her, like we were a married couple enjoying a late-night meal together. I'd forgotten how small she was.

"I can feel it, yes. Not so bad."

"Where have you been?"

"Istanbul just now. Your people flew me in. Budapest before that. Russia. Siberia a couple of years. Around."

"Did our people do that? Your head? Your hair?"

"No. It was an accident. It did not go well, after I last saw you. It will grow back. A part of who I am."

"What do you mean, a part of who you are?" I asked, but she waved a hand as if it were too obvious to go into.

"How have you been, Dick? You look good," she said.

"I'm the president of the United States now."

"Congratulations. Although I know this, I hear them talk about you. Are you liking it all right?"

I shrugged. "We went to the moon."

"How is Pat?"

"Pat is—she's unhappy. I don't think she likes any of this. I don't know how to talk to her."

"Always you think she is stupid and untrusting. But what is she to do, not knowing the truth?"

"And how am I supposed to—never mind, this isn't what I came here for." I glanced at the impassive Secret Service agent hovering outside the door. How far did sound travel in this place?

"What did you come here for?" she asked.

"Look, Tatiana, you're in a tricky position. They grabbed me out of the White House for this. I'm the leader of the free world now. They think you've got fresh intelligence. They might try to interrogate you. Probably you should be thinking about what you can offer them."

"I could always offer them you."

"That's not funny."

"You and me. You and Arkady. The KGB president."

"What do you want, Tatiana?"

"I'm still thinking. It has been an eventful few weeks. But don't worry yourself, I have all kinds of spy stuff for them. Missile placements, intelligence assets around the world. They'll be satisfied."

"Are we...enemies? Are you still loyal to the Soviets? Are you with us now?"

"I'm a very good liar, Dick. If this"—she turned her burned face toward me—"does not convince you, I don't know what more I can do." I stared at her unhappily. What wasn't she capable of? But if she wasn't my friend, who was?

"Just give me a story to tell," I told her.

"All right. When I returned to Russia in 1961 they were not happy with me. I was given long debrief session. Several weeks.

Many repetitions of my story. They want to know what happened to Hiss. Where my subsequent intelligence came from. This causes me great difficulty at first. They do not know you are my agent, and I keep it that way, do not worry. I tell them it is Hiss, then I invent other sources, people who are dead now. A little here, a little there. I can play these games better than they can.

"Or so I thought. Always in the past I was successful in the Russian system. Smarter and tougher, and willing to do what is necessary. But when I get back, all doors are shut. I lost my rank, my fancy apartment, my access. I was given menial work. Then it got worse. There are irregularities in my service record and they were found. Things no one should know. But the explanation was not hard to find. Gregor, who you tried to kill, is not dead. He is highly placed now, the Nth Directorate. Dark places."

"I know."

"He used his influence to make things difficult. I was taken for tests, medical tests. They started to notice things about me. I have more secrets than you might guess. My face, my age."

I looked more closely at her and realized what had seemed wrong from the start. I'd known her for more than twenty-one years now, and when I'd first met her she was in her early thirties. For the luckiest people, time gently suspends itself between, say, twenty-five and the midforties. Skin, hair, weight stay, with only a little charity involved, the same.

I thought of the changes in my own face over the last twenty years. I'm not a vain person; there was no mistaking what happened. The hairline had stayed where it was, but it had thickened, coarsened; lines had been graven deeper. George Orwell said that at fifty, everyone has the face he deserves, and I was evidently less deserving than most. Tatiana, though—she had to have been in her fifties, but, apart from her injuries, she looked exactly the same as she had two decades ago.

"What is this? What do you want, Tatiana?"

"Tell your Secret Service man to check outside the window," she said. "Walk over and tell him you heard something." I did, and as he left I turned back and saw her standing there in front of me, and without warning she kissed me.

It had been a long time since anything like that had happened to Richard Nixon. Maybe it was that, or maybe there was some other reason why it was so exactly perfect, the soft, tender, furtive Russian-spy fantasy kiss of my dreams, her body pressed against mine, the very wrong life-ruining kiss, hope and worry over in a long, loveless public marriage. The kiss you starve yourself for. It went on seconds or minutes, until she heard the screen door close and sat down quickly and I did the same.

"What if I asked you to run away with me?" she said.

"That's not possible."

"Yes, it is. Run away with me before it's too late. From dumb-ass job, from stupid Pat who cannot love."

"But I'm the president."

"Yes, you are. Hurrah and good for you. Now you can maybe live your life and not eat your heart out anymore. You have money. I do too. We could live anywhere."

"You don't just leave the presidency."

"They'll kill you," she whispered. "You think Kennedy was an exception?"

"Who will?"

"Gregor will; 1972 is coming and they plan to take advantage. Gregor has had a long time to prepare. They couldn't get to Eisenhower but you are no Eisenhower. And if Gregor doesn't get you, there's your own Dr. Kissinger, and you don't know what he is but I have my strong suspicions. I watched him a long time in the fifties and he does not mean well. You're a lit-tle chicken in a world of foxes. They'll tear you apart between them. Your wife too."

"I have to stay. I'm the president."

"Oh, Dick. We both know what you are."

I stood up so fast the chair fell over, and Connors was there in an instant.

"Is everything all right, sir?" he asked.

"The prisoner is ready to talk," I said. "I'll be returning to the White House. Good-bye, Tatiana." I said this last on my way to the door, not turning around. Gary was in the car with his hideous satchel, working on a crossword, and we pulled back onto the highway.

"How'd it go, sir?" he asked after a few minutes.

"You know, Gary? Go ahead and send those launch codes out whenever you feel like it. All of them. Any time is fine for me."

"Right, sir," he said.

CHAPTER THIRTY-EIGHT

DECEMBER 1970

PROXY WARS, RECESSION, a new offensive building in Vietnam. Approve: 52 percent; Disapprove: 34 percent; No Opinion: 14 percent. A five-point drop in approval, a new low. I mumbled to Rose about a last-minute diplomatic crisis and she knew enough to invent the rest. Then I gave the signal to activate Arkady.

It should have gone the usual way. The limousine pulled up at the embassy and there was a quick, awkward minuet with a body double, and I transferred myself to the second limousine, which took me to a back entrance of the Jefferson Hotel. If the Secret Service thought I had a mistress, that was the least of my worries.

I ducked into a dim, roped-off section of the empty hotel bar and took a seat in the booth. Arkady slid in a moment later, a half-full bottle of vodka and two shot glasses gripped in one hand.

"Is not as easy as it once was," he said.

"The Secret Service can keep their mouths shut. They do it for everyone."

"Is not what I mean. You are burned but good, my friend, I must tell you. Do you not know you are followed this time?"

"What?" I half stood and Arkady gave me a swift kick under the table. "Why didn't you wave me off?"

"I think it has reached a point that we do not solve it this way."

"But this can't be known. Us, I mean, it just can't." I could hear myself panicking but there was no way to stop. "Is it another Soviet branch? MI6? The *Post*? What do we do? Arkady, you've got to fix this." I waited for him to nod but he just stared at me.

"Get it . . . taken care of," I said. More staring. I whispered in his ear, "You know. Liquidate the issue. Can't you do that?"

"Is hard target. And also taste issue of killing wife? I think you come out now, Mrs. Nixon," Arkady said loudly.

After a few moments, Pat stood up rather shakily from behind the bar, hair untidy, her face a mask of shock. Wearing a trench coat over a powder-blue ensemble and Jackie O sunglasses, she looked just as much a cartoon spy as Tatiana had when I'd met her in the California diner. Pat gripped a small revolver in one hand as if it were her last hold on a sane reality.

She walked stiffly around the bar and toward us, revolver pointed straight at me, until it was maybe two feet away. She stood by the booth as if she were a waitress taking our order.

"I am Arkady, who you have met before, yes?" Arkady said. She ignored him and stared at me.

"So this is where you go," she said. There was nothing of the chirp and swoop of her public voice. This was another Pat entirely.

"Dick and I have many locations of drinking," said Arkady. "Is an aid to relaxation and bonding of man to man."

"I would like you both to put your firearms on the table," she said.

"Weapons? But I am humble diplomat," said Arkady. "Emissary of peace."

"I don't have a gun," I said. "Since when do you have a gun?"

"Since I realized I don't know who my husband is. For a long time I thought I was going crazy, you know. Where is Henry?" she asked, lowering the gun slightly.

"Henry?" I asked.

"The national security adviser does not know of this meeting," Arkady said.

"Why don't you tell me who you work for, Dick? The Russians?"

"They're just my friends," I said.

"And that Tatiana woman? Are you 'just friends' with her, too?"

"Yes, her. And Arkady." I started to slide over toward Pat but she jerked the gun up.

"Hands on the table; let's do this properly," she said. "How long? Since the presidency? Since Eisenhower? Since the very start?"

"Mrs. Nixon," Arkady said, "I must tell you, I am feeling this is awkward marital conversation and perhaps I am not belonging."

"You go over there. The bar. You sit." He got up slowly, hands in view.

"Is great mystery, marriage," he remarked, "of which I have not the happiness to know. But I wish its greatest blessings to you both." Pat waited for him to take his seat at the bar.

"So you're a traitor," she said. "After all this time. Have you told Alger Hiss?"

"Pat, these things are complicated." I was sweating torrentially in my wool suit, sweating like a man losing a televised debate.

"Because you're in love with Tatiana?"

"No!" I blushed even though I didn't want to. Was I in love after all? Was it possible to be elected president and still not know how to tell if you're in love?

"Dick. I know we're not anything anymore. Maybe not even friends," she said. She sat down opposite me, the gun still in her hand. "I know that. I just don't want to be lied to."

"I admit that in a very technical sense, I am a spy," I said. I closed my eyes as I said it, not wanting to see her expression. But instead of a gasp of shock, I heard something that sounded like a badly suppressed snort of laughter. I opened my eyes.

"No, you're not," Pat said. She smiled, a little patronizingly, I thought. "You can't be!"

"I'm sorry, but yes, I am." She shook her head. "Why am I not a spy?"

"Spies have to be — well, you have to be good at things. You have to be able to shoot a gun. Run a mile in a reasonable fraction of an hour. Speak languages. Hold your breath underwater."

"I can speak French."

"Well, then, you have to be brave," she said, and now there was ice in it. "Are you brave?"

"I'm investigating a threat to the United States that very few people know about." At least she wasn't pointing the gun at me anymore.

"Is that what you're spying on when you go get drunk on Thursday nights? Is that the only time this threat is available?"

"Pat, there is no possible way you would understand."

"Show me, then," she said, apparently in no hurry to finish torturing me.

"There's nothing to see, Pat. Nothing at all."

"So you never got the magic to work, then?"

"The . . . what?" I stammered, waiting for my brain to tell me she hadn't said what she said.

"I know, Dick."

"How do you know about any of this?"

"I got a letter from Ike. A long time ago, fifteen years maybe. It said not to open it unless he died, but then I did anyway."

"What did he say?"

"He said the Constitution was special, that it was magic. That he was magic, because he was president, and that he'd done unspeakable things. It went on and I thought he'd gone crazy. He said he killed Stalin."

"What else?" I said. "Did he talk about a plan? Anything we're supposed to do?"

"He talked about you. He said he didn't understand you. He said you had secrets from him, and it shouldn't have been possible. But you did, didn't you?"

"Yes." I nodded slowly.

"He said you were powerful, that you might be the greatest president in history. And he said there was a terrible thing coming for us—he couldn't describe it, only that it was a hideous darkness. He was afraid of you. He didn't know if you would defeat the terrible thing, or if you were that thing."

"So you know. You really know." I scrutinized her face, trying to guess what she would do. You'd think after thirty years, I could. "Why didn't you say anything?"

"Because when Ike was gone I would have to be the one who watched you and decide what to do. I didn't tell you because by that time I didn't know who the fuck you were." She said the curse word experimentally, in a way that made me remember my very first time firing a rifle: squeezing the trigger, waiting for the bang. "What if he was right? You weren't much of a husband, so what kind of president were you going to make?"

"And you believe it all? The magic? The lineage of presidents? The Soviet necromancers?"

"Not at first, no, not fifteen years ago. But I talked to people. I learned Aramaic, which you never bothered to do. There are at least five forms of magic operating in America and at least nine in the world. Did you know that, Mr. President?"

"No. How do you know that?"

"I have friends you don't have, Dick. You don't have many friends at all right now." I glanced at the gun on the tabletop; she saw me watching and rested her small, pale hand on it. "God, Dick, why do you always think you're the smartest one in the room? You don't know your own mother was a powerful witch on top of being a terrible, terrible person. And, okay, last one, I swear." She gave the snorting laugh she never did in front of cameras. "I'm what's called a New Deal Democrat. I've never voted Republican in my entire life."

CHAPTER THIRTY-NINE

DECEMBER 1970

A COLD WAR keeps going even when you can't see it; even when it's miles under the ice. Armies glare over the border and jockey for advantage; factories strain to outproduce one another; proxy wars are won and lost; new technologies are invented and change the strategic landscape. But one way or another, a cold war has to end, even if it takes decades, or centuries, or millennia.

Maybe a common enemy appears and the opposing sides unite for the sake of self-preservation. Some cold wars flare up into hot ones; a border commander loses his temper; missiles fly, and mutual annihilation takes its course. Or maybe the conflict just drains more and more resources from both nations, a mutual grinding into nothingness that goes on and on until both sides simply collapse.

Or sometimes there is just magic.

It was a very odd Christmas Eve celebration at the White House that year. Afterward, everyone else in bed, Pat and I sat in the Green Room and talked, sipping incredibly old bourbon we found in the back of an ancient cabinet, the label in Gothic script. I cautiously told Pat about Alger Hiss, Eisenhower, Arkady, Tatiana. Gregor.

"Eisenhower liked you. He just knew you had secrets, and he couldn't figure out how you were keeping them. He said it shouldn't have been possible, not the way the power works. I couldn't figure them out either."

"All those years. Why did you stay? Why the hell didn't you leave me?"

"God knows I thought of it, every day. Then I'd tell myself it was nothing, or that I'd stay just another week. Maybe I just don't know to leave people.

"But there were good days, and there were times when I thought: Well, Dick has to be in there somewhere."

"I was."

"Remember the day Ike came to see us, the first time? And we waited for you? I spent three hours making tea and listening to his stories about war and golf. And I happened to be at the window and I saw you come up the street. You saw the black cars and the Secret Service and I'd never seen a person so afraid, so clutched by shame and terror. You'd done something wrong and you thought you'd been caught."

"I'd just come from the farm at Pawtuxet. It was the first time I spied for them."

"But then you turned back and you walked to our door. You thought no one was watching but you did the brave thing, just that once. It wasn't much to go on for the next decade and a half of marriage. If I'm telling the truth, it was starvation wages." She took a sip of her whiskey. "But I tried to remember it, and I did. Even when they told me not to."

"Who told you not to?"

"The Democrats, silly. Even Eisenhower never understood. It's a much older party—your people didn't get started until the Outworld Horror Kings—excuse me, what you call the Civil War, which was when so much was lost. You'd be surprised who turns up at society séances and tarot readings. Those people at the Lincoln Memorial were my friends."

We walked along the colonnade through the snowy night to the Oval Office.

"What have the Democrats really been doing all this time? What do you know?"

"I know about how FDR's plan for the modern version of the Oval Office came to him in a dream. About historical anomalies around Grover Cleveland. And Woodrow Wilson. The plagues of 1918 were his work, you see. His final words were never written down, but it was a kind of ghastly antiquarian curse."

"What did you say about the Oval Office?"

"He dreamed it. You haven't thought, then, about the shape?"

She traced the wall with one hand, feeling the numinous curves.

"Why is it not a circle?" she said. I stared bleakly around myself, as I'd done every day of my tenure there.

"I don't know. Because it's an oval. I don't know why it's an oval."

"The first time you saw Ike do his ritual, he wasn't alone, was he?"

"No, he had the secretary of defense with him," I said. I leaned on one of the low-backed couches, which is what low-ranking cabinet members do when they're being left out in meetings.

"Eisenhower guessed, then, that it would need a second person to make any of this work. Now I'm going to teach you what they've learned on the other side of the aisle. The office isn't just an oval, is it? It's an ellipse, which means it has two focal points. You only have to measure to figure out where the points are. Here, and here." We marked spots on the carpet with tape. "I think FDR didn't want one person to have all that power."

"Why didn't Eisenhower just tell me that himself?" I asked.

"Maybe he didn't know. Or maybe, dear, he somehow got the idea you were an asshole."

We stood on the points we'd taped, maybe twenty feet apart. "What now?" I asked.

"Well, what did you try all the other times, Mr. Chief Executive? Or was it all just 'Yankee Doodle Dandy'?"

We started with the Constitution. I never found out exactly what did it. An activation code, a resonant sequence of words or syllables, a gesture. I'm not a technical magician; two-thirds into the backward reading of the Declaration, Pat stopped me.

"Dick? How long has that door been there?" she asked.

I turned, slowly. Without the room's seeming to have expanded at all, there was now enough space between the fireplace and the grandfather clock to fit two doors instead of one. One led back to the residence. To its left was a large white-painted wood door in the style of most others in the West Wing, unremarkable except that it had never been there before.

"What now?" I said. No one implied this wasn't going to be dangerous.

"I think we have to," she said.

The door opened inward onto a simple flight of stone steps curving down and out of sight to the left, lit by dim electric bulbs strung along a wire stapled to the wall. The walls were unadorned plaster, their age impossible to determine. Outside it was silent, early Christmas morning. Pat took my hand and we descended.

Past the first turn the plaster walls gave way to brick and the air grew colder. One turn and we were level with the lowest subbasement, and then below it. Who had come this way last? Did Eisenhower descend these steps, in the earliest days of the Cold War? Did FDR force himself to make the trip down and up on his crutches and halting, crippled legs?

A second turn and the brick grew older, mortar crumbling.

Far off I heard a sound like constant rippling thunder, or an enormous river cascading into the depths. Another turn and the stairs stopped in front of a door just like the one above.

"It's the real Oval Office," Pat said. "The true one. It must be."

I opened the door. It was the same room but it wasn't. Oval, yes, but the details had shifted.

The presidential desk was solid New England granite, carved, more altar than workspace. The chair behind it was high-backed and seated there was a skeleton, long dead, in an outdated wool suit suggestive of the 1940s. Its posture was skewed left as if by a sharp blow or bullet impact, its bones shattered at the shoulder joint. One hand still clutched at the receiver of a red telephone. There was a black phone as well, its cord severed, and next to it a white phone, and a sapphire-blue one. I lifted the blue receiver to my ear and a voice spoke in musical tones, urgently but too quietly for me to understand. I felt a numbness spreading up from the hand that held the phone, and I slammed it back down.

The painting of Lincoln gazed empty-eyed, somehow devoid of expression. The portrait of Washington hung just as it did upstairs, but its face was seared away almost entirely.

The high windows were obscured by green velvet curtains. I eased them back and looked beyond the windows. A vast white cavern of marble, the neoclassical architecture of the American Capitol expanded to inconceivable size, a city of white stone hewn into enormous blocks. A broad flight of steps gave onto a massive causeway flanked by gigantic fluted white columns whose breadth and height I couldn't estimate. It might have been beautiful, but it seemed somehow hideous. We saw in the distance a vast plaza, crowned with an empty white throne like the seat of the Lincoln Memorial. An enormous sphinx crouched on its left, its massive face was Washington's. A second sphinx sat on the right, its face in shadow but as I strained to see I thought I discerned a long bulbous nose and angry sloping brow.

I closed the curtain. This was the madness that America made itself forget. The madness of King George Washington the First, the king who never was.

Pat had been pulling books off the shelves, checking titles and stacking them on the floor. Many of them were half burned, a few were just loose pages bound in twine. She'd stopped and laid one flat on the dead man's desk.

"It's a manuscript copy of Bradford's history of the colonies, but there's another set of writing in the margins. Listen to this," she said. "'At first the wind blew against us, day after day, and then it died altogether and we drifted, sails slack, on a current of black water, under stars that no man of us knew. When we landed we were some two hundred miles north of New Amsterdam, and—as we were to learn—it was by no accident. By whose unseen will, we were soon to learn.'"

The unknown narrator had left us a fragmentary portrait of the founders' first year. They were brilliant in their way but they were not like us. They believed in a predestined elect, an original depravity, and an agonizing afterlife for all but a few. They spoke Latin and German and Aramaic and there were some who had read widely in profane and pagan texts now lost. It was 1620 and Europe still lingered on the threshold of the century of Descartes and Galileo. But for all their knowledge and bravery, these people who'd come to the New World were dying.

The Pilgrims looked on their problem with cold eyes and a breathtaking intellectual flexibility. Long ago, kings and princes and the nations of the world had made peace with old things neither angel nor seraph nor demon, but the Pilgrims had crossed a great ocean to a place where no treaty or contract shielded them.

They would forge a new one, with stolen Native American knowledge and Old Testament thunder and the scraps of learning they'd brought from Europe and much else they invented for themselves. Somebody walked into the forest and summoned the terrible old ones and made a deal. The Pilgrims would live and the old contracts would be broken. The principals of those old contracts, the Pequot and Narragansett and Wampanoag tribes, would lose both their protection and their title to these strangers.

Reading between the lines it seemed clear the four surviving women were the instrumental parties: Eleanor Billington, Mary Brewster, Elizabeth Hopkins, and Susanna White Winslow. I have a dark suspicion that in some way, the women who didn't survive made their own contribution. I believe the members of the Roanoke colony were either reluctant to pay a similar price or unable to live with having done so.

It was not a small thing they bought. Everyone thinks of the Enlightenment as the end of superstition, the breakdown of religion and magic and the beginning of a new and rational order. The United States is the standard-bearer of that order, a nation founded not on superstitions about bloodlines and myths of swords in stones but on sound civic principles and contracts rationally entered into.

Everyone is wrong. The dawn of modernity wasn't the end of enchantment, only the beginning of a new and more terrible one. The Plymouth elders made a bargain and brought forth nothing less than a new American sorcery, the casting of a vast invisible spell great enough to bind the darkness of the New World. The settlers lived, and prospered, and over time their work was given the name by which we now know it—the

Constitution, the thing that opened the way for the master enchanters of the nineteenth century, Lincoln and Whitman, and for the obscene magical forces that would one day push us all the way to the Pacific.

The Pilgrims' bargain bought them a continent, and we were the inheritors of a contract bound into our land and our nation and infused again and again into the flesh of its principal executive, the president of the United States.

No one ever matched the power of the events and conjurations described in the first generation of founders. American magic may have reached its peak with Washington, the desperate man who married wealth and was given command of the Continental army only to see it on the verge of starvation until, in unknown fashion, he contrived to come into his power. After him the line of chief executives waxed and waned, scholars of the Constitutional arts. But after the disasters of Grant and the Civil War so much was lost, and the result was wilder spikes and surges in executive force, diminishing until even McKinley couldn't save himself. Taft had begun his project of retrieval too late. The presidential seal had certain properties, yes, and the signing statement, and the blood of the sworn, but all of these varied from decade to decade, president to president. So much depended on the officeholder. Or was it something else? The decade? The electoral mandate?

The seal of the president was sketched on the final page, and the same one lay on the floor of the office. Here the eagle was monstrous in aspect. This was the eagle of Lincoln's tattoo and my own. In one claw it held a tree torn up by the roots; in the other, a struggling human figure. On impulse I touched the circle, the angry form, and felt an odd charge in me. I tasted copper and sank to my knees.

We sealed the room again and staggered back up into the

light. Outside in the rose garden I squinted into the sun just above the horizon. The air felt night-cool.

"Dick?" Pat said. "What are you looking at?"

"The dawn."

"Dick, look at your watch. It's only four in the morning."

She was right. I held up a dollar bill, its face clearly readable in the blackness. My first taste of power, at last. I was an American president. I could see in the dark.

CHAPTER FORTY

FEBRUARY 1971

WE DROVE NORTH in one of the black cars with tinted windows that Tatiana, as a spy, seemed able to conjure at will. My body double—Pat and I each had one now—was at the moment in the Bahamas dutifully letting himself be photographed. It was the end of February, late in the New England winter, just warm enough to rain without freezing, cold enough to make everyone miserable.

Tatiana drove, expertly. In the passenger seat next to her, Pat pretended to sleep. Arkady and I sat in the back. After a full hour in which nobody spoke, Arkady brought out an edition of Herodotus and read silently, underlining passages as he went. I looked out the window trying to decide if there was any point in telling the truth to anyone. I'd told Pat the whole story of myself and the KGB, of Tatiana and Arkady. I'd told her because I felt I had to—after all, the four of us would be spending three days together. If Pat felt inclined to elaborate on her cryptic revelations, she didn't see fit to act on it. If Tatiana felt inclined to forgive me for outing herself and Arkady to the First Lady as KGB spies and assassins, she didn't act on that either. Telling the truth had only ensured that I'd spend the next three days with people who disliked one another.

The trip north looked almost the same as it had twenty years ago. Brighter, more built up, new cars, but it still got older and more wooded as we went north. As we crossed into Massachusetts, the forest seemed to rise up and swallow the road around us. Towns were smaller and farther apart and somehow meaner.

We reached Pawtuxet after dark and stayed in the same motel I'd stayed at before. I couldn't show my face at the window, and neither could Pat. Arkady got out to go book our rooms, took a few steps on the rain-slick gravel, and then turned back to Pat, a question on his lips. Pat raised four fingers. Four rooms for the night.

In the morning Tatiana knocked on each of our doors in turn. No one said anything about getting breakfast, and we drove out again in the gray rain to the farm. If there was any place left to teach us about the paranormal in America, this was it. We drove until I pointed out the shoulder where I'd been dropped off before. We got out, our collars turned up to the rain, our hats pulled down, except for Tatiana, who smiled and shook her wet hair and didn't seem to notice the damp at all. She looked no older than she had in 1948.

We followed the decrepit chain-link fence that led at right angles away into the dripping silence of the woods. We walked single file, ducking sodden branches. The winter forest was thawing, smelling richly of rot and rain. On the other side of the barrier, grass had grown up untended, and there were already slender saplings springing up where acorns had fallen and taken root. When we reached a spot where an entire tree had toppled onto the fence and collapsed it for a dozen yards, we abandoned the already dubious notion of stealth, crossed into the hummocked, untidy field, and walked toward the cluster of low makeshift buildings I remembered from two decades ago.

"Wait," Arkady said, almost the first word anyone had spoken that day. He crouched in the dead grass and pulled up a thick hank of it. Underneath was what I took to be a stone, but he lifted it to show it was hollow, and metal. A helmet, and a skull underneath. Arkady began ripping out the grass around it to find the rest of the bones. If Pat was shocked, she did a good job of hiding it.

"See. Facedown, feet go that way to the farm," he said. "He dies running away."

I looked at the buildings for movement, for any sign of life, but there wasn't any.

"It does not seem dangerous now but let me go first," he said. "I am not so easily killed."

Rain drummed on the cheap hollow metal roofing of maybe two dozen temporary huts that were well into their fourth decade. They clustered around a broad square pit marked by blackened granite blocks, the foundation of what used to be the farmhouse. In places the earth was still darkly stained, and the rain made ashy mud. Tatiana knelt and sniffed and made a face. "It started inside. And it was set on purpose."

"Excuse me," Pat said, "how the fuck can you tell that?"

It is something to be surprised by one's wife of thirty years.

"I can tell because I have an excellent sense of smell and adequate psychic abilities," Tatiana said. "Blood and gas and sweat and rotten flesh, and absolute terror. They fought. It was a last resort."

"Bullshit," Pat said. "I don't smell anything. It had to have been years ago."

"Would you like me to tell you your perfume? Or what your clothes are made of? Or how long ago you—"

"Okay!" Arkady said. "I think we search the buildings now. I say we split up. Yes, Mr. President? You second this?"

"Seconded," I said.

"I take Tatiana. You take your wife."

Inside the first hut, we heard the rain drum louder. This had been the library but roof panels were cracked or missing. The old books were scorched and sodden lumps, lying on the ground or on sheet-metal bookshelves standing askew. We moved on to the next hut, an abattoir of rusted surgical equipment and stained mattresses. The bare séance room was a small pond. I tugged at the drawers of rusty filing cabinets. In the barracks I found ruined clothes, personal effects, photographs, all scattered. Parts of the base had been emptied out, others left untouched. Four more skeletons littered the avenue outside. My good shoes were long since ruined.

"Here!" Pat called. I followed her voice to what had been McAllister's office. In one corner his safe remained, closed and intact. We tore the old wooden desk apart but the keys to the safe weren't there. I pulled at the handle of the safe; it snapped right off.

"Can we move it out of here?" I said. I gave it an experimental shove, or tried to. Arkady was pretty strong, but the road was a mile off.

"Just a moment," said Pat. She rummaged in her purse and came out with a tiny penknife. With a quick jerk she drew it across her thumb. I watched as she faced the wall and brought her arm down hard, casting a drop of blood.

"One for lies," she said, low and not to me.

"Pat, what in God's name?"

She turned a careful ninety degrees on her heel and did it again. "And one for truth," she said, and turned. "One for lost things. And one for sweet youth." She finished her last turn and sucked the cut. "One from across the aisle. The keys are underground."

The stone steps down into the basement were charred but intact. A trickle of water ran through the barred gate at the bottom. Arkady stopped and heaved; the grillwork bent, then snapped. His strength must have been prodigious.

"This is a bad idea," he said, panting. Pat pulled a flashlight from her purse as Tatiana brushed past her.

Through the gate were catacombs formed partly of poured concrete, and they gave onto older brick passageways. Some of the corridors had cells built into the sides. Pat shone her flashlight into one of them and drew back, shaking her head. For a while the passageway crisscrossed above an underground river, intermittently visible through a grating until it plunged down to some deeper level away from us.

Tatiana stopped in front of another barred cell whose door swung open easily. She pointed inside, and Pat nodded.

They'd chained McAllister up before he died—of what, no one could say. Evidently he'd lived several years after the burning of the farmhouse. The skeleton of a dog lay near him, and his keys.

The safe contained more paperwork, now pulpy with water damage, and notebooks secured with rubber bands. A few of its pages, written in Eisenhower's spiky penmanship, survived. A list of agents identified by code names with annotations and commentary. Strengths and weaknesses, protocols for contact, and an index to a clandestine network of paranormal entities. Code names like Pendragon and Optical told me nothing, and it was clearly out of date. But at the very least, it indicated that not so long ago, magic had been alive and well in America.

CHAPTER FORTY-ONE

IN THE END the notebooks told me very little I could use. Clues and fragmentary records point me to the Blue Ox project's persons of interest. Colonel McAllister had been thorough, if undiscriminating. People in government service touched by the unhallowed presences that survived in America and the world beyond. One I knew; the rest had served without distinction and then sunk out of sight.

There were five of us present in the Oval Office when I started it off. Agent Hunt had seen a lot in the past decade. He'd been part of the Bay of Pigs and there were photographs of him on the scene in Dallas when Kennedy died. At fifty he looked a haunted sixty, and none of the others were particularly young. They were all fleshy older white guys, a circle of blue and gray suits, patriotic neckties, and thinning hair. In fact, they looked terrible. All men with promising careers that had disintegrated into eccentricity, obsession, and dangerous extremism. The Plumbers.

H. R. Haldeman, forty-five years old but perpetually boyish with his brush-cut hair, a campaigner and a former ad executive. I'd made him chief of staff but never spoke to him outside of work. He'd attended UCLA and started out as a Near Eastern studies major but had changed shortly after an incident involving a noise complaint, campus police called to the department library on Portola Plaza. Report of a strange smell, unusual plant growth. In the end, four students were dispatched to psychiatric services.

George Gordon Liddy had been an FBI bureau supervisor in DC at twenty-nine. One day a work crew laying the foundation for a parking garage uncovered unusual remains, and Liddy was called to the scene. Subsequently brought in were a forensic team, a hazmat team, and a paleobotanist. The excavation went unusually deep.

John Ehrlichman had served in the South Pacific, part of a squadron out of the Philippines tasked with surveying low-lying reefs in a certain island formation, coincidentally during a month of extraordinarily low tides. They returned with reports of lights burning under the ocean and vast and dark forms moving among them. Seven men, navigators mostly, were hospitalized and subsequently discharged from the unit.

"I'd like to welcome you all to the Presidential Task Force for Vaguely Important Matters. The point is, it's a secret task force. Doesn't officially exist. Nobody talks about it. Okay? One of those." They nodded. Everyone here, I had noticed, liked to be on a secret committee. They also shared, in addition to everything else, a twitchy, depressed affect.

"You all have a certain amount of intelligence background, legal background, or military background. None of you are particularly distinguished in your fields. All of you have been sent for psychiatric evaluation more than once. All of you had involvement with the now-defunct Blue Ox program, and, even more extraordinary, you are still alive and more or less functional.

"You are here in case I should happen to have a problem I don't know how to explain, or would prefer not to mention, or don't want to admit exists. We all know these kinds of problems are out there. There are sections of the government that were set up to deal with—the kind of things we're talking about. I believe some of them are gone; others have left the direct control of Strategic Air Command.

"If you tell another living soul about this I'll probably deny ever having spoken to you. I will certainly pay people to make you look crazy.

"I can offer you only one thing: The things you know, the things you've seen that you can never tell another living soul? The president knows them and has seen them too."

There was never any great hope that the Plumbers were going to cover themselves in glory. They were Nixon men. Ambitious strivers, failed agents, and failed civil servants. They were well known to be corrupt, vulgar, incompetent, intermittently criminal. They were the remnants of the remnants, the last and least of the United States supernatural research corps.

They were there when the end began and the trap started to close.

"We are here to discuss a national security risk that has been detected," Henry said.

"Do you mean Ellsberg? I think I can deal with it," I said. I realize that no one is going to back me on how I handled that one, even in hindsight, but what was I supposed to do? I had a great deal to hide at that point. It wasn't going to help anything if people realized Kissinger was—what?—a thousand-year-old necromancer.

"That is heartening but it is not what we discuss on this day," he said. His eyes shifted around the room. Ehrlichman was there, taking notes. Haig was there too, scowling, his oath and basic loyalty preventing him from telling anyone that the top of the executive branch was an occult cell.

"I have learned of the existence of a massive insurgency within our borders. Organized and malevolent and possessed of the knowledge and, moreover, the will to strike at us with devastating swiftness," Henry said. His eyes continued to dart around the room as he spoke. Was it me, or was he getting more and more manic lately?

"You want to give me these people's names?" said Haig. "Shouldn't be hard to round 'em up."

"I speak, naturally enough, of the Democratic Party's National Committee," he said. "They have been meddling with friends of yours, Richard. If the old gods rise, it will represent a significant realignment of the electoral landscape. And not necessarily in our favor. You know how important the Christian demographic is, so we'll lose most of the southern states. Maybe not Georgia."

"What do you suggest we do, Henry?" I asked.

"Is there a UN policy on domestic use of the thermonuclear arsenal? In the name, perhaps, of public order?" someone said.

"You know I'm going to end up looking crazy over this," I said.

"It is not to our disadvantage," Henry said, "if we appear irrational to the Soviets in this regard."

"I think there must be other options," I said. "I'll speak to my people."

"The one you call Gregor has approached the Democratic National Committee. They have proven surprisingly cooperative. A pact was made. A process of spatial distortion and hybridization has commenced. They are developing their candidate as we speak."

"How is it possible they could agree to a thing like that?"

"The election is approaching, Mr. President, and you are favored overwhelmingly. As is so often the case in such conflicts, they believe you are capable of taking steps similar to theirs and that perhaps you have already done so."

"But to make a pact with Gregor . . ."

"Surely you of all people must understand. There are those who wish so very badly to become president, they would do anything to make it happen."

I didn't tell them everything, mind you. Just enough to get them through the missions. I didn't want to tell them exactly how bad it was. I didn't want to tip my hand to any particular side. It was becoming obvious that none of the enemies of my enemies were my friends.

Did we have an enemies list? We did. Gregor could operate in the United States and he could look like anyone and he had no reason to be kind to us. Many of his cells had been replaced by those of an elder god and that did nothing to enhance my appreciation for civil liberties. Yes, Paul Newman was on the enemies list. It was Ehrlichman's call and I wasn't going to second-guess him. Was Barbra Streisand on that list? We flagged her for good and sufficient reasons, is all I will say. Judge me if you must.

Did I have multiple meetings with Elvis Presley? I admit that I did, and that I deputized him in the name of the Federal Bureau of Narcotics and Dangerous Drugs. The deeds he performed in the name of that office will remain retracted for another century, but they will one day be told.

On September 9, 1971, did we break into the office of Daniel Ellsberg's psychiatrist? Everything is so clear in hindsight. We could just as easily have been right on that one too. We were right about Watergate.

CHAPTER FORTY-TWO

JUNE 16, 1972

I COULD SEE well enough in the dark, not as if it were daytime, but I saw a kind of vivid moonlit outline of things. Night by night we tested and discovered there was more.

Why did I ever think I'd have a soldier's powers? Eisenhower did, and rightly. My affinity was with shadows, with conceal-ment. Pat and I tested the idea by playing hide-and-seek with the Secret Service. If I concentrated hard enough I could oc-casionally confuse them, forcibly lapse their attention while I walked away unnoticed. There were moments when I could vanish into the shade of a pillar before their eyes, and emerge to startle them. I could cloud men's minds, it seemed. What evil lurks in the hearts of men? The shadow president knows.

This is what sparked the idea of the grand plan, the deception in the plain sight of history, but before we acted we would have to run a field test. No games in the White House; it had to work anywhere. The form was my idea: the most famous face in the world would spend one night in the open.

I prepared in mundane ways. I practiced moving my shoulders and head more when I spoke. Applied putty to build up my cheekbones. A heavy layer of foundation made the jowls less ap-parent. There was nothing whatsoever to be done about the nose.

I trained my voice to be half an octave higher, more nasal, less of the signature guttural growl that anchored my public speaking. Finally the dirty-blond mop of the wig; awkward, but I'd need it for only a night. For clothes, a pair of blue jeans, a white T-shirt, and a canary-yellow shirt bought from the Salvation Army. The shirts were a size too small and showed off a pair of biceps the world didn't know about. Seventy dollars cash and a false passport out of an old emergency kit, with a photo of my disguised self painted in, grinning as broadly as I could. A harmless goofball with a terrible haircut.

I dispatched the body double to a children's concert for the evening. And finally there was the car, a 1969 Ford Thunderbird painted a sparkling gold. Borrowed from the younger brother of one of the social directors on the White House staff, ostensibly for intelligence purposes. I slipped into the visitors' parking lot and fumbled with the door lock. It had been so long. The last time I drove a car was before I won the presidency four years ago, and I'd never driven a car like this one. I got the thing open and ducked inside to find myself much lower down than I thought, practically supine, feet splayed. I pulled the door shut and sat for a while inside this silent, dark, cushioned pod, breathing the smell of leather, cigarette smoke, a stranger's sweat.

I turned the key and the car shuddered and vibrated. The wheel was broad and turning it felt like steering an ocean liner. The sudden sense of physical ease was overwhelming; the car seemed to say to me, *Anything you want, guy, anything at all.* I briefly laid my head against the steering wheel. I broke into an involuntary, profoundly un-Nixonian laugh that built into a spasm remarkably like a sob. It was so, so good to be somebody else for a moment.

Time to go. I yanked the stick and put the car in reverse, eased it out past the checkpoint and into the nighttime Washington, DC, streets. Richard Nixon had escaped the zoo.

It was only nine o'clock; I had the whole night ahead of me. I cruised, took easy lefts and rights through the grid just for the pleasure of it. I had an itinerary, a map with addresses marked, but for a while it was enough just to drive. A few guys looked me over when we pulled up at a traffic light. I froze in panic until one of them yelled, "Nice car!" It *was* a nice car. I had one of the most recognizable faces on the planet, but just for tonight it wasn't about me. No spark of recognition, no applause, no jeering. Bored indifference, or a thumbs-up.

I was a Guy with a Nice Car. What if this was who I was meant to be, on the most elementary level? What if years of deception and ambition and horror and accomplishment were utterly separate from the person I basically was? A lost, forgotten Nixon who ought to have been. Dick Nixon, just a guy in a city with a shitty job and a cool car and a mellow attitude.

I pulled up at a convenience store to give the outfit its first test under fluorescents. A Hershey bar and a Coke. Panic again; I had no idea how much these things cost. I shoved a twenty at the guy at the cash register and then scooped up the change. He didn't even look at me. I stammered out "Th-thanks, man," snatched up my purchases, and fast-walked back to the safety of the car, afraid of breaking character completely. I peeled out of the parking lot, gleeful again the moment I hit the streets. The sheer administration-wrecking potential of the evening's plan was sharply apparent. The night could end in a police standoff or at the emergency room or with any number of other unpleasant outcomes, each a first in the annals of the presidency.

A few blocks down I pulled into the lot of Jerry's, a bar promising beer and color television. The tires scraped and popped on the gravel, and I skidded to a stop. I resisted a Nixonian impulse to fix a shitty parking job. That's not what I was there for.

It was dark inside, and crowded, and I aimed for the neon light over the bar. Bathed in moist, beery air I almost backed out again at the sheer peril of walking into an utterly unvetted crowd, one that the Secret Service hadn't checked, cleared, and saturated with undercover operatives. I tried to concentrate on being inconspicuous as I stood in the doorway cataloging faces and firing angles until finally a guy in an *Easy Rider* T-shirt shoulder-checked me into motion again. I stumbled toward the bar. Easy Rider walked on, and I realized nobody was going to tackle him. We were just a couple of guys, and it was Friday night. I could get used to this.

The younger faces looked like the ones I'd seen on TV lately: men with drooping mustaches and masses of hair, women dressed sloppy-sexy, smiling and knocking back shots at the bar. Not for the first time I observed that I had no idea what country I was president of. I ordered a Budweiser, and, in the unfamiliarity of the moment, I did it in my own voice. The bartender did a mild double take but that was the end of it. So what if the dude sounded like Nixon? People sounded like all kinds of things. Men and women crowded in around me and I made room. Everyone chattered and laughed, and, invisible among them, I waited for my moment.

I watched the television, scarcely able to process it. *The Brady Bunch,* then a variety music show. Who the fuck was Ziggy Stardust? Then the late news, the news about me. I'd hoped for something on the SALT conference, but it was yet another piece on the sagging economy. I turned to the man next to me, gestured with the bottle at my face on the television set, and uttered my one line for the night in a way that was supposed to be hearty and casual but came out sounding like something from a gangster movie:

"Whaddya make of that guy?" I said and then I turned back,

looked straight ahead, heedless of the response. It was the bartender who answered, his handsome face earnest and manly serious and disconcertingly young under its mustache and beard, younger than I remember feeling, ever.

"I think he's an asshole," the bartender said.

I nodded and muttered, "You got that right," chugged the rest of the beer, went out through the crowd and into the parking lot, and almost made it to the car before starting to cry, big uncontrolled jerks of the body.

"You okay, man?" said the voice of a stranger.

"Fine, man, I'm fine," I replied in I don't know what voice this time. Just a voice.

Three more bars, three versions of the same answer, and I was done. I left the car in the White House lot with the keys inside and a note saying thanks and that the mission had been a success.

I could have run off, taking the car west as far as I could, trading it in for another. Drifting from place to place, keeping just ahead of the massive cloud of ill omen that was my life's legacy. Focus on being that unknown guy with the cool car. It was just that a long time ago, Cool Car Guy started making the choices that turned him into Richard Nixon.

CHAPTER FORTY-THREE

JUNE 17, 1972

MY MEMORIES OF the night of June 17 will never be complete, and the various wild and hallucinatory accounts of what happened cannot be reconciled. The only certainty is that some went into the eighth floor of the Watergate Hotel, and some fewer walked out.

The Democratic National Committee had fatally overreached. Gregor had contacted that fool McGovern and sold him on a plan for electoral victory, sold him as only a Kremlin-trained operative could. The Politics of Spirituality or some such hippie line, tailor-made for the New Left.

As it was, they were almost too late. When Arkady tore the door off the room on the sixth floor, the air inside felt frigid, felt like dawn over Russian permafrost. Several DNC staffers were found frozen to death, still standing in the postures in which they had completed the ritual, victims of their own naive understanding of power politics. The suite was soaked in blood, caked in feathers, and strewn with candles, paper, the debris of the summoning.

American magic is haphazard, a thing of *genius loci* and wild talents. The Russians had set their most inventive minds to the problem of travel through frozen, starry places beyond their gates. When they came, the eight military shamans who stepped out onto American hotel carpeting were hardened from service in Afghanistan and stranger places, and ready to die to establish their beachhead.

While six shamans dug in behind desks and chairs, the final two prepared the way and its cold breath pervaded the room. Pat glimpsed it but would say little, a dark shape rising from the Russian steppe, spilling millennia-old snow from wings that could shroud a city. It needed only to empower a proxy in the land of its enemy and it could bring its will to bear. And then, its host in power, it could at last shake off its bonds and take flight over the pole to the New World, its form a gargantuan blot on American radar before it descended to breed in its new satellite nation. A McGovern presidency would end the Cold War and unite the rival powers in one savage, blasphemous coalition.

I wish I could have seen the fight. Tatiana unrestrained, a blur to the eye, at last free of the pretense and control of civilian life.

I'd begged Pat not to go but she wouldn't hear of it. As I heard it later she was capable of far more than she ever confessed to me. I believe she had spent time in the subterranean White House without me, reading the Democratic disciplines that had belonged to that party long since, battle magics perfected in the War of 1812 and on the fields of the Revolution itself. Pat reportedly shone so brightly it was impossible to look at her; it was as if the world had been torn open to show the light behind it, a fracture in the shape of my wife.

Henry loomed in the fray, the dark beast of the Bavarian forest at last unleashed. His origins will never be understood and whether he was profoundly good or evil, human or not, it was his legalistic sorcery that turned the tide and closed the gate, though the effort nearly killed him. He did his duty that night; his only mistake was to miss that crucial last card I would deal from the very bottom of the deck.

A numbed and semiconscious George McGovern was apparently central to what they'd hoped to accomplish. We also recovered several spheroid objects, each two feet across, whose composition was later found to be an inexplicable match with lunar rock formations. But Gregor was nowhere to be found.

I, of course, was nowhere to be found either. In fact, I was in the lobby, disguised and safe from harm, only waiting for the outcome. Eventually, I went to the restroom, walked to a stall, and sat down to wait in privacy. Just for a minute, face in hands, trying not to wonder how much time it would take. After a few seconds, I heard the restroom door.

I thought maybe Gary had come to tell me the world was ending after all. I opened the stall door just a crack. A little old man in the red-and-gold uniform of a Watergate Hotel valet lingered in the restroom doorway.

It was a shock to see how much Gregor had changed. The sleek young man of 1948 had withered and puckered; his skin had a deep permanent tan and age spots. He still wore his thinning hair combed straight back, but there was now a circular scar on his left temple, the skin roughened, the surface visibly cratered. It appeared he'd once been shot in the head and it hadn't worked.

"Richard?" he said. I didn't say anything. There were no other exits. It wasn't going to be hard to find me, but I couldn't bring myself to step out of the stall. I was only seconds away from a very unpleasant thing happening. I wanted those seconds. I wished with all my heart I could fight him. Eisenhower would be gathering thunderclouds by now, preparing to strike the man dead.

"Richard, I don't have much time. I wanted to do this properly and have a good talk but Kissinger's made it hard. I was going to run for office against you. If you think Kissinger played it rough, well . . . you should see how we do it back home." True, the restroom had only one exit, but the space was palatial in scope. A line of stalls ran down each wall, with a marble island of sinks, soaps, and mirrors in the center. I was in a middle stall and watched while Gregor strolled along the stalls opposite me, stopping and nudging each one open, taking deliberate care, one and then the next. I waited breathlessly for him to pass the midpoint.

"But you've come on your own, and it's too much to pass up. I truly can't wait till he sees me wearing your face. What a time we'll have then. East and West united. Down comes the Berlin Wall. We'll go to the moon. All comrades together." Now Gregor had reached the middle, and then he passed it. I was closer to the door than he was.

Behind him, I eased the stall open and took my first step along the tile. Gregor was making headway. He could turn at any moment. I took another step, as silent as I could be in stiff presidential shoes. I tried to calculate my odds. The moment I began to run, he would hear my footsteps clattering. He still walked like a young man, and I had never been fast. A desperate scramble across the tiles with the devil himself at my heels. For some reason that was the thing I couldn't stand. What if I slipped? What if he caught me?

Two more gingerly placed steps. In ten seconds he was going to turn around and see me standing there. The thirty-seventh president would die creeping through a public restroom. Where were my fucking powers? The real ones? I'd thought I was going to be able to fly.

Five seconds. Just up to the mirror with the light switch. I should probably have started running by now. Eisenhower would have backed Gregor down and laughed him out of the room. I was nowhere near the door. Could I get back to a stall?

No. It was a joke. It was over. Three seconds. The awful thing was going to happen and I didn't know what to do.

I turned the lights off. I heard a soft "Oh" from across the room. Had Gregor noticed where the light switch was on his way in? If he had, then I'd just told him where I was. I stood frozen and waiting for it but it didn't come. I watched as Gregor felt his way along the row of sinks to the door.

"All right, comrade. I'll wait. I'm at the door now. You may come to me when you're ready."

I felt my way forward to the sink and turned one of the taps on, and the water hissed out, the white noise masking every other sound in the room. I slipped my shoes off for good measure.

"What are you doing, Mr. Nixon?" Gregor said. I looked for something I could pick up, anything at all. It didn't seem like anything in the room was going to kill Gregor. I lifted the heavy ceramic lid off one of the cisterns, hefted it; the man who controlled North America's nuclear codes was going into battle armed with a toilet-tank lid.

I remembered being dragged, long ago, toward that hole in the wall and the frightful thing beyond, and I remembered begging them to stop, and I watched now as the shadows around Gregor darkened further. He was becoming less human as I watched, features contracting and lengthening into that hideous beak.

And there was nowhere to hide now. I was going to die alone with the darkness inside me that had always been there, inescapable. The night in Yorba Linda, the train whistle, dark shapes in the depths of the reservoir. I had written once of the black thing in a tree, and the dark swarm that came out of it, and the good dog Richard who ran from it, ran all the way home.

I saw now that Gregor stood in the darkness too, blind and

deaf and very far from his home. Gregor, the monster I made. He didn't see me as I hefted the cistern lid and swung, hard, but it was only to get his attention. I let it drop and shatter on the tile. I'd lived in that darkness for so long and I knew it now. I was the blackness of a particularly cold winter night in 1620, and although Gregor was a frightening man, there were worse things in the world. There were in particular four women still out there in the dark forest under the snow who had never quite died after all, had they? And they knew what to do with Gregor.

CHAPTER FORTY-FOUR

AN HOUR LATER the second team entered the Watergate Hotel. Their mission, to shift the night's drama from tragedy to farce. A group of young and highly competent men meticulously cleaned and reconstructed the offices of the Democratic National Committee to make them look only mildly ransacked and then stood in the middle of the suite and waved flashlights around until, at 2:30 in the morning, the police were finally called. They disclosed their names and handed over their surveillance equipment, cameras, emergency cash, and at least one incriminating phone number and then proceeded to deny everything. The curtain on the final act of my low-comedy political demise had risen, and the masquerade, the bizarre double game whose story has been told and retold, was afoot.

I egged them on, all of them. "Come and get me," I said. The ones whose phones I'd tapped, whom I'd lied to, slandered in the press, stolen votes from. I'd spent a lifetime making enemies, and here they were. They were coming for me and they were going to have themselves a grand feast.

But Richard Nixon would fight them first. I brazenly declared my innocence. I lied. I told them it was a matter of national security. I threw John Dean to the wolves, and then the rest of them, denying their friendship, loyalty, credibility. I pleaded for time and clemency. I cursed them. I'd go kicking and screaming, ducking and dodging and, ultimately, crying. I'd go out like a Nixon.

It took them a year. In July 1973, they began asking for the tapes. What tapes? No one had any tapes. Well, in fact, everyone had tapes. Johnson did, Kennedy did. We all made them. And no, they couldn't have them, subpoenas be damned. I invoked executive privilege. The tapes were a sacred trust, to expose them would compromise anyone's ability to speak with the president. The court told me to give them the tapes. We appealed, lost, appealed again. I wouldn't go quietly. I couldn't.

Four years later I would sit for my interview with David Frost. We had scarcely met before we were thrust together under the lights, and he smiled, mousy and sharply discerning. He asked, for his very first question, why I didn't destroy the tapes. Pat Buchanan had told me to destroy them, everyone had. I was startled and very nearly told the truth, at least part of it, which was that I deserved them. I deserved to be brought before the judgment of history and damned in my own voice.

But I did not necessarily want what I deserved, not yet. In October I fired the special prosecutor, and in response, the attorney general and his deputy both resigned, the famous Saturday Night Massacre. They called it the most poorly judged act of my political career. They hadn't seen anything yet.

CHAPTER FORTY-FIVE

NOVEMBER 17, 1973

WHAT HAPPENED IN those few seconds birthed the modern idea of the inopportune sound bite, the career-defining gaffe. Millions have watched it, probably hundreds of millions. In a few seconds I made the presidency a joke in a way that the obese Taft or the pathetically corrupt Harding never could.

It was already far from my best day. I would never have gone back to Disney World if I had had a choice. The setting lacked dignity and there has always been something uncanny about the location, one of the nation's primordial swamps. But the lawyers advised it and Henry was getting desperate. He didn't understand why I couldn't gain any ground. So we decided I would do a question-and-answer session at the annual convention of the Associated Press Managing Editors Association, held at the Contemporary Hotel at Walt Disney World.

I'd flown in the night before and had stayed up till dawn looking out at the lagoons, at the strange artificial landscape of the Magic Kingdom, and remembering Agent Reindeer. I arrived at the convention and was shown to the front of a long, low, claustrophobic ballroom, and immediately they clustered around, firing questions. The talk veered from Watergate to the *Pentagon Papers* to the tapes to illegal surveillance, and I struggled to focus. Watching myself on videotape, I see I was obviously tired, angry, possibly a little drunk. I leaned into the lectern as if into a high wind. I was needled, harangued, cross-examined. I was punch-drunk when it began, that car wreck of a paragraph.

"Let me just say this, and I want to say this to the television audience: I made my mistakes, but in all of my years of public life, I have never profited, never profited from public service—I have earned every cent." Here it was, the warm-up to the crash, to the fishtail and skid. I still had a decent rhetorical rhythm going but I was stalling; time was slowing down inside me.

"And in all of my years of public life, I have never obstructed justice." Why did I even say this? On the videotape there's a little head shake for emphasis at the end, as if I'm daring somebody to contradict me, to ask me if I had any idea what constituted justice at that point. As if I'm rhetorically steering straight for the guardrail and the cliff beyond.

"And," I found myself saying, "I think, too, that I could say that in my years of public life, that I welcome this kind of examination." I welcomed it? This was the fuck-you, and as I said it, I threw up my hands to prove it, essentially saying, *Shout me down, if you will, given that I'm virtually staking my career on a doomed lawsuit over the privacy of the executive branch.* I said it because I could see what was coming, a lifetime of this hedging and prevaricating, a fighting retreat unto death.

And I said it because I was waiting for the questions that weren't coming, that no one knew to ask. About Alger Hiss's true secrets, about Eisenhower's lost plan. About the terrible truths of our reality, the shattering gulfs of time haunted by alien intelligences. And then the wave broke, and I lost control, and I said the rest of it.

"Because people have got to know whether or not their president is a crook." People have accused me of lacking political instincts, of having a tin ear, but I knew at once what I'd done. I could already see the bullies of the press corps light up, the corners of their mouths twitching. They had the purest school-yard sadists' instincts for the inadvertent and the off-script, the screwup, but whether or not I was a crook was the question I would be asking for the rest of my life. I said it and then I gave the answer. You'll see me say it on the video, bitter and res-olute, then step back and look at their faces and wait for the laughter. Watch me. Knowing I'd crafted the perfect cover-up at last, the ruse that ensured I'd never be believed, I flung it straight in their teeth and fooled them all.

I would have skipped the following day if I could have. I didn't even like Disney World. I was, in fact, slightly afraid of it. When Khrushchev visited Disneyland in 1959, he wasn't al-lowed in. It was said that the American authorities couldn't guarantee his safety inside. And whatever else Khrushchev was, I would have backed him against an infantry division.

I'd met Walt himself in 1954. Eisenhower had called me into his office and introduced me to a gentle, slightly stooped man with a wispy mustache and hair combed straight back. "Meet Agent Reindeer," he'd said. Reindeer had a weak chin but extra-ordinary heart-warming eyes, liquid and intelligent and sly. He shook my hand earnestly and said, "How do you do?" Of course I knew him at once.

"Reindeer's a great technician," Eisenhower said, "the man in charge of Negate Crystal. He's building the greatest military fortification the world has ever seen."

"You're from California, Mr. Vice President?" Reindeer said. He had a genteel manner from somewhere that I couldn't place, and the magnetism of a film star. I wondered how he'd been re-cruited.

"That's right. Yorba Linda."

He froze a moment, then looked at me carefully.

"How did you like it?" he asked seriously. Like an examining physician.

"I had my childhood there. Good folk," I said. It was a presidential answer, the kind I'd been trained to make, impenetrably bland and folksy.

"You didn't notice any manifestations?"

"I'm not sure what you mean. Manifestations?"

"The soil there . . . never mind, never mind," he said, but he took a noticeable step back.

"Reindeer's been active in your area for quite some time. You'll go out and see the facility when it's operational," said Eisenhower. "I can't explain how it all works. Geomancy is a very technical field. It's principally a defensive installation, although there may be offensive capabilities down the road."

I sat through a long briefing then, none of which I understood.

On Reindeer's way out, I stopped him.

"You do mean the magic . . . of the imagination, right?" I said. "The look in a child's eyes and that sort of thing?"

"Oh, no, none of that nonsense," he said. He glanced down shyly. "I'm a sorcerer, Mr. Nixon. Come see me when my work is complete and you've come into your power, and I'll show you. I'll show you wonders."

He'd said that. But then he'd died in 1966, years too early. No magic, no kingdom.

Still, a trip to Disney World couldn't truly be the worst day of my presidency. Except insofar as, at this point, every day of my presidency seemed to be the worst day.

The management came out and greeted us and we were ushered in through the turnstile. Everything felt wrong. Even the optics were wrong. Shouldn't we be paying? We looked like visiting royalty, not regular small-town Americans, and that was my brand. And *Disney* was a byword for the kind of trumped-up sentimental Americana believed in only by children. I'd be "the Disney president" in a hundred penny-ante op-ed pieces this week.

Julie was bored; Tricia was embarrassed. And I walked around feeling like shit, trudging from one cheap photo opportunity to the next, my grinning Nixon mask firmly in place. It was as if the whole operation were designed to make a real person, a grown-up person, feel bad about himself. *This is how you're supposed to feel,* it seemed to say, *good and wise and pure. See how great that is? How do you feel about yourself now?* We'd been handed a few younger children, cousins or friends of cousins, I wasn't quite sure, and they trotted along. They were locals. Gary was there too, eyes wide and evidently having the time of his life even as he hauled his payload through the amusement park. The straps of his satchel looked a little frayed to me, but I didn't mention it.

I wanted to like it too; honestly, I did. I wanted at least to feel like I was standing there. Jesus, all I could think of was my approval rating. Haldeman had called; the Gallup poll had come out that morning. A 32 percent approval rating. I'd sat with the phone, feeling the silence stretch, as I tried to think of an answer to 32 percent.

"What—what do they actually ask when they call a person on the phone?" I asked. "What's the question people are answering?"

"The exact words are 'Do you approve or disapprove of the way Richard Nixon is handling his job as president?' And so, that's the choice."

"So . . . disapprove. Not much room for ambiguity there," I said.

"No."

I had a list of the things people were unhappy about: Vietnam. The Russians. The Chinese. The protest movement. Now I'd come into my power, and what was the point? Maybe this was Eisenhower's joke on me.

"What did Eisenhower have this month? End of fifth year?" I asked. I knew Haldeman would know.

"Look, sir, those were different times."

"Just roughly."

"He'd had a bump, so . . . fifty-eight. But Eisenhower was—it was a different metric for someone like him."

"Someone like him? What does that mean? What about someone like me? How exactly are we different?"

"Never mind, sir."

"Well, what do we do?"

There were a lot of possible answers to this. A speaking tour with the goal of connecting with ordinary Americans and their concerns and then crafting legislation to address them. Social welfare to the neediest. Sitting down with the warring camps in our divided nation and looking for places to compromise.

"Henry's got the letter writers going. The *Times,* the *Wall Street Journal.* Letters in protest. A couple experts questioning their methodology."

"Well . . . well, carry on, then."

It was how we did things. Approve or disapprove? Honestly, it was hard to say.

"Where do you want to go first?" Pat said, watching me a little cat-like. I don't think I ever told the truth to a single soul until I met Pat, and I'm not sure I ever regretted it more than I did then, stewing in self-loathing.

When you go into Disney World, it starts with a rustic town square, fire station and city hall and movie theater. A cozy little town of friendly faces and homespun wisdom where no one was ever spat on, where three-toed feet never lurked outside one's living-room window only to vanish with the dawn. A place I'd never been.

We window-shopped a little as we strolled Main Street, U.S.A., displays of toys and country scenes, eerie Victorian dolls and bric-a-brac. Was this Eisenhower's childhood? The street opened out into a wide circular plaza, and beyond it, dominating the skyline, was Sleeping Beauty's Castle, absurd and delicate and beautiful.

They'd repurposed the look of a Bavarian folly, a nineteenth-century German monarch's Romantic idea of an ancestral dwelling. What was it doing here? How was this American at all? Wasn't the point of America to not have a king? To not have magic? I remembered what Eisenhower said about the place: "It is the engine of our phantasmal dominion. I believe that as long as it stands, America cannot fall."

We soldiered on through the main plaza, crossed a drawbridge, and entered into Fantasyland, a crammed-in ghetto of folklore. King Arthur's sword stuck in a rock, Peter Pan's London town house, and Toad Hall. A wicked queen (monarch of what country?) peered out of a lit window. The crowd was densest here, the atmosphere somehow more crushing. One of the masked dwarfs took my hand in his (hers?) for a photo opportunity and I glanced around to find a Secret Service agent, for a terrifying moment certain he (or she) was dragging me off to either subterranean revelry or ritual punishment, I could scarcely decide which. In fact, we walked a few awkward paces until I pulled away, averting my human eyes from his (or her) platter-size ones. I wondered whether one could buy a drink anywhere on the grounds or how a president might even raise the subject. A king, I supposed, could just raise a jeweled goblet and beckon.

Inevitably, Liberty Square and the Hall of Presidents. I walked there like a prisoner going to trial. This had to be Agent Reindeer's last shot at me, and a venomous bolt it was.

It was as if Disney knew my ancient nightmare and had rewritten it. A ponderous speech played but I didn't hear the words; I was just looking at the thirty-six presidents staged like figures in Raphael's *School of Athens,* Washington and Lincoln framed by the lesser lights. I set my face in a pious mask, trying to look like a man ennobled by an encounter with his great forebears. They looked at me and I looked at them, the brotherhood. All captured in their most essential aspects. The dying patrician FDR's noble languor. Andrew Jackson's foppish menace. James Madison's hollow-eyed stare, pregnant with mortal knowledge. Taft's vital glare. A lineage of grotesques and homicides, slavers and geniuses. A fistful of dead presidents. The silent majority.

A crowd of angular faces, scowls and beards and the occasional sly smirk. And they began to speak as the light shifted from one to the other, at first voicing only a chorus of patriotic platitudes.

I seemed to hear more, now in whispers, faster than I could catch. Washington mused, "I will not become a king. I will be . . . something stranger." James Polk anxious and unpleasantly fervent: "There is a cancer at the heart of our Republic. Yea, a living god!"

Ulysses S. Grant keening, *"Iä! Iä!,"* the model staggering to its feet. McKinley stretched out a warning hand: "I fear what I have become. My blood will poison the ones who slay me!"

Teddy Roosevelt stuttered, "It's s-so bright in here. My eyes—can nothing be done?"

Taft, rapt: "I have made a most extraordinary discovery."

Eisenhower's voice, heartbreakingly familiar: "There is one who will come after me."

At last they fell silent; the lights dimmed and then rose again. No one else seemed disturbed. Had I fallen asleep?

It was getting dark. We were taken to see what was meant to be the showpiece of my visit, two rides that were new since the last time I'd been here. Was this, I wondered, to be the completion of Agent Reindeer's work? Or were they going to keep building this thing forever? There was a hushed humid bayou, a summer evening. Lanterns glowed over the black water; an old man sat in a rocking chair. We got into a boat and bumped along down a sudden declivity and into a cavern and then rapidly passed a series of allegorical tableaux. Skeletons sprawled on a sandy beach, the outcome of a long-ago frenzied melee. A sunken rowboat. A skeleton posed in the midst of limitless wealth plundered from all the civilizations of the world, studying a map. Each one a memento mori. A dilapidated tavern room where two skeletons faced each other across a chessboard. Was this Cold War symbolism? "Dead men tell no tales," a voice said. He's not going to say anything? Then what was I doing here?

The ride went from dream to memory, it seemed to me—the old man of the bayou thinking of his past. Now we witnessed the terrifying sack of a Caribbean port. Pirates ransacked the city, tortured its inhabitants, auctioned the rest into sexual slavery. The situation worsened. Now the marauders set the city afire and got roaringly drunk. The other passengers looked charmed. The winding river of debauchery at last took us beneath the city into its dungeons, past prisoners certain to die. Even its supporting timbers were on fire, on the point of collapse, as drunken pirates, singing, laughingly shot at one another in a subterranean room full of gunpowder in a scene of blackest nihilism.

And the final pirate perched on top of a pile of gold, drunk as I wanted to be, clearly the double of the earlier skeleton. *You will die, Mr. Nixon, just as I have,* it seemed to say. *Rich as I am, powerful as you are.* This was entertainment? I stumbled out of the boat, mocked by piratical laughter. I couldn't leave fast enough. I was going to die, I knew.

The children ran to and fro and I took Pat's arm, pulled her down one of the narrow streets of the absurdly faux-sordid New Orleans French Quarter, into an empty little forecourt. We were alone, just for a moment.

"I have to talk to you," I said.

"What is it?" She sounded more surprised and annoyed than interested.

"I know you don't really love me anymore," I said. What was the point in lying?

"What?" Pat said.

"I know it—I've known it for a while. Years. I know I've turned into—"

"Sir, excuse me," said a voice. It was Gary. "We may have a crisis."

What followed took half an hour and $11.85 fed into a pay phone when the radiophone died, the money curried from Secret Service agents, journalists, and passersby. Ultimately it was, I think, sunspots and not a partial preemptive launch.

That took us on to the Haunted Mansion, which I had been avoiding. Surely if the ghost of Agent Reindeer was going to pull a fast one, that would be the venue. I sat with two tiny cousins who bounced up and down with anticipation. I waited glumly through a nonsensical introduction that included (could they be serious?) a staged suicide. I thought of the haunted mansion waiting for me at 1600 Pennsylvania Avenue. Was Walt trying to tell me something?

The ride that followed was meant as, I guess, a sort of musical carnivalesque romp through an accursed plantation home, but the farther we got, the stranger it seemed. After a portentous front hallway, we lost all architectural coherence and seemed to be sliding into a terrifying vision of the afterlife. A ruined dining room; an attic cluttered with the debris of countless atrocities. And then I stared into a black abyss out of which spirits ascended in a never-ending throng. We had left the house now—were we outside? How was this possible? We trundled through a graveyard alight with singing dead men and women. This was Disney World? A clockwork abattoir? I felt I'd been returned to Pawtuxet Farm.

Pat caught my hand to slow me down.

"Try to have a little fun, Dick," Pat said. "Act normal, maybe? We're at Disney World. You're the president."

"I'm sorry," I said. "About what I said earlier . . ."

"Come on, the fireworks are starting in a minute. We just have time to get to Main Street."

Julie and Tricia had wandered off together, taking the children, and Pat and I fled toward the exit as explosions began behind us. I turned and saw fireworks towering above the illuminated castle. We stopped in the town square to watch. I've never liked fireworks, but I felt a patriotic duty to look attentive and happy. Everyone was watching me, after all. This was the people's moment to see fireworks a few weeks before Christmas at Disney World with Richard Nixon, whatever his approval rating. And I felt, maybe, a little of what I was supposed to feel.

It was a stage set and we were supposed to be in the mythical small-town America I'd grown up reading about. Not the dusty, miserable housing development of Yorba Linda, but a town out in the plains somewhere, far from any oceans, far from conspiracies and lies. A place you could grow up in and not want to leave. A place with springs, summers, falls, and winters instead of rain and mud and sun.

And finally the music came to a crescendo and the fireworks did the enormous airburst that signals the end of the show. But when it fell silent, I heard a hissing above us and then felt a cool prickling on my face. What was happening now?

It was, impossibly, snow, falling past the mock-ups of buildings with their forced perspective frontages and—wait . . . where were we? We weren't in California. Where were we? Pat took my hand, smiling. Just a clever piece of theater, I thought, as my features convulsed and I looked down, hiding sudden tears. And then I sobbed, ducking the cameras as an unfamiliar feeling swept through me. I felt homesick for a place that had never been and I felt another thing, the impossible sorcery that Agent Reindeer had placed here for me to find. Absolution.

In March of 1974 a grand jury indicted Haldeman, Ehrlichman, and a host of others for their role in covering up the break-in at the Watergate. I was, legally, an "unindicted coconspirator." None of them ever spoke to me again.

The subpoenas continued to come. I gave them transcripts, made and edited under my supervision. Why not? And I took my case to the Supreme Court, that mystic body now invisible to me but apparently still present to the rest of the world.

I was with Henry when we received the news. The Supreme Court had unanimously voted to overrule our claim of executive privilege.

Henry looked to me, his blue eyes liquid and of infinite depth. I couldn't help feeling a little sorry for the man who had won me the presidency, who was, in fact, loyal almost to the end.

"I do not understand," Henry said. "How can they connect you with this? How can you let them do this?"

I shook my head. "I always thought we could win this one." Was I performing a mournful shame, or feeling it, or both? It was impossible to know.

"The impeachment will come," he said.

"Pray with me, Henry."

"What?"

Once I was on the floor he really had no choice. Two grown men kneeling on the carpet in the room where Lincoln had held his last reception. Did we actually pray? I certainly didn't know how, or what to pray to. Of Henry, I can only speculate about whom or what he might have called upon. I couldn't even quite laugh at him, he looked so earnest and awkward and sorry. I was his only chance at power and he'd just never conceived I'd be this bad at it. He had, in his way, been the one who believed in me the most.

CHAPTER FORTY-SIX

AUGUST 8, 1974

"I HAVE NEVER been a quitter. To leave office before my term is completed is abhorrent to every instinct in my body. But as president, I must put the interests of America first . . . Therefore, I shall resign the presidency effective at noon tomorrow. Vice President Ford will be sworn in as president at that hour in this office."

Beyond the camera lens, I could see, Kissinger was scowling, and I believe it was in that moment that he understood what we'd done to him.

The recording sessions took place over several grueling months, produced between one and four in the morning daily, aided by Arkady's and Tatiana's unheralded abilities as mimics and their gifts for improvisation.

Thus was born the true Nixon, the behind-closed-doors, off-the-record Nixon. We invented him and his voice on the tapes we'd made during all those late nights, halfway or fully drunk, declaiming into the microphones, standing or sitting or lying on our backs in the Oval Office. His brusque misanthropy, his legalistic diction, his vocabulary utterly impoverished except in the area of profanity. He was a chimera of Pat and me, Haldeman and Ehrlichman and Haig, of my mother's sly secretiveness and my father's warmth-less profane jocularity with his customers.

We created the long lie by which the world would always know me. We'd do three or four tapes in a session, carefully noting the notional place in the timeline of evasion, venality, criminality, and cowardice among the off-the-cuff diatribes against Jews and blacks and homosexuals, liberals and hippies and reporters. Pat was the silent partner but displayed a particular genius at urging the rest of them on by scribbling lines on a legal pad or miming the next twist in the conversation in a Harpo Marx turn. We'd made it all up, solemnly or, more often, doubled up with silent laughter, laughing until we cried at the buffoon we were making for ourselves. I'm proudly the funniest president, a punch line for as long as the great Republic stands, but we were always our best audience. And then, inch by inch, we let them tear the tapes from us, savagely battling while inviting the legislature and the judiciary to come and rip our guts out. They'd trapped Gregor and Henry and most of all me, and like Samson in the Temple, I brought the house down.

Now Pat stood behind Kissinger and watched without expression as I spoke to the camera.

"As I recall the high hopes for America with which we began this second term, I feel a great sadness that I will not be here in this office working on your behalf to achieve those hopes in the next two and a half years."

Could I even do this? Just by saying the words, could I cease to be president? None of the former presidents I knew could answer this. Johnson never knew what he had. Kennedy was shot down. Eisenhower's mind was ruined. Roosevelt died in harness. Most who left this office were dead a few years later.

"But in turning over direction of the government to Vice President Ford, I know, as I told the nation when I nominated him for that office ten months ago, that the leadership of America will be in good hands."

I would go, Ford would speak the oath, and probably history would continue. Would the dark power leave me? Would it chase me to the end of my legal term in office? Or to the end of my life?

The speech trailed off; I mouthed regrets, hopes of peace, best wishes, and have-a-good-summer-everyone. In twenty-four hours I would have no political existence beyond the ability to vote in federal and local elections.

I signed the letter, which read, in its entirety, *Dear Mr. Secretary: I hereby resign the Office of President of the United States. Sincerely, Richard Nixon.* Henry shuddered and signed as well, witnessing as the power departed us both, leaving him with nothing but his preternatural rhetorical powers and a shared Nobel Peace Prize.

And with the pardon in place there wouldn't be a trial and I'd never get to testify in my own defense. Soon it would all become muddled in the collective mind and I'd be viewed as not quite guilty, neither a traitor nor an innocent man, just an infamous kind of weasel, a national regret, a comedy gangster. A crook forever.

Arkady and Tatiana disappeared into the uncharted bureaucratic vastness of the Soviet Union. I've been largely cut off from my intelligence sources, but lately several declassified papers have hinted at the existence of a true shadow czarina of the old blood roaming the outback with her bodyguard and counselor, righting wrongs, investigating mysteries, and still waiting for the moment the once and future savior of a troubled nation will be found.

I had my own nation and I continued to haunt it, not least the Republican Party. They gasped to see me and Pat arrive, erect and defiant, to ruin political fund-raisers and photo opportunities. Our mere presence made a joke of things. Pat in particular,

I think, enjoyed the pained expressions that propagated through the crowd.

And no pain was more acute and baffled than Ronald Reagan's, the one they'd praise as a saint, the man who lost to me, the slack-jawed impostor who never managed to grasp the historical coincidence he lucked into. None of them did; the great secret of the Cold War was kept, and that is its own sort of victory. Meanwhile, I angled myself into every conceivable formal photograph and no one quite had the gall to keep me out. Give me an asterisk if you must; I was once the president.

It was at one of these occasions that Mikhail Gorbachev, deep in conversation with someone, caught my eye and—I will always believe it happened—raised his glass an infinitesimal amount in my direction. The knowing tribute of a man who, six years later, would disassemble his own empire and bring the great ridiculous drama to a close. Just as he was the last of the general secretaries, I am the last of the American sorcerer-presidents—the line ends with me.

Or at least it stands in abeyance until the fated day that I read of in the sealed chamber, the day when Richard Nixon's true successors at long last will arrive. I, for one, await their coming.

AFTERWORD

DECEMBER 1983

IT WAS A wintry morning in the late fall of 1983. I looked up from my window at an iron-gray sky.

I'd been gone for a little over nine years. Nine years since the entire planet had tuned in to watch me quit my job as leader of the free world, walk to the helicopter, and vanish into the sky over Washington, DC, crowds cheering and waving their fists and razzing my departure. And today I would go back to public life. The nation had had nine years to get over it.

I prepared alone, fussing until the knot in my tie was perfect, my hair combed and dyed to a pristine blackness. I turned to the mirror and faced what I had to face, the daily reality, the famous visage, a commedia dell'arte mask crafted for avarice and comedy. The Secret Service men followed me into the elevator, and there were a last few seconds of peace before the long mid-morning trek across the lobby of the hotel.

And there it was, the bow wave of astonishment that rolled out before me when I passed through public space anywhere on planet Earth. Hotel staff glanced up and then looked away, but civilians stared in open amazement. In nine years I'd become a figure from a tall tale, like Ichabod Crane or Rip van Winkle. *Trick or treat, ladies and gentlemen,* I thought. *Happy Halloween.*

Pat was waiting for me, and we walked out to the limousine that was idling by the curb in the light snow, the driver barely out of his teens. A crow cawed at me and I flinched, even after all these years. I caught the driver's smirk in the rearview mirror.

He let us out into a puddle of slush at the foot of the broad icy steps of a modest Georgian building where the mayor of Des Moines waited with a cluster of assistants and school officials.

"Mr. President and First Lady, it's an honor." She stumbled over it, caught in the basilisk gaze of celebrity. I took that for a good sign. This was an easy one, a softball venue for a man like me.

They led me in by a side entrance, took me through quiet corridors to a steel door. I could hear the hum and chatter of the excited crowd as the mayor went in and gave them one last reminder of who they were about to see. She told it well. The Environmental Protection Agency. Title IX. Peace in Vietnam; détente; the voyage to China. Then, as usual, a slight faltering through last bits, edging past the salient details like a man on a narrow ledge.

And then: "Please welcome our thirty-seventh president, Richard Milhous Nixon."

I squared my shoulders and made my entrance, walked solemnly to the lectern on the podium. There was a hush as I looked out at the eighth-grade class of the Des Moines Martin Luther King Jr. Middle School.

I saw Pat standing at the back of the gymnasium, watching it happen. I let the silence drop and settle, breathed in, and leaned forward slightly to the microphone. And then, as I pronounced the first syllable, every nonadult person in the room began to yell at the top of his or her lungs.

I was looking up into a solid wall of gyrating arms and bellowing faces and children screaming at me. I'd miscalculated badly.

At first I couldn't hear individual words. But then, I didn't need to, did I? Every single monstrous one of them was in the same identical pose. Arms locked rigid overhead, second and third digit of each hand spread in an ecstasy of inspired mockery. Shoulders hunched, shaking phantom jowls. All shouting the same thing. Chanting it. Saying it like I'd never said it: Not. Crook. I am not a crook. I am *not* a crook. I am not a *crook*. I. Am not. A crook.

"Boys and girls," I began. It was like speaking into a high wind. I stood stranded on the podium, waiting for the deluge to recede. If anything, it grew louder. I looked down at the cheap wood of the lectern. I remembered other, better lecterns.

"Boys and girls," I started again. It just kicked them into higher gear, but I kept on. "It's an honor to be here today at Martin Luther King Jr. Middle School. It's truly marvelous. I couldn't possibly be any happier.

"I was once just like you. I went to a small school in Yorba Linda, California, in a time long distant, but my hopes and dreams were the same as yours. I worked hard, and in 1946 I was elected to Congress." The sound was dying down a little.

"In 1948 I was catapulted to national—"

"*Tricky Dick!*" yelled a red-faced boy, and the cry was taken up and mere anarchy was again loosed upon the gymnasium. The boy wore a T-shirt with the word *Supertramp* on it. What the hell did that mean? The principal hopped onto the stage and made as if to take over, but I waved her off.

Down below, children ran left and right and objects were thrown and offenders were dragged from the room, the Chicago riots in miniature. They had Richard Nixon himself here, and they were going to make the most of it.

"It's all right," I told the principal. "They're just having a little fun." It wasn't her fault. If I hadn't wanted to be mocked by young teenagers, I could have protected and defended the Constitution like I'd said I would.

"You know, boys and girls, I like a joke as much as the next man, I really do," I said. "Politics is a tough business, and you don't get through without a thick skin. It's—it's not always easy. I ran for vice president in 1952 with Dwight Eisenhower, and, well . . . we had our own trouble with the Communists in those days." Did eighth-graders know who Eisenhower was? They had at least heard the word *Communist*, a sort of socialist goblin to the Reagan youth.

"We faced great—great challenges. A nation divided against itself. The Soviet Union threatening to expand everywhere. Spies on our doorstep. Nuclear missiles. The Cold War. But so much opportunity. To come to power then . . ." I groped for words. What could I tell them? What did these kids know? I looked out at the blank half-pubescent faces. They knew Reagan, the ignorant pretender. They didn't know who Eisenhower was. Or Stalin. Or me.

"For Christ's sake, I was president!" I shouted into the microphone to a howl of feedback. In the back of the room, Pat winced and made a slight shushing motion with a pale and trembling hand. But I wasn't done. Who knew the truth now? No one but her and Kissinger, a creature so far from human as to scarcely matter. A being who might never die at all. No, I had to tell them the story.

"Your mothers and fathers voted to make me their supreme leader. The highest office in the land, the most venerated position an American can aspire to. Laugh if you want to, but believe it, you little shits, I was your fucking president!"

When had the crowd gone silent? I heard the last words ring three times through the gymnasium, like Peter denying Jesus.

And all at once, I understood them. At their age I didn't even know what a president was, really. Just that the people of our country decided who the best person in all of America was, and that person got to make the decisions. And I, the boy they'd one day call Tricky Dick, wanted to be that person. God, I wanted it, and I cannot tell a lie. I don't know why, but I did.

So I knew why they were laughing. I'd taken the idea of the presidency and I'd turned it into a joke. And it's not that it wasn't funny, because whatever else I am, I am history's funniest president. But these children were laughing at me to turn the thrust of a disappointment. They were laughing at me because I had hurt them in a very personal way. I was president the year they were born, the president their parents gave them. The best person in America turned out to be me, and they were still trying to laugh me off.

After I signed the letter of resignation, Pat and I walked to a waiting helicopter clutching our suitcases like newlyweds, and the concrete chambers beneath the White House were then sealed forever. I am the last chief executive ever to have seen them or practiced the vile sorceries to which they gave me access.

I looked at Pat. She shook her head no. Leave it. The Cold War was a lie, and far beyond the Iron Curtain, the blacked-out science cities lay frozen and empty.

There are truths so awful they can't be told, and words so dense and alien and malign that they take eighteen and a half minutes to say and even digital tape cannot reproduce their accursed sounds. The runes of the sealed chamber hold all these truths—last and least among them, that once I wanted to be the president, defender of the Republic, the true one that was promised long ago, holder of the highest office in all the land. Even if I am a crook.

ACKNOWLEDGMENTS

I'd like to thank the extraordinary team that took me through this writing process: my agent Luke Janklow and the indomitable Claire Dippel at Janklow and Nesbit and, on the publishing side, Josh Kendall, Wes Miller, Pam Brown, Ben Allen, Tracy Roe, Ruth Tross, and all the rest who first believed in this book and then hauled it across the finish line.

ABOUT THE AUTHOR

Austin Grossman is a video-game design consultant who has worked on such games as *Ultima Underworld II: Labyrinth of Worlds; System Shock; Flight Unlimited; Trespasser: Jurassic Park; Clive Barker's Undying; Deus Ex; Tomb Raider Legend; Epic Mickey;* and *Dishonored.* He is also the author of *You* and *Soon I Will Be Invincible,* which was nominated for the 2007 John Sargent Sr. First Novel Prize. His writing has appeared in *Granta,* the *Wall Street Journal,* and the *New York Times.*

MULHOLLAND BOOKS

You won't be able to put down these Mulholland Books.